Discover Me and You

A Devil's Kettle Romance
Book Two

Susan Sey

OTHER TITLES BY SUSAN SEY

Money, Honey

Money Shot

Kiss the Girl

Taste for Trouble (Blake Brothers #1)

Talent for Trouble (Blake Brothers #2)

Touch of Trouble (A Blake Brothers Novella)

Time for Trouble (Blake Brothers #3)

Picture Me & You (Devil's Kettle #1)

Author's Note:

Welcome to Devil's Kettle, readers! I'm so glad you're back! As most of you probably know, Jax and Addy found their happily ever after in PICTURE ME & YOU, but there's a whole lot of story left to unpack. The scandals run deep in this little town, and Willa Zinc lives right in the heart of the biggest one.

Willa's not looking for love, of course. Neither is Eli Walker. But secrets don't keep forever, and nobody escapes when true love comes calling. Willa's a fighter, though, so pull up a chair and put on the kettle. This should be a good one.

As always, all my love and thanks to Bryan (whose patience and support appear to be bottomless), to Claudia (who is navigating her teen years with a genius-level blend of grace and sarcasm), and to Greta (whose dinner table antics are the stuff of legend, and probably not just in our house, lord help us).

And to Inara, of course, whose editorial eye is invaluable, exacting and — for lucky, lucky me — only an email away.

Chapter 1

WILLA ZINC PULLED her rusty old pickup into a parking spot on Main Street and let the engine idle while she considered her options. She didn't have to do this. She could call in sick. She could make up an emergency. She could leave Bianca Davis and her precious gallery twisting in the wind a bare week before Devil Days. She dropped her elbow onto the warm ledge of her open window and pondered the thought. She could. She could turn around right now and go home.

"I don't have to do this," she said to nobody in particular. "I mean, I work for myself. If a call sucks, I don't have to take it, right?"

Across the street, the late-summer sun had made a mirror of Lake Superior, and a handful of obscenely cheerful boats bobbed at anchor in the harbor, admiring themselves. Willa scowled.

"What do you know?" she said to them. "You don't even work."

The lake winked at her and jiggled the delighted boats. She rolled an irritable shoulder and turned her scowl on the steering wheel, which had the good sense to look as worn and dismal as Willa felt.

"I hate my job," she decided. But even as she said it, she knew it was a lie. She actually kind of loved her job. "Okay, I hate *today's* job. How's that?"

The steering wheel was unhelpful, the lake withheld comment, and she was clearly beneath the boats' notice, so Willa killed the engine and pocketed the keys. But she didn't open the door. Not yet.

"It's not like I won't *do* it," she muttered. Grudges went deep in small towns, and deeper yet in Devil's Kettle. They went right down to the bone in Willa, but indulging those grudges was no way to stay in business. Plus she really did love her job, and the Department of Natural Resources had finally approved her request for licensure. All Willa had to do now was rock three supervised removals — which she felt confident she would — and give up her client list along with her permission to cold call any one of them for a reference. She wasn't as confident on that part. Her work spoke for itself but so did her last name, and grudges really did go deep in Devil's Kettle.

So, yeah, she was going to do the damn job, and do it well. But first, she was going to take one minute — one small, pathetic minute — to feel sorry for herself.

Thirty seconds later, Willa bailed out of the truck, sweating. Even with the windows down, she'd been baking like a brownie in there, damn it. *No brood for you!* the boats chirped gleefully. She sighed. Today was clearly out to screw her. She should probably just accept it.

She slammed the door with heartfelt violence and headed for the equipment box in the truck bed. She didn't bother to lock up, or even to roll up the windows. Everything worth stealing was locked in the equipment box, and she was perfectly willing to give up her empty styrofoam cups and granola bar wrappers to whatever petty criminal wanted them.

She retrieved a black duffle bag from the box and heaved it onto her shoulder. The jangle of tools was a familiar music to Willa, a sweet reminder of why she loved her job. She was good at what she did, sure, but more importantly? She worked for herself and by herself. She had an unusual skill set and it gave her that rarest of all things — true independence. Willa decided when, where, and for whom she worked. And while her heart sang at the very idea of refusing Bianca Davis' royal summons — and oh, lord, it was tempting, especially with Devil Days just around the corner — Willa had worked and sweated and bled for a professional reputation spotless enough to make people forget she was a Zinc, even temporarily. She wasn't about to throw it away on a personal grudge.

She loved her job, she reminded herself yet again, today's job included. What she hated was the woman writing the check for today's job.

She hated Bianca Davis.

It felt good to get that straight.

She locked up her equipment box, tossed her jingling bag of tools into a more comfortable cross-body carry and headed for the Davis Gallery.

Chapter 2

WILLA PAUSED ON the sidewalk and considered the block-long stretch of glass and pine that made up the Davis Gallery. One part of her brain — the rational part — was scanning the foundation for any crack or flaw an animal could turn into an unauthorized entrance. But the other part of her brain — the part where instinct lived — was stalling. She didn't want to go in there. Why would she? Diego Davis had been powerfully handsome, ridiculously talented and astonishingly selfish. He'd lived fast, died young and left a smoking swath of damage in his wake several dozen women wide. And Willa ought to know; she'd been one of those women. It had been a lifetime ago that a teenaged Diego had talked her out of her panties, and yet here she was, undeniably avoiding a job because her peace of mind couldn't take the sight of his paintings.

Either that or she was still afraid of his mommy.

Which was stupid. *She* was being stupid, and stupidity wasn't just inconvenient. It was expensive, and Willa had been poor too long and hungry too often to let a little discomfort come between her and a paycheck. She tightened her mouth, pulled the brim of her ball cap nice and low, and walked into the gallery.

It sucked her in like a vacuum, the light bright yet diffuse, seeming to come from nowhere and everywhere all at once. The floor was a pale, gleaming pine, the walls a creamy white that looked both surgically clean and somehow appetizing. Like it might taste good if you were insane enough to lick it, which Willa definitely wasn't. It put her in the mind of vanilla lattes, that was all, to the point that she could almost smell the bitter tang of coffee and the dusty warmth of cinnamon under the cream.

And now she was overthinking the paint, for heaven's sake.

"Bianca?" she called, her voice disappearing into the hushed space rather than echoing the way it should in such a big room. She studied the ceiling, wondering about acoustic panels but really just avoiding eye contact with any of the framed canvases on the walls. Diego's paintings — much like the man — sucked you in. They grabbed you and demanded that you look and keep looking until you'd given up whatever they wanted from you. It had become a point of private pride for Willa to refuse that demand. She couldn't blame him for every bomb that had ever gone off in her life — she was a Zinc, after all — but saying yes to Diego had lit some of the worst fuses. So if she didn't want to look at his damn paintings, she wasn't going to look.

A white curtain twitched at the back of the room and Bianca Davis swooped out like the angel of stylish doom.

"Willa, you're here," she said briskly, surveying Willa with every appearance of satisfaction. "Good."

Willa blinked at her, startled. "Good?" Diego's mother was tall and golden, all long limbs and elegant bones with a pair of bright dark eyes that had never looked at Willa with anything less than stone-cold dislike, even when she was paying for the privilege of Willa's presence.

"Yes, good." Bianca nodded firmly. "Thanks for coming on short notice. It's back here."

She turned, her hair swinging expensively, and led Willa toward the curtain from which she'd emerged. She wore a pair of slim dark pants and a striped top with a wide neckline and elbow-length sleeves that would've made Willa look like a demented sailor. On Bianca, it looked vaguely French.

She followed the older woman through the curtain and into a wide, shallow room at the back of the gallery with another vanilla latte wall that ran the length of the building.

A jumble of boxes and crates crouched in one corner and framed canvases were everywhere — hanging on the wall, propped on the floor, leaning against the boxes. At the far end of the room, yet another white curtain had been hitched to one side, revealing the emergency exit.

"Sorry about the mess." Bianca waved a hand and sighed. "We normally use this room for storage and staging but Addy insisted we house the *Diego After Dark* series here during Devil Days." Her lip curled. "Heaven forbid that unsuspecting people should be accidentally exposed to actual art."

"Or a boob," Willa said. She hadn't meant to look but it hadn't taken more than a glance. Then again… She squinted at the framed painting that had caught her eye on the wall in front of her. "Wait, *is* that a boob?"

"Not the entire thing, no." Bianca gave the painting a loving glance. "Only the aureole. And my God, just look at his use of light and color!" Grief passed over her face like a cloud over the sun, momentarily dimming the force of her presence. "In some ways, Diego was such a typical boy. He must've been fifteen when he did this one." She smiled softly, and Willa tensed. The Bianca she knew didn't smile. Not like this. Her smile was a weapon, not an expression. "I was still his primary teacher at that point and he was rebelling. Trying to shock me, I suppose." She lifted her shoulders, let them drop. "But all he did was remind me that he wasn't a typical boy." Her gaze drifted over the long wall, touching on every frame, each image naughtier than the last. Her smile sharpened. "He wasn't a typical boy at all, was he?"

"Oh good heavens, no. Not just any boy would think to paint *boobs*." Willa nodded wisely while her stomach knotted with a rage she thought she'd digested years ago. "He was clearly very special."

Even as the words fell from her mouth, Willa regretted them. Diego Davis had been dead for nearly four years now, but he was still the single hand feeding the entire town. Nobody was brave enough — or stupid enough — to bite that hand, especially not with his mommy looking on. Nobody but Willa, evidently, and she damn well ought to know better by now.

"That reminds me." Bianca smiled again, but this time it was the smile Willa recognized — sharp as a blade, twice as dangerous. "We should talk."

Foreboding swam greasily into her gut. "About what?"

"Addison."

Willa blinked, startled. Bianca wanted to talk about Diego's young widow and celebrated muse? Right now? "What about her?"

"She likes you." Bianca said this with an air of sincere bafflement, and perhaps some faint pity. Not pity for Willa, of course, but for Bianca's poor, widowed daughter-in-law who'd clearly lost her mind if she was befriending the likes of Willa Zinc. "She seems to have gotten it into her head that Georgie and I are somehow responsible for your social standing, or lack thereof."

"You are." Georgie Davis — homecoming queen, long-legged fashionista, and Bianca Davis's pampered only daughter — had been the author of much of Willa's high school misery.

"Perhaps partly." Bianca sent a pointed glance at Willa's dirty jeans and t-shirt. "But even you have to admit, we don't deserve full credit on that score."

True enough. Social status was dictated by some complicated calculus in small towns. It wasn't good to be on the Davis family's bad side but Willa knew it was hardly the only nail in her coffin. Just the biggest one.

"You don't like my outfit?"

"Addison is important to me," Bianca said tightly. "She's family."

"Ah." Willa nodded slowly, the light finally dawning. Addy *was* family to Bianca, and not just through Diego.

Bianca had three other children as well, and Addy meant the world to each of them. To the youngest, Matty, she was a beloved bonus sister. To Georgie, she was a live-in best friend. And to the eldest, Jackson, she was quite simply everything. Addy might as well be Bianca's own child at this rate, and Willa knew only too well how far Bianca would go to keep her children happy. "And since Addy and I are friends—"

"—she won't be happy unless we're all friends." Bianca's smile was frigid.

Willa stared at her. "You and I aren't ever going to be friends."

"Amen. But we can be civil, can't we?" Willa's skepticism must've shown on her face because Bianca blew out an impatient breath. "Our history is…complicated, I'll grant you, but surely we can agree to coexist without quite so much open hostility."

Willa considered that in silence.

Bianca scowled. "I'm making an effort here, Willa. You could do the same."

"Why?" It was an honest question. "Why would I expend even the tiniest bit of effort to make your life easier?"

"Because Addy is the best person we know." She said it bluntly. "Because she's happy — truly happy — for the first time since she came to Devil's Kettle, and the people who love her have a responsibility to keep her that way. So we, Willa Zinc—" She bared her teeth in a brilliant smile. "—are going to get along."

Willa frowned. She agreed wholeheartedly in principle. Addison *was* the best person she knew. The girl was a stubborn bundle of freckle-faced sunshine, and the closest thing Willa had had to a friend in years. In practice, though? It was unsettling to find herself in agreement with Bianca Davis. It was unprecedented, in fact, and left her groping for an appropriate response.

Then, inside the wall, something thumped, and the

unmistakable sound of nails skittered frantically along the baseboards. Bianca whirled like a gunslinger and shot a lethal finger toward the noise.

"But that—" She glared at Willa, a familiar glare Willa found deeply reassuring. "—is why you're here."

Willa dropped her bag and pushed Bianca out of her mind. Pushed this bizarre conversation and this universe-altering proposal out of her mind, too, and focused on whatever was inside that wall.

"When did you first hear it?"

"This morning." Bianca stared at the wall as if she could burn through it with her laser eyes and incinerate whatever unlucky mammal was hiding back there.

Willa pushed a stack of cardboard boxes to the opposite wall and knelt at the baseboards. She put the flat of her palm against the wall where she'd heard the scrabble of tiny nails and tapped with the knuckles of her other hand. The wall came alive under her palm, and she could almost smell the tiny creature's panic. It was a thin, electric scent, like bad wiring, and Willa's heart ached for the poor thing. She rose to her feet and headed for the emergency exit.

"Where are you going?" Bianca was hot on her heels. "It's in here!"

"I know." Willa stepped into the alley and squinted at the cinderblock foundation, then at the eaves. "There." She pointed to a rotten spot just under the overhang. "See that? It's an open invitation."

"Well close it."

"Let's see if we can get your little house guest to come out the way he came in first."

"How?"

"I'll wedge a trap up there and bait it. Give it a few days — a week, tops — and I'm betting we'll have a live mammal in custody."

"Devil Days is a week from now." Bianca's eyes were dark and calculating. "I don't have time for manners. I want that thing out of my gallery today."

"Okay, but I'll have to open the wall."

"Today, Willa."

She shrugged. "It's your wall."

Half an hour later, Willa had boarded up the hole in the eaves and returned to the gallery's back room. She had her live trap out, ready to slide it in front of the hole she was about to cut in the wall. She plugged in her reciprocating saw and gave the trigger a testing pull. The saw roared to life and Willa smiled. She did enjoy opening a wall. She turned her ball cap backward, snapped her safety glasses into place and prepared to make the first cut.

Behind her, Bianca said, "For God's sake, Willa, be careful."

"Don't worry, ma'am," Willa said. "I'm a professional."

"I'm more worried about my wall than your fingers," Bianca said dryly. "I have an important showing in this room in exactly one week. Do *not* destroy my gallery."

"Would I do that?"

Bianca's silence spoke volumes. Willa triggered her saw and went after the wall, hiding a smile in her shoulder.

A few loud, dusty minutes later, Willa had her live trap plugged into the wall where there had once been a neat square of vanilla latte drywall. Bianca eyed the trap distrustfully.

"What do we do now?"

Willa pushed the safety glasses to the top of her head, wrapped the cord around the saw and tucked it back into her bag. "Now we wait."

Bianca frowned. "How long?"

Willa shrugged and hitched herself onto a sturdy table. She let her boots dangle and gave Bianca a guileless smile. "As long as it takes."

"Well, how long do you usually wait?" Bianca asked, all exaggerated patience.

"Depends on how long that little fella's been in your

wall. If he's hungry—" Which she kind of thought he was, given the panic she'd sensed earlier. "—it'll be sooner rather than later." She pointed at the gob of peanut butter sitting in the back corner of the trap. "That's an invitation he won't be able to resist."

Bianca sighed. She propped an elbow on the stack of boxes Willa had moved and turned her attention to the trap as if she could force rodents out of her wall through sheer will power. If anybody could do such a thing, Willa thought, it was Bianca Davis.

The emergency exit swung open suddenly and Matty Davis appeared. The youngest Davis was all enormous shoes and perfect cheekbones as he wrestled his lanky teenaged body, a duffle bag, and a lacrosse stick through the narrow doorjamb.

"Hey, Mom," he said to Bianca while Willa's heart tried to leap out of her chest. She drank in the sight of him. She had so few opportunities to study him up close. He was almost fourteen now and so tall, probably approaching six feet. Skinny as a rail, though, and still learning to manage his newly endless limbs. His face was pure Diego, Willa had to admit, from those cheekbones to all that dramatic black hair, and lord knew that always put a cramp in Willa's stomach. But those gun-metal gray eyes weren't Diego's and there was a sweetness in them that Diego had never possessed. It eased Willa's stomach but it also opened up a pit of yearning in her soul that had never, not in all the years it had existed, shrunk a single inch.

"Hey, Ms. Zinc."

"Hey, Matty," she managed over her stupid heart wedged in her mouth.

He eyed the hole in the wall and the empty trap. "What's going on?"

"There's a thing in the wall," Bianca told him. "Willa's getting it out. Are you ready to go?"

"Yeah. The bus leaves the school at two. I'm heading up

there now."

"You have your passport?"

"Yep."

"Snacks?"

"Yep."

"A jacket?" Bianca frowned and reached for his bag. "It's Canada, you know. It'll get chilly at night. You should have—"

"Mom, I have a jacket." He caught Bianca's reaching hands and rolled his eyes, the way only a teenager could. "It's a field trip with my lacrosse team, not a voyage to the Antarctic. I'll be with Coach and like fifteen other guys. We'll be fine."

"Of course you will." Bianca patted his cheek with an open affection that had Willa blinking hard at the floor between her boots. "But I'm your mother. Worrying's my job."

"Well, don't." Matty leaned in, kissed her cheek. "I'll be back on Thursday."

"Make sure you are." Bianca smoothed his t-shirt. "Devil Days starts on Friday and we'll need all hands on deck."

"That's the plan." He drew back to grin at her. "Okay, gotta go."

"Travel safe, sweetheart."

Willa was never quite sure, later, who to blame for what happened next. A number of things happened almost simultaneously. First, a chipmunk bolted out of the wall and into the live trap, its striped tail straight up like a racing pennant. It was willing to die but it was going down with full stomach, by God. It launched itself face-first into the gob of peanut butter with a kamikaze leap that rattled the cage.

Matty gave a startled yelp. Willa jumped off the table and Bianca backed into the stack of boxes beside her, tumbling them to the ground. During this little comedy of errors, at least one person — possibly more than one — kicked the live trap, dislodging it from its cozy hole in the wall. The chipmunk looked up from its peanut butter binge, smelled freedom and made a break for it. Only it mistook Matty's leg for a tree trunk and raced for the skies.

Matty froze, likely paralyzed by his lack of good options. He seemed reluctant to slap at such tiny bones, which spoke well of his soul, but he was clearly uncomfortable being climbed by a wild animal. He turned wide, panicked eyes on his mother, who apparently didn't suffer any such qualms. She scooped up a sketchbook from the tumble of papers at her feet, took a double-handed backswing worthy of the LPGA and delivered a blow to Matty's thigh that would have rendered a less worthy chipmunk unconscious if it didn't deliver him directly to his ultimate reward.

But this, Willa discovered a split second later, was no ordinary chipmunk. This chipmunk not only survived, but maintained consciousness. It arrowed through time and space like a furry little bullet, a line-drive of furious survival instinct that landed square on Willa's crotch. She said, "Oh, hell."

Then those little claws — so handy for tree-climbing — found purchase on Willa's jeans and suddenly there was a dazed ball of speeding-heart panic *inside* her t-shirt.

"Jesus!" She indulged in several sweaty seconds of intensely personal self-groping before finally just giving up and ripping the shirt off over her head. She twisted it into a pouch, trapping the chipmunk inside. "Got it!" She held up the wadded t-shirt in triumph, her heart racing, her ball cap on the ground. Only then did she realize that she was now standing in the Davis Gallery in nothing but a pair of dirty jeans and a boob-squashing sports bra, her hair a wild tangle around her shoulders, her ponytail holder having abandoned its post during the fracas. "I, uh, got it."

Chapter 3

BIANCA AND MATTY both stared at her, open-mouthed. Bianca, at least, had the grace to look down at the sketch pad in her hands, then dropped it as if it had burned her. It hit the floor with a bang that broke the spell, and Matty turned to his mother.

"Thanks, Ma." He grinned. "Always looking out for me."

Bianca scooped up the sketchbook again and folded it carefully shut. "I'm your mother," she said lightly. "It's my job."

"Concussing chipmunks is in the job description?" Willa asked. She dropped to her knees and deposited her shirt in the live trap. She carefully eased the chipmunk out of the make-shift pouch, dropped the door on the trap and pulled the shirt back on.

"It's under *other duties as necessary*," Bianca murmured, her knuckles white on the sketch pad.

"Well, this has been awesome," Matty said, still grinning, and rocked back on his big boots. "But I really do have to go now."

"Have a good time," Bianca said.

"Yeah, have fun," Willa told him.

"Will do."

He kissed his mother's cheek one more time, and then he was gone, leaving Bianca and Willa ankle-deep in spilled papers and awkward silence.

Finally Willa said, "I'll put the wall back together then find a new home for the chipmunk."

"You can't do that," Bianca said.

"I can't?"

"I don't mean the chipmunk. You can do whatever it is you usually do with the chipmunk." Bianca shoved the sketchbook into one of the boxes at her feet and straightened to face Willa. "I mean Matty. You can't look at him that way."

Willa froze with one hand deep in her duffle bag, rummaging for the wood screws. "What way?" she managed, though her throat was suddenly painfully tight.

"The way you do."

"I don't look at him any way. I don't look at him at all."

"Most of the time, that's true." She inclined her head stiffly. "But sometimes — just now for example — you do. And when you do, it's…"

"It's what?"

"It's obvious." She drew herself up, peered down her regal nose at Willa. "You need to stop it. For his sake, if not for your own." She folded her hands at her waist and smiled politely. "I'll expect your bill in the mail whenever it's convenient."

And then she was gone, leaving Willa alone with her confusion, her pain, and a concussed chipmunk.

"I know how you feel, buddy," she muttered, and began putting the wall back together when all she wanted was to break something.

An hour later, the chipmunk was halfway to Duluth and Willa was strolling down Main Street toward her truck. She walked slowly, still chewing on the sort-of olive branch Bianca had extended when she spotted Addison Davis. The woman breezed out of the Devil's Taproom at the end of the next block and Willa's stomach clenched. Shit. Normally she enjoyed running into Addy but she wasn't ready to talk to her yet. She needed a few hours — days, weeks, decades? — to consider the cease-fire Bianca had proposed and all the implications thereof.

Maybe she could just say a quick hello, plead a super-busy day and escape. Addy was nothing if not mannerly. It might just work.

Then Georgie Davis strolled out of the bar, too, all six skinny feet of her, her silky-straight, Vogue-ready hair glistening in the sun, her smile an exact replica of her mother's — cold, sharp and quietly furious. Willa's hope abandoned her. Addy might cooperate out of pure niceness but Georgie wouldn't. Georgie hated her, a circumstance that generally didn't bother Willa. She hated Georgie every bit as much as Georgie hated her. The only difference was that Willa hated Georgie for a very, very good reason whereas Georgie hated Willa as a matter of principle. This was assuming, of course, that you could call hating all things ugly or poor a principle, in which case Willa qualified on both counts.

Then there was the fact that Georgie's engagement to Willa's brother Peter had recently imploded spectacularly. Given that Peter ran the taproom, they'd almost certainly just had a public run-in. The wise Zinc would play least-in-sight right now, and Willa was no dummy.

She hung an abrupt right into the Wooden Spoon Diner. She'd buy a sandwich or something. That was a normal dinner-time sort of thing to do. If Addy found her, she could just be like, *Oh, hey, buying a sammy, super busy, got to run—*

The crack of an open palm meeting somebody's cheek stopped Willa dead. It was a sound she knew too well to ever mistake for anything else. She had a fleeting moment of craven gratitude that it wasn't her face in the line of fire this time before her humanity kicked in. She didn't care who'd done what to whom. She was a healthy, strong adult and refused to stand by gawking while somebody did violence in front of her. It occurred to her in a vague sort of way that in trying to avoid one fight, she'd inadvertently walked into another one.

Today really wasn't her day, was it?

The real drawback to having your face slapped, Eli Walker mused, was that it made you feel things. And not just the fire racing across his abused cheekbone, either. No, having your face slapped in public opened up that big, putrid pit of shame inside that was always whispering *you deserve this*. This, and probably worse.

Eli had no argument. If there was a reason he was still walking this earth, whole and healthy, when so many of the men who'd worked beside him were dead, he didn't know what it was. Nor did he know why Gerte Torsen — the sweet little pie lady of Devil's Kettle — had just cracked him a good one.

"How dare you?" Gerte breathed, her soft jowls trembling with outrage. Or maybe with the aftershock of that slap she'd laid on him. She'd really put some muscle behind it, Jesus. Not that he should be surprised. He'd bused tables here at the Wooden Spoon Diner for a couple of unremarkable weeks back in the spring, and it had taken him about two shifts to spot the rattlesnake under Gerte's tourist-friendly veneer. "How *dare* you show your face here, after what you did?"

Eli touched his throbbing cheek. The whole diner had fallen shoot-out-at-the-OK-corral silent. He raked his memory for anything he might've done while *in situ* that would provoke this kind of fury. He shot a glance toward the kitchen where Gerte's daughter Lainey ruled. She'd made a pass at him one night after closing, a clear signal to his inner vagabond that it was time to move on. So he'd moved on. It was a simple enough thing to do. You rolled up your sleeping bag, laced up your boots, shouldered your pack and walked out. You didn't, as a rule, think much — if ever —

about what you'd left behind but his throbbing cheekbone was curious. What exactly had Lainey told her mother about the night he'd taken off?

"After what I did?" he prompted. The door jingled behind him and a blast of sticky summer air hit the back of his neck. More spectators, great. "What exactly did I do?"

She slapped him again. Christ. His ear rang and he tasted blood this time. Gerte had herself one hell of a swing. Then again, if he let her slap him hard enough and often enough, would that pool of shame inside him start to drain? Worth thinking about.

"You nearly blew this place to smithereens!" she snapped.

"I did?" He blinked, sincerely shocked. He'd been expecting something more along the lines of dishonoring her daughter, which he hadn't. Not that Lainey hadn't lobbied for it.

"What?" she sneered. "You've forgotten that your grand exit included torching my Dumpster?"

Behind him, somebody breathed, "Oh hell."

"Not to mention burning Peter's resort to the ground!"

Eli held up a staying hand. "Wait, I burned down a resort?" A Dumpster was one thing but a whole resort? "Which one?"

"The Hideaway, Eli! You only slept there every night while you were here?"

He considered the bat-infested squirrel hotel in which he'd parked his sleeping bag for the bare week or two he'd been in town. He supposed it might've been a resort. Once. When he'd slept there, it had been an abandoned fire hazard. Evidently, he wasn't the only one who'd thought so.

"You could've just said no." Gerte's soft mouth pinched into a damning line. "To Lainey. To what she asked you. That's what a normal person would have done, you know. A decent person. But not you. Not Eli Walker. Because you're not decent, are you? You're poison."

Her words rang inside him like a bell, sank into his accepting soul like the unvarnished truth they were.

There was an impatient huff behind him and a woman said, "For Christ's sake, Gerte. Are you still going on about that Dumpster fire? It was months ago, and there wasn't one penny of damage done to this place. When are you going to get over it already?"

Gerte's eyes sharpened with dislike on the woman who'd spoken behind him. "When somebody's guilty butt is in jail," she said, "and not a minute sooner."

"So you're just going to hold impromptu witch hunts every time a stranger passes through?"

Eli turned and found his champion just inside the diner's glass door. She was smaller than he'd imagined. It took guts to stand up for a total stranger, more when you were just barely this side of tiny. She wore a baggy t-shirt and dirty jeans with boots to match, and a St. Paul Saints cap pulled so low he couldn't see much more than a pointed pixie chin underneath it. A thick, dark ponytail snaked halfway down her back and the arms she'd folded across her middle looked slender and breakable.

And yet that slippery pool of shame inside him went strangely still. Because this woman — whoever she was — didn't shift on those sturdy boots of hers. She didn't blink or smirk or speak. She simply waited for Gerte's response with a patient calm that spread into the air around her, wrapped itself around the violence of Gerte's slap, and laid it serenely on the cool cement floor to sleep.

"It's hardly a witch hunt," Gerte sniffed, but she stepped back. Out of slapping range, Eli realized with a twinge of relief. "Not when both fires happened within hours of Eli skipping town without a word to anybody." Those hostile eyes swung back to him. "Aside from the ugly ones that passed between him and Lainey."

Eli didn't recall any particularly ugly words, unless you counted *no*. Which Lainey might. Rejection never felt good.

"Far as I know," his champion said evenly, "there's no law against turning a girl down."

"What about torching a Dumpster? Burning down a resort?" Gerte continued to glare at him. "He might've been behind the Davis Place fire, too, for all we know!"

The other woman didn't blink. And that eerie, watchful stillness of hers only deepened. "That happened, what, a solid month after the other fires? You think he waited until the heat was off, sneaked back into town and did one more, just for fun?" She let that sink in. "You're reaching, Gerte."

"I'm not saying he did it himself." Gerte lifted her chin. "But he definitely gave somebody ideas."

The woman stared at her for a long moment, then finally moved. She flicked her cap back far enough to drag a weary palm down her face. "Okay, listen, Gerte. Listen, all of you." She glanced around the room, took in their avid audience. "I'm only going to say this once and I want all of you to pay attention. This man—" She stopped, pointed at him. "What's your name?"

"Eli," he said. "Eli Walker."

"Great. Hi, Eli."

"Hey."

"Eli Walker didn't start any fires. The fire marshall examined both the Dumpster and the Hideaway. The sheriff was consulted. Peter — my brother, mind you, and the owner of record on both properties? He's dealt with his insurance company, the fire marshall and the sheriff. Everybody's satisfied and the cases are closed. Gerte's got no cause to accuse anybody of anything, let alone the right."

She made hard eye contact with three or four individuals — high value social targets, he imagined — and Eli watched their eyes slide guiltily away from hers.

She was good, whoever she was. He had to wonder why she was spending whatever social capital she had for a stranger, though.

"As for Davis Place?" She nailed Gerte with the eye

contact this time. "That one was my fault."

Gerte's mouth dropped open and an audible gasp filled the room. "You burned down Davis Place?"

"Not on purpose, Gerte, geez. Get a hold of yourself." She waited a beat, as if giving Gerte a moment to truly get back in touch with reason. As if she had every confidence that, because she'd given an order, it would be obeyed. And something in Eli yearned.

He blinked, startled. He hadn't wanted anything in so long, he barely remembered what wanting felt like, let alone yearning. He wasn't even sure what he could possibly want. But he felt certain that it had something to do with this small, strange woman and that radical *stillness* she commanded.

The room waited breathlessly for her to speak and Eli had to wonder who on earth this woman was that she could bespell Gerte and a potential mob into rapt silence. If he was going to be here for a while — and God help him, it looked like he was — it would definitely pay to find out.

"How?" Gerte bleated, clearly bewildered. "How did you burn down Davis Place?"

The woman said, "Addy got this big, fancy espresso machine, and I was helping her figure out how to use it. Evidently, we left a rag over the fan intake when we wiped it down. That plus some wonky wiring she was still having worked on and next thing you know, you've got yourself a house fire." She shrugged. "It happens. But Addy has also settled everything with her insurance company, and there's no open case with either the fire marshall or the sheriff." She gave Gerte another beat or two of that uncompromising eye contact. "Which means it's no business of yours. So why don't you check your own hands before you go calling other people poison?"

Willa judged the sidewalk was clear, and since Gerte had

stopped talking — and slapping people — she turned and went outside. Besides, she'd said everything she needed to say and she wasn't in the habit of hanging around once the work was done.

Her truck was half a block up Main Street, right outside the Devil's Taproom where her stupid brother was probably tending bar and pretending he liked it, as usual.

"Hey!" The Wooden Spoon's door jingled behind her and then boots were thudding up the sidewalk toward her. "Hey, wait!"

She turned and found the guy Gerte had been whaling on jogging toward her. Eli, she reminded herself. Eli Walker. He was about average height. Maybe average plus an inch or two, she saw as he drew up in front of her, but not tall enough to loom over her. Not that he seemed inclined to loom, having stopped a solid two yards away. He frowned down at her nonetheless, his eyes achingly blue and set wide over broad cheekbones. She frowned back. Those eyes were gorgeous, ridiculously so. Giant, extravagantly lashed and so desperately sad. She wondered if he was aware that sorrow clung to him like a scent.

"Who are you?" he asked.

"Willa."

"Eli Walker." He didn't hold his hand out to shake and she was glad. She didn't want to touch him. Not yet. Not with that sorrow of his trying to snake its way into her head. She studied him carefully. He wasn't a handsome man, not exactly, but there was something appealing in the way he was put together — in the sharp planes of his face, the precise angles of his bones. He looked like a marathoner, all lean muscle and long limbs, every move engineered with maximum efficiency in mind.

"Was that true?" he asked. "What you said back there? About the house fire? The way it started."

"No."

"I didn't think so."

She gave that a moment and when he didn't seem inclined to elaborate, she turned and started for her truck again. He fell into step beside her.

He said, "You didn't need to lie for me."

"I didn't."

"But you lied."

It wasn't a question so she didn't answer it.

"I don't want any favors, Willa. I don't need anybody to protect me."

She reached her truck and crossed to open the driver's door. She'd left the windows open but even so it was like opening a blast furnace. She hiked herself up on the runner and met his eyes over the top of the cab. "I wasn't protecting you," she said.

"Somebody else, then."

Again, no question so she didn't feel obligated to answer. But Gerte had taken that Dumpster fire damn personally, and she'd already accused Matty of lighting it once. Willa wasn't about to let her do it again. She got into the truck. The vinyl was like lava under her thighs, burned through her worn jeans like they didn't exist. She fired up the old engine. Eli put a hand on the open passenger window and leaned in.

She gazed deliberately at his hand on her truck, then lifted her eyes back to his. Didn't suck in a breath at the punch of all that deep, sad blue, but it was a near miss.

He said, "I owe you one anyway."

She put the truck in gear and said, "No, you don't." And drove off, leaving him on the sidewalk outside her family's bar, watching her go with those eyes of purest sorrow.

Chapter 4

IT WAS AFTER midnight when Willa's phone rang. Late night phone calls were rarely a good thing but in Willa's line of work, they weren't unusual. In fact, they weren't even bad news. Not for her, anyway. The caller was almost certainly having a bad night but to Willa that ringing phone was like money knocking on her door. And she wasn't rich enough to ever wish it would knock on somebody else's.

She snatched the phone off her nightstand and shoved her hair out of her face. "Zinc Pest Control."

"Hey, my name is Eli Walker. I'm staying out at the state forest campground just north of town, Cabin 6. There's a snake in my toilet and I'm hoping like hell you can send somebody out to deal with it because I honestly didn't think you grew snakes this big this far north."

Eli Walker. Her mind supplied a pair of achingly blue eyes and the sound of Gerte's open palm connecting with a sharp cheekbone. Guy was having himself one hell of a visit. "We can grow a sizable snake on the North Shore, Mr. Walker, but we keep the venomous ones down state."

"Yeah, well, this one shook its tail at me, so maybe your guy can discuss it with the snake when he gets here."

Willa suppressed a sigh. New customers always assumed they were speaking with the receptionist. Doing battle with entrenched sexism wasn't really her job, though. The snake in the toilet was.

"We'll be there in fifteen minutes," she said.

"Thank you, Jesus."

Fifteen minutes later, Willa was on state forest land. She pulled up to a glorified toolshed with an extremely questionable veranda tacked to the front and the number six painted beside the screen door. It was cute and rustic, she supposed, with that sharply peaked roof and a gingerbread-house-shaped bird feeder hanging from the eaves. But between the seed the feeder leaked and the foundational cracks she could see in the dark, it was no wonder the guy had snakes. She wouldn't be surprised if he had wolves, honestly. Moose, too, except they wouldn't fit. She eyed the warped shingles. He almost certainly would have rain if they ever got any, which they hadn't. Not all summer.

She killed the engine, dug the necessary equipment from the lockbox in the truck bed and considered the porch steps. There were only two but they looked more questionable than the veranda. She doubted she'd die if she busted through but a broken ankle wasn't on her agenda tonight. Not now that the DNR had finally agreed to audit her and approve her license.

The screen door flew open while she was still considering her options and suddenly Eli Walker was there, framed in a rectangle of light. He was wearing a pair of ratty cargo shorts that had clearly seen better days if *better days* was code for crawling around in a blast zone. They hung low on narrow hips, the plaid boxers he'd probably been sleeping in showing plainly through a rip in the thigh. He was still pulling on a t-shirt as he opened the door, and Willa found herself eyeballing a torso that was exactly what she might've imagined, had she spent any time imagining Eli Walker's torso.

Which she hadn't. She wasn't an eye candy kind of woman. She preferred her men fully clothed, actually, and at least six feet away. Ten was better. But all that lean, efficient muscle shifting under skin the sun had kissed deeply gold? Willa stared, a little mesmerized, while something warm and interested uncurled inside her tense belly.

Eli's head finally appeared and he said, "You're here for the snake?"

Willa closed her mouth. She'd been gaping, she realized, disgusted with herself. "Here for the snake," she confirmed and mounted the iffy steps. They creaked but held and Eli stepped back to allow her into the cabin's bright kitchen.

He froze. "Willa?"

Good for him. He not only noticed she was a girl but recognized her from earlier. Remembered her name, even. He didn't smile, though. He only blinked those big sad eyes at her in surprise.

"Mr. Walker." She didn't smile either.

"Eli. You're Zinc Pest Control?"

"Owner, operator."

"Huh. Fancy that."

Her smile took her by surprise. Who said things like *fancy that* anymore?

"Fancy that," she returned. The cabin was about twelve feet by twelve feet, a tiny kitchenette with a two-burner stove against the front wall and a twin-sized bed shoved up against the back. A stingy little peninsula counter poked out of the wall to her left, separating the stove from the bed, and a cheap accordion door stretched across an opening in the back wall. She nodded toward it.

"The bathroom, I assume?"

"If you can call it that." Eli shoved both hands through hair buzzed so brutally short it was more like a five o'clock shadow than hair. "There's a toilet in there but if you want to sit down on it, you'll have to leave the door open to account for your knees being six inches into the bedroom."

Willa eyed him. "Did you try to sit down on it?"

"I don't have a snake bite on my ass, if that's what you're asking."

"I was more concerned about the snake than your ass, but good for both of you."

Eli's hand dropped protectively to one butt cheek and he tipped his head to study her. "I hadn't considered it from the snake's point of view, but you're right. Good for both of us."

Willa rounded the stubby counter and unlatched the accordion door. It retracted with a sullen snap and sure enough, there was an ancient toilet in harvest gold, a cast iron dutch oven sitting on the closed lid. She raised a brow at Eli.

"It was the heaviest thing I could find," he said.

"Good thinking."

A rueful smile ghosted over his face. "I now feel compelled to admit that I had already done a few laps around the cabin with my shorts around my knees screaming like a little girl before the thinking started."

An answering smile tugged at Willa's lips. "You're not a snake guy?"

"Nope." He admitted it easily. "Just call me Indiana Jones."

"*Snakes*," she said solemnly. "*Why did it have to be snakes?*"

He blinked at her. "That movie was old when I was born."

"It's a classic for a reason." She shrugged. "Now tell me what's happening in your toilet."

"There's a snake in it." He blinked again. "What else do you need to know?"

"What did it look like?"

"Big."

"Color? Markings?"

"Uh, dark? Maybe some stripes?"

"Horizontal or vertical?"

"Hang on, I have to think past the horror." He dragged a hand down his face, blew out a breath. Opened his eyes and said, "Okay, yellow stripes running from head to tail. Which it shook at me. Did I mention the tail shaking?"

"Yeah." Willa kept her face solemn. "Many snakes do that, Mr. Walker, not just rattlers. Think of it as a friendly warning."

"Eli," he said again. "And I'm from Colorado. When a

snake shakes its tail at you in Colorado, it's not friendly."

"Fair enough."

"So what do you think it is?"

Willa's money was on a harmless little garter snake, but based on the nerves still jittering all over Eli's face she doubted he'd welcome the news. "Why don't we have a look?"

"I already did, thanks. My heart may never recover." He sat on the edge of the bed, which creaked mournfully. "You go ahead, though."

"Okay." She reached into her bag and pulled out an old pillowcase. She flapped it open and draped it in the tiny sink beside the toilet. She pulled out her snake tongs next, a telescoping pole with a pincers on one end and a grip on the other that controlled the pincers.

She could feel Eli's eyes on her as she moved, and it was strangely unsettling. It wasn't that he was watching her work. People often hung around while she dealt with whatever wild thing had invaded their home. They might not want her there but they all wanted to be damn sure her services were rendered.

Eli's gaze didn't feel like that, though. It touched down gently, almost curiously, like butterflies landing all over her. Hair, hands, wrists, throat. It should disturb her that he seemed to see through the cloak of invisibility she thought she'd perfected. But those deep, sad eyes of his wandered over her body without any of the nasty appetite she'd learned to fear. This felt more like an animal sniffing at an unfamiliar scent — no malice, no aggression, just wary curiosity. It made her want to stand still and let him learn whatever there was to learn from the sight of her.

Instead, she put one boot on the toilet lid and slid the dutch oven to the floor. She glanced back at Eli, found him staring at the lid under her boot with a tense implacability.

She said, "Ready?"

"As I'll ever be." He stood up. "What should I do?"

A funny rush of tenderness tightened her throat. She could all but smell the fear on him but he'd stood up, grimly prepared to do whatever she told him.

"Nothing," she said. "I just wanted to make sure you were braced for this. I didn't want to surprise you into running around the cabin with your shorts around your knees again."

"Oh. Sure." He heaved out a hugely relieved sigh and sat back down. "Once a night is my limit on that kind of thing, but thanks."

"You're welcome," she said and opened the toilet lid.

Suddenly, he was right there behind her, peering over her shoulder into the toilet bowl. The tang of his fear mixed now with the clean scent of grown man, and the warmth of his body reached out to touch her bare neck. She wished, fleetingly and for possibly the first time in her adult life, that she'd worn her hair down. His body heat on her nape felt dangerously intimate. But *he* was afraid, she reminded herself, not her. At least when it came to snakes.

Willa took a moment to focus and sure enough, there was a garter snake curled up in Eli Walker's toilet bowl. It lifted its tail from the water, gave it a weary shake.

"Yeah, I hear you," Willa murmured. "Not your night, either."

"Why is it doing that?" Eli asked, his voice like rough velvet against her vulnerable nape. She itched to scoot forward, to put a few more inches between them but there was nowhere to go. The only way out was through. "Why is it shaking its tail?"

She considered the time this snake had probably spent in the state forest's ancient plumbing system. "I imagine he's had a crappy night."

"There's a three-foot-long snake in my toilet, I'm sweating bullets here and you're making poop jokes?" He let out a soft huff of laughter. "I don't know whether to fire you or propose marriage."

A bolt of uncertain awareness shot from her nape to low in her belly and smoldered there. "Two and a half feet, tops," she said briskly and snapped her snake tongs out to an appropriate length. Put her elbow in his gut while she was at it. It was hard to breathe with the *scent* of him — all cool pines and warm earth shot through with that bright, metallic fear — wrapping around her. "Sorry."

He stepped back. "No, that was me. I'm crowding you. Sorry. But that beast is at least eighteen feet long."

"If that's how you want to tell it, I won't contradict you."

A pause. "I'm leaning toward marriage. Just FYI."

Willa eased her tongs into the bowl. The snake flickered its tongue at her, tasting the air, testing her intentions. Willa concentrated on exuding calm, peace, strength. She brought an image to mind of the secret little clearing deep in the forest where she intended to release the snake. She didn't necessarily believe in the power of visualization, and had no ambitions to speak to the animals Dr. Doolittle style, but she did believe deeply and strongly in non-verbal communication. Animals understood scent, movement, sound, and depended on them to intuit strangers' intentions, animal or human. It only made sense, then, that putting her intentions in the forefront of her mind while picking up a frightened animal would help her send the right signals.

The snake seemed to agree because it didn't move as she eased the pincer around its body just behind its head. It seemed relieved, actually, and Willa didn't blame it. The state forest plumbing system was ancient but well used. This snake couldn't have had a good couple of hours. She lifted it gently from the toilet bowl, let it hang there a minute, dripping. She sent Eli a look over her shoulder.

"You want to measure it?"

"Twenty feet," he breathed, his face caught somewhere between fascination and revulsion. "Easy. Maybe thirty."

She chuckled. "Try thirty inches."

"I'll tell it my way, you tell it yours."

"Deal." She moved the tongs to the sink and lowered the snake into the waiting pillowcase. It curled into the bottom with what she'd have sworn was a sigh of relief. She concentrated on her favorite clearing again and twisted the top of the case shut, fastening it with a length of twine she pulled from her pocket. She hefted the case and eased it over her shoulder so the poor snake could at least enjoy her body heat until it was free again.

"So that's it?" Eli said. "I'm alone in my cabin again?"

She eyed him. "You do know what snakes eat?"

"Ah, hell. Mice." He palmed his face, scrubbed the stubble on his scalp. "I must have one hell of a mouse population if a snake was willing to crawl through miles of shit to get at it."

"It's just a theory."

He thought about it. "I don't mind mice. Definitely lived with worse."

"Me, too." She touched the brim of her ball cap. "Goodnight, Mr. Walker. I'll bill the landlord."

His grin was a bright, unexpected flash, transforming his face from interesting to compelling. "My landlord is the DNR."

"Yep. Should be a fun bit of paperwork."

He nodded at the pillowcase. "What are you going to do with it?"

"Normally I wouldn't release a snake on state forest property but since I found it here, I'm within my rights to do just that. There's a place I know that would be perfect for him."

"You're going to take him tonight?"

"I'd planned to." She tipped her head, suddenly wary. "Why?"

"I need to go with you."

She narrowed her eyes. "Again, why?"

"Because if I do, then you can count this against the three observed removals you need for your license."

She stared. "Oh, hell. You're a DNR agent?"

"I'm *your* DNR agent."

Chapter 5

IF YOU'D ASKED him a couple hours ago, Eli would've said that the only thing in this world he wanted was to fall face-first into any available bed and sleep for forty-eight hours. That was before Willa Zinc had rescued him from the kind of situation that he'd previously believed existed only on the internet. Before she'd walked into his tumble-down cabin with that cool air of devastating competence. Before she'd quoted *Raiders of the Lost Ark* unprompted. That was before she'd pulled a dripping nightmare from his toilet and all Eli had been able to see was the delicate curve of her exposed nape, a whisper of fine hair sliding out of the ponytail she'd threaded through the back of a no-nonsense ball cap.

Which was insane. Eli was finally losing it. His therapist would be thrilled to know it. At least he was making progress, one way or the other. Too bad it was toward crazy town — because what else could you call being seized by lust when there was a forty-foot snake in the room? Those were the breaks, he supposed.

"You're my DNR agent?" Willa said. "Last I heard, you were an itinerate bus boy."

He tried a winning smile. "Not to mention a potential arsonist. Now there's a story I'd like to hear."

"Explain," she said, that pixie-pointed jaw of hers at a terse angle that didn't bode well for the marriage Eli had nearly offered.

He wished he could explain. The circumstances leading up to his relocation to Devil's Kettle were a little unclear still even to him but he could give her the broad strokes.

"I'm actually a Forest Service guy," he said finally. "US Department of."

"I thought you said you were DNR."

"I'm on loan."

"You can borrow a forest ranger?"

"Ever heard of the Good Neighbors Act?"

"Nope."

"It pretty much allows just that between state and federal agencies with shared interests."

"Like adjoining state and national forest lands?"

"Exactly. Good neighbors, see?"

She only stared at him but he felt confident that she saw just fine. She might not be the bubbly sort but Willa Zinc was definitely firing on all cylinders. He suspected she fired on more cylinders than most folks even had.

"As it happens," he went on hastily, "the DNR needed a guy up here to do your observed removals—" Or so Ben had insisted when Eli tried to call bullshit. "—and I was available." Because desperately trying to hike your head straight for the third fire season in a row surely didn't take up *all* his time, or so Ben had argued with remarkable efficacy. "So here I am."

"I see." She studied him and he wanted to reach out and nudge that ball cap up a little higher. He wanted to see her eyes with an urgency he didn't understand and couldn't have explained. He just did. "And you didn't mention this when you called for an emergency snake removal because…?"

"Because I was in a cold sweat about the fifty-foot snake I nearly peed on?" She gazed at him, stone-faced. He sighed. "But even if I weren't, I'd probably have done the first one blind anyway."

"Why?"

"Because I wanted to see you in action before you knew it counted. Pest removal's a weird line of work. A lot of cowboys in it, people who shouldn't be allowed to own a dog, let alone wrangle wild animals." Her nod was stiff but at least she nodded. "I wanted to see how you treated animals when you didn't know it mattered."

A long pause. "Are you really afraid of snakes?"

"Straight up."

She nodded again, as if she'd known it all along but he'd passed some kind of test by admitting it. She jiggled the shoulder the snake-sack was slung over. "Are you going to be okay riding shotgun with this fella?"

"Oh, Christ. Do I have to?"

"It's not safe for me to drive and be in control of a wild animal," she said primly. "And it's afraid. It would really be a lot happier on your warm lap."

"Hell, no." He eyed the sack. "I'll hold the tied end, and it can sit on the seat next to me."

"Fair enough," she said, and he couldn't stand it anymore. He reached out and nudged the brim of her cap up. She jerked back like he'd threatened her with a loaded pistol but he only nodded.

"I thought so," he murmured.

"Thought what?" she snapped, snugging her cap back down and glaring at him.

"You're laughing at me." He smiled, unoffended. "I couldn't tell with that cap pulled so low but I thought as much."

"I'm not laughing," she muttered. She spun and stalked toward the door.

"Not now." He fell in behind her, more cheerful than he could remember being in months. Years. "But you were."

"I was not." She glared over her shoulder at him. "I don't laugh. I'm not a laugher."

"Okay."

She stalked to the beat-up pickup parked just off the porch. "It's open," she said and yanked open the driver's side door. Eli helped himself to the passenger door and slid onto a worn vinyl bench seat. The truck smelled like sunscreen and night air and wild things. Just like her. Willa dumped a sack full of snake on his lap and said, "Buckle up, Mr. Walker."

"Eli," he managed and obeyed orders.

"I thought you said we were releasing this beast on state forest land," Eli said as Willa pulled onto the highway. She didn't turn to meet his eyes but she felt them on her, just like she had in the cabin. She was starting to get used to it, the whisper-light touch of his attention.

"We are."

"Then why are we leaving the state forest?"

"The place I have in mind?"

"Yeah?"

"You can't get there from here."

"Where can you get there from?"

She sent him a cool look. "I'm taking you there."

He gave a soft laugh. "You're the first person to tell me to shut up in three years."

"I didn't tell you to shut up."

This time the cool look was his, and the soft chuckle was hers. Because she totally had told him to shut up. It was to his credit that he understood as much and wasn't offended. It was even more to his credit that he did indeed shut up. The silence was comfortable and broken-in somehow. Sliding into it was like lacing up her favorite pair of boots, which should've freaked her out except that it didn't. He wasn't happy about the snake snuggled up to his leg but he was dealing. Aside from that, she was reading him as…content? Yeah, sitting there in the passenger seat of her old truck with the night air swirling through the open windows, all rich earth and sharp pines, fading heat and dark secrets, Eli Walker was content.

Strangely, so was she.

She pulled up in front of her own cabin a few minutes

later and killed the engine.

"Where are we?"

"Other side of the state forest." She took the snake from him and shouldered open her door. He followed suit and met her at the front bumper.

"Private property?"

"Mine."

He studied the neat one-and-a-half story building in front of them with grave care and Willa wondered what he saw. She'd replaced the roof and repainted last summer, but otherwise it was identical to hundreds of other cabins planted along the North Shore. The only significant difference was that her foundation was solid as Split Rock lighthouse and she'd put up a bird feeder the day she decided to invite every mouse in the neighborhood into her attic. It wasn't fancy or even decorated, really, but it was home to Willa. It was her retreat. A stronghold. Safe, solid, secure. It probably just looked grim to him, though. Cold and square and unadorned. Just like her. Just as she'd made herself years and years ago.

"Yeah," he said finally. "I can tell. It feels just like you."

"*Feels* like me?" She wanted to bite her tongue off. She really didn't want to know what he thought she felt like. Did she?

No, absolutely not. She turned and headed down a path she'd worn into the forest floor decades ago. Eli fell into step behind her, still not remotely offended by her abruptness. Most people were but she was coming to understand that Eli Walker wasn't like most people.

"I only meant that it felt very still and serene." His voice was low and rough in the darkness, like a cat tongue against her skin. It prickled and smoothed all at the same time. A shiver seized her nape and shimmied down her back. "You have such a stillness to you, Willa."

Longing was an ache in his voice, a poignant desire that had nothing to do with her and everything to do with that endless sorrow filling his eyes. He'd been broken, she knew suddenly, and badly. She had no objective reason to think so but she knew it nonetheless. She recognized it. She'd lived with it herself, hadn't she? Lived with grief and shame buzzing relentlessly inside her, filling her skull every day and every night until she thought she'd go mad with it. It had driven her out of her room, out of her home, out of her very self. She'd gone to the woods, to the night, walked for miles among the small creatures that hid from her and the large ones that didn't. It was there that she'd finally found her measure of that stillness Eli was talking about.

Her bones ached with his pain but she didn't know what to say. Didn't think saying anything would help anyway. So she let the night surround them as they walked to the one place she thought might help.

Eli lost track of time. He simply followed Willa through the night. He didn't wonder where they were, didn't ask where she was taking him. He genuinely didn't care. He simply put his boots in her tracks and drank in that blessed *stillness*.

He didn't know how she was doing it. Didn't really care. All he knew was that this woman was like a drug, smoothing out the jagged edges and broken pieces that had been rubbing and ripping inside him for the better part of three years. And for the first time in recent memory, there was quiet inside his head. There was peace.

Jesus Christ, it had been so long. He would've cried if he'd remembered how.

When she finally stopped, it was to send him an unreadable look over her shoulder. The shoulder over which she carried what must by now be a very confused snake.

She took the sack from her shoulder, cradled it to her stomach and murmured, "This is it, buddy."

He wondered if she was talking to him or to the snake.

Decided it didn't matter because he was at the edge of one of the most beautiful meadows he'd ever seen in his life.

He looked up and found a star-shattered circle of night framed in spiky pine crowns. He lowered his eyes and saw that the clearing was perfectly circular as well, centered on a massive boulder. It, too, was circular but flat and low, like some whimsical god had wanted a coffee table right here in the woods.

No, not a coffee table. An altar. Eli had never been much for church — no god worth praying to would allow half the shit that went on down here — but if he'd been inclined that way, this was the kind of place that would drop him to his knees.

He might end up on his knees anyway.

Willa crossed to the boulder and he followed her, unable to do otherwise. She knelt by the edge and he knelt beside her. A part of his brain — separate, amused, detached — thought, *shit, that was fast.* But the bigger part, the part that had turned off everything else in favor of simply being here, now, with her, watched her reach out and place her palm on the rock.

She smiled and he lost his breath. "Touch," she said and he almost did. He desperately wanted to. Wanted to put his fingertips to the smooth curve of her cheek, to the sharp edge of that pixie jaw. He wanted to trace the delicate curl of her ear, the clean line of her collar bone. He wanted to touch the deep dip in her upper lip, the one that made a pretty bow of her mouth.

But he obediently placed his hand beside hers on the smooth surface of the rock and found it warm against his fingers. Warm and something else. Alive, maybe, though not alive in the sense he'd always understood it. Something pulsed there, something more than alive. Something older than time and wiser than knowledge. He hissed in a breath and she sighed.

"You feel it?" Her eyes were shadowed by the brim of

her cap but they were sharp on him, urgent. "You feel how *old* it is?"

"Willa," he said finally. "What is this place?"

"I don't know. A fairy ring, maybe. A thinnie?"

"Holy hell, you're a *Dark Tower* fan?"

"Stephen King is the Shakespeare of our era."

"Marry me." He was more than half-serious.

She ignored him. He didn't know if he was relieved or devastated. "I love the idea of a thinnie," she said. "Of a place where the usual barriers between worlds, between times, are so delicate, so permeable you can almost hear that other time or place singing to you."

"Dangerous," he murmured. "Like sirens singing sailors to their deaths."

"Or to their greatest adventure," she returned. She lifted the pillowcase and placed it on the warm rock between their hands. "Not that anything even slightly paranormal has ever happened here."

"It hasn't?" Again, Eli wasn't sure if he was relieved or disappointed. "Never?"

"I've never seen so much as a fairy dancing." She unwound the string and opened the bag, folded back the edges and revealed the snake curled loosely upon itself. The instinctive dread Eli had always felt, that bolt of adrenaline and terror, was still there. It lived in the part of his brain that was as old as this rock, so it was there but it was strangely muted. Present but not overwhelming. He could think over it without any trouble. Could look into the strange flat eyes of the snake flickering its tongue experimentally at this new air, and understand it as nothing more or less than a fellow being. A random spark of life, just like Eli, riding its ticket as long as it lasted. As long as its luck held out.

The snake uncoiled slowly, glided out of the pillowcase in that unearthly way of snakes, moving without any obvious means of propulsion. Fascination twined with the background hum of fear and Eli reached without thinking to lace his fingers through Willa's. She let him. Her hand was small and cool even as it was callused and tough. And the horror buzzing at the back of his brain, the relentless shame and guilt and agony, muted down to almost imperceptible. They watched together while the snake curled slowly over the surface of the boulder. It paused once it was free of the pillowcase, seemed to absorb the rock's warmth, age, strength, whatever. Then it streamed over the far edge in a liquid ribbon of movement, and was gone.

Chapter 6

THE NEXT MORNING found Willa at the Devil's Taproom, extricating a box of straws from the jammed-tight supply shelves with the same focus a bomb technician might give an IED. Devil's Kettle was built on a basalt lava flow several hundred feet thick, which meant basements weren't a practical option. But lake-view real estate wasn't cheap, so you didn't complain when you scored some. If that meant storing an entire bar-and-grill's worth of inventory in what amounted to a broom closet, well, those were the breaks.

Not that Willa was particularly concerned with the taproom's straw supply. The day to day running of the family bar was Peter's responsibility but he'd insisted she take one shift a week. He'd actually written it into that 60/40 ownership deal they'd worked out four years ago when he'd sailed back into town for the circus that had been Diego's funeral. Peter would run the place — among others, as Peter intended to amass an empire that ranged far and wide in Devil's Kettle — but she had to vote her shares (she had *shares* now, for sweet lord's sake) on any major decisions, and she'd pull one shift every week. To stay in touch with the business, Peter claimed. Not because he was a pretentious jerk with delusions of grandeur. Definitely not because he wanted to sleep in on Saturdays.

Willa didn't care. She wasn't much for sleeping in anyway. Even if she wanted to, she doubted she could. Once the sun was up, the ravens nesting in her yard were loud enough to wake the dead. Plus, if she were being perfectly honest, she had to admit she didn't actually mind Saturday mornings at the bar that much. The breakfast crowd hit the

Wooden Spoon or the Sugar Rush for doughnuts, and the serious drinkers were still sleeping off Friday night. This left Willa alone with the mop bucket, some restocking and her thoughts, which suited her far better than customers.

Usually. Today was an exception. But if her thoughts weren't easy company this morning, it was because of last night. It was because Eli Walker had knelt beside her in the woods. It was because he'd given her thinnie the same reverence she did, the reverence nobody else ever had. And when she'd given that poor, frightened snake its freedom, when the snake had trusted her and taken it? He'd held her hand.

It sent a slow shock rolling through her to even remember it, the way his fingers had threaded through her own. The strength and gentleness in them. The uncompromising masculinity of that broad palm against her own smaller, more feminine one. The way it had made her breathlessly aware of that femininity for the first time in years.

She'd buried it deep, her sexuality. That was what you did with dangerous things. You put them deep in the dirt where they'd draw no notice and hopefully just sleep. Because once people saw that primitive appetite in her, once *men* saw it, they wanted it. Oh, they didn't want *her*. She wasn't a fool. She knew what she looked like. But she also knew that looks didn't matter much once men got a good sniff of the earthy lust that lived inside her.

So she'd hidden it. Hidden herself. Done such a good job that nobody in this town even remembered the half-wild girl she'd once been. The one who used to laugh and dance and attack the world with wide-open arms and a wider-open heart. The one whose hair had flown like birds in the air, like bare feet over the grass. The one who'd loved a boy whose wild streak had put her own to shame. A boy whose wildness had been veined with a cruel selfishness she hadn't understood and so hadn't seen or even imagined. Not until it had been far, far too late.

But nobody else had seen the cruelty in him, either. How could she be blamed for not seeing something nobody else had? But even if they had, who would have stopped him? The Davises were the closest thing Devil's Kettle had to royalty, and Diego had been their crown prince. Willa had been nothing but a pretty bit of trash.

Now she wasn't even pretty. She'd made sure of it.

But Eli had taken her hand last night like it was something precious.

He'd nudged up the brim of her ball cap because he'd wanted to see her eyes.

And when she'd dropped him back off at his rickety little cabin in the woods in an agony of confused awareness, he'd said nothing more than, "Thank you, Willa." And left her alone in the darkened cab of her truck wondering what the hell had just happened.

She was *still* wondering, damn it.

She shoved through the swinging door into the front of the bar and stopped dead, the box of straws clamped tight in one armpit. "Addison."

"Hey, Willa." Addison Davis grinned at her from a bar stool, the late morning sun bouncing off her wild auburn curls. In all the years she'd lived with the spit-and-polish Davises, Addy had never even tried to tame those curls of hers. It was just one of the reasons Willa actually liked Diego's young widow. Another was that she suspected he'd been just as vile to his pretty little wife as he'd been to Willa.

"What are you doing here?" Willa asked. But she knew. After yesterday's baffling exchange with Bianca? Of course she knew.

"I've been looking for you." Addy's green eyes danced under that disarming bird's nest of curls and she wrinkled a pert nose sprinkled with the most innocent freckles known to man.

"Why?"

"Because I want to ask you something."

"Like what?" She took the box of straws from her now-sweaty armpit and shoved it under the counter. She kept the swinging door open with one boot just in case. An escape hatch seemed like an extremely good idea just now.

Addison slid off the stool and raised both hands. "Now, Willa, don't panic. And don't say no right away."

"To what?"

"Take your foot out of that door first. Heaven's sake, I'm not going to shoot you."

"Am I going to wish you had?"

She smiled and dread gripped Willa by the throat. "Maybe."

"Oh hell." Addy nailed her with a look that had Willa pulling her boot out of the door. "Okay, okay. Fine. Sorry."

Addy favored her with a sunny smile — cheerful as a daisy now that she was getting her way — and said, "Come out here."

Willa did as she was told. Now that Addy had her, there was no point trying to get away. Might as well just get it over with.

"Sit," Addy said and pointed to a stool. Willa blinked at the pretty diamond winking and burning on Addy's ring finger. It was a far cry from the massive heirloom diamond that had lived there until earlier this year, the one Diego had put on her finger when she hadn't even been twenty-one.

"Jax finally got his ring on your finger, I see," Willa said, desperate to distract her.

Addy smiled smugly. "That's exactly what I wanted to talk to you about."

Willa sighed. She was so bad at this. She thought she'd been changing the subject and instead had walked right into the jaws of the trap. But how could Addy's engagement to Diego's older — and far better — brother possibly be any of her business?

"Um, okay." She sat. "Why?"

Addy hopped up on the stool beside hers and grabbed one of Willa's hands. Willa flinched, startled. Why was everybody *touching* her lately? But she didn't pull away because, once she got past the shock, Addison's delight was overpowering. It buzzed in the air all around her, enveloped Willa like a bouncy hug, all but vibrated in her bones. There wasn't a hint of darkness in it, though. Willa smelled nothing of ambition or manipulation. Addy was just straight up happy and Willa felt her resistance crumbling under the sheer force of it.

"Because I need a bridesmaid and I want it to be you."

Willa didn't think she could've been more shocked if Addy had produced a girl-sized hammer from her purse and rapped Willa smartly between the eyebrows with it.

"*What?*"

"I want you to be my bridesmaid."

"Why?" Horror dripped from her voice. Willa didn't even care.

Addy laughed. "Willa, my goodness. What a question! Because you're my friend."

"I am?" she asked automatically. It still surprised her, Addy's friendship.

"Of course you are." Her face softened and she let go of Willa's hand to pat her knee. "After what you did for Matty the night Davis Place burned? You're mine for life."

"I didn't do anything but keep my mouth shut."

"Exactly. Do you have any idea how rare that is in this town?" Unfortunately, Willa did. "And I heard what you said to Gerte the other day when she was trying to slap Eli Walker's face off his head at the Wooden Spoon. The way you took responsibility for the fire."

That slow, hot shock rolled through Willa again at the mere mention of Eli's name. She carefully squelched it. "She needed to stop harping on that damn fire, that's all. She was after Eli right then, sure, but it was only a matter of time before she worked her way back around to giving Matty the stink eye, so I—"

"—protected a kid." Addy beamed at her. "A kid I happen to love like he's my own. And you protected a stranger, too. Best of all, you shut Gerte's mouth for her, which is no easy task."

"Tell me," Willa muttered.

"I love you double just for that."

Willa narrowed her eyes. "And you're demonstrating this love by asking me to wear a fancy dress and let some sadist at my hair?"

Addy gave her a patient smile. "No, I'm inviting one of the best people I know to stand for me while I do one of the most important things I'll ever do."

"Oh, hell. When you put it that way, how am I supposed to say no?"

"You're not." Addy gave a watery little laugh and launched herself at Willa without warning, wrangled her into a fierce hug. "I'm getting *married*, Willa!"

"Okay, okay." Willa patted Addy's back with uncertain hands while Addy squeezed her like a tube of toothpaste, rocking her side to side, half unhinged with that mad delight Willa could all but smell. "And to somebody I actually love this time."

"You didn't love Diego?" Willa had no idea why she'd asked. It wasn't any of her business.

"No, I did." Addy drew back and swiped her fingers under her damp eyes. She took her own barstool again — thanks be — and beamed at Willa. "I loved Diego the way you only ever love the first one, all wild and passionate and impulsive. But it was shallow. There were no roots, and real love needs those." Her eyes softened and Willa understood that whatever Addy felt for Jax had sunk those roots deep into the bedrock of her being. "But I'll never regret marrying him. How could I, when it put me here, right where I belong?"

"You couldn't," Willa conceded. She herself could and

did regret many things, but she could see that Addison was made of sterner stuff. "Of course you couldn't."

"But this one's forever and I want to do it right." She gripped Willa's hand and locked her in the tractor beam of that uncompromising gaze. "And that means making my promises surrounded by the people I love and who love me. My folks will come and they're good people, they really are. But they don't do family the way my heart does, and I need *family* around me this time."

"I'm not family—" Willa began.

"Oh yes you are." Addy's eyes blazed and she seized Willa's hand again. "You're tough, Willa. Smart and funny and sharp. And what's more, you're *true*. You have more courage than everybody in this town combined. I see it every time you protect Matty, one of the very Davises who treat you like garbage."

She paused, eyed Willa thoughtfully. "I don't know why they do that, you know. I don't know why you allow it. Why anybody in this place allows it. All I know is that there's a story there, a complicated, painful one that nobody's told me yet. That maybe I haven't earned yet. But I do know one thing. Earlier this spring? When people went bonkers about Diego's lost paintings? When everybody else in this town stepped away from me? You stood for me, Willa. You stood for me, even though it also meant standing for a family you must hate. That makes you family in my book, and believe me, I've made sure that the Davises know it. Know it and accept it. So I'd be deeply honored if you'd stand for me one more time while I marry the man I love."

Willa stared at her. Addy had just said more words out loud about the tragedy of Willa's own childhood than all the people in Devil's Kettle combined. And each word had lifted a stone off her soul. The space underneath was just as dark and slimy as you'd think the underside of a rock might be, but there was no denying the exquisite relief of having that weight lifted.

And it was tempting, so tempting, to heave off the rest of them. To tell Addison — to tell anybody — that story she so obviously wanted to hear.

But it wasn't as simple as just telling the story, was it? The truth came at a price, and it wasn't only the guilty who would pay. Innocents would pay, too, and Willa couldn't be party to that. She'd been an innocent once herself. She had a strong back. She could bear the weight of a few secrets.

All she said to Addison was, "You're going to let Georgie have me, aren't you?"

Addy laughed, wicked and satisfied. "I'm sorry but yes."

"I thought you said you loved me."

"I also said you were strong and courageous." Addy's eyes danced merrily. "Are you really going to tell me you're afraid of a little makeover?"

"You put a sharp and/or hot implement in Georgia Davis's hand and leave her alone with me, there's going to be bloodshed."

"You and Georgie shed blood just having a conversation."

"That's why we don't have conversations."

"Well she's my sister—"

"Sister-in-law." Willa paused. "Do you double down on the in-law bit since you're marrying another of her brothers? Is she going to be your sister-in-law-in-law?"

"She's going to be my maid of honor," Addy said firmly. "Which means you'll have to follow her lead until the wedding."

"Wait, follow her lead on what?"

Addy's eyes skated to the side. "Well, dresses and hair and makeup and such."

"Define *such*."

"There might be an event or two in the run up to the wedding." Addy gave her an innocent smile. "A shower or bachelorette party. Things the bridesmaids usually...plan together."

Susan Sey

Willa closed her eyes. "Kill me now."

Addy patted her knee. "I already have Walt at the Sugar Rush thinking about a doughnut tree."

"What in the holy hell is a doughnut tree?"

"Just an idea right now but maybe the best bridal shower centerpiece in the history of bridal shower centerpieces?"

Willa eyed her. "I thought you were a pie girl."

"That was before Gerte went after Matty."

"Ah." Willa could respect that.

"Please say yes, Willa. I need you."

She clamped her jaw shut on the *no* trying to happen and thought about the new lightness Addy had put in her soul. Solitude was Willa's natural habitat but honest friendship was a gift. It wasn't something she could walk away from without regret, and Willa didn't need even one more regret.

"Listen, I'm not making any promises," she said finally. "I won't start anything but if Georgie starts something—"

"—you'll finish it. Understood." Addy caught her up in yet another hug. Addy being Addy, she'd probably give out three dozen more before lunch but two hugs was more than Willa had had in...well, more years than she wanted to count. So she hugged her back. If standing by one real friend cost her several months in the company of her bitterest enemy, it was worth it. Enemies were a dime a dozen, even those with Georgie Davis's talent for meanness and taste for theater. Friends were far more rare.

Or so Willa had to assume. She'd never had one before. How would she know?

She was still pondering the question several minutes later while untapping the kegs so she could give the lines their weekly flushing. Everything under a bar was sticky but the keg of hard cider was always the worst. Any little spill, and sugar sludge cemented everything together for the ages. Willa was down on her knees with a wrench and some creative language when a waft of fresh lake air struck terror into her heart.

Lord, please let it not be Georgie already. Wasn't it enough for one day that she'd agreed to let Trust Fund Barbie dress her? Did she really have to live through her first consultation with a shirt full of sugar sludge, reeking of old beer?

She stayed where she was and went after the tap line with renewed vigor. Which wasn't hiding, she told herself. It was simply good strategy. Don't engage the enemy under unfavorable conditions. That was a rule or something, wasn't it?

Footsteps approached the bar and paused. Willa could all but feel the eyes on her back but she counted to twenty and kept wrestling with that stubborn hose. Thirty. Forty. Then the wrench slipped and she smashed her finger and that small, new pain glided into the everyday pain she'd just gotten used to carrying. She gave up on the hose and pushed to her feet. Pointed the wrench at Georgie and said, "Listen."

Then she stopped. The words just died and she stared. Because that wasn't Georgie, smirking at her from the other side of the bar, all mascara and despair over the hopeless task of making Willa pretty.

It was her father.

Chapter 7

IT WAS ALMOST noon and Eli had been on his feet for over seven hours. The sun rose at about 4:30 a.m. this time of year in the north country, and the birds along with it. Birds and whatever the hell else lived in that cabin of his. Willa had implied he might have a mouse issue and Eli didn't doubt it for a minute. When it came to Willa's job skills, Eli had seen everything he needed to see last night. She wasn't just good at what she did; she was gifted. He could sign off on her license right now with perfect confidence.

It was everything else about her he couldn't figure out.

And he wanted to.

The mystery of her had eaten at him as he lay in his lumpy excuse for a bed after she'd dropped him off. She'd spun through his brain, chewed at his dreams and eventually driven him out of his bed and into his boots. He'd laced up in the dark and been three miles into the other reason he'd been stationed here in Devil's Kettle before the sun had even broken through the pearly morning fog. And still she'd simmered there in the back of his mind. Even as he hiked and photographed and documented, he thought of her. Of the way her appeal hadn't faded with the rising sun.

He'd expected it to. She'd been like a dream last night, her footsteps silent in the living night, the moonlight streaking that thick tail of dark hair a witchy silver, that self-possessed, preternatural *stillness* of hers singing to him, calling to his aching bones.

She should've faded from his mind the way a dream did, leaving nothing but incomprehensible fragments that eventually disappeared altogether. But a dozen and a half miles of hard hiking later, it was still there. As was the urge to touch her, to smell her, to unwrap that cloak of stillness she wore. To peel it open layer by layer until he saw how it worked, how he could fashion one of his own. It was all still *there*.

He was going to see her again. Outside of the two supervised removals he had left, he was going to see her again. He *wanted* to see her. Didn't know if he could resist seeing her. He'd planned to steer clear, to give last night's strangeness a few days to settle more comfortably in his gut before he risked it. But he didn't want to wait. She'd been on his mind for coming up on twelve straight hours now. He didn't just want to see her. He needed to.

He checked his watch. Nearly noon, and he'd already put at least fifteen miles on his boots this morning, and had documented enough of what he'd come here to see to concern him. He was sweaty, he was hungry and having just wrapped up a singularly unimpressive conversation with the DNR guy managing the region's state forests, he was mildly pissed off. A shower, a meal and a phone call, he told himself. Then he'd let himself drop in on Willa Zinc.

He slid into the insulting excuse for a car the DNR had issued him. No wonder their employees were assholes. Eli might be an asshole, too, if he had to drive around an underpowered tuna can like this come winter. He fired it up — it coughed pitifully but caught — and dialed up his boss at the Forest Service.

"Ben Bayfield."

"Hey, Ben." Eli put the accelerator on the floor. His tuna can eased half-heartedly toward the exit of the state forest parking lot. "Eli."

"Eli." He could all but hear his uncle Ben sit up straight. "How's Devil's Kettle?"

He pulled up to the state highway intersection and checked traffic with more than his usual care. Fully loaded logging trucks were as common as minivans up here and his tuna can needed a good while to achieve cruising altitude.

"Interesting."

"You've been there one day, Eli," Ben said, all bluff and hearty. "How much trouble could you possibly have gotten into?"

Trouble was an old song — Eli's theme song, actually — sung in the key of *boys will be boys*. But lately his family had started injecting it with this determined note of hope, like maybe if they sang it loud enough and long enough, Eli would suddenly remember the mischievous kid he'd been. A troublemaker who'd always managed to land just on the right side of true trouble.

"I stopped in town for a sandwich on my way in," Eli said obligingly. "Got my face near slapped off my head."

Ben's laugh was loud and relieved. "I don't even want to know. But you always did like the ladies."

Gerte was fifty if she was a day — closer to sixty if Eli was any judge — and he didn't particularly like her. "Did my first supervised removal, too."

"That was quick."

"There was a snake in my toilet."

Ben paused. "I thought that only happened on the internet."

"Me, too. Turns out it's a thing."

"Who knew?"

"Not me. Willa Zinc did, though, so good on her."

"Zinc Pest Control is a girl?"

"I believe they like to be called women these days, Uncle Ben."

"Stuff it, son."

Eli chuckled. That was the Ben he'd grown up worshipping. A cigar-chewing, scabby-knuckled hotshot who didn't care how you were plumbed so long as you got the job done. A man who now rode a desk with the same blunt authority he'd once used to run an elite crew of wild land firefighters. A crew that would've followed Ben straight into hell, which was essentially what wild land firefighters did.

Once upon a time, Eli had wanted nothing more than to grow up to be Ben. To have his own crew that would follow him to hell and back.

He'd gotten that wish. Half of it, anyway. He'd gotten a crew, all right, and they'd followed him into hell. But only Eli had come back.

Shame gripped him by the throat and his chuckle died. He knew he should say something. Ben was waiting and it was his turn to talk but he couldn't squeeze any words past the guilt and pain. Ben finally took pity on him.

"So what about the fire potential up there? Did you talk to that bastard O'Malley yet?"

Eli cleared away the old guilt, focused on the job. "O'Malley, yeah. And I did. He's not the proactive sort."

"Shit." Ben's chair creaked and Eli could picture him shoving away from his desk to pace and scowl. "I knew it. When is the Department of Natural Resources going to get on the stick and force that fucker into retirement? How long does Minnesota keep dementia patients on the job?"

"He doesn't have dementia, Ben."

"How else do you explain refusing to do any kind of controlled burn for the better part of four decades then?"

Eli didn't have an answer for that one.

Ben sighed. "How bad is the fuel load?"

"Bad. Like you said, there've been no burns up here — controlled or otherwise — for nearly forty years. I probably pulled better than fifteen miles this morning and if the rest of the forest is anything like the little bit I saw today, this place is teed up for a hundred-year burn. And given the fuel load, it'll burn hot."

"Too hot?"

"Borderline. Either it happens by itself and under whatever weather conditions fate ponies up, or you plan the burn, pull in resources and pull the trigger when the conditions are optimal."

"Wait, don't tell me. O'Malley wants to leave nature to itself. That way when four hundred square miles of forest is burning at six thousand degrees and all the basalt up there is turning back into goddamn *lava*, he can play the above-my-pay-grade, act-of-God card."

Eli nearly smiled at that. "He didn't use those exact words but that was the impression I got, yeah."

Ben swore with an inventive fluency that had never failed to impress the boy Eli had been. "Convince him otherwise, Eli. We're supposed to be good neighbors now, the states and the feds. Convince this cowardly asshole to steward the damn environment, or we'll do it for him and screw neighborly relations."

"I'll do what I can."

"Do more."

"Goodbye, Ben."

"Later, kid."

Eli disconnected. Half an hour later, he trundled into Devil's Kettle proper. It was about three colorful blocks of courageous charm curled up next to the fierce glitter of that vast inland sea the locals called a lake. A great one, to be sure, but still just a lake. That was what you got, Eli mused, when you threw a bunch of French fur trappers and Scandinavian farmers into the local Native American population. They'd name everything with an oddball combination of radical understatement, sly humor and stylish insouciance.

He could actually learn to like it up here.

His stomach rumbled as he parked on the street in front of the Davis Gallery. It was a glass-and-pine building that stretched the entire length of the northern-most block of Main Street, and it glowed with a soft light that made even Eli who knew exactly nothing about art want to investigate. Oh, he'd heard of Diego Davis. Who hadn't? But he'd never

felt any inclination to visit a gallery before. He'd have to
swing in sometime.

It was more likely, he had to concede, that he'd be
visiting the hot-pink doughnut shop on the north end of the
block first. Maybe even today. But today's hike required
more fuel than a bear claw could provide so he locked up his
tuna can, hit the sidewalk and headed south. He squinted at
the sun, consulted his mental map. Southwest, he amended.
The lakeshore ran from the northeast to the southwest, and
Main Street followed suit.

The middle block of town started strong with a giant
papier mache fish leaping through what Eli assumed was a
false second story of the cinderblock building that ran the
length of the block. It was Soren Buck's idea of advertising,
and since the guy ran a bait and tackle, it was a good one. Eli
had made it a point to skim lightly over the towns and trails
he'd visited these past couple years. He didn't want to know
them, and didn't want them to know him. But even so, he
knew where to go if he needed a bucket of night crawlers in
Devil's Kettle and who to ask for them. Which meant Soren
Buck knew exactly what he was about.

There was a pretty little gift shop nestled between Buck's
Bait and Tackle and the Wooden Spoon, but Eli skipped all
three and aimed for the Devil's Taproom. It was the last
business on the block and while he wasn't typically a day
drinker, he wouldn't say no to a beer if it came with a
cheeseburger.

It was early, just after noon, but maybe he'd get lucky
and the place would be open for lunch.

He pushed through a heavy wooden door and stopped
dead. Because Willa was there, behind the bar. She was all
but glowing with the golden sun pouring in through a
generous plate-glass window fronting the bar. It ran over her
like a river, picked out reddish strands in that midnight
ponytail of hers, spotlit a filthy t-shirt that spoke of an epic
battle with…something, and given her line of work, Eli

didn't even want to hazard a guess as to what.

But none of that mattered because what struck Eli was her stillness. It was wrong. This wasn't her usual stillness. There was nothing of that blessed peace or centered calm in it. This was the frozen caution of a prey animal when a shadow glides by overhead. It wasn't quite fear but it was something close. He could all but smell it hanging in the air.

A tall man stood with his back to Eli, and he was the opposite of still. He shifted on cheap running shoes, twitched inside clothes so new they still looked creased and stiff. His hair was prison-guard short, a look Eli appreciated and cultivated himself but when you put it together with the twitch and the brand new clothes it added up to the other side of the coin. Not prison guard. Prisoner.

"Hey, Willa," he said and moved into the empty bar. He kept himself at the stranger's back, trusting the guy's prison instincts to do the heavy lifting for him. Sure enough the guy turned to put Eli in his peripheral. It backed him off Willa a few feet but it also gave Eli a good look at the guy's face. He was somewhere between fifty and seventy, Eli judged, depending on how hard the miles and the years had been on him. Still a good-looking guy but weathered. Used. But there was something child-like and wounded in those dark eyes that gave him pause. He'd known guys who'd done time and for all sorts of reasons. Some came out hard, some came out mean but they all came out damaged. This guy just looked sad.

But something about him had Willa worried and that couldn't be an easy thing to do. She knew something Eli didn't know, clearly, and Eli wouldn't leave her alone with it.

He nodded to the stranger, propped a dirty boot on the rung of a barstool and dropped an elbow on the bar. It put his fingers within brushing distance of the hunting knife he kept in the side pocket of his cargo pants.

"Hey, Eli," she said. She snugged her cap down on her

head and seemed to gather herself. Whatever he'd smelled on her — worry, caution, unhappiness — she gathered that up, too, and wrapped her cloak of stillness around all of it. "What are you doing here?"

"I could ask you the same question."

She flicked a glance at the man standing silently at Eli's side. His eyes were wide and inexplicably wounded, his mouth in a tight line that was the next thing to a flinch. As if he were waiting for Willa to hurt him, not the other way around. As if he'd almost welcome it.

"My family owns this place," she informed him shortly. "I pull the early shift on Saturdays."

Eli blinked. Her family owned a bar? And not just a bar but one of Devil's Kettle's flagship institutions? He couldn't digest it. Willa was so *alone*, so perfectly self-contained. Running a family restaurant was a messy, loud, complicated, twenty-four/seven endeavor, as Eli well knew. He'd grown up in one, hadn't he? He'd bused tables, done dishes, taken orders, run the bar. He'd helped his mom build something she'd hoped to pass along to him, and the whole time he'd just been waiting for the moment when he could break her heart and follow Uncle Ben into hell.

So he knew exactly what a family business was, how it wrapped you up and held you fast. He hadn't sensed any of that on Willa. He hadn't sensed anything on her but that deep, complete aloneness. So he asked the only question that made sense.

"You have family?"

"Not much." Beneath the brim of that damn cap, her mouth went tight. "Just a brother. You've probably met him. Peter Zinc? The Donald Trump of Devil's Kettle."

"Haven't had the pleasure."

"Lucky you."

"So it's just you and Peter?"

"Was." She tipped her head toward the strange, silent man to Eli's left, a gesture so slight somebody not used to her stillness might've missed it. Eli slid his hand into his pocket to touch the hilt of his knife. "Have you met my dad?"

Chapter 8

"YOUR DAD," ELI said carefully. He didn't know what the hell was going on, only that something was and it wasn't anything good. "No, I don't believe I have."

"You wouldn't have," Willa informed him. "He just got out of prison."

"I see."

"He'll be staying with me until he gets himself squared away."

"You're all right with that?"

"He's not dangerous." She smiled but it was anything but amused. "You might hear otherwise but people in this town like to talk and they aren't overly attached to accuracy."

"I see," Eli said again. He eyed the man silently watching Willa with all that bewildered pain and tentative hope. He took his hand from his pocket and held it out. "Eli Walker."

The man cleared his throat, like speaking was a new thing and he was still trying it out. "Brett Zinc," he said and took Eli's hand. The guy was easily six-two, if not six-three, with the beefy sort of build that said he'd probably been a football hero once upon a time. But he took Eli's hand with determined gentleness.

"Good to meet you, Mr. Zinc." He turned to Willa, who was still standing serenely as a tree in the forest on the other side of the bar. He wondered how she did that. How she pulled it all in and wrapped it all up like that. She was like a black hole, all impenetrable darkness wrapped around the mysteries of the universe. That craving seized him unexpectedly by the throat again, that desire to *know* her. "Hey, I was wondering, do you do food here? I'm starving to death and I'm afraid of Gerte."

She considered him. "I was just flushing the tap lines when Brett showed up, so I can't give you a beer but I could do a burger and fries."

"Make it a cheeseburger and you can have my firstborn."

"You have a firstborn?"

"Not yet. It would have to be an IOU. Unless you're offering?" He leaned into the bar and gave her a roguish twinkle he hadn't tried since before...well, since before.

She blinked slowly. "No. I'm not."

"An IOU, then. I'm just racking those up with you, aren't I?"

She gazed at him impassively. "You don't owe me anything."

"I disagree. Especially if there's a cheeseburger in the offing."

"I'll go start the grill. It'll be a few minutes."

"That's fine. I'll sit here and chat with your dad." He took a stool and Willa disappeared into the kitchen. He nudged another stool with one boot and cocked a brow at Brett. "Seat?"

Willa's dad eyed the stool with a resigned sigh. "Spent a lot of time on one of those in my misspent youth."

"Too much time?"

"Yeah." He glanced at the kitchen door. "She suffered for it." His mouth tightened. "A lot of people did."

"I'm sorry to hear it."

"Couldn't be sorrier than I am." He shook his head. "Not that sorry's worth a damn. I was always sorry once I sobered up. Then one day I sobered up in jail and learned I'd near killed a man." He gave a weary chuckle. "To this day, I don't even know what for. We were both black-out drunk but I woke up in a jail cell with a hangover for the ages. He woke up in the ICU with a brain bleed. I got ten years for it, served eight. He got a life sentence, though, didn't he?"

"Sounds that way."

Brett sank onto the stool finally, eased into it like it was an old friend, a perfectly broken in pair of jeans. "I haven't had a drink in over eight years but God help me, when I sit here I can almost feel the glass in my hand."

"The worst habits are the hardest to break." Eli rose and walked behind the bar. Found the coffee pot he'd smelled and poured them both a cup. "Start by changing the whiskey glass to a coffee mug. Cream? Sugar?"

"Never did acquire a taste for coffee."

Eli ripped the tops off at least five sugar packets and dumped them in. Found creamer in the little under-bar fridge, added a generous stream of that, too. "Acquire it now."

Brett eyed him. "You look comfortable behind a bar."

"I am." Eli slid the coffee Brett's way.

"I am, too. Or was." Brett lifted the coffee, sipped cautiously at it. "That's not bad."

"My barista sister would weep bitter tears over the abomination I just served you." He lifted his own coffee, black as night, for a taste of his own. Angels sang in his mouth and he found himself smiling. "She might actually like your daughter, though."

"Do you?"

Eli set down his coffee and met Brett's eyes. They were dark and cool and watchful. "You asking about my intentions, Mr. Zinc?"

"You've been here long enough to piss off Gerte, so longer than five minutes, but not long enough to know if we serve food or to meet the guy who runs this place day to day, so probably not quite ten minutes. And yet you're awfully comfortable behind my bar, and awfully friendly with my girl. And she's not the friendly sort."

"She isn't, no."

"I know I don't have the right to ask. Gave it up years ago, way before I woke up in that jail cell." Brett met his eyes steadily, and there was regret in them but also grim determination. "But I'm asking anyway."

"I don't have any intentions toward Willa, Mr. Zinc. I hardly even know her."

Those dark eyes were shrewd. "But you want to."

"I do."

"Why?"

"Hell if I know. She doesn't want me to."

"Don't take it personal."

Eli laughed at that. "Wasn't planning to."

"Plan to be kind to her, then. Plan to treat her like she's worth something."

"She is. I don't know much but I know that much."

"You'd better. I learned some shit in prison."

Eli laughed again. It was a goddamn record. "Do I want to know what kind of shit?"

"Pray you don't find out." But he smiled with the faded charm of a guy who'd stopped drinking but had bartender in his bones.

Eli propped his elbow on the counter as the blessed scent of hot grease wafted in from the kitchen. "So Willa says you're staying with her until you get squared away?"

"Yeah." Brett sipped cautiously at the coffee again. "I could get used to that," he decided and went back for another sip. "According to my parole officer, I'll be squared away when I have a permanent address and gainful employment."

"What kind of work are you looking to do?"

"Any kind I can get hired for." He gazed into his coffee cup. "Keeping a bar's the only thing I was ever any good at, the only thing I know how to do. But it's not anything I'm looking to do again. I'm not going backward, Eli. Not ever. I wasted too much of my life looking at this place through the bottom of a whiskey glass. And after the last eight years? I don't even want to be inside four walls again if I can help it."

"You got any kind of education?"

"Criminal justice." He sent Eli a sideways smile. "How's

that for irony? In the event I didn't make it to the NFL, I was planning to be a cop. Was one, too, for a while. Till my temper got the better of me." The smile died. "I've got a temper when I've been drinking."

"I gathered."

"My plan is to get to Willa's place, borrow a laptop and some internet, and figure something out. I'm not young anymore but I'm sturdy enough for construction, road work, something."

"You want a ride out there? To Willa's?"

"Nah. I'll walk."

Eli lifted a brow at that. "It's a good ten miles."

"I know that." Brett lifted a brow of his own. "How do you?"

"Pete's sake, Brett. I haven't ravished your daughter."

Willa pushed through the swinging door, slid a cheeseburger onto the counter in front of him. It was almost buried under a mountain of fries, still glistening with hot oil and sparkling with salt. "I might, though, if that burger tastes anything like it smells." He snatched it up and shoved it into his face. Closed his eyes and chewed blissfully. "Oh, yeah." He pointed at Willa. "You're getting yourself ravished just as soon as I finish this. You might want to brace yourself."

"I'll take an IOU," she said drily. Her phone buzzed and she pulled it out of her jeans. "Zinc Pest Control." She listened intently, then grabbed an order pad from under the bar. Uncapped a pen with her teeth and started scribbling. "Uh huh. Yeah, I know where it is. I'll be there as soon as I can."

She pulled back, tapped the screen of her phone a couple times, then put it back to her ear and waited with that economical watchfulness of hers. Brett frowned at the phone. "I hated cell phones before I went in," he mused.

"Can't avoid them now," Eli said. "Especially if you're job hunting."

"Hell."

"Peter, it's Willa," she said into her phone. "I just got a call on a cabin south of town. I have to deal with it. Get down here and take over your empire." She hung up. "He won't call me back."

"No?" Eli was down to fries now, his stomach placated to the point that he could chew and enjoy instead of just swallow by the handful. He eyed the disconnected tap lines. He'd kill for a Coke. "Why not?"

"Because he's Peter. And he recognizes my number." Her lip curled and Eli understood that, should he ever have the misfortune to meet her brother, he'd probably end up punching the guy in the face on principle alone. He considered the prospect. Wasn't overly disturbed by the idea of assaulting a stranger. Not if the guy made Willa's lip curl like that. "Bastard."

Eli couldn't agree more. "Is there anybody else you can call?"

"I don't call anybody about this place. It's Peter's responsibility. That's why he makes the big bucks."

"Peter makes big bucks these days, huh?" Brett's eyes roamed the bar, skating over the shiny wood, the polished brass, the gleaming mirrors, all of it bathed in sunlight so thick you could almost touch it. "Definitely looks more expensive than in my day. That big front window was a good call."

"He's a bastard who knows how to make money," Willa conceded. "But I've got a cabin owner with a van full of scared kids and something alive in the attic she didn't invite in. Keeping Peter's empire staffed isn't my job. Dealing with whatever's in that lady's attic is."

The door opened and a handful of tourists breezed in. They paused uncertainly at the sight of all the empty tables but Brett waved a hand. "Anywhere's good, folks. Menus on the tables."

Chatter resumed and they took a sunny four-top near the window.

"No." Willa narrowed her eyes and pointed at her father. "You've been out of prison what, twelve hours? I'm not leaving you in charge of the scene of the goddamn crime."

"This is where it happened?" Eli asked, startled.

Brett's smile was faint, regretful. "Of course this is where it happened. When you're serious about your drinking — and I was — you have to put in your hours on the stool. And when you have a bar of your very own, well. I doubt I was anywhere else those days." He turned to Willa. "I apologize. This place is yours now, yours and Peter's. I have no intention of trying to take it back, or even of asking for a job here. It was force of habit, that's all." He spread big, helpless hands. "You can take the man out of the bar, but I guess you can't take the bar out of the man."

Willa sighed. "I can't go anywhere until I get the lines flushed anyway, and that damn cider line is practically welded on there."

"All the sugar," Eli said. "It's like cement."

"Tell me," Willa said. "By the time I get it off, flushed and reattached, my shift will be over anyway." She snatched a clean white apron off a peg by the kitchen door, dropped it over her head and began filling water glasses for the customers. "Here's hoping they don't want a beer." She frowned at the array of disconnected hoses. "Or a soda." She hefted the tray with an easy strength that interested Eli almost as much as her stillness. Eli wasn't a tall guy himself but Willa's head barely hit his jaw. If she was five-two he'd be amazed and yet she hefted that tray like it weighed nothing. When had she decided she needed to be so strong? Was it a matter of principle, or had she learned the hard way that small people couldn't afford to be weak?

He wondered how many people he'd be inclined to punch before he unraveled the mysteries of Willa Zinc.

He spotted a wrench on the floor next to the tap lines. He didn't know a lot of things, but he knew tap lines. He slapped his greasy hands clean on his cargo pants and picked up the wrench. Brett leaned over for a look while Willa took orders at the front window.

"You do know what you're doing back there."

"Family restaurant." He fitted the wrench to the coupling and put some muscle behind it. The coupling all but laughed at him. "I hate hard cider."

"Is that a thing people are drinking these days? Hard cider?" Brett sat back. "I'm out of touch."

"It's a thing girls drink," Eli informed him, shifting for better leverage. Something soaked into the knee of his cargos. Nice. "And kids who want their alcohol to taste like candy."

"Ah."

The coupling finally gave and Eli grunted with satisfaction. Willa already had the flushing solution ready to go so he hooked it up and started pumping it through. She lifted the pass-through and arched a brow at the tap lines.

"You got the cider line off?"

"We're half flushed already."

"Good, because we need two pints of the Angel's Blond and a Diet Coke. Think you can get those tap lines reattached before I get their burgers out?"

"If you pay me in Coke, I'll do anything you want."

"You're on." And she sailed into the kitchen to do her magic thing with the grill.

"Willa's still getting squirrels out of people's attics?" Brett asked casually but Eli heard something hungry underneath it. Something that echoed his own frustrated desire to *know* a woman who'd made herself so unknowable.

"She's Zinc Pest Control," Eli said simply and started running fresh water through the lines.

"Not surprised, I guess. She spent more time in the woods than in the house when she was a kid. Barefoot and wild, all hair and knees and elbows. Like a little raven, and twice as noisy."

"Really?" Eli took up the wrench and began reattaching

lines. Coke first, of course. A deal was a deal but he had his priorities. "Can't picture it."

"No, I imagine not. She's...quiet now."

"That she is."

"Something happened to her."

Eli stopped tightening couplings and met Brett's eyes. "What kind of something?"

"I don't know." He lifted big shoulders and wrapped both hands around his empty coffee cup. "I never knew. I was too busy feeling sorry for myself and drinking my way to the bottom of it to pay much attention to my kids, and I'll regret that until the day I die. Because she was a bright flame of a girl, Eli. Shouldn't have blazed so bright with hair that black, but she did. Bright enough that when she went dark even I noticed. But then Shay disappeared and—"

"Shay?"

"My wife," Brett said. "Ex-wife? Late wife?" He laughed bitterly. "I don't know what to call her, since I don't know if she's alive or dead. If she's divorced me, I never got served papers. All I know is she disappeared when Willa was, I don't know, fourteen? Fifteen? Shortly after Willa went dark, anyway."

"Where did she go?"

"What, you haven't heard? You really haven't been in town long, have you, son?"

"Guess not." Eli reached under the bar for a couple of pint glasses, tested the keg labeled Angel's Blond Ale. He discarded a glass and a half of foam before it started playing nice.

"Well, ask around. Everybody's got a theory. Most popular is that I killed her in a jealous rage, a drunken fit, or out of just plain meanness. Probably dumped the body in the big lake. Superior doesn't give up her dead, you know. Too cold for the bloat-and-float, as the cops say. No, bodies just sink down, down, down to the rocks and they stay there forever. Which, of course, I'd know as I'd been a cop once upon a time.

"Then again, some folks are more inclined to think I threw her into the Kettle. You been here long enough to get a gander at Devil's Kettle? The pothole, not the town?"

"It's what brought me to town in the first place," Eli said carefully. He set the two requested pints on the counter and started on the Diet Coke. "Who hikes through this town without taking a look at a disappearing river?"

"Yeah, all that water." Brett toasted Eli with his empty mug. "Scientists have studied it, you know. They've measured the volume of water that goes down that hole. They've measured the volume of water that comes out of the cliff below, too. And you know what? They don't match. Only about half the water that goes into the hole comes out the falls."

"Where does the other half go?"

"That's the question, isn't it?" Brett set his cup down carefully. "Nobody knows. It just disappears. And if you had a body you didn't want found…"

"You might toss it in the Kettle in the dead of night."

"You're practically a local already."

Willa pushed through the swinging door from the kitchen, her tray loaded with burgers and fries. Eli put the drinks in the spaces she'd left for them and smiled at her expression of mild surprise.

"Family restaurant," he told her.

"You're just full of surprises, Eli Walker."

"Yeah. You, too."

She shot Brett a glance. "Been telling stories, Dad?"

Brett shrugged. "Assumed he'd heard most of them, unless this place has changed more than I thought."

Willa sighed. "Probably not."

She moved away to deliver the food to the table. The door opened, letting more tourists in. Eli waved them to a table and threw on an apron. He grabbed Willa's arm as she stashed her tray behind the bar. "I know my way around a grill, too. Family restaurant, remember? Go see about the mom and her van full of scared kids. I can handle this."

She glanced at her watch. "Peter's shift doesn't start for an hour."

"I can do an hour of this in my sleep."

"Are you sure?"

"You have at least three of my IOUs already."

"Stop saying that."

"Stop doing me favors, then."

"I haven't been."

"So let me do you one."

She narrowed her eyes at him, and he wanted more than anything to nudge up the brim of her ball cap, to get a better look at those suspicious eyes. "Why?"

"Because I'd like to."

"Again, why?"

He nudged up her ball cap — couldn't resist — and met a pair of pale gray eyes, startlingly light against the raven's wing of her hair. They were suspicious, sure enough, but also a little baffled. He was trying to help her for no reason other than that he liked her, was intrigued by her, and wanted to be closer. And she truly couldn't understand that.

"Have dinner with me," he said.

She blinked, bafflement deepening into straight-up incomprehension. "What?"

"Consider it a favor if you really have to balance the scales."

"How is having dinner with me a favor to you?"

"You're absolutely fascinating, Willa."

"And you make absolutely no sense." She scowled at him and snugged her cap back down. "And stop messing with my hat."

"Is that a yes?"

She hesitated and he glanced at his own watch.

"Van full of scared kids with something in their attic, Willa."

"Damn it. Fine. Dinner."

"Tonight."

"Tomorrow."

Eli smiled, delighted with her. "Tomorrow then."

Chapter 9

SEVERAL FILTHY HOURS later, Willa found herself pushing through the heavy wooden doors of the Devil's Taproom one more time. Peter hadn't returned her calls — the predictable bastard — so they were going to have to have this conversation in person, in front of a crowd. Not her first choice, but then neither was Peter. Life was what it was, and so was family.

The yeasty musk of spilled beer rose up from the floorboards as the door thunked shut behind her. It twined together with the hot-grease-and-salt scent of a grill in action, and suddenly she was eight again. Eight years old, her skinny thighs stuck to a cracked vinyl barstool, her eyes wide open, her mouth shut tight but cold and sweet from the pop her dad had shot into a fancy glass with that gun he had on a hose under the bar. Ten-year-old Peter was beside her, the ice melting in his own pop because he was too busy trying to impress the cops who had been her father's friends (until they hadn't been) to drink.

The door opened behind her, snapping her back to the present while nearly sweeping her into the crowd of tourists enjoying a craft brew with a lake view. (It was, she had to admit, a nifty tag line. Say what you would about her brother; the guy knew how to sell stuff.) A fresh batch of drinkers breezed in, and Willa stepped aside to let them pass. And took a moment in the shadows to root herself in the present.

She was twenty-eight, she reminded herself, not eight. And the Devil's Taproom — for all that it smelled the same — wasn't the dim, shabby clubhouse for serious drinkers her father had cultivated. Peter had been back in town about three minutes — had been in charge of the family bar for about two — when he'd driven them both yet further into debt with that big-ass plate glass window that was currently lavishing lake-shattered sunshine on the early dinner crowd and painting the floor a thick, August gold. He'd pitched the cheap chairs and sticky tables, too, in favor of a mix of high-tops and cozy booths, and a gleaming oak bar that ran the entire length of the back wall. A small stage and sleek sound system stood where the jukebox had once reigned. About the only thing he'd left alone were the floors — wide pine planks dark with age and warped with countless spilled beers. Because a bar, Peter said, ought to smell like a bar.

Her brother of the firm opinions and fearless mortgage applications was right there behind the bar where she'd expected to find him. He was slinging drinks, chatting up tourists and wiping up spills with the easy charm of a bartender born. Unless you looked closer, of course. Then you'd see that he despised everybody in this place.

It was so obvious to Willa. She wondered why nobody else ever seemed to see it. Peter was as slick and glossy now as the bar he was working behind but there was no changing your bones. He was just as desperate for approval as he had ever been, only now he was self-aware enough to know it. And to bitterly resent the very same people whose approval he craved. It was right there in the tight edges of that easy smile, in the dark eyes that scanned constantly for the next angle, the next sale. People weren't fellow humans to Peter; they were potential profits.

He lifted a friendly hand when he spotted her and jerked his chin in what might've looked like welcome, but wasn't. She knew her brother still, knew what that chin jerk meant. Normally she'd just flip him the bird and leave him to sleep in the bed he'd shit. But this wasn't normal, was it? Normal had left the building the instant she'd heard the word *parole*. No, it was war now. It always was, getting Peter to do

74

anything that didn't line his pocket. It wouldn't hurt to have his IOU in her pocket before the discussion they were about to have.

So she slid through the crowd like a fish through water, propped her elbows on the bar at the waitress station and waited for Peter to ask her for that favor. It took about thirty seconds.

"Walt's running late," Peter told her as he pulled a handful of pints. "Could use a pair of hands to get us over the dinner rush."

She hefted the pass-through and snagged an apron off a peg. "Grill or stick?"

He hesitated, his dark eyes shooting longingly toward the kitchen door for the briefest of instants. Then India Grace arrived at the bar, a tray riding the full sleeve of tattoos on her arm, her magenta hair in a Rosie the Riveter do-rag. She slapped a handful of grill tickets on the bar and rattled off half a dozen drink orders. At the same moment, a trio of sorority sisters propped their cleavage on the bar and batted their Kardashian eyelashes at Peter.

"Christ." He snatched up the tickets and shoved them at Willa. "I'll stay on the stick." He wiped the irritation off his face between one instant and the next, replaced it with a naughty sparkle. He turned to the boobs and said, "Welcome to the Devil's Taproom, ladies. How can I help you get into trouble this evening?"

Willa headed for the grill while the girls giggled. She wondered, not for the first time, how the hell he did that so quickly and so well. Shed his skin, his emotion, like a snake. Like there was something underneath it, something different just waiting for him to be next.

It was a mystery, she decided. One she'd probably be better off not solving. She went to the back and settled into the familiar rhythm of flipping burgers and dunking fries.

Half an hour later, Walt Kovacz showed up, six-and-a-half feet of painfully skinny hipster, from his clunky glasses frames to his Sperry Top Siders.

"Hey, Willa." He swung on an apron with the efficiency of a guy who knew his way around a grill. He whipped a bandana from his pocket and fashioned himself a guy-friendly hairnet. "Thanks for covering. Meeting ran over. I told Peter it might."

He held out his hand and Willa slapped the spatula into it like she was a sprinter passing the baton. Even over the hot grease, she caught the scents that always clung to him, butter and powdered sugar and kindness. It went down to the bone in him, that kindness, just like Peter's need. She couldn't help breathing it in while she was up close and personal.

"Willa."

"What?"

"Did you just sniff me?"

She suppressed the wince. This, she thought grimly, was why her school years had been such a disaster. Behavior exactly like this, plus Georgie fucking Davis. "Sorry," she said and stepped back. "You smell like doughnuts."

He did, too. He'd only last year opened the Sugar Rush, a tiny doughnut shop housed in a ramshackle little fishing shack right next to the Davis Gallery. He'd painted it blazing pink, too. That alone would've made Willa's day. A hot pink fishing shack shoulder to shoulder with Bianca Davis' hallowed shrine to her late and utterly unlamented (at least by Willa) son? Nice. It was icing on the cake that Walt was genuinely good at what he did. And he smelled like it.

"I do? Still? It's been hours since this morning's bake." He lifted his sleeve to his nose and inhaled deeply. Grinned. "Well how about that? I even took a shower before the meeting with Addy."

Willa wasn't surprised to hear that it was Addy who'd held Walt up tonight. As the CEO of Devil Days — Devil's Kettle's annual tourist bash — Addy was pleasantly and persistently harassing every shopkeeper in town about something these days. Then a grim thought struck her.

"Was it about Devil Days or the doughnut tree?" Willa asked suspiciously. "The meeting."

"You heard!" His eyes sparkled and he flipped a burger. "I didn't know if Addy and Jax were telling anybody yet." His grin went sly. "Guess I'll be seeing a lot of you and Georgie in the near future, what with you being co-bridesmaids and all."

Willa scowled. "It's a prospect that frightens even me, Walt, and I'm the one who got that bear out of the liquor store last year." The buzzer went off over the fries and Willa snatched them out of the hot oil.

Walt laughed and hit the glistening fries with the salt shaker even as he flipped a burger with the other hand. "Be brave, Willa."

"There's brave," Willa said darkly, "and then there's stupid."

"And then there's love," he returned mildly, one eye already on the new order slips coming in, "right there in the middle. Weddings make strange bedfellows. You're doing a kind and loving thing for Addy, and she totally deserves it. Still—" He brought the spatula to his chest in a kind of line cook salute. "Respect for your sacrifice."

"Yeah, thanks." She pointed her chin at the sizzling grill. "You got this?"

"I got this."

She left Walt to his burgers, shoved into the bar proper and pointed a bad-tempered finger at her brother.

"You."

Peter ignored her to slide a beer and a smile to a guy leaning on the bar whose grease-stained nailbeds said both *mechanic* and *straight* to Willa. The guy smiled back in a way that said Willa's call was no more than seventy-five percent accurate. And she was pretty sure about the mechanic bit.

"I need to talk to you," Willa said to Peter.

"Figured." Peter turned to the waitress who was

restocking glasses under the bar. "India, can you take the stick for a minute?"

"Sure. Hey, Willa."

"Hey, India. We'll be in the office."

"Oh boy. Privacy." Peter leaned toward India and stage whispered, "If I'm not back in ten minutes, call the cops."

"Don't bother," Willa told her. "They'll never find the body."

"Does she mean that?" India blinked at Peter then at her. "I can't tell if she means that."

Willa hefted up the pass-through and gave Peter some uncompromising eye contact.

"Ten minutes, India," he said. "Seriously."

"Oh, hell, no." Five minutes later, Peter kicked back in the squeaky old office chair that had been their father's. He linked his hands behind his shaved-bald head and stared at her. "No way in hell."

"It's the conditions of his parole," Willa said grimly. "He needs a permanent address and a job. I told him he can move into the cabin for the time being, so there's the housing thing taken care of. The least you can do is give him a job."

"What, in a bar?" Peter dropped his elbows to the desk and shook his head. "In what universe is that a good idea? He's an alcoholic with violent tendencies who just got out of prison, Willa. For killing a guy while under the influence."

"He didn't kill a guy. He brain damaged a fellow drunk," Willa muttered. "It was a lucky punch, that's all."

"Lucky for who?" Peter wondered.

"Given his blood alcohol content," Willa went on doggedly, "it's shocking he even landed that punch. He should've been out cold."

"Well, he practiced."

Willa couldn't deny that. If drinking was a sport, their

dad was a goddamn Olympian. Or had been, eight years ago. "Given the other guy's BAC, he shouldn't have been on his feet either," she said. She hated the taste of the lawyer's words in her mouth. *Hated* them. But family was family, and Brett — for better or worse — was hers. So was Peter, goddamn it. "His skull had a date with that curb one way or another."

"The jury evidently didn't agree."

"There was no jury." A fact he'd know if he'd bothered to come home when Brett had been arrested or charged. Bitterness curled inside her like smoke but she kept her face perfectly blank, her tone even. "You know what Sober Brett is like. He *wanted* to go to jail. Said he *deserved* to go to jail, and God knows there was nobody in this town who'd argue."

"Nobody but you, and I don't know why you'd bother. Brett's been heading for jail his whole life. By the time he actually got there, most folks around here figured he was due." He paused significantly. "Long overdue, in fact."

Willa didn't miss the implication. "They were wrong."

"Were they?"

Willa held his gaze. "He was a crappy father and a worse husband, probably, but he didn't kill Mom, Peter. She took off."

"You know that for sure?"

Willa hesitated. Ninety-nine percent wasn't the same as one hundred, and nothing was ever one hundred percent sure where Shay Zinc was concerned.

Peter smiled grimly. "That's what I thought. So come on, Willa. Consider the facts. If Dad jumped at the chance to do time for a minor pushy-shovey that took a bad turn, isn't it possible — probable, even — that he knew what he was doing? That maybe Drunk Brett really did disappear Mom, and Sober Brett was finally ready to pay for it?"

"Sober Brett is a child, and you know it. People take advantage of that."

"And you're going to protect him, is that it?" He steepled

his fingers and gazed at her with their father's gypsy-dark eyes. "Why would you do that? He never protected you a minute of his life."

"Neither did you."

"You weren't my responsibility."

"I was a child. I was everybody's responsibility."

"Everybody's is the same as nobody's."

"Tell me about it." She planted both hands on the desk, looked him dead in the eye. "Which is why finding Brett a job is your responsibility." She smiled. "I'm making it yours."

"And I'm telling you, there's no way on God's green earth I'm giving him a job in a bar."

"So give him a job somewhere else. You're the king of the financial world. You own a piece of everything in this town. Surely you can find him something somewhere else in your vast empire."

His smile was sleek and ugly. "Your information's a little out of date, sister mine. That vast empire of mine? It's been downsized."

"What, did you sign a prenup? Sign away half your assets if you failed to follow through on that gaudy engagement ring you gave Georgie Davis?"

His smile went bitter. "Something like that."

She blinked, startled. "How bad?"

"My fabled empire now consists of—" Peter spread his hands, indicating the office and the bar. "—exactly one bar." He frowned. "And a goddamn sheep farm nobody will buy."

Willa stared. "You own a sheep farm?"

He shrugged. "Artisanal, locally-produced, earth-friendly milk, butter and cheese. It hit all the trends and seemed like a good move at the time. It actually might've been one if that asshole hipster farmer who pitched it to me had had any clue how to actually fucking farm. Or shepherd, or what the hell ever." He waved that off. "I'll sell it, don't worry. Just like I'll sell this place."

"You're selling the bar?"

"My stake, sure. Soon as possible so I can get the fuck out of this inbred backwater." He smiled at her suddenly, a flash of charm and unholy glee. "You want to buy me out, partner?"

She only barely suppressed a shudder. "No. This place is your headache. That was the deal when we agreed to a sixty/forty split."

"Well you can't have it both ways, Willa. Either I'm running this place or you are. Which is it?"

She ground her teeth and spit out the words he'd expertly maneuvered out of her. "You are."

"That's right. I am. And while I am, you can forget about Daddy dearest working here."

Chapter 10

TWENTY-FOUR HOURS later, Willa stepped out of the shower, wrapped herself in a towel and grabbed another one for the mess of her hair. She gave it a good scrubbing, reached for the door and hesitated. Her dad was out there. That was going to take some getting used to. Her days of waltzing through the house in nothing but a towel were over, at least for the foreseeable future.

She grabbed a thick bathrobe from a hook on the back of the door and threw it on. She immediately began sweating. There was a reason she viewed the robe as winter-only wear. No help for that though. She yanked open the door and set herself on a direct course to the nearest pair of shorts. Brett was seated at her kitchen table, pecking away at her laptop with a resigned competence she assumed he'd acquired in prison. There were probably a lot of skills you acquired against your will in prison.

He looked up. "Your phone dinged." He turned his attention back to the screen. "Didn't know if you'd want me to interrupt you in the shower."

Willa picked up the phone she'd left on the counter. She had one new text from a number her phone didn't recognize.

Seven o'clock, my cabin. It's just dinner so stop scowling. You'll survive and then there'll be only two IOUs to go. Anything you don't eat?

Willa sighed. Eli. She'd managed to put their date out of her mind earlier while she'd squirmed her way into a crawlspace designed to admit only gymnasts and toddlers. Then she'd been too busy to think about him, what with convincing a mama raccoon and her clutch of pink, naked babies to find alternative accommodations. And then she'd been too filthy and sweaty to think about anything but a shower.

But now she was clean and Eli wanted to know if she was allergic to anything because this ridiculous dinner he'd somehow talked her into would be taking place at his cabin. At seven, evidently.

Eggplant's not a favorite, she texted back and checked the time. Nearly six.

"It was nothing," she said to her father. Phone still in hand, she headed for the staircase at the far end of the living room that led to her bedroom. All slanted ceilings and dormer windows, Willa's room took up the cabin's entire — if modest — second story. The space you could stand up straight in was just barely big enough for a full-sized bed, a dresser and a few bookshelves, but it looked out over the rolling forest in all four directions which made it her favorite indoor space in the world. But even if it weren't, she'd adore it as it held all the shorts.

"Okay," Brett said absently. "Your friends are upstairs."

She froze, one foot on the steps. "What?"

"The Davis girl — Georgie? — and I forget the other one's name. Pretty little thing with a head full of curls? She's getting married to the oldest Davis kid, I hear?"

"Addison." Willa stared. "Addison and Georgie Davis are in my bedroom?"

Brett looked up from the screen again, blinked uncertainly. "I — yes. They stopped by while you were in the shower, said you had bridesmaid stuff to talk about. I didn't know you were close with the Davises."

"I'm not."

"You're not standing up in this Addison's wedding then?"

Willa pinched the bridge of her nose. "No, I am."

"Oh." Brett closed his mouth, clearly confused by the intricacies of female social interaction. Willa sympathized.

"I'm sorry. I should've asked them to wait down here. I just thought—"

"Don't worry about it, Dad." Willa yanked the tie of her robe tight, gripped her phone in one shaky hand and marched up the stairs. Like Sober Brett could've stopped Georgie Davis from going any-damn-where she wanted. "Not your fault."

And it wasn't. This showdown with Georgie had been bearing down on her like a runaway freight train since the moment she'd agreed to stand up in Addy's wedding. She only wished she'd been allowed to wear more than a sweaty robe when it finally caught up with her. Evidently, fate wasn't done screwing with her yet.

There was no door at the top of the staircase. People could — and did, apparently — walk up the stairs and right into Willa's bedroom. The lack of privacy hadn't concerned the wild little girl she'd once been, nor had it much concerned the adult she'd become, as she hadn't ever imagined sharing her snug little story-and-a-half in the woods with another living soul. She might have to consider getting a door, though, now that she had Brett in the house.

If she kept coming home to find Georgie and Addy elbow deep in her dresser drawers, she'd get a damn lock, too.

She leaned against the bannister that kept people from plunging from her bedroom straight into the living room and watched them paw through her underthings. "Having fun?"

"Willa!" Addy clapped a hand to her chest and whirled to face her, a guilty flush on her cheeks. Georgie didn't flinch, just continued picking through drawers with two squeamish fingers, as if Willa stored anthrax in there instead of perfectly ordinary socks and underwear. "You startled me!"

"Isn't that my line?" Willa folded her arms over her robe and gave her a good, hard stare. "Pretty sure you're the ones ransacking my dresser without permission."

"Yeah." The flush deepened and she sent Georgie a swift glance. "About that."

Georgie wiped her fingers down her undoubtedly expensive skirt like it was a common dinner napkin and turned to Addy.

"She's a disaster." She flipped a yard of gleaming blond hair (surely as expensive as the skirt) over one bony shoulder and spoke to Addison as if Willa didn't exist. Fine by Willa. "I told you she would be."

"Georgie, for goodness' sake, we talked about this." Addison folded her arms and glared. "Be *nice.*"

Georgie cut Willa a sideways glance from under long, dark lashes, a look that weighed, measured and condemned in a split second. "Remind me why again?"

"How about common human decency?"

Another dismissive glance. "No, it wasn't that. It was the other thing."

"The thing about how I'm the bride and I asked you to?"

Georgie sighed. "That was it." There was a long pause while Georgie digested the idea. Addy waited her out. Georgie, everybody knew, sometimes needed a good while to get her neural pathways fired up.

"Nice is too big an ask," Georgie decided finally. "I'm going to aim for neutral. As a special favor to the bride."

Addy frowned and opened her mouth but Willa said, "Quit while you're ahead, Addison. I'd like to get dressed sometime this century."

"Believe me, nobody wants that more than I do." Georgie tapped the dresser Willa had tucked between the two dormer windows overlooking the drive. "But nothing in this wasteland qualifies as clothing."

Willa smiled sweetly. "Naked is the only other option, Ms. Davis."

"Please." Georgie pressed a hand to her stomach. "I have dinner plans later."

"Oh, sorry. I didn't know you ate. Aren't there an awful lot of carbs in food?"

"Yes, there are and thank the good lord," Addy said

seriously. "Carbs are life."

"Amen," Willa said just as seriously.

"I eat," Georgie informed them loftily. "Once, maybe twice a week, or if I have a date, which I do."

Addy stared. "You have a date? With who?"

"A real estate agent from the cities. He's listing a hobby farm down the road from Hill Top House and stopped by to meet the neighbors." She lifted a lock of silky hair and inspected the ends. "He suggested dinner, and since I haven't let a man buy me so much as a drink since Willa's asshole of a brother gave me a bottle of French champagne and a diamond ring, I said yes."

Willa let that one skate by without comment. She could've told anybody who'd asked that Peter was a bad bet but Georgie hadn't asked, nor would she have listened if Willa had offered the information up. Not that Willa had been tempted to do anything of the sort. Even if Georgie had had a heart to break — which Willa sincerely doubted — Peter hadn't put a scratch on it. Georgie wasn't hurt; she was pissed off, and Willa wouldn't waste an ounce of pity on her.

"So I'll be damned," Georgie went on, "if I'll let Willa spoil my appetite with this train wreck she calls a wardrobe."

Willa's phone dinged in her hand with an incoming text, and she suppressed a jump by force of sheer habit. Georgie might not be overly bright but she was shrewd and she was mean, which made her dangerous. A display of nerves would be like blood in the water.

"Who is it?" Georgie asked, all big innocent eyes. "Or should I say what is it? Wait, don't tell me. Is there a muskrat in the basement? A skunk in the garage? A bear in the liquor store? You lead such an interesting life, Willa." She said *interesting* in exactly the same tone another woman might say *contagious*. Willa had to smile. Georgie was a lot of things, many of them deeply unappealing, but she gave good spite. Kept you on your toes.

"I did a snake in a toilet the other night," she offered.

Georgie's perfect face went momentarily blank and Addy said, "That's a real thing? I thought that was just on the internet."

"It's a real thing," Willa informed her and checked the phone.

Not a favorite what? Because nobody actually eats eggplant, do they? I meant food, Willa. Is there a food you don't like?

Her lips twitched. Eli Walker had himself a sense of humor.

Omnivorous, she texted back. She considered the women in front of her and added, *I also drink.*

"A snake in the toilet," Addy mused, frowning into the middle distance. "My imagination is never going to unsee that."

"Just like I'm never going to unsee the abomination of this underwear drawer." Georgie gave the drawer in question a look of the purest dislike, then turned that gaze on Willa. In spite of the heat, goosebumps broke out on Willa's arms. Because that wasn't dislike in Georgie's eyes now. It was speculation. Perhaps even ambition. "You know what? I take it back. I'm glad she's naked."

"What?" Willa yelped but Georgie was still talking to Addy.

"I'm even gladder she's just showered. I love you and all, Addy, but I have my limits and I know what she does for a living."

"You have no idea what Willa does for a living," Addy said fondly.

"And I'd like to keep it that way," Georgie returned, seemingly unperturbed by the gaping holes in her own logic. She turned her attention back to Willa and said, "Lose the robe."

Willa was three steps down the stairs before Addy managed to hook a warm little hand in her elbow.

"Willa, wait!" And because Addy was a lot stronger than

she looked, Willa did. "Georgie didn't mean that the way it sounded."

"I absolutely did." Now there was another hand in her elbow — a cool, expensive one this time — and Willa found herself being hauled back up the stairs. It was either that or risk losing the robe, something Willa had no intention of allowing. "I have a damn good eye but I'm not psychic. If I'm supposed to dress you, I need to know what I'm working with."

"You already put your hands all over my underwear," Willa pointed out. "What else do you need to know?"

"Measurements."

Willa opened her mouth but Georgie threw up a stop-sign hand.

"Which I can't get through a bathrobe. That travesty you call an underwear drawer isn't going to give me any worthwhile information either."

"Well, I don't have anything else so—"

Georgie shot a manicured finger toward a small mountain of shopping bags on the bed. "We guessed." She smiled, slow and evil. "Why don't you try a few things on?"

Willa opened her mouth to tell Georgie exactly where she could stuff her rich-girl pity-buys then happened to catch a glimpse of Addison behind Georgie's skinny shoulder. She was all but wringing her hands and sidling from foot to exquisitely unhappy foot. Georgie would exploit any excuse to heap shame on Willa's head but Addy actually liked Willa, and didn't have a problem telling her sister-in-law (-in-law?) where to step off when she was misbehaving.

But Addy wasn't telling Georgie to stuff it. She was just standing there, throwing off big, fat waves of…what? Empathy, Willa thought. Understanding. Solidarity. She knew exactly what it was to be in a situation that stung but couldn't be helped. That's where she saw Willa now, fighting the good fight but waging an ultimately losing battle. Like a toddler resisting nap time.

Fuck.

She tossed her phone onto the bed and said, "I have to be somewhere by seven."

"Christ," Georgie said. She snatched a bag out of the pile and threw it at Willa. "Start with these."

Chapter 11

GEORGIE LISTENED TO Willa stomp down the stairs — presumably to some room in this godforsaken hovel that had a door on it — then turned back to her dearest friend and sister-in-law. And gasped in horror.

"Jesus, Addison! You're sitting on its bed!" The one person outside of blood whom Georgie had ever known to be completely and sincerely loyal was sitting cross-legged on Willa's quilt, gnawing on her lip, staring at the empty stairs. "Get off there. You'll catch something."

Addy ignored that and continued to chew on her lip. "Her dad is staying here." She shifted that clear green gaze to Georgie. "Do you think she's safe?"

Something uncomfortable stirred in Georgie's gut and she rolled an irritable shoulder. "Why wouldn't she be?"

Addy dropped her voice. "Even I've heard the rumors about Brett Zinc. People think he killed his wife!" She hopped off the bed and came to Georgie, grabbed her hands urgently. "I know you don't like her but think about that, would you? What if your dad did something awful while he wasn't himself, while he was too drunk to know better? What if it cost you your mom?"

That stirring in her gut edged toward actual cramping and Georgie filled her lungs with cool, calming air. She released the air on a deep sigh that was gratifyingly languid and unconcerned, then commanded her wonky innards to settle the fuck down. "My dad died less than a year before Matty was born, Addison. I know what losing a parent is."

"So you should know how awful it would be to have to cut off the other one. That maybe you couldn't do it, even if you ought to. Not even to keep yourself safe. He's her family, Georgie."

And here came the cramping. Lovely. Georgie drifted to the bed Addy had abandoned, made a show of smacking clean a space on the quilt and sank gracefully onto the edge.

"Believe me, Willa doesn't have any particular reverence for family." She smiled but her voice was as hard as her words. "I dated her brother for two years and never saw them exchange so much as a Christmas card."

"But you hate Willa, and Peter wanted to marry you."

"He wanted to marry my money," Georgie pointed out and breathed through the fading cramp.

"Which is exactly why you can't depend on anything he told you."

Georgie smiled tightly. "Yes, thank you. I've come to understand that."

Addy sighed and sat next to Georgie. Wrapped a warm, strong arm around her and tipped her curly head onto Georgie's shoulder. She smelled like sunshine and mint shampoo, and Georgie felt her plastic smile melt away and the last of the pain drain from her stomach. "I'm sorry, honey. I really am. For what it's worth, I think you're right. There's no love lost between Willa and Peter."

"Thank you."

"But that means the night Davis Place burned, the night Matty burned it down?"

"The night my fiancé blackmailed my baby brother into burning it down so he could commit insurance fraud, you mean?"

"Exactly." Addy gripped Georgie's hands and leaned back to look her square in the face. "Willa heard everything that night. She knows exactly what really happened, and she didn't say a word. She's never said a word. Not to anybody."

"No, I know," Georgie murmured, and a warning twinge fluttered in her stomach again. "Believe me, I know."

"And if we accept that she's not protecting Peter, which I

propose we do—"

"Agreed," Georgie said reluctantly.

"—and if we accept that the hatred between her and your family remains intact, for whatever impossible reason nobody's seen fit to reveal to me?"

"We definitely do."

"Then we have to accept that Willa's protecting Matty, the beloved baby of the family she hates and that hates her right back."

"It sure looks that way, doesn't it?" Georgie said, frowning blindly at Willa's horrible dresser.

"Why would she do that?"

"I have no idea," Georgie said. And it wasn't for lack of thinking it over, either. The question chewed endlessly at her gut while she pushed uneaten food around her plate, while she stared fruitlessly at submissions to the gallery, while she passed countless sleepless hours in her bed. It sat there in her stomach even now, Willa's refusal to hurt them through Matty, a foreign idea she could neither digest nor throw up. It just *sat* there, wrong and stubborn, eating at her like an ulcer. "But I'll tell you one thing I do know."

"What's that?"

"It's not respect for family — even a family she hates — driving her."

"How do you know?"

"I just know."

"So what is driving her?"

"That I don't know." Georgie pressed her lips together. "But I'm going to find out."

Addy frowned. "How?"

A muffled ding sounded in the pile of shopping bags behind them and Georgie smiled. "I'm going to start by reading her texts."

"What?" Addy leapt to her feet. "You can't!"

"Of course I can." Georgie told herself not to think about rabies and shoved a hand into the closest mountain of bags.

Came up with Willa's phone and prayed it hadn't been asleep long enough to require a passcode.

She swiped the screen and the text message program opened cooperatively. She smiled and read the most recent thread.

"Oh good heavens." She stared at the screen, dumbfounded.

"What?" Addy danced from foot to foot in an agony of nerves. "What?"

"Willa the Skunk Girl has a date."

Addy grinned hugely. "Really?"

The stairs creaked but Georgie didn't put down the phone. She made a decision instead. She knew what people thought when they looked at her — rich, spoiled, lazy, entitled, beautiful, stupid. Some of those titles she'd earned, some of them had come with her name. The rest were misperceptions she'd either cultivated on purpose or allowed to stand because she didn't care. People could think what they wanted; she knew who she was. She knew she wasn't stupid, nor was she pointlessly vindictive. She had principles and she lived by them, that was all.

The most important one was family. Family came before everything and everybody else. Being a Davis was a privilege and a responsibility, and she'd been brought up to give thanks for the one and to honor the other.

Willa Zinc, on the other hand, had no concept of loyalty, no sense of honor and no commitment to responsibility. She didn't understand family on any level, but somehow fate — in its infinite bitchiness — had connected her indelibly to Georgie's family. Georgie could hate her for that alone, for sticking her dirty fingers into something that Georgie held precious, for trying to take for her own something she didn't deserve. But she didn't. No, what Georgie really hated Willa for was letting go. She'd had the balls to reach. She should've had the balls to hang on. If she knew what love was, what loyalty was, what *family* was, she wouldn't have been able to let go. Not for any amount of money.

But she'd let go. And Georgie wasn't about to let her grab on again.

But Willa — so predictable for so long — was suddenly making moves that Georgie didn't understand and that made her deeply uncomfortable. The game had changed and Georgie was by God going to understand why. And that would mean shifting stances on one of the other guiding principles of her life — hating Willa Zinc. At least in public.

"You wanted me to be nicer to Willa, didn't you?" she said now to Addy, who was still grinning at the idea of Willa's date.

"You know I did."

"I'm going to do it."

Addy blinked, startled back to the present. "You are?"

"I am." She smiled and rose as Willa hit the top of the stairs, smoothly tucking the phone into the clever side pocket of her skirt. "There you are, Willa. How did everything fit?"

Willa only frowned, her hands going protectively to the belt of her bathrobe, her wet hair starting to wave around that small, suspicious face.

"Addy and I had a good talk while you were changing," Georgie went on conversationally. She pulled her hand from her pocket and brought out a seamstress's tape measure.

"Did you?" Willa's eyes fixed warily on the measuring tape.

"We did. Worked out a few things." Georgie flicked a hand toward the center of the room. "Stand over there."

Willa didn't move. "Talk first, measure second."

"Fine." Georgie gave a theatrical sigh. "So here's the deal, Willa. I don't like you and you don't like me, and I don't see that changing. But I decided that I love Addy more than I hate you."

Willa's gaze flicked to Addy. "She loves you a whole awful lot."

"You have no idea." Georgie shook back her hair with a

long-suffering sigh. "So I'm going to give her a gift. A wedding gift."

"What's that?"

"You." Georgie smiled, sleek and brilliant and just a little bit sharp. Sharp enough that Willa would recognize the cutting edge and relax, thinking everything was *de rigueur*. "Only better. A you that won't embarrass her on the most important day of her life."

"I would never be embarrassed of Willa," Addy said stoutly.

"Of course not," Georgie murmured. "And I'm going to make sure of it. Which means you and I, Willa, are going to work very closely together these next few months. When it comes to your face, hair and body, you're going to do exactly what I tell you."

"I own power tools, Georgie. I'm not afraid to use them."

"And that complete cooperation," Georgie went on as if Willa hadn't spoken, "is going to be your wedding present to Addison."

Willa clamped her jaw shut and descended into fuming silence.

"Agreed?" Georgie unfurled a length of the tape measure and snapped it between her fists like a strop.

Willa looked to Addison, who clasped her hands together under her chin and said, "Please? I don't care what you look like but an honest cease-fire between my bridesmaids would be the best present in the world."

"Ah, hell." Willa stalked to the center of the room.

Georgie said, "Drop the robe."

"I hate you."

"Back at you, sister."

Willa dropped the robe.

"Holy Moses," Addy breathed, "everything fits exactly. You're good, Georgie. You're very, very good. How on earth did you guess the sizes so well?"

"It's a gift." Georgie narrowed her eyes and considered

Willa standing there in the bra and panties Georgie had purchased for her. She'd gone with combed cotton in a gun-metal gray that matched her eyes, the eyes people rarely saw under the brim of that stupid ball cap but that Georgie saw every day looking out of her baby brother's face. Georgie might hold her fire for the next few months but she would never forget what Willa had done to Matty. Would never let Willa forget either. "But I'm going to measure anyway. Arms out, Willa."

Willa stood there, all but naked, while her bitterest enemy wrapped a measuring tape around every conceivable body part with shocking competence. And she knew she was making a terrible mistake. She didn't know how letting Georgie take her measurements was dangerous, only that it was. Nearly as dangerous as wearing the bra and panty set Georgie had picked out to match her eyes. Hers and Matty's. That was no accident, and neither was this unexpected truce.

Now Willa just had to figure out what the hell Georgie was playing at.

"You don't have a bad figure, you know," Georgie said. "I would've been less generous with the cup size but Mom says you gave her quite a show at the gallery the other day."

"There was a situation with a chipmunk," Willa muttered, her cheeks burning. "It got in my shirt."

"And you got out of it, which is why you're wearing a bra right now that actually fits quite nicely. Those sports bras you wear don't do you any favors, you know."

Of course Willa knew. That was the point of sports bras — to flatten those attention-seeking curves into complete overlook-ability. It wasn't something a Davis would ever understand, so Willa didn't bother to explain. Georgie didn't seem to require a response. She just dropped to her knees and jammed the business end of the tape measurer into the business end of Willa.

"Jesus, Georgie!"

"Inseam," she muttered, entirely unconcerned, and shot the other end of the tape to the floor. "Okay, all done. You can get dressed."

"Finally." Willa bolted for her dresser, found herself nose to sternum with Georgie.

"What did I say about wearing anything from that toxic waste site?"

"What else do you propose I wear?"

Georgie tucked the tape measurer into her pocket and drew out Willa's phone. "I'm so glad you asked. Whoever you're meeting at seven is going to be even gladder." Georgie arched a brow. "Why didn't you tell us you had a date?"

"It's not a date," Willa muttered and snatched her phone back.

"There's a person on the other end of this text thread who might disagree. I'm sure she's very nice, too."

"Lesbian jokes," Willa said evenly. "So clever."

"Almost as clever as anorexia jokes."

Willa eyed her consideringly. "You're not as dumb as you let people think, are you, Georgie?"

"I'm as dumb as you are ugly."

Willa considered that. "I liked you better dumb."

"I liked you better ugly."

Addy said, "For heaven's sake, Georgie. She's meeting her...person...in half an hour."

Georgie took a handful of Willa's damp hair — starting to wave up in the humidity — and sighed. "We'll go for the natural look."

"You'll go for the exit," Willa said. "Out."

"Fine by me." Georgie shrugged and said to Addy, "She's breaking the deal, though, not me. You're witnessing this, right?"

"Willa, come on." Addy held out one of the shopping

bags, gave it an encouraging little shake. It sounded luxuriously heavy and Willa wanted whatever was in it. She hated that she wanted it, hated herself for wanting it. But she was only human and she'd poured every last cent into the business — and into the lawyers — for the past decade. Clothes came somewhere below bills and food on her list of priorities. And pretty, delicate clothes? They were listed with high heels and European vacations in the *Things To Admire In Magazines* category. They weren't things she could ever actually buy. Not with her life, and the budget that went with it. "It's just a few things so Georgie can see how different styles work with your body type."

"I'm five foot two, I weight one hundred and fifteen pounds, and evidently I wear whatever size bra this is."

"How can a grown woman not know her own bra size?" Georgie wondered aloud. "How does that even happen?"

It happened when little girls suddenly developed big boobs which caught the attention of skeevy men. It happened when said little girls decided not to even think about, let alone show off, such things. But Willa wasn't about to hand Georgie that little bit of ammunition.

She turned back to Addy. "Seriously, how much more information could she possibly need?"

"It's six eighteen, Willa," Georgie announced. "Just put on the damn clothes and let me at your hair or you'll be late for your lady date."

"It's not a date," Willa muttered, but she took the bag Addy handed her. "And I'm only doing this so you people will go away."

"It's as good a reason as any," Addy said soothingly.

Willa shot a finger at Georgie. "But no makeup. I draw the line at makeup."

Georgie blanched. "Mascara isn't makeup. It's...necessary."

"Power tools," Willa reminded her.

Georgie scowled. "Just give me the damn comb."

Chapter 12

ELI STOOD OVER the miniature grill cemented into the yard outside his cabin and admired his glowing coals. He'd spent the last forty-five minutes coaxing these babies into emitting a perfectly even five hundred degrees or so, ideal for grilling the gorgeous steaks he'd found at a butcher shop down in Hornby Harbor yesterday.

He lifted his sweating beer bottle toward what he judged to be the southwest, a silent toast to the woman who'd insisted he put in his time at the family restaurant irrespective of his career ambitions to the contrary. Fighting wild fires was a young man's game, she'd told him, but grill skills were forever. Were mothers ever wrong? He doubted it.

He checked his watch. Seven on the button. He figured Willa for the punctual type so he'd wrapped a couple of potatoes in foil an hour ago, tossed them in the dinky little oven in the cabin and cranked the dial to four hundred. He planned to unbag the salad and open the wine when she arrived. Then they could both stand sweating over his perfect fire and grill until the steaks were just barely unable to moo. Then he'd feed her.

Something uncurled inside him, something deliciously edgy and sharp. There was a reason people usually chose restaurants for a first date. Restaurants were polite, safe. They were a neutral place to feel each other out, to decide if there was anything between you worth exploring.

Cooking for a woman, though? Feeding her from your own hand? That was a show of strength, deliberate proof of your ability to care for her, both of which any woman worth having would require before she'd even consider an invitation to your bed.

Not that Eli had any intention of asking Willa to his bed. Not tonight, anyway. Oh, he'd like to satisfy her body in every way imaginable but tonight he'd satisfy her stomach. He'd start there, then take his time with the rest of it. If he decided there was even going to be a *rest of it*.

That pleasant tension in his gut coiled tighter. He hadn't felt anything like this for so long he barely recognized it. But he did. Some things you didn't forget, and wanting a woman was one of them. And he wanted Willa. Wanted her with a fierce intensity that should be making him nervous but wasn't. She simply spoke to him on a level so fundamental he didn't know if he could even articulate it. She sang to him like that damn thinnie of hers, and something deep inside him, something ancient and wise, heard her and answered.

Who was he to argue with something like that?

Her truck rumbled up the two-track in the woods while he was still pondering the question and he grinned at the sight of it. It wasn't fancy or flashy but it got the job done and would probably run forever. It suited her perfectly.

Then she opened the door and slid to the ground and Eli realized he didn't know a damn thing about her. He didn't know a damn thing, period. He simply stared, his nervous system thrown into chaos.

The small, tough, no-nonsense woman he'd asked to dinner had disappeared. The woman who'd scowled at him from under the brim of a ball cap and didn't care about the cider sludge on her t-shirt was nowhere to be seen. In her place stood a gray-eyed warrior-fairy. Where the hell had she been hiding all that hair? It poured down her back in a luxurious tangle so thick and black it looked like ravens tumbling out of the sky. Women paid gazillions of dollars for hair like that, he thought stupidly. Hair that implied she'd just crawled out of some seriously tangled sheets. Hair that made even a stodgy man want to sink his hands into it and his teeth into some other things. And Eli wasn't the stodgy sort.

He blinked and tried to focus on the whole picture. Maybe it would kick-start his brain if he could get past the hair. She was wearing a flippy skirt the color of storm clouds, he saw finally, that ended only a few inches north of her pretty knees. There was a matching strappy tank top, too, with something a shade lighter thrown over it. It had sleeves, so a woman might call it a sweater but it was so gauzy that Eli could see straight through it to the warm skin glowing underneath.

He stood there for a long moment trying to remember how to swallow. Willa turned and gave her truck door the mighty heave it required to shut. That flippy skirt did its thing and Eli's heart tried to leap out of his chest. He rubbed a hand over it, and let his eyes follow those slender legs all the way down to the ground. Where he discovered that Willa had paired that pretty-floaty-girly outfit with her scarred old work boots. Everything in him settled down into a deep, hungry glow. He liked the skirt, no question. Liked the hair even better. But he liked them both a lot more now that he recognized her.

"Hey," she said shortly. Was she nervous? His heart lurched dangerously toward tenderness.

"Hey yourself," Eli said and let his eyes drift back up. She was a curvy little package, wasn't she? Strong and lean, built for endurance and surprise, but the good lord in all his wisdom hadn't skimped on the curves. It was enough to make a believer out of Eli, and he'd had some serious doubts over the years.

And that was just her body. Her face was...

He drifted off again, taking it in. Lord, her face. All those angles and edges. That chin, so ready for a fight. That mouth, so soft and curvy and vulnerable, right next door. And those huge gray eyes, alive with wary pleasure, impatience and...something else he didn't have a name for but wanted to erase. And maybe punch whoever had put it there in the first place.

"What?" she snapped. "It's just a skirt."

"With your boots," he murmured. "I know. I love those boots."

"Then why are you staring at me that way?"

"I've never seen you without your ball cap," he said helplessly. "Your eyes are really—" He stepped closer, lifted a hand toward her cheekbone but stopped short of touching it. Didn't know why. Maybe he was afraid she'd disappear if he did. "Are you sure you've never seen a fairy?"

"Pretty sure."

"I have."

"Is that so?"

"Yeah, just now." He feathered one finger over her cheekbone. "If there's not a fairy somewhere in your DNA, I'll eat my hat."

Her lips quirked. "You're not wearing a hat."

"I'll eat yours then."

"I'm not wearing one either."

"So I see. That's probably why I'm not making any sense."

Those huge gray eyes searched his, a tiny frown pinching together her black brows. "You're doing fine," she decided. "We're both doing fine."

"Aren't we?" He grinned at her, charmed by the serious evaluation. "Let's keep doing fine, shall we?"

"Okay by me." She blinked up at him. "What's next on the agenda?"

"Grilling." He nodded toward the coals a few yards away, turning the air wavy with heat. "I have a couple steaks inside just waiting to be transformed into dinner. I thought we could see about that while the potatoes finish baking. You can tell me how you got turned into a fairy since I saw you last."

She scowled and he wanted to kiss it right off her curvy

lips. "I got hijacked by a love-sick bride and her evil henchmaid."

"That sounds like a story best told over a drink."

"It might take more than one." She shoved a bottle into his hands. He hadn't noticed it there. Too busy gawking, he supposed. "Here. The henchmaid said I had to bring a hostess gift — she thinks I'm a lesbian, by the way — and I definitely deserve a drink for not punching her in her stupid, perfect face when she stuck her tape measurer up my hoohah, so here you go."

"Wait, *she* stuck the tape measurer up *your* hoohah but she thinks *you're* the lesbian?"

Willa shot a finger at him. "Thank you!"

He smiled. "I have a corkscrew inside."

"What are we standing here for?"

"No idea." He settled a hand in the small of her back which was tidy and warm and custom designed for his palm, and nudged her toward the porch.

Willa marched up the cabin steps, exquisitely aware of Eli's eyes on her bare legs. The silky fabric of her skirt whispered against her thighs and that tumbling awareness that had been simmering in her belly since he'd taken her hand in the thinnie a few nights ago churned into wild life. It set her nerve endings on fire until she could feel each super-charged particle of air swirling over her skin.

She definitely needed a glass of wine. Something to do with her hands anyway. Something that didn't involve spearing her fingers into the brutally short stubble of hair covering Eli's scalp just to see if it would feel as deliciously rough against her skin as she thought it might.

Her palms tingled with anticipation, so she gripped the doorknob hard enough to bring herself back to reason and twisted. She breezed into the house with what she hoped was charming nonchalance.

She stopped short in the doorway, her throat closing on the unmistakable stench of burnt fur. Eli froze behind her and she turned to meet his stricken eyes. He knew, too. He recognized the smell. Many people didn't but Eli did. She wondered again what had put that unbearable sadness into his eyes, the sorrow she'd understood before she'd known anything else about him.

Smoke leaked out of the oven to her left and she rushed to it. Snatched up a dishtowel and yanked the door open. Eli reached over her to spin the dial to off. Smoke billowed out of the black cavity of the oven and she flapped the dishtowel to get a better look. Nothing inside but a pair of foil-wrapped lumps she assumed were the potatoes Eli had intended for dinner. They didn't look burnt, plus potatoes didn't have fur. Not usually.

"What is it?" he asked behind her, his voice taut. "It was empty when I put the potatoes in, I swear it. I checked. After the snake in the toilet, I checked."

"I believe you." She kept flapping. "Open the windows, will you?"

Eli jogged away to open every window in the cabin, all three of them. The smoke appeared to be leaking from the burners as much as from the oven itself and Willa said, "Oh no."

"Oh no?" Eli was back at her side in an instant. "What's oh no?"

Willa held a hand over one of the burners. Hot. Very hot. "No insulation between the burners and the oven," she informed him grimly. "Eaten away by mice, probably."

"Okay."

"Leaving a nice warm space where they might then build a nest."

"Oh hell."

Willa located a metal spatula on the counter, chose the smokier of the two burners and pried up the heating element.

She pulled out the aluminum liner beneath it and sure enough, there was a blackened lump of paper and cotton and who even knew what else. Mice were handy little scavengers when it came to building their homes. But this wasn't just a home, she saw quickly, her heart sinking. It was a nursery. There were at least four tiny bodies in the smoldering remains.

"Oh *hell*," Eli said again, his voice ragged, his distress sharp in the smoky air. "Jesus help me, I baked the babies."

"You didn't know." Willa scooped up the smoking lump and laid it carefully in the burner plate she'd removed. She turned to face Eli, and the naked pain in those gorgeous eyes stopped the breath in her lungs. She didn't think about it, she simply reached for him. She slid both hands up his arms, smoothed them over shoulders tight with dismay, and took his jaw in her palms. "Eli, look at me. You didn't know. How could you know?"

She wouldn't say anything as stupid as *they were just mice* or *it could've been worse*. His pain was a living thing, thick and oily in the air around him. She could smell it all around them, as acrid as the smoke clinging to the cabin's ceiling, and just as hard to breathe through. If this was about mice, she'd eat the hat this time.

She rubbed a thumb over one sharp cheekbone. "Eli," she murmured. "Come back."

"It's following me," he said softly, his gaze still on the smoldering remains of the nest.

"What is?"

"Death." He shook his head. "I missed my stop, Willa. I was supposed to get off the bus with everybody else but I didn't, and now it feels like every breath I take I'm stealing from somebody else." He stared blindly at the stove. "I can't even make a fucking baked potato without killing something."

"Do you think it works that way?" she asked. His pain was so thick she could barely breathe through it but this was an important question. She'd never thought to ask anybody before. Had never had anybody to ask. "Do you really think there's somebody up there balancing the scales, spinning and cutting our threads? Do you really think we're part of a plan? Do you think we matter that much?"

"I don't know. Christ, I wish I did." He brought his eyes to hers finally and her throat closed. It simply clamped shut in the face of his agony. "Do you?"

"I don't know either." She gave in to the low-grade hum of need still itching and pulling at her, and slid one palm into the rough rasp of stubble covering his scalp. He closed his eyes and leaned into her touch like a big cat. "Wouldn't that be nice, though?" She closed her eyes, too. It was more private this way. She could drop her words into the darkness between them like wishes into a well. "It would be a comfort, wouldn't it, to think our pain meant something? To think we mattered somehow?"

"You think we don't?"

"I didn't say that." She pulled her palm slowly down the curve of his skull to rest against the nape of his neck. It was smooth and warm and so tense. She drew her finger lightly down the line where his spinal column met his skull and back up again. "We might not matter to some higher power — if one even exists — but we can matter to somebody else. Pain is a fact of life. We can't escape it but we don't have to deal it out ourselves. Not on purpose. Life gives us choices every day, and we can choose to be kind. We can choose to be honorable. We can choose to use whatever we're lucky enough to have to protect somebody who wasn't so lucky. We can matter, Eli. It's just a question of to whom."

Chapter 13

"YOU MATTER TO me," Eli told her. Her fingers were firm on the back of his neck, as if she could command out the demons of grief and guilt with nothing but her touch. And the funny thing was, it was working. Eli fully understood how ridiculous that sounded, even within the confines of his own head. But whatever she was doing to him, it was totally working. "I don't know why you matter, Willa, but you do. You're so damn still."

Her breath was sweet in the space between them and he could feel her absorbing his words, pondering them in that calm, serious way she had. "That's a good thing?"

"It's a goddamn miracle." He lifted his hands and placed them unerringly on the curve of her waist. He didn't even have to open his eyes. He just knew where she was, like there was some kind of primitive echolocation thing at work feeding him her location with exquisite, constant accuracy. In his mind's eye, she was simply *there*, always.

Touching her was an instant and astounding relief. He'd needed this, needed *her*, and satisfying that need nearly put him on his knees. It unstrung the muscles grief had yanked so pitilessly tight, and he lowered his head until his forehead rested against hers. Calm lapped at him like Lake Superior licking at the rocky beach. "It's so noisy inside my head, Willa. It's constant and exhausting and I can't get away from it, no matter how far I walk. Do you have any idea how many pairs of boots I've worn through looking for even a second of quiet?"

"Too many," she murmured, and that curvy mouth was so close he could feel as much as hear her words. They touched his lips, his jaw, his chin. Hunger stirred inside him, tangled into the precious stillness she'd laid over him like a blanket, and wove itself into something new. Something unknown and potentially dangerous, but radically compelling.

"Too many," he agreed. "I probably would've worn out a thousand more but I ran face-first into you instead. And all the noise in my head stopped. It all just stopped and I fell into you. I'm still falling. I'm drowning in you and I don't care."

He had no idea where the words were coming from, they just boiled up and poured out. He'd been desperate and angry and defeated and she'd reached for him anyway. Her touch was a gift, unexpected and undeserved, and had lanced some wound nobody else had ever touched. And everything that had been trapped inside, poisoning him, killing him mile by mile, was released.

"I don't know what you are, Willa, but I need it. I need you. Stay with me."

He didn't even know what he was asking. He hardly knew what he was saying. And then it didn't matter because she was kissing him. Words disappeared. Thought disintegrated. Reality suspended itself and there was nothing but her mouth on his, warm and curvy and real. She was a fairy queen, kissing him with a fierce demand that sent flames rippling across his mind. He hauled her into him, crushed her body to his and she was so small in his arms, so breakable and yet so vibrant and strong. He pushed one hand up under the back of that gauzy sweater of hers, until he could spear his fingers into the living heat of her hair, thick and warm and alive against his skin. He found the delicate curve of her skull, fitted it into his palm and angled her mouth under his, searching for the fit that some corner of his mind knew was there.

Then there it was. She came up to her toes, met him in the middle and the stray flames that had been chasing themselves through the forest of his mind leapt into roaring life. Her mouth opened under his and he fell thoughtlessly into her, spinning and drifting like ash on the updraft. He'd seen this before, he thought hazily. He'd seen fire leaping from tree to tree like a voracious monkey, devouring whole forests from the crown down. He dipped his tongue into the deep, delicious curve of her upper lip, the one he'd been watching with hungry eyes since the moment he'd seen it, and then the fire was in him. It was a vicious, devouring need that created itself even as it slaked itself. He fisted his hand in the living thickness of her hair and let it feast.

Willa had never been kissed like this. She hadn't known it was possible to be kissed like this. Some hazy bit of her mind wondered idly how that could be. If whatever Eli was doing to her was even remotely within the scope of normal, shouldn't she have at least heard about it?

Then again, did it really matter? And why was she wasting time thinking about it when his hands were so fierce in her hair, anchoring her to his hot, hard body? And his mouth, oh good God, his mouth. It took and it took. It demanded and commanded. It reached down deep into the place where she'd buried that wild girl, the girl she'd once been who'd danced and shouted and *wanted*, and resurrected her. It breathed her back to life and the weight of her want was stunning.

Willa twisted her head and broke free, gasped in a whistling breath. Her mind was white and blank, her body a pulsing tangle of need. She needed to think. Oh God, she just needed a second to think, to breathe, to—

Then Eli's mouth landed on her neck, his lips hot and ravenous on the tender, vulnerable curve where it met her shoulder, and desire detonated low in her belly. It raced outward in seismic waves, crashed over her head in a punishing blow of lust. She whimpered and clenched her thighs together against the pulsing need.

And somehow Eli understood. He understood what she wanted before she did.

Suddenly the countertop was at her lower back, and Eli's thigh was between her own, tight against the throbbing center of her want. Stars exploded inside her head and suddenly she didn't want to think. She didn't want to wait and she didn't want to even breathe. She only wanted to be closer.

She arched herself into him. Her new bra slid silky and unfamiliar over the aching buds of her nipples, and she pushed them helplessly into the broad heat of his chest. Her nervous system shattered in a shower of sparks and she gasped. Eli caught her mouth with his, his tongue hot and demanding. She met him halfway, answered his demand with one of her own.

More. She wanted more. She'd been starving and hadn't even known it. Hadn't understood that she wanted anything at all until she'd tasted Eli's mouth and stood in the center of his desire. Until she'd stood at the center of his sorrow, too, and given him respite. He'd shown her what it was to be needed. To be desired. To be revered. He'd made her important, given it to her like a gift.

And he'd awoken her desire. He'd reminded her how to want, and now all she wanted was more. Whatever he needed, she wanted to give it to him. Peace, quiet, stillness, satisfaction. She had it within her power to *satisfy* him, and in doing so, satisfy herself. She knew it was too soon, knew it was dangerously impulsive. But she also knew that life was damn stingy with the good stuff, and Eli was unquestionably the good stuff. He'd walk out of Devil's Kettle as abruptly as he'd walked in. He wouldn't take her with him, and she had no desire to go. This was her home.

But this radical sense of being cherished, nearly worshipped? She'd never felt anything like it before. What if she never did again? She'd be a cowardly fool not to snatch it while it was in front of her.

Willa was no coward, and she was no fool. She was going to take every last thing Eli Walker could give her. And when he laced up his boots and walked out of her life, she wouldn't regret a damn thing.

The decision sent a thrill of pleasure up her spine, where it twined into the darker pulse of her need. She slid her palms over the taut angle of his shoulders and into the rough scrape of stubble covering his scalp. Lust shuddered from her palms straight to her belly, to her nipples, sparkled through her bloodstream and curled her toes inside her boots. She lifted her mouth to his, offered it up and circled herself shamelessly against his thigh. Her thin skirt and silky panties did nothing to protect her from the tough canvas of his cargo shorts, and the friction was unbearably delicious.

And she wanted more.

She found his elbow, tight and trembling, and hooked her hand into it and tugged. He let go of the counter — he'd been gripping it, caging her between two strong arms and drew back. He blinked down at her, his eyes hazy and unfocused, as if he'd surfaced too fast from a deep, deep dive.

Then he zeroed in on her and leapt back. "Willa, Jesus. I'm sorry. I totally jumped you."

"Jump me some more." She took his hand and pressed it to her breast.

"Oh, Christ." His hand trembled against her, and something broke inside her. Something delicate and achingly tender. He cupped her breast like it was fragile. Like he was holding something beyond value, something he didn't deserve but wasn't about to let go of. "I want to see." His eyes met hers in the still-smoky air. "May I?"

She nodded and lifted her arms. He eased the sweater over her head, then nudged the straps of her tank top down her shoulders. He peeled it down to her waist and sucked in a breath, his eyes hot on the plump curves cupped prettily in gun-metal gray. And Willa, who'd had very few reasons in her life to be grateful to Georgie Davis, sent a brief mental thank you her way.

Georgie had intended the lingerie as a clever dig, of course. The bra and panties were lovely and undoubtedly expensive, falling cooperatively in line with Addy's let's-all-get-along agenda. But they played up the generous proportions Willa took daily pains to play down, and the color was a deliberate slap. It was a subtle reminder that Georgie would never forget or forgive Willa's most spectacular failure. But if the appreciative hunger filling Eli's gaze was anything to go by, even *fuck you* was stylish when Georgie Davis said it.

He reached out with one tentative finger and Willa stopped breathing. Her nipple beaded and begged, pushed against the fine material impatiently. And when he touched it, she felt it everywhere. In her palms, in her feet, low and hot in her belly. It unleashed a wave of desire in her that was too big, too lavish to be contained. It shattered her like a swollen river smashing through its banks, and she flowed with it. She simply let it carry her.

Suddenly his hands were everywhere, his mouth wet and open on her skin, on her throat. He boosted her up and the counter was cool under her bottom. She wrapped her legs around him, pushed herself hungrily against the hard thrust of his desire. Her hands were greedy, too, flying under his t-shirt to find his skin, the muscles fluid and smooth under her palms. He dragged the cup of her bra down, exposed her aching nipple, and took it between his teeth. She arched into him and cried out, curled her nails into the lean muscle of his shoulder. He made some noise, something deeply satisfied and inherently hungry all at the same time, and took her other nipple between his fingers. She tugged at his t-shirt until he flung it off, then his hands were back on her. He curled them under her thighs, jerked her to the front of the counter and swept aside the fragile barrier of her panties. He pushed a finger into the needy heat at her center and she dropped her forehead to his shoulder and moaned. He added another finger and she bit him. Sank her teeth into the meat of his shoulder in naked demand.

Her core quivered for more, for release, but she didn't want his fingers. She wanted *him*. She shoved him back and tore at the button closure of his cargo shorts. Worked the zipper, pushed away his boxer-briefs and hissed at the sight of him, thick and hard and hungry. For her.

"Now," she said. "Now." And wrapped her hand around him and put him where she needed him. He lifted her with an easy strength, put his hands under her bottom and sank into her. The breath left her body as he filled her in one hard, assured stroke. There was no room inside her for oxygen, for thought, for ideas. Everything in her — spirit and body — obeyed a single imperative.

She wrapped her legs around his waist, dug her heels into his buttocks and said, "*Move.*"

He did. He held her with merciless hands and drove into her with a fierce demand that sent her shooting up to a bright, tight space. She stayed there, her body suspended in an agony of blinding tension, her legs quivering, her arms shaking, as she reached, reached, reached.

Then he wrapped an arm around her waist, propped one hand on the counter behind her, and dragged her to a new angle, one that had him cursing and pounding into her with desperate ferocity. One that snapped the tension like a tightrope, sent the severed ends singing dangerously through the air and shattering her into a supernova of brilliant dust.

He shuddered and froze, his body whip-tight but curled protectively over hers, as if to shelter her from the storm that had broken over both of them. Even in his release, she realized, he thought of her. Cared for her.

If this was a mistake, it was the best one she'd ever made.

<hr />

When Eli came back to himself, he realized two things. Well, three things. First, it was utterly and completely still inside his head. His body hummed lazily, and satisfaction was like warm honey in his veins. But beyond that, the low-grade buzz of guilt and shame that propelled him out of bed before the sun every morning, and kept him on his boots until he could fall unconscious back into it? It was gone. He didn't know for how long, but he was stupendously grateful for it, and to the woman in his arms who'd granted it.

Second, he had a woman in his arms. A semi-naked, sweat-slicked woman, whose body he was still balls-deep in, whom he hadn't had the courtesy to even fully undress before he'd taken her with all the finesse of a wild badger.

Third, he'd taken her with wild-badger finesse right next to the carcasses of the mouse family he'd killed with his potatoes.

The quiet inside his head broke, gave way to the usual hum of guilt and shame. A muted version to be sure, but it was definitely the same old song.

Willa stirred inside the circle of his arms and he immediately straightened, taking her carefully with him. He disengaged their bodies gently, handed her his t-shirt to tidy up. She simply held it and gazed at him with wide gray eyes surrounded by a halo of rumpled raven hair.

"Still so sad," she murmured and reached out to tap a feather-light finger on his cheekbone under one eye. "It smells like rain."

"What smells like rain?" He took the t-shirt from her hand and gently tidied her up before doing the same for himself. All he could smell was cooked mouse and savage sex.

"How sad you are." She straightened her skirt and leaped lightly down from the counter. She went about the business of putting her bra back in place, hiding those generous pink nipples from him before he could do something stupid like stop her.

"You can smell sad?" He hitched up his shorts before his dick got any other bright ideas.

"You can smell lots of things if you pay attention." She smiled at him, friendly and warm, and the shame inside him crested like a wave. She reached up, put her hand on his bare shoulder and he had to suppress a hiss of renewed want. He'd just had her but he wanted more. He wanted her again. He just wanted. She rose to her toes, pressed a kiss to his jaw and said, "Now where's that corkscrew?"

Chapter 14

IN THE END, they ate steak and drank wine sitting on the iffy front steps of Eli's even iffier cabin. And when the sun gave way to darkness, when loons called wildly over the water and owls went hunting in the forest, Willa set her jam jar of wine aside (the DNR's claim of *fully furnished* was a little optimistic in Eli's opinion) and leaned her shoulder into his.

"Tell me."

Eli didn't set his wine aside. "I don't want to."

"I know. Tell me anyway."

"You tell me something first." He was stalling. He didn't care. "Why me? Why tonight?" He didn't look her way. They were both giving each other the essential courtesy of not forcing eye contact. Two wary animals, circling and sniffing. "I know you don't sleep with men on the first date."

"I don't sleep with men, period."

He sent her a startled glance. "Women?"

She laughed, low and appealing in the warm darkness. "I don't sleep with anybody. I don't have first dates. I don't have dates."

Shock was a hollowness in his belly, sick and guilty. "Good God, Willa. Why didn't you say something? I'd have—"

"I wasn't a virgin, Eli. And I didn't want whatever you'd have done. I wanted exactly what you did."

"Why?" He gripped his own jam jar fiercely, wanted to crush it to dust in his hands. "What I did to you, it wasn't—" His throat closed. He couldn't bring himself to put into words what he'd done to her, the primitive, frantic coupling that was the farthest thing from romance he could conceive of. "Why would you want that?"

"Because you wanted me." She rubbed her cheek against his shoulder like an affectionate cat. "Because everybody else who's ever wanted me has wanted me *for* something. They wanted me to do something for them, to be something for them. They wanted me to give them something, to give *up* something. It was a competition. Somebody would win, somebody would lose." He felt her smile against his sleeve. "I always lost. I always do. I'm not great at people."

The urge to punch some sanctimonious faces rose up in him again. Willa was so generous and warm, so unstinting and alive. Eli was fifty-fifty at best on the existence of a higher power but it struck him as flat-out sinful to take advantage of that generosity for some generic sex, or to rack up points in a sick social competition.

"I'm going to get arrested before I leave this place," he muttered.

"But you," she went on, as if he hadn't spoken. "You didn't want me to be anything but exactly what I was. You didn't ask for a thing. Just being who I was, how I was, was enough for you. No, it was more than enough. The way you held me felt...reverent." Her hand slid around his biceps, rested there trusting and warm. "You didn't ask for my secrets, or my panties, or any other proof you could carry home as evidence you'd bagged the Lumberdyke of Devil's Kettle."

"Lumberdyke?"

"People are so creative, aren't they?"

"I'm definitely going to jail."

"Why?"

"Never mind. Go on."

She shrugged. "The only thing you asked was for me to stay. Just stay there and let you hold me. Let you breathe me in. Let whatever stillness you find in me soothe the noise that won't let you sleep. Do you have any idea what a gift that was, Eli?"

"To me? Yes," he said promptly. "I don't know what you are, but whatever it is is magic. It's just…" He shook his head. "You're just so still," he said again helplessly. "I don't know how else to describe it. You just reach out and wrap yourself around all the noise and lay it down to sleep. You're amazing."

She laughed again, soft in the darkness. "And that's exactly why I wanted exactly what you gave me." She drifted her fingers down his forearm, laced them through his own. Something bruised and dark shifted inside him and he pressed his palm to hers. "You don't want me to change. All you wanted in that moment was me, exactly as I am. Pretty skirt, ugly boots and all."

It was a devastating combination as far as Eli was concerned. It broke his heart that she didn't know it. He wanted her to know it, damn it. "Keep it up and you'll find that skirt around your waist again and those boots in the air."

"Sweet talker."

This time he laughed, surprising himself. It was chainsaw-rusty but it worked. "Would you believe that used to be true?"

She gave that a moment of thoughtful consideration. "You know, I just might."

"I didn't give you any sweet words."

"I didn't want them."

"Why not? You deserve them."

"I don't trust them."

"Do you trust anything?"

"Only what I can see and smell. And you, Eli Walker, smell like rain. It's been the driest summer on record and you still smell as sad as rain."

He didn't know how to argue with that so he didn't try.

"What happened to you?" she asked quietly. "What took away all those sweet words you used to have and put all that noise in your head?"

"Nothing happened to me. That's exactly the problem."

Her silence was calm, endless. She'd have sat there forever, waiting serenely for him to go on without being remotely tempted to throw in a word or a thought of her own. Which was maybe why he started talking.

"I have this uncle," he said finally. "My mother's brother. Ben. He was a Black Canyon Hotshot when I was growing up, which gave him a cool factor somewhere between a Navy SEAL and an Olympic snowboarder. Hotshots are like the Marines of the wild land firefighters, you know? Smoke jumpers parachute into the fight, which is wicked cool and has its own challenges, I'm sure, but hotshots get there the hard way. They hump in on foot, carrying half their body weight in equipment and gear. They're the toughest bastards on the fire line, and that was who I wanted to be.

"My mom, on the other hand, ran an Irish pub in Denver. And no, we're not Irish. But nobody does a better pub than the Irish and my mom's just like my uncle. She doesn't do second best, not at anything. She put everything into that place after my dad died. She wanted to build something for my sister and me, something that would be there for us after she died, too."

"Did she?"

"Die? Hell, no. Mom's as tough as Ben, and Ben's a stick of goddamn jerky. But did she build something? Yeah, she did. And my sister Julie is just like our mom. The instant she graduated college — college was Mom's one nonnegotiable — she went to work at the pub full time. She talked Mom into buying this incredibly expensive espresso machine and—" He cut himself off, dragged a palm down his face. "And I'm stalling."

She squeezed his hand but held that dark, inviting silence of hers. He pulled in a deep breath and it was full of her stillness. It settled him. It didn't solve him but it settled him enough to go on.

"The restaurant business wasn't for me. I wanted to be

Ben. My mom knew it, and she didn't fight me. By the time
I graduated from high school, I'd been working as an EMT
for two years. I still pulled shifts at the pub but my heart was
set on fire. I went to Colorado State University for a Forestry
degree, with a concentration in Forest Fire Science. Applied
to hotshot crews for two years after college before I finally
got on with a brand new crew out of New Mexico, the Silver
Creek crew. Oh, I wanted to be one of Ben's Black Canyon
boys but I knew I needed to prove myself. Black Canyon
was a legend and Ben was the next thing to a dad to me.
Hell, for all practical purposes, he *was* my dad, and I wanted
to prove myself to him as much as to myself. Probably more.
I wanted to come up the hard way, just like he had. So I
landed on the Silver Creek crew and took my damn lumps.

"That first season was hell on earth. I'd never been
filthier or more exhausted in my life. I'd never been happier,
either. Hotshotting is sixteen hour days, fourteen of them in
a row sometimes, cutting fire line. That's essentially ripping
a path the size of a decent highway through a forest but
instead of using a bulldozer, you do it by hand. You take out
every tree, every bush, every root, even the damn soil,
anything that could possibly burn. It's twenty guys building
a fuel-free strip between a fire and anything the government
doesn't want to burn. And I loved it.

I started as a scrape, just like everybody else does,
trailing the chainsaw teams, chopping out and raking away
anything the sawyers and their swampers left behind.
Worked my way up to swamper, dragging felled trees off the
line. Then I was a sawyer, felling those trees. Then I was
squad boss for the sawyers. By the time I was twenty-five I
was the captain of Silver Creek, answered only to the
superintendent. And our supe — Vic — he was kind of a
dick. That's what we called him, in fact. Vic the Dick. He
was old school. Very military, right down to the crew cut."

Eli scrubbed a rueful hand over the stubble covering his
scalp. It was a reminder every day of his hubris. Every chill

breeze was a warning — don't get too comfortable, too confident. Don't forget that you're still above the earth in the sun, breathing and eating and living while nine good men aren't.

"We were on a fire in the mountains a couple hours outside Sedona. I had half the guys and Vic had the other half," he began and stopped. Had to swallow and start again. "It was a beast of a fire, hot as hell and faster than lightning. It was tough country, all pockets and canyons and peaks, and the fuel load was staggering. It hadn't burned since 1971 and it was dry as hell. My crew and I were cutting line on the heel of the fire down in a valley—"

"The heel?"

"Behind the fire."

"Why would you do that? I mean, if the fire's going one direction, why wouldn't you put all your resources into cutting line in front of it?

"Because there's no guarantee the fire's going to keep moving that direction. Forecasts are handy but when a fire starts making its own weather, all bets are off."

"A fire can make its own weather?"

"Sure. There's a shitload of water stored in even the driest forest, and when it burns hot and fast, that's not just a column of smoke you're seeing in the sky. It's steam, too. And you know what happens when a bunch of hot, wet air meets a bunch of cold dry air somewhere way the hell up in the atmosphere?"

"It comes down," Willa said wonderingly. "The steam condenses into water and it comes down as rain."

"It sure does. The actual rain evaporates before it gets to the ground but the wind it generates would put a hurricane to shame. And that's when shit gets dangerous because nobody can predict which way that wind's going to blow. A fire that's been creeping west all day will suddenly double back on itself and tear up five hundred acres to the east that nobody was even looking at." He shrugged. "The heroes with a track record get to be on the front lines, but when the government's fighting a fire, they hedge their bets and put a team on the heel, too."

"I see."

"Heeling's a shit job but that's what the young, unproven crews like Silver Creek are for. But we were hot to change that."

"How?"

"By being fearless motherfuckers with balls of steel, of course. So we'd been heeling for three days already, watching the smoke and steam climb like a damn skyscraper." A mental picture rose up in his mind's eye, as vivid to him now on a midnight porch in the north woods as it had been on a sweltering July afternoon in the mountains. A towering column of brackish smoke arrowing into the sky, like the fire itself giving you the finger. Dread and terror balled together in his throat but back then he'd only felt awe and anticipation. "It was going to crash down, all that steam. Everybody knew it, from Uncle Ben — who'd been named incident commander of the whole fire — on down to the newest scrape on Silver Creek. And when it did, the shape of the valley would probably funnel the wind — and the fire — right back the way it had come. Back toward my crew."

She said nothing, but her hand was a warm, reassuring presence on his thigh. He cleared his throat and went on.

"When you're heeling a fire and it turns on you, you have two options. You either run toward the fire or away from it."

"Why on earth would you run toward it?"

"After a fire rolls through a section of forest, there's nothing left to burn. That area's called the good black and there's nowhere safer. The good black is always your first option when the fire you're heeling turns on you." He let out a breath — had he been holding it? — and forced his shoulders to relax. Forced himself to go on. "Your other option, of course, is to run away from the fire and hope like hell that the line you've been cutting buys you enough time to get to some other previously identified safe zone. It's riskier, of course, but sometimes it's the right call."

"Was it?" she asked quietly. "Was it the right call?"

"No," he said, just as quietly. "But we made it anyway."

Chapter 15

WILLA CLOSED HER eyes and concentrated on breathing, slow and even. The hair on her arms lifted and the air smelled electric, as if the thunderstorm in Eli's memory were gathering in the skies above them, here and now, threatening to break. But it wasn't. Willa knew it. The only thing that would break tonight was Eli.

She thought of her thinnie, of its impossible age, of the serenity born of that age. She put her mind in the center of it, even as her heart stayed and bled with Eli. She focused on that ancient calm, and pushed it from her pores into the air between them. She was a catalyst for the coming storm; she understood this even as she tried to comfort him. She acted on Eli like a trigger of some sort, pulling something from him he had no desire to give up, something he wouldn't thank her for demanding.

But there was no going back, not now. Whatever it was he needed to say next — and she dreaded it — it was poisoning him. It was killing him, minute by minute, and he needed it out. He was like an animal in a trap. He could either lie down and wait for death, or he could start gnawing off his own leg. She had the impression that up until this moment, up until this night, he'd been resigned to death. Had been waiting for it, in fact. Might even have welcomed it. But something had changed in him tonight, something she'd triggered somehow, and now he was circling the idea of living instead. Sniffing at it, gathering his courage for the unspeakable violence he'd need to do his own soul to earn it.

And that violence was swirling and growing, snapping and snarling in the air like an impending storm. And Willa was the lightning rod. She only hoped she was strong enough to bear the strike.

"What happened?" she murmured, and tipped her head onto his shoulder. Rubbed her cheek against the living fact of him, breathed in the scent of sharp pines and clean man and unbearable sorrow. "Tell me."

He paused for a long moment, so long she wondered if he was going to go on. Then he spoke.

"We had talked about it, me and the guys. We'd talked it through all day and we all agreed. When the fire turned, we weren't going to trot over to the black and wait there like good little boys for the fire to blow by us so we could get on its tail and start heeling again. Not when there was a high-dollar development not a mile behind us full of people standing on their million-dollar roofs live-streaming the action. Not when, with the help of a little conveniently timed radio trouble, we could be the kind of steel-balled motherfuckers who were already cutting line for the cameras before any of the other crews — including Black Canyon — even showed up. All we had to do was get to that development before the fire did."

His voice was thin, far away. She knew he was back on some sun-baked mountain in the southwest, dripping sweat and breathing smoke. "I hiked over to this knob of rock off to the north where I could have eyes on both my guys and the fire. I watched the smoke column grow this ugly, lightning-streaked mushroom head, then I saw it drop out of the sky onto the fire. It was goddamn textbook, and it shoved the fire right back the way it had come."

"Toward your crew."

He nodded, cleared his throat. "I was on the radio the instant I saw it turn, gave my guys the go. Two seconds later, the radios fucking blew up. I didn't even have to fake radio trouble. If Ben or Vic tried to order my crew to the black, I never heard him. Every captain, every supe, every squad boss was trying to raise his own crew to confirm that they were executing their exit strategy. It was chaos across the channels but I had gotten the jump. I'd already put my guys in motion and I could see them doing exactly what we'd talked about, exactly what we'd all agreed on. They were hauling ass for that fancy development. Except I could also see the fire, and it was moving fast. Too fast. Faster than I'd ever seen a fire move."

He laughed then, short and bloody. "Twenty-seven years old and I thought I knew how fast a fire could move. Jesus, I was an arrogant little dick. Nobody has any idea how fast a fire can move. You can't possibly imagine it. But maybe I'm still that arrogant dick, because even now I believe my guys could've outrun it. They were beasts, and they knew they were running for their lives. They should've won."

They hadn't won. Willa didn't need to hear him say it. He didn't need to hear her speak that ugly truth, either, so she stayed silent. Eli didn't notice. She would've wondered if he was even aware of her anymore, except that her fingers were crushed inside the vise of his own.

"There was a set of tennis courts right on the leading edge of the development, and we'd IDed them as our worst case scenario option. If worse came to absolute worst, if the fire was right on our asses, we could deploy our fire shelters there. It would be humiliating — the idea is to never be stupid enough to have to deploy — but at least we'd be alive." He paused, and the silence was so awful Willa didn't know if she'd survive it. "They were less than two hundred yards from the courts when the fire caught them. Later on, when they sent a crew up to retrieve the bodies, they found eight fire shelters deployed, feet toward the flames, just like we always practiced. Eight shelters, Willa, but I had nine men on my team."

She rubbed her cheek against his shoulder again, this time to wipe away her tears. His voice was dry as the desert floor, raw as an open wound.

"They found Thomas in Ollie's shelter," he said quietly.

"They were a sawyer/swamper pair, Thomas and Ollie, and I swear they shared a brain. They could clear a hundred-year-old ponderosa without a word and make it look like a fucking ballet. But here's the thing, Willa. If you can get into a sleeping bag, you can deploy a fire shelter, but those things aren't designed to hold two fully grown men. There shouldn't have been two guys in one shelter, not even guys as close as Thomas and Ollie."

"So what happened?" she asked. "Why would they buddy up?"

He shifted his shoulders, resettling the weight of those nine deaths like a hiker adjusting a heavy pack. "I've been asking myself the same question every second of every day since. And I don't know the answer, not for sure. But Thomas had been sick the week before the fire with one of those nasty flus that leaves you on the bathroom floor, praying to die. When we got the call about the fire, he insisted he was totally fit, 100 percent." A smile ghosted across his face. "He was probably eighty percent at best but for those three days we fought that fire, he made up the missing twenty with sheer grit. He'd be damned if he'd stay home watching Netflix while the rest of us were off covering ourselves in glory." The smile died. "But that kind of grit doesn't leave much in the tank, not even when you're running for your life." He dropped his head. "I doubt he did much running, though. If he was too weak to even deploy his own shelter, he was probably too weak to even hike at speed, let alone run. And that means nobody else was running, either, because my crew would rather die than leave a brother behind. They'd probably been carrying him by the time they realized they weren't going to make it and deployed."

"You couldn't have known," Willa said helplessly. "He worked for three days without flagging. He didn't give you any indication—"

"I was the captain," he said simply. "My job was to make

the right call. My job was to honor grit like that. To protect it, even from the guy giving it to me. Instead I abused my position—"

"You think you abused your position?"

"I think I wanted to be the guy who showed the world — who showed my uncle — that the Silver Creek guys were heroes, not heelers. That when a fire turned nasty, we had the balls and the vision to get in front of it instead punking out and scampering for the black. I wanted Ben to show up with his Black Canyon crew and find Silver Creek already there putting a leash on that bitch." He shifted again, still searching for some way to carry that load, and Willa's heart bled for him.

"You said the fire moved faster than anything you'd ever seen. What if you'd been more conservative and run for the black? Would you have made it?"

"I don't know." He pulled his fingers from hers. Dropped his elbows to his knees and released a shuddering breath. "I'd have been with my guys, though. If the fire caught us, it would've caught us together. Maybe we'd have died, maybe we wouldn't, but it would've happened to all of us together."

Willa's throat clamped shut. He wasn't just guilty or ashamed, she realized suddenly. Eli Walker was *lonely*. He'd been a cocksure, incredibly fit young man pursuing a dangerous profession in the company of other young men exactly like himself, and collectively they'd made a bad decision with terrible consequences. But Eli had gotten lucky. He'd survived, and his shame and guilt over that were immense. But underneath them both was a staggering loneliness. He'd lost his *brothers*.

"I was the captain, Willa. I was their leader and I failed them. If anybody had to die on that mountain, it should've been me." He closed his eyes. "It should've been me."

For a long time, Willa said nothing. She simply leaned into his shoulder and stayed with him. She knew what regret was. She knew how bitter bad decisions tasted, even if no good decisions had existed when you made the bad ones. Even if you weren't making those decisions by yourself. She knew exactly the hell Eli was living in. And she knew that you didn't find your way out of that kind of hell. You just learned to bear it.

She lifted a hand and placed it in the center of his back. It was tight under her hand, the muscles rigid with shame and pain. She moved her hand in slow circles, smoothed it over all that guilt and sorrow. Over the aching loneliness. "You didn't make that decision by yourself, Eli, but even if you did, there's no changing what's done. Those men — your brothers — are gone, and you can't buy back their lives with yours. No matter how much pain you bear, no matter how much you suffer, you can't undo what's done. And wishing yourself dead won't change that."

"How am I supposed to live with that?" His voice was tight, choked. He trembled under her hand, the storm gathering, flashing and howling. "If I can't die, how do I *live*?"

"You just have to bear it, Eli. You can't keep running from it. There aren't enough miles in the world, and trust me, I know. Killing yourself won't balance the scales. Neither will refusing to live. But people make mistakes, and you didn't make this one alone."

"I was the captain," he said again, almost desperately. "It was my responsibilty to—"

"You were twenty-seven years old," she cut in gently. "And probably trying to lead a team of bullet-proof cowboys just like you who'd been your peers and equals a year or two before." He shut his mouth and frowned. It had been a guess but had evidently hit the target. "You're no better or worse than any of the men who died on that mountain, Eli. You were luckier, that's all. And the price you pay for that luck is that you get to keep this mistake. You get a future, but you also get to carry that mistake. It's yours to carry and yours to honor. So honor it. Let it teach you how to be better. Let it build you into somebody stronger, somebody wiser. Somebody who would make a different decision if given the chance. But you *live*, Eli. You didn't die, so you have to live."

He sighed and tipped his head until his cheekbone rested on the top of her head. They sat that way for a long time, Willa's hand on his back, his breath in her hair.

"One day," he said softly, "you'll tell me."

"Tell you what?" She'd let her eyes close, let contentment drift through her veins, make her limbs heavy and warm.

"How you learned all this." He put his hand on her knee, and it was heavy and warm, too. "Why you can talk about it with an authority that makes my throat hurt."

"It's an old, sad story," she said lightly, even though it put its claws into her soul at random moments. "It's behind me and done."

"Do you ever think about what you'd do differently?" he murmured. "Do you ever wonder what you'd do today if you were given a second chance?"

She tried like hell not to let her mind even wander into such dangerous territory. "I made my peace with it a long time ago."

"Did you?"

The ache was old, almost sweet. "I like to think so, yeah."

Some days she wasn't so sure, though.

Eli told himself to stay away. He told himself to give Willa some space. He didn't know what the hell had happened between them the other night, didn't know what it meant or what kind of black magic she'd worked on his soul but he did know he needed some time alone to figure it all out. Because for the first time in nearly three years, his head was quiet. It wasn't silent, not by a long shot, but it was quiet enough for him to breathe, even when he was standing still.

And he wanted to know — he needed to know — if it would stay that way without her.

In the end, the mice forced his hand.

Two days after the first-date-turned-horrifying-therapy-session, Eli pulled his tuna can up to Willa's cabin. It was morning, early enough that he thought she might still be at home, but not so early that he'd look desperate. Though, Jesus help him, he *was* desperate. Maybe his head was still quiet — quiet-ish, anyway — but he was a desperate man. Desperate for the sight of her, the scent of her, the feel of that warm, strong hand of hers on his back, on his scalp, on other parts of his body she hadn't gotten around to exploring, probably because he'd been in such a goddamn hurry the other night.

So, yeah, he was definitely desperate. But he didn't want to *look* desperate, so he made himself wait until eight-thirty. That was almost business hours. He could get away with eight-thirty, especially as he was bringing her a gift. That had to count for something.

Her dad sat on the front porch steps as Eli pulled up, a laptop balanced on his knees, a cup of coffee steaming beside his boot. Eli got out of the car, his gift carefully cradled in both hands.

"Hey, Mr. Zinc."

"It's Brett."

"Brett, then. I'm Eli Walker. Willa's friend from the bar the other day?"

"I remember."

He stopped at the steps and pointed his chin at the laptop on Brett's knees. "How's the job search coming?"

"About like you'd expect." Brett lifted his coffee cup for a long sip, eyed the beautifully crafted nest in Eli's hand. "That for Willa?"

"Yeah. She around?"

"You know, most men would bring flowers."

"I'm not most men."

"I guess you're not." A corner of Brett's mouth twitched into a faint smile. "Not if you're courting a woman with a mouse nest made of—" He tipped his head. "What is that, anyway?"

"Best guess? Half a box of tampons and my favorite pair of socks."

Brett blinked, then shook his head slowly. "You have a lot to learn, son."

"Trust me. Willa will like this better than flowers."

"I wish she were here so we could find out but she's not."

"No?" Disappointment flooded him and he gave himself a stern mental slap for visible desperation. *Pull it together, Walker.* "I'll just leave it for her, then. Kitchen okay?"

"Okay by me, especially if you bring the coffee pot out here. You got me damn addicted."

"I know the feeling," he muttered and went inside. A minute later, he was back with the coffee pot and a mug of his own. Brett lifted a brow.

"Help yourself," he said.

"I did, thanks."

"You didn't bring the cream or sugar," Brett pointed out and held up his mug. Eli obliged him with a refill.

"Real men drink it black, especially when Willa makes it." He treated himself to his first sip and sighed. "Woman's got a gift."

Brett's sigh was more resigned. "I was working my way up."

"Congratulations. You're there."

"Shit." He took another sip, then set aside the mug to poke at the keyboard on his knees.

"Any luck?" Eli asked.

"On the jobs? Nah." Brett scowled and poked some more. "I hate computers."

"Me, too. That's why I hike for a living."

Brett clicked and cursed. "Jesus Christ, I don't even know what I did just there. Let's assume I'm not getting that one." He shut the laptop's lid and set the thing aside. "Tell me how to hike for a living, Eli. I don't even care if it makes me so addled I'd give a woman a mouse nest and call it a gift. I'm that desperate."

Eli knew enough about desperate to recognize the thread of utter sincerity inside the frustration. "You a hiker?"

"Never was, but after eight years inside walls and fences? I am now."

Eli considered that. "The other day, after I met you at the bar. Did you really hike here?"

"I did. And every day, after I spend two hours on that godforsaken thing—" He sent the computer a look of pure dislike. "—I take myself on another little walk-about."

"Walk-about?"

"A mile or six. It blows the cobwebs out. Had mandatory anger-management in jail. Didn't put much stock in it except I had this one shrink. Dude lived through Vietnam, three tours. Said when he got back, he ended up on the shrink's couch, too. Lady told him to exercise and journalize. That was it. That was therapy. Exercise to wear out the body and journalize to bleed off the crazy in his head before it took root and started making sense. Exercise and journalize. It was like his religion." Brett's smile was rueful. "Saw a lot of shrinks when I was inside, but he was the only one who looked like The Rock. Only one who ever said anything useful, either."

"You journalize?"

"Hell, no. I never had two thoughts to rub together. But I had a lot of strength when I was angry or drunk or, hell, let's face it, both." He met Eli's eyes directly. "I was both a lot of the time."

"Okay.

"And when I was?" He moved his shoulders. "Well, it's

like Sinatra says. *Regrets, I've had a few*."

"How many miles do you think you cover a day?"

Brett sent him a sideways glance, a flicker of something cautiously interested in those dark, weary eyes. "We in a competition now, boy?"

"Maybe. How many?"

"At least five. Sometimes ten. Why?"

Eli lifted his coffee cup. Sipped and considered Willa's dad. Considered that tentative spark of hope in eyes he'd have sworn were dead. He knew something about how hard it was to die, even when you wanted to. Eli would be damned if he'd do anything to snuff out something so determined to live.

"Get in the car, Brett. You impress me today, you've got yourself a job."

"Doing what?"

"Hiking."

Chapter 16

WILLA STEPPED INTO the Davis Gallery, and immediately wished she hadn't. Willa's family situation had never been particularly stable, but Diego Davis' selfishness had kicked its last, tottering legs out from under it. Loving him — or what passed for love in the heart of a lonely young girl — had cost her plenty. She avoided worshipping at the shrine of his talent when she could.

It had been one hell of a talent, though. She had to admit it, if only to herself, as she wandered farther into the airy space, bright with morning light. The gallery didn't open until ten but Georgie's summons — no other word for it — had demanded Willa's presence at nine sharp. But when you didn't know what the hell was going on, it was never a bad idea to catch the other party off-guard, so it was still a few minutes shy of nine when Willa paused in the center of the gallery to ponder *Diego's Angel.*

It was the masterwork that had shot Diego to celebrity, a portrait he'd done of Addison when he was still stupidly, besottedly in love with her. Willa didn't know much about art, but she knew when a painting shoved its hand into her chest, grabbed her still-beating heart and yanked it out.

Diego's Angel was that kind of painting.

The rest of his stuff wasn't far behind.

The faint scent of iron and ice drifted over her shoulder and Willa knew that Georgie had arrived. She didn't need to see her; nobody smelled as cold or as beautiful as Georgie Davis.

"It's a classic for a reason." Georgie stood beside her, gazing at the *Angel.* "When Diego fell in love, he fell in *love.*"

Willa wouldn't know. "Sure looks that way."

"Too bad he fell out of love the same way."

Willa pointed her chin at the painting. "You got to keep the prize."

"Addy's a peach, all right." Willa would never like Georgie but she had to give her credit for assuming — correctly — that Willa hadn't been talking about the painting. Georgie was wearing some silky tunic-like thing in a soft lilac over a pair of slim white pants. She folded her arms and studied the painting as if she didn't see it every damn day. "Wouldn't have minded keeping my brother, too, though."

A pulse of hatred surprised Willa. She might not like Georgie but she'd also given up truly hating her years ago. She'd refused to let any of the Davises matter enough to hate, except maybe Bianca. Hating Bianca went deeper than Willa's self-control. But was Georgie really expecting Willa's sympathy? Georgie, with her big house, her piles of money, her perfect face and her intensely loyal family? Willa had never been in line for any of those things, nor had she ever expected them. But she'd had a family once. It had been a little trashy and drama-prone, sure, but she'd had a family nonetheless. Now she had none. Maybe that wasn't Diego's fault per se, maybe her family had been primed to blow, but he'd sure lit the fuse. So she wasn't sorry he was dead, and she'd be damned if she'd say she was.

Georgie sent her a sly sideways glance. "Nothing to say, Willa?"

Willa met her eyes with perfect indifference. "Nothing you want to hear."

"You might be surprised at what I want to hear."

"I'm sure I would be. I just don't care."

Georgie smiled. "I wonder why we don't chat more often. It's always so pleasant."

"For you, maybe. I get bored."

Georgie tipped her head and gave her a narrow study. "Sometimes I can almost see why Addy likes you." She let her gaze drift over Willa's well-worn jeans and *Zinc Pest Control* t-shirt. "Then I look at your outfit and horror chases everything else from my mind."

"It's a short run."

Her lips twitched. "Nice one." She shook back a sheet of silvery hair with a satisfied flick. Formalities observed, it was time to get down to business. Whatever the hell that business might be.

Georgie turned on the heel of what looked like a ballet slipper and headed toward the back of the gallery. "Come on," she said. "I want to show you something."

Willa followed, curiosity at war with foreboding. Georgie slipped past the white curtain that separated the gallery proper from the staging area where Bianca was planning to show Diego's naughty paintings for Devil Days. There was a table against one wall holding several pieces of pottery and a couple wooden sculptures but Georgie led her to the other wall. A series of frames stood propped on a narrow shelf that ran chest-high along the length of the wall. Track lights on the ceiling bathed the frames in warm, generous light, and even Willa — no art lover — recognized the artist.

"Welcome to *Diego After Dark*," Georgie said.

"This is the final line up, then? This is the display that has Gerte all heated up?" Willa asked. Rumors had been circulating for months now that the Davises were planning to show some of Diego's previously unshown works for Devil Days, and Diego being Diego, Gerte was utterly convinced it had to be porn. She'd whipped herself — along with most of the town — into a torches and pitchforks frenzy over it. Willa squinted at the painting in front of her. "I see the boob made the final cut."

"Along with its companion piece." Georgie indicated a matching frame right next door.

"Huh." Willa stepped to the next painting. Tipped her

head. Blinked. "Is that what I think it is?"

"Probably." Georgie nudged her with a pointy elbow. "Speaking of which, how was your date the other night?"

"Shut up."

"Got all dressed up for nothing, huh?" Georgie laughed. "Well, not everybody can be as lucky in love as our Diego."

Willa glanced down the row of paintings. "Is that why you asked me to come here? So you could show me a bunch of vagina paintings?" She paused. "Wait, has Gerte seen these?"

"Are you kidding?" Georgie rolled her eyes. "I'm no Gerte fan but even I don't want to be responsible for the stroke that takes her out of this world." She paused thoughtfully. "No, I don't," she decided. "Not yet, anyway. Addy will want pie at the reception."

"She told me she was thinking about a doughnut tree."

"What in the holy hell is a doughnut tree?"

"How do I know? She already talked to Walt about it, though. Or, wait, maybe that was the shower, not the reception?" She shrugged.

Georgie scowled and produced a slim phone from an invisible pocket somewhere. Maybe from thin air. How the hell did Willa know? Georgie's clothes existed on a plane outside Willa's experience. Definitely outside her budget. Georgie opened an app and thumb typed something with shocking efficiency. "For cripes sake, Addison," she muttered under her breath, "I'm only your maid of honor. Keep me in the loop, why don't you?" She tucked the phone away and smiled brilliantly. "But no, I didn't bring you here to rub your nose in your lack of romantic success, nor to discuss the wedding. I want to talk to you about my mother."

Willa sighed. She'd wondered when Georgie would get around to this conversation. "She thinks we should be civil to one another for Addy's sake."

"It's more than that." Georgie's mouth was grim. "I think she wants to tell Matty about you."

"What?" Shock was a bright white light, and suddenly Willa's brain was a blank sheet.

"She hasn't said as much but I think she's toying with the idea."

"Why?"

"How do I know?" Georgie rolled an elegant shoulder. "Mom's mind follows its own twisty paths. Maybe she wants to get ahead of the story. I mean, he already knows Mom isn't his biological mother. He knows *I'm* not his biological mother, either, which is more than I can say for most of the other idiots in this town, your asshole brother included."

"My asshole brother has a lot of idiotic ideas about you," Willa said faintly.

"Had." Georgie's smile was chilling. "He's been disabused of the most egregious."

"Nice vocab." She wondered if Peter had been aware of precisely who he was dealing with when he'd screwed over Georgie Davis.

"Even magazines with shiny pages use big words sometimes."

"Mmm."

"My point, Willa, is that Matty's at the age where he's going to start asking questions. And with the wedding coming up, he's going to be seeing a lot more of you. You and those goddamn eyes you two share. He's not a dumb kid, for all that he does dumb things. So it's entirely possible that he'll put two and two together and end up asking you some interesting questions before Mom decides how she wants us to answer them." Georgie folded her arms and gazed at Willa, flat and cold. "If that happens, I want to know what you're going to tell him."

Willa's heart crashed into her rib cage like a bird mistaking a window for freedom. It lay stunned inside her chest, not beating, not bleeding, just suspended somewhere in between. She waited for it to make up its mind — hope or

resignation? But even as she waited, she knew the answer.
The truth was her burden. She carried it the way Eli carried
those men's deaths, a nonnegotiable weight she'd learned to
live with. She'd made her bargain years ago, and she'd held
up her end. Even when the loneliness was a physical
presence inside her, grinding her soul into dust, she hadn't
reached for Matty. Hadn't reached out to the one person who
shared her blood who hadn't rejected or abandoned her. The
one person she could honestly say she loved with her whole
heart, whatever was left of that poor, battered thing.

Love, she knew from bitter experience, wasn't about the
lover. Love — true love — was about the beloved. And
Willa knew she had nothing to offer Matty. Nothing but
damage. Nothing but a family tree full of violence,
corruption and dysfunction. Revealing Matty's true
parentage might give Willa some faint claim to family, but
there was nothing but shame in it for Matty. And she loved
him too much, too purely, to do that to him. Not unless she
had to.

Besides, her silence had been bought and paid for.

"I'm going to say exactly what I've always said," Willa
told Georgie. "Exactly what your mommy paid me to say."

"What's that?"

"Not a damn thing."

Willa's truck was in the drive when Eli and Brett pulled
up in the tuna can late in the afternoon. The sun was still
high in the sky and it glinted off what little chrome was left
on the rusty old Ford. In the passenger seat, Brett shook his
head.

"I can't believe she still drives that thing. I got it before
she was born, and it wasn't new then."

"I get the impression that Willa knows how to hold on."

"Yeah. Me, too." Brett compressed his mouth into a hard

line. "But she ought to learn to let go. No sense holding onto things you've outgrown, things that aren't good for you."

Eli eyed him. They'd hiked mostly in silence for the better part of eight hours. Eli had set a moderate pace that Brett had easily matched, and he hadn't flagged. His eyes had proven sharp once Eli explained what they were looking for, and Brett hadn't been lying about his appetite for the miles. Whatever was inside his head, whatever his personal noise was, the rhythm of his boots on the rocks seemed to quiet it. He'd been relaxed, almost easy, when they'd folded themselves into the tuna can for the ride back to Willa's place. Each passing mile had wound Brett tighter, though, and now he was staring at Willa's truck as if it was personally responsible for the mess Brett had made of his life and of his daughter's.

"And yet," Eli pointed out softly, "here you are."

"Here I am," Brett agreed, just as softly. "One more junky old thing she's hanging onto."

"You're letting her."

"I know." His mouth twisted. "I never claimed to be strong, or to be good. That's Willa you're thinking of."

"You're not weak. Not from what I saw today."

"There's different kinds of weak, Eli." Brett pushed open his door, put one boot on the ground. "I'm the kind of weak that'll lean on anything sturdy enough to hold me when the need arises."

"Need arises, does it?"

"When you're fresh out of prison, you got nothing but need, and no choice but to ask for help where you don't deserve it." Brett planted the other boot on the ground, looked back at Eli. "But I'm not the kind of weak that'll keep leaning when I've got my feet under me."

He shoved out of the tuna can — the piece of crap rocked like a small boat on a large ocean — and leaned back down to speak. "You coming in to explain about the tampons and hiking socks on the counter, or are you throwing me under that bus?"

"Oh, I'm coming in all right." Eli stepped out as well, headed for the porch. "I'm presenting that beauty in person."

Eli chuckled. "This I've got to see."

"You're just jealous you didn't think of it yourself." Eli had one boot on the porch steps when the front door opened and Willa appeared above him, the mouse nest in her hands, her face cool and closed. "Hey, Willa."

"Eli." She turned to her father. "Dad. Where have you been?"

"Hiking with Eli."

Her brows rose slowly. "All day?"

Brett winced. "I guess so, yeah."

"You're supposed to be looking for a job."

"I was doing just that when Eli showed up." Brett slipped his fingers into his pockets. "I'd been at it for at least a pot, pot and a half of coffee when Eli showed up with..." He nodded at the nest. "That."

Willa switched that cool, remote gaze to Eli. "You brought me a mouse nest?"

"Not just any mouse nest." Eli mounted the steps and leaned against the pillar holding up the roof. "That there is a one-of-a-kind, paw-crafted, multi-media masterpiece."

"Multi-media?"

Eli smiled. "Best I can tell, it's mostly my favorite hiking socks plus half a box of the tampons somebody left in the bathroom."

Willa blinked. "You brought me a mouse nest of dirty socks and clean tampons?"

"Who said the socks were dirty?"

"You said they were your favorites."

Eli grinned at her. "No flies on you, honey."

Her face went as blank as a sheet of fresh paper. "I'm not your honey."

"Sure you are. I brought you a mouse nest."

"Is that what it takes these days?" Brett mused. "I was in

prison longer than I thought."

"Times change," Eli observed.

"I guess." Brett rocked back on his heels, studied Willa's face — still blank as a snow bank, Eli noted with concern — and said, "You know, I could use a shower. Knock off the trail dust."

"Good hiking today," Eli said to him. "You want the job, it's yours."

"I want the job," Brett said.

"What job?" Willa said.

"The job I just gave him," Eli told her. "I'll pick you up at seven tomorrow," he said to Brett. "There's a section of state forest I want to have a look at, and it's damn near in Canada."

"What kind of job?" Willa asked, each word icy and distinct.

"Super," Brett said, backing toward the door. "I'm hitting the shower." Then he was gone. Coward.

Willa arched a brow. "Well?"

Chapter 17

ELI LOWERED HIMSELF to the porch railing and patted the wood next to his thigh. "Sit with me?"

"No." Willa held the mouse nest in both hands, still as always. But there was a coldness to it now that Eli didn't care for. A contained edge. The warmth, the generosity of it was missing, and Eli cursed himself for leaving her alone. He should've called, come over. For God's sake, she'd given him everything — her body, her stillness. She'd given him peace. And in return, he'd gone dark, thinking of nothing but his own damn skin again, as relentlessly self-centered as always. Shame touched him with cold fingers. "What job, Eli?"

"Well, there's a little more on my plate here in Devil's Kettle than those supervised removals of yours," Eli told her carefully. "I'm also doing a fire risk assessment on the state and national forest lands up here."

"A fire risk assessment." She didn't make a question of it, only repeated his words with a cool care that stuck unpleasantly in his throat.

"Yeah. There's a DNR guy running the regional assessment team up here — a Paul O'Malley? He should've retired about a hundred years ago, and my uncle Ben has some concerns about the quality of his work. He's at Boise now, Ben is, and—"

"At Boise?"

"Yeah. At the National Interagency Fire Center there. It's an alphabet soup of all the agencies that fund wild land firefighting but since nobody could come up with a nifty acronym everybody just calls it Boise." He tried a smile that she didn't return. He cleared his throat and went on hastily. "They assess fire risk across the country, rank all open fires in order of importance, and deal out the resources accordingly. Ben basically gets to boss around every federally funded hotshot crew in the nation. He's in heaven." Willa only continued to gaze at him, her stillness growing into a chill that touched his soul. "You might think I'm outside Ben's jurisdiction now that I've spent a couple fire seasons hiking instead of hotshotting but you'd be wrong. When I gave him my resignation letter, Ben just turned around and gave me a new job title — fire risk assessor."

"What does that mean?"

"It means that wherever I happen to be hiking, I pay special attention to the fuel load. I take pictures, I make notes. If I start seeing too much ladder fuel—"

"Ladder fuel?"

"You know how you build a campfire? You start with dried grass or bark and then add in the twigs, then the sticks, then bigger sticks, until you're finally up to logs?"

She nodded.

"Ladder fuel is like that, only for a forest fire." He leaned in, warming to his subject even as he was aware that her chill only deepened. "Forests are supposed to burn, Willa. They're *designed* to burn. And if you leave them alone, they will. They'll do it often enough to clear out the scrubby underbrush that's trying to choke them to death. And when we let that happen, everything's cool. That brush is like kindling, see? It can't burn hot enough to do any real damage to established trees. You can't light a hundred-year-old oak tree with a match, right? But if you put out the fire every time the forest tries to clear that shit out, that scrubby underbrush survives. It gets taller and bigger, and bigger fuel burns hotter. Pretty soon, another layer crops up underneath the first one, and another one underneath that one until you have a ladder of fuel, from tinder all the way up to actual trees. And when a forest in that situation catches fire, the entire thing goes up. It burns hot enough to kill the trees when it should have only cleared the choking brush. The forest gets destroyed. Everything gets destroyed." He paused, had to take a second. His throat was too tight and hot to continue unless he swallowed down that omnipresent lump of shame and guilt. "People get destroyed."

"That's what you do now?" She tipped her head and studied him, so remote. So closed. "You hike through forests all over the country and you report back to your uncle if you think they're getting ready to burn that way?"

"Yeah. I do it mostly alone, but I'm allowed to hire per diem help when I feel like it's necessary."

"Convicted felons?"

He shrugged. "The Forest Service isn't so fussy on that point. You'd be surprised how many convicts end up on hotshot crews. Some crews are prison-based, in fact. The inmates volunteer, and get bused to the fires in—" He cut himself off. Her eyes were deep in the shadow of the ball cap he'd decided he hated but it was clear that dropping Forest Service factoids into this conversation wasn't doing him any favors. "Listen, I can't work a crew again, not ever. I had brothers and I lost them. I don't deserve to have more. Which is why I'm not offering your dad anything permanent. But the guy's legitimately a monster hiker, a quick study, and could use a purpose. I have the budget to give him one even temporarily, and if I can prevent anybody else's crew from facing the kind of shitstorm my crew faced a couple seasons back, I'll do it."

She nodded slowly, her eyes never leaving his. "You're going to be fine, Eli."

He frowned at her. "What does that mean?"

"I was worried about you the other night. You hurt so much. You carry such a massive load. I didn't know if you could keep going."

"I don't know if I can." And the admission itself was a weight off his shoulders. A slice of his brain wondered idly if she had any idea what she was doing to him. That she was busting effortlessly through a reserve that had held four separate grief and trauma counselors at arm's length. That she was pulling things out of his soul that had been burned there so deeply he wasn't even aware of them anymore, only of the infection they caused. "I really don't know if I can, Willa."

"You can." She handed him his nest.

He reared back, hands up. "No, that's yours."

"I don't want it."

Pain shot through him, unexpected and agonizingly sweet. He hadn't felt anything in so long before Willa. She went straight to the heart of him, though, and stripped him bare. "Yes, you do." He didn't know why he said it, only that it was true.

"No, I don't."

"Of course you do." She was lying to him. Why was she lying to him?

She gazed at him, her silvery eyes wide and blank. "I don't want anything from you, Eli. You have to understand that."

"But I don't understand. I don't understand at all. No, wait." He palmed his face, shame renewing its grip on his soul. "Actually, I do. Willa, the other night was—"

"—was lovely. Thank you."

"Lovely?" He stared at her, aghast. "Thank you?"

"Yes, thank you. It was one of the better dates I've ever had."

"Jesus Christ. Willa, I banged you on the kitchen counter like I paid for the privilege. Then I let *you* pour *me* a drink while I unloaded my whole sad, sordid story on you. And then — just to prove what a prince I am — I maintained strict radio silence for the next several days, just in case you were harboring any romantic delusions that needed dispelling. For fuck's sake, Willa. You gave me your body. You gave me your stillness. You gave me *peace*. And I took it. I thought of myself and I took, just like always. I should be thanking you." He paused, shame rising sickly in his throat. "I should have thanked you."

"No, you shouldn't have. That's my point. We both got exactly what we wanted from that night. So just stop." She set the mouse nest beside him on the railing. "Just stop, please. You don't owe me anything. If you used me, I used you right back. So you don't need to give me presents. You definitely don't need to give my jailbird father a job assessing ladder fuels or whatever the hell it is you said you were doing. I don't want anything from you, Eli." She stepped back, tucked her fingers into the pockets of her filthy jeans. He wondered with that same detached slice of his brain what she'd been doing today that had rolled her through the muck again. Seemed like she spent a lot of time crawling through other people's trash. "I don't want you."

I don't want you.

Denial roared through him. Of course she wanted him. How could she not, when he wanted her so badly? How was that even possible?

"We had a nice night," she told him evenly. "We both needed something and we got it. It doesn't need to be any more complicated than that."

"But it is." He blinked at her, reeling. "It's incredibly complicated." Complicated enough that he hadn't had the courage to give her the *thanks-for-a-fun-night-but-this-can't-go-anywhere* speech she was now giving him. A speech he realized — too late, of course — that he didn't want to hear.

"No," she said with gentle finality. "It isn't." She nodded at the chewed up tampons and hiking socks beside him. "I'll deal with your mouse problem. You can call it the second supervised removal. I'll call you when a good opportunity for number three crops up. Otherwise, I think it would be best if you went back to radio silence."

Willa made herself turn and go back into the house while
Eli was still sitting on the porch, staring at her. His eyes
were enormous and blue over those sharp cheekbones.
Baffled and a little bit pissed off but not hurt. Not sad. Not
anymore. Willa would hold onto that, she decided, and
slumped against the door she'd just shut on him. She'd hold
onto that and let it comfort her. What had he said? That
she'd given him her stillness? She'd given him peace?

Yes, she decided, her throat tight and aching. She had.
She could see that much for herself. That vast sorrow that
lived in his eyes, the scent of rain that clung to him even in
the baking sun? It wasn't gone, but it had eased. And she'd
done that for him. Not on purpose, either. Simply by being
herself, her truest self, she'd lifted some of the burden that
was grinding him down day by day, mile by mile.

That, she told herself, was enough. It had to be enough.
Hell, it was practically a miracle. Because the conversation
she'd had with Georgie that morning had rubbed her nose in
the incontrovertible facts of Willa's life: maybe she wasn't
poison herself but she came from poison, which meant the
best thing Willa could do for other people was to leave them
alone. Forming connections with other people was just
asking for tragedy. Somebody was going to get hurt.
Abandoned. Rejected. Ridiculed. Swindled. Possibly
murdered, depending on who you talked to. Which was
definitely taking things a step too far, considering that even
Drunk Brett was no match for Shay's ravenous survival
instincts. But when had the truth ever mattered in this town?

No, her history was just too complicated, her family too
toxic. It was better to keep good people, innocent people,
well clear of it. Of her.

Oh, she wasn't her family. She knew that. She was better.
She was a decent person, and she proved it every time she
weighed her crushing loneliness against Matty's bright
future and held her silence. She'd proved it again just now
when she'd come home to find that Eli had brought her a

mouse nest. He'd given it pride of place on her kitchen counter, putting it right where another man might put a dozen roses. He'd understood that to her, it might as well be.

He'd *seen* her.

The realization had landed in Willa's chest like a hand grenade, dangerous and unpredictable. They'd had sex and some deep conversation the other night, but Willa hadn't expected anything else. She couldn't have anything else. She'd crafted her life as carefully as the mouse had crafted the nest Eli had left her, and one of the foundational pieces was her invisibility. Willa walked and talked and ate and worked right in plain sight but she'd mastered the art of invisibility. People saw her every day but they didn't *see* her. She'd withdrawn the essence of herself years ago, tucked it under ball caps and dirty jeans and boob-squishing bras and silence. She'd wrapped it up tight and hidden it away, kept it only for herself. It was how people could see Willa's eyes in Matty's face — which was in all other respects identical to Diego's — and not see the connection. They didn't want to see the connection. They wanted to see only Diego in Matty — his talent, his charm, his limitless potential — so they did. Nobody wanted the Zincs to have anything to do with that beautiful boy's bright future, so they simply didn't see.

And Willa was grateful. She didn't want the Zincs to put their ugly fingerprints all over that beautiful boy, either.

But if she had done something to Eli, something that eased his terrible burden of guilt and grief and lord only knew what else, he'd done something to her as well. He'd seen through the jeans and the caps and the dirt and the silence straight to the heart of her. He'd brought her a mouse nest made from tampons and his favorite hiking socks without a single doubt that she'd love it. And she did. God, she did. She loved it, and she loved him for knowing she would. For knowing her. For *seeing* her, in spite of everything she'd done to prevent it.

And that was dangerous. Because if Eli could see her,

maybe other people would start to see her as well. She'd realized this as she'd stared at that lopsided nest sitting on her counter. She'd thought about Addy and those impulsive hugs she tossed at Willa with bewildering regularity. She thought about Georgie's astonishing ability to buy her pretty clothes that fit perfectly. And she knew with grim certainty that there was no *maybe* about it. Whatever Eli had done to her, it was unraveling her. It was revealing her, and she couldn't afford that. Not now, not with Matty due home any day.

Matty. Oh, God. Her lungs locked up and she had to press a hand to her chest to breathe. This was why Bianca was threatening to upend their arrangement, the one that had protected the boy for so many years. This was why she was considering revealing the boy's true parentage to him. If she didn't do it, surely somebody else would. Because Willa was coming undone. The realization pushed the remaining air from her lungs and she leaned her forehead against the door.

She'd never hated the Davises for taking Matty from her, or for keeping him from her. But they'd hated her for letting them, or so Willa had assumed. They'd spent years judging and dismissing her, as if they needed to prove to themselves that they'd done the right thing. As if they needed to prove it to her, too. Why they'd bother, Willa didn't know. She *agreed*. Matty was better off never knowing who his mother was, or what kind of family he had.

But now she wondered if Bianca hadn't hated her at all. What if she'd simply been creating a social gulf between the Davises and the Zincs so wide and so deep that people could look straight at those Zinc eyes in Matty's face and never see them?

If that was the case, Willa had to give Bianca props. She'd played a long, deep game that would've put Willa's own mother — a master manipulator if ever there was one — to shame. A game that Eli, by unraveling Willa against her will this way, threatened to undermine.

She didn't know how long she'd stood there, staring dismayed at that damned nest on her counter, but by the time Eli and Brett pulled up, she'd known what she had to do.

So she'd done it. And she'd been right to, because good God, he'd given Brett a job. She didn't imagine for one second that Eli particularly wanted to hike all over creation in the company of a barely-dry ex-con, but he'd taken one look at her situation and stepped in with a magical job offer. Which wasn't a job at all, but a gift. A gift for her.

There was nothing Willa could do about the job — that was between Eli and Brett— but she could make Eli understand that she didn't want his gifts. That she wouldn't accept them. That he'd gotten everything she was willing to give him, and it was time for him to go away. It had hurt like hell, but she'd done it. And he must've gotten the message because Willa finally heard his little car trundle away up her drive.

Suddenly the house felt too small. There wasn't enough air, enough light. Willa's lungs constricted and her skin itched and she wrenched open the door to let the outdoors in. She needed to breathe before her heart simply broke. Or maybe she needed to breathe while her heart broke. She gripped the open door frame with both hands and leaned out, desperate for oxygen. Then she stopped breathing altogether.

There, in the center of her porch, sat the perfect mouse nest.

He'd left it for her.

Chapter 18

GEORGIE DROPPED HER purse on the sideboard at the end of a very long day and headed for Hill Top House's great room. Aside from the four years she'd spent at college, she'd never lived anywhere but Hill Top House. Unlike her brothers, she'd never wanted to live anywhere else, and walking into the great room reminded her of exactly why that was.

Sun spilled fiery and golden across the endless glitter of Lake Superior, and Hill Top House framed the cliff-top view within a towering wall of windows. Narrow panels ran through the glass from floor to ceiling, supporting the soaring peak of the roof without detracting from the view. And, God, that view. It just grabbed you by the throat. It had nothing on the paintings hanging on the narrow walls between the panes, though. Inside those frames, her brother Diego's violent brush strokes masterfully echoed the lake's brutal beauty.

The sight of them had Georgie lifting a hand to her own throat and she smiled. Diego had always gone for the jugular, in art and otherwise. She still missed him. Even knowing exactly what he'd been capable of, she still missed her brother.

She drifted into the room, found the sunniest corner of the massive white sectional facing the view and sank down into it. She toed off her ballet flats, curled her legs under her and laid her head on the cushions to think about Diego, and about Willa Zinc. About the conversation she'd had with Willa earlier that day.

"Georgie?" Her mother's voice came down the stairs,

interrupting the kaleidoscope of colors shifting behind Georgie's closed lids. "Are you home?"

"Hey, Mom." Georgie hauled herself upright and wondered if she'd drifted off. She eyed the sunset bleeding ever redder and deeper into the water. No more than a minute or two, if that. Georgie had a habit of getting lost in her thoughts. A consequence, she figured, of her face. People freaked out over beauty, and tended to talk to you like you were stupid. Slow pace, small words, limited range. Georgie's interior landscape was vastly more interesting than that sort of limited interaction, and as people tended to give pretty girls a pass on holding up their end of the conversation, she'd gotten into the habit of drifting off sometimes. "Yeah, I just got home."

Bianca sailed down the stairs with her usual regal air, her silver-streaked blonde hair just skimming her shoulders, her eyes dark and bird-bright over the same cheekbones Georgie saw in the mirror every day.

"Did you speak with her?" Bianca settled onto the end of the sectional nearest the view, still wiping her hands on a paint-stained rag. A waft of turpentine and wildflowers reached out to Georgie, her mother's signature scent. "With Willa, I mean?"

"I know who you meant, Mom." Georgie yawned. "And yes, I did."

"Well? What did she say?"

Georgie shrugged lightly. "Not much."

Bianca leaned forward, pinned Georgie with that gaze, sharp and dangerous. "Did you tell her I was considering telling Matty who his mother is?"

"No, Mom, we had coffee and chatted about the weather." Georgie rolled her eyes. "Of course I told her. Just like you asked me to."

"What did she say?"

"Nothing."

"The girl doesn't ever say anything."

"And that's how it's going to stay forever, according to her."

"I see." Bianca narrowed her eyes and studied Georgie closely. "How did she react otherwise?"

Georgie sifted through her impressions slowly, savoring the weight of her mother's attention. Bianca was one of the very few people — aside from Addie and maybe Jax — who treated Georgie like there was a brain inside her head.

"She was…I don't know, honestly," she said slowly. "When she first came in, it was just business as usual, you know? A couple good insults both directions, a little posturing on both sides. Then I told her that you were thinking about getting the jump on the gossips and telling Matty everything, and whoosh." Georgie drew a flat hand over her own face. "She went blank. Like an emotional black hole opened up and swallowed her reaction. I could almost feel it trying to suck me in, too, like some weird dementor."

"Dementor?"

"The soul-suckers from *Harry Potter*?"

Bianca flicked an impatient hand. "I never read those."

"How can you claim to be culturally literate and not know *Harry Potter*?"

"How can you claim to be culturally literate and still reference children's books in your conversation?"

"I'm a Davis," Georgie said airily. "I don't follow culture; I make it."

Bianca smiled. "There's my girl."

"Anyway." Georgie rolled a lazy shoulder. "Whatever's going on inside Willa's head? She's not going to share it. Not with me, not with you, not with anybody."

Bianca considered that. "She's never been one to seek out attention."

"Or even human contact," Georgie pointed out. "When's the last time you saw her with anybody? A friend, a date, a family member?"

"I haven't," Bianca admitted. "Although I hear her

father's home."

"And living with her at their little cabin in the woods," Georgie said. "I spoke to him the other night."

"You did?"

"I did." Georgie wrinkled her nose. "He wasn't nearly as big and scary as I remember. Then again, when I was a kid, we were all convinced he'd murdered his wife and was just waiting to do one of us next." She shrugged that off. "He was still tall but he's...smaller now. It's hard to describe. He's wary. Hesitant." She frowned. "I think it might be the first time I ever saw him completely sober."

"Why on earth were you at the Zinc place?" Bianca frowned, too.

"It was an emergency. Addy asked Willa to stand up in the wedding—"

"Oh, lord, she really went through with that?"

"She really did. We went over there to assess the wardrobe situation and ended up staging a mini-intervention." Georgie's lip curled involuntarily. "It was awful, Mom. Willa's closet is as bad as she is. I hate her *and* her clothes."

"I know, darling." Bianca gave her a sympathetic pat. "You'll just have to get over it."

"Why should I?" Georgie was perilously close to pouting. "Just because Addy likes her, the rest of us have to like her, too? What kind of madness is that?"

"Georgie, please. Use the perfectly serviceable brain God gave you. Willa's the only person outside our family — besides Peter, of course — who knows that Matty's the Arsonist of Devil's Kettle."

"He's not an arsonist," Georgie snapped. "He was *blackmailed* into arson, and by my own ex-fiancé."

"Who will, I'm sure, keep his mouth shut about the whole affair," Bianca said placidly. "As much as I'm sure Peter would love to see us squirm, he must know that going public with Matty's involvement in those fires will hurt him far more than it would hurt us. But why would Willa hold back? One conversation with the appropriate authority, and Willa could not only embarrass us tremendously, but maybe even put her brother in her father's old jail cell."

"Let her do it. Peter can go straight to hell for all I care." Georgie discovered her hands in hard fists on the soft suede beside her knee. She loosened them deliberately, and gave her hair a lazy toss. "And since when are we afraid of a little scandal? I've been staring down gossips since I was fourteen and people decided Matty was my love child."

"And you do it brilliantly. You get that from me." Bianca gave Georgie another fond pat. "But circumstances have changed."

"Addy's changed," Georgie said darkly. "We could change her back, you know. She thinks Willa's some kind of hero just for keeping her mouth shut about Matty."

"Addy told me Willa also took the blame for the Davis House fire the other day. Gerte was blaming some poor man who used to work for her, but it was only a matter of time — or so Addy claims — before she circled back around to accusing Matty again. Evidently, Willa scotched it right there."

"Yeah, I heard that, too." Georgie set her jaw. "Which is why she thinks Willa's such a hero. But what if we tell her the truth? What if we tell her how we really got Matty? How Willa and her family sold him to us like he was a farm animal or something? Addy loves Matty like he's her own kid. Surely, she'd be horrified, and start to see that Willa's nothing but a—"

"Georgie, stop." Bianca sighed. "It isn't just Addy driving this decision."

"What is it then?"

"It's just time, darling. All lies have an expiration date, and I'm frankly surprised this one has lasted so long. I'd hoped to wait until Matty was eighteen before having this particular conversation but maybe it would be better for all of us if we just made a clean breast of it now." Bianca sighed wearily, but Georgie could almost see the gears in her brain turning dangerously. "It's just…I don't want to drop this bomb on Matty without knowing exactly how Willa's going to respond."

"Mom." Georgie waited until Bianca looked up. "What aren't you telling me?"

Those dark, shrewd eyes narrowed. "I don't know what you mean."

Georgie grinned. "God, I love it when you do that stare-down-the-upstart thing. I'm good but you're in a league of your own."

She gave a haughty sniff. "Thank you."

"You're welcome. Now tell me why you're suddenly so hot to tell Matty a secret we've kept from him for fourteen years. Because I believe that it's not only to make Addy happy, but I'll be damned if I'll buy that it's just *time*." She leveled her own version of the stare at her mother and waited.

Seconds ticked by, taut and unrelenting, while Bianca held that stare and considered her.

Finally she said, "Come upstairs. I want to show you something."

Chapter 19

ELI HELPED HIMSELF to a table in the sunny front
window of the Devil's Taproom. It had been nearly twenty-
four hours since Willa had given him the kiss off, twenty-
four hours during which he hadn't slept for shit and had lost
another pair of hiking socks to the mice along with a tube of
toothpaste. The socks he understood, but toothpaste? What
the hell did mice want with his toothpaste? Clearly their
teeth were already in top condition.

He should ask Willa. She'd know, and she couldn't blow
him off because it would be a purely professional question.
And if Eli was desperate enough to ask about such a thing,
surely she'd be professional enough to answer. It wouldn't
be the conversation he wanted to have with her but it would
be a start. And he had to start somewhere because sometime
before dawn, between thrashing around on his skinny, lumpy
bed and listening to the mice laugh at him and chew shit
with their obscenely healthy teeth, Eli had reached a
decision: He wasn't letting Willa blow him off.

Whatever had bloomed between them, whatever it was in
her that spoke to him? It was too important to back away
from. Because he'd thought about it. He'd had plenty of time
over the course of a long sleepless night for thinking and
he'd arrived at a startling conclusion. Whatever magic Willa
worked on his soul? He must work some kind of
corresponding magic on hers. Because if he understood
correctly, Willa didn't sleep around. She didn't even date.
From what he could see, she barely spoke to people who
weren't him. Human connection wasn't her thing, either by
choice, by nature, or because she'd learned the hard way that

life was cruel and people were shitty. But she'd connected with him, and in every possible way.

That kind of miracle didn't come along every day. Eli had been in a tough spot these past few years but had been generally a lucky guy before that. Good family, stable home, plenty of friends. Clear goals, plus the brains and strength to achieve them. Mentors who paved the way when they could, beat his ass when they had to, and pushed him farther, longer and harder than he believed he could go. He'd been an arrogant son of a bitch, sure, but never so arrogant that he imagined he'd achieved success on his own. He'd been lucky in innumerable ways. Which was probably why it had felt like such a betrayal when that luck had run out.

Which was probably also why he recognized luck when it dropped back into his life. Why he recognized Willa for the gift she was. Eli wasn't about to shrug and let her toss what was between them in the trash. He didn't believe she really wanted to for one thing, but even if she did, she'd be wrong. He wasn't about to drop to one knee and beg for her hand in marriage either — did people even do that anymore? — but he was definitely grabbing hold and not letting go until he understood the mysterious forces at work here. Until she did, too.

He wondered what Willa would say when he informed her of this development. He smiled just thinking about it.

He was still smiling when Paul O'Malley of the Minnesota Department of Natural Resources and his uncle Ben's worst nightmares walked into the bar. Eli stopped smiling and lifted a hand to the guy.

O'Malley walked to the table, a solidly built man in his early-to-mid-seventies, with a full head of white hair and big-knuckled hands that spoke to a lifetime of working with them. He also had small, darting eyes that spoke to a life lived in a defensive crouch. Eli wondered briefly if he'd been born that way or if some tragedy had taught him to be afraid. He rose and extended a hand.

"O'Malley," he said as he gripped that wide palm. "Thanks for meeting me."

"Walker," O'Malley returned, those eyes darting and dipping.

Eli gestured him to the chair across the table and sat. "So I've been spot-checking your fuel load in the region."

"Yes." O'Malley's lips compressed into a flat line. "I know."

"What you might not know is that I also spent the spring through-hiking the Superior Hiking Trail."

A waitress appeared at their table with bright purple hair spilling from the top of her bandana turban and a *Devil's Taproom* tank top showing off the impressive sleeve of tattoos on her left arm. "Hey, Paul," she said to O'Malley, and turned a friendly smile to Eli. "Eli Walker, isn't it?" Her smile brightened. "The guy Gerte slapped before he could even put his bags down?"

"That was me."

She laughed. "Welcome to the Kettle. Your first beer's on me."

"Thanks. What do I want?"

She studied him. "Let's start you with a pint of the Devil's Handmaiden and see where we end up."

"It's a deal."

She turned to O'Malley. "The usual, I assume?"

"Yes, please. Thank you, India."

The waitress sauntered off into the growing crowd and Eli said, "What do you suppose a Devil's Handmaiden is?"

"I wouldn't know." O'Malley leaned back in his chair and studied Eli. "I don't drink anymore. Haven't for years."

"Ah." Eli leaned back in his own chair and studied O'Malley in return. "You mind if I ask why not?"

"If there's a lifetime limit on alcohol, I hit my quota back in the seventies."

Eli nodded to a tattoo he could just see peeking from a rolled back shirt sleeve. "Vietnam?"

"Spent a few years there, yeah. Then spent a few years back here trying to get *there* out of my brain."

"Hit your quota in the trying?"

"Exactly." O'Malley leaned back, folded his arms. "What are you chasing yours out with?"

"Excuse me?"

"I know who you are, Walker. I may be old but I do know how to use the internet. Plus you'd have to be dead or stupid not to recognize your name in our line of work. You were with the Silver Creek Hotshots at the Cathedral Hill fire. You're the only guy on your entire crew who walked out of that mess, and rumor has it you had the radio and the command. Now how do you suppose a thing like that happens?"

The waitress reappeared and slid what looked like a gin and tonic onto the table in front of O'Malley. She set a glass of pale, hazy beer on the table in front of Eli.

"Careful with that one," she said, grinning. "It's as dangerous a blonde as you're going to find in this town, and we're got us some dangerous blondes."

"Do you?" Eli murmured, his eyes on O'Malley, his chest tight and hot.

India laughed. "Just ask Peter." She tipped her bright purple curls toward the bar where Willa's brother was laughing and chatting with tourists, his dark eyes cold as ice. "He used to be engaged to one." She tapped the table lightly. "Anyway, let me know how you like it." And she swung off into the crowd once more.

O'Malley lifted his drink and inspected it in the golden sun streaming through the window. "Tonic water with a twist of lime," he told Eli. "It makes drinkers feel more comfortable when the guy across from them gets his fizzy water in a highball glass."

"I don't get the feeling you're overly concerned with my comfort here, O'Malley."

His smile was small, calculating. "I'm not. I'm concerned

about my forest and my town."

"Bullshit. If that were the case, you'd have been doing prescribed burns yearly for the past two decades or more."

"You've seen the fuel load out there. It's a keg of TNT."

"Exactly."

"I inherited it in pretty much the condition you're seeing now."

"So why the hell haven't you been doing something about it?"

"Have you looked at the historical weather data for the region?"

"Of course I have."

"We're in a serious, long-term drought. I know it's hard to believe, what with all that water right there—" He waved a hand toward the endless expanse of Lake Superior, flirting and winking at the tourists from the tidy, picturesque harbor across the street. "—but meteorologically speaking, we've spent the last ten years in a water deficit. If the conditions had ever been right for a burn, I'd have called for one. But I'm not going to be the guy who drops a match in a fuel load this big and this dry. There's no way you could control it."

"So you'd rather wait for a lightning strike or a careless campfire? You'd rather let it go up when you're unprepared and understaffed and every hotshot crew in the country is busy somewhere else?" Eli leaned forward, anger licking at his brain, making fists of his hands. "You really call that protecting your forest and your town?"

"At this point, there's no protecting anything." O'Malley spread big, helpless hands. "Only God can do that. When He decides it's time, He'll drop the match Himself."

"And absolve you of the responsibility?"

"Do you really think you're qualified to talk to me about responsibility?" O'Malley's eyes flickered with sly triumph. "Tell me, Walker, where was this righteous sense of responsibility when your men's lives were on the line? From what I understand, your boys were practically on top of the good black but you sent them the other way trying to impress your uncle and be a hero. Where was your abundance of caution then?"

Eli swallowed, his throat hot and dry with remembered smoke, with aching grief.

"Seems like you're pretty free with other people's courage but if you think you can come onto my turf and start telling me how to handle the forest I've lived in and loved my whole life, you've got another think coming." O'Malley set down his drink and leaned forward. "And if you think you can force my hand, you'll want to think again. Gerte's still mostly convinced you were behind all those fires we had back in the spring. That little scene she pitched a few days ago, when she rang your bell for you in front of God and everyone? It only reminded the entire town that we still don't know who was responsible for lighting us up like that. So if my forest happens to catch fire while you're still here — and I don't care if it's a lightning strike, a campfire accident or a troop of evil Girl Scouts that starts it — everybody in town is going to look at you. And I'll have nothing to say except that you seemed awfully anxious to see our forest on fire. What happens next will make Gerte's face-slapping look like a day at the beach, and I happen to know that girl packs a wallop."

O'Malley rose, tossed a five on the table.

"Time to move on, son." He smiled unpleasantly down at Eli. "Tell your uncle I said hello, won't you?"

Willa checked the equipment box in the bed of her truck for the seventy-fifth time and tried to tell herself she was only sweaty because it was hot. She was lying. And she *knew* she was lying, which only added to the mortification. She could've been working in an ice box and she'd have still been in a flop sweat from the underwear out.

She was going to Eli's cabin.

Yesterday she'd told him she didn't want him — another dirty lie. She did want him. She wanted him like she wanted her next breath but she knew better than to take him. She'd already taken more than was reasonable or safe. She knew when she'd pressed her luck far and hard enough, just like she knew that, given her druthers, she could press a lot harder and a lot farther on Eli Walker.

A hot shiver skipped across her skin that had nothing to do with fear and everything to do with what she was afraid of.

She ignored it and went back to making absolutely certain that she had everything she needed to chase the mice out of Eli's cabin. Because she had the courage to go there one more time. She had the strength for one more show, for one more convincing *no*. After that, she didn't know how long her good intentions could hold.

Her phone buzzed in her back pocket and she nearly tumbled out of the truck bed. She snatched at it with slippery hands, saw Addy's photo on the screen and breathed through a curious mix of disappointment and relief. She swiped the screen to answer.

"Hey, Addy."

"Hey, Willa."

"What's up?"

"Not much," Addy said lightly. "I was just calling to see what you're up to tomorrow night. Thursday."

"Why?" Willa knew better than to admit to free time. Not when Addy was looking down the barrel of both Devil Days and her own wedding.

"Because Devil Days opens on Friday."

"Right. So?"

"So *Diego After Dark* is also opening on Friday, and you know how controversial that showing has been. We thought it would be a nice gesture to the local business owners to do a special preview for them the night before we open to the public, so they can see there's really nothing to fuss about. I want you to come."

"I don't think Zinc Pest Control has any pressing interest in *Diego After Dark*."

"You're as much a member of this community as anybody else," Addy said stoutly. "If I'm inviting them, I'm inviting you. Besides, I could use a friendly face in the crowd. *Diego After Dark* is the racy stuff. That's going to be an after-hours, ticketed-admission-only event. But we're showing something else, too."

"Like what?"

Addy hesitated. "Remember those paintings of Diego's I found back in the spring? The ones that Gerte was all upset that Bianca wanted to show?"

She did, actually. It would be tough to forget Addy risking her life to pull those canvases out of her burning garage. They were rumored to be works of such staggering emotion and technical brilliance that even *Diego's Angel* paled in comparison. Nobody but the Davises had ever seen them but everybody in town had an opinion. Gerte was certain they were dirty, of course, while Bianca had assured everybody they were pure genius even as she conspicuously refused to remark on their content. Addy and Jax had been suspiciously close-mouthed about the whole affair, and Georgie had just floated around on her usual cloud of entitled nonchalance. Willa didn't care about the paintings, not really, but something about Addy's guarded attitude toward them had inclined her to believe they hadn't said anything particularly nice about Diego's views of marriage, love and fidelity. All of which had been wrapped up in Addy.

"I remember," Willa said cautiously. "You rescued them from the garage fire only to have them burn down with Davis Place a couple months later."

"As to that." Addy cleared her throat. "There was one that didn't burn."

"Was there?"

"Yeah. It was called *Broken*. We're hanging it right next to the *Angel*."

"Like it's the *Angel*'s opposite number?"

"Exactly like that."

Willa's gut clenched. "Why would you do that?" she asked. "Why show it? You already have a fresh collection in *Diego After Dark*. Why drag up whatever shit Diego put you through toward the end?"

Addy sighed. "It's a long story, but bottom line? I took off Diego's ring months ago. Before I can get married to Jax, I need to take off the halo, too."

"And showing *Broken* will do that?"

"Big time."

Shit. Willa hated being right.

"I really could use the backup, Willa."

"Do Georgie and Bianca know you're inviting me?"

"Yes. Bianca said it was as good a time as any to test drive your new peace accord. Georgie took to her bed. Said she needed to conserve her strength if she was going to make you presentable for a gallery preview."

"Fuck me."

"You have a very fashionable fairy godmother," Addy told her primly. "You should embrace her."

"Fuck her, too."

Addy laughed, and it actually sounded genuine enough to make Willa's discomfort worthwhile. Almost.

"Hey," Addy said, still chuckling, "you should bring your person."

"My person?"

"Yeah. Like a date. A plus-one? You had one just the other night, remember?"

Another hot shiver chased itself over Willa's already super-heated skin. "Yeah. I remember."

"Bring him. Her. Them. I don't care. Just come." Her voice softened. "For me."

"I don't want to."

"I know."

Willa sighed. "What time?"

Chapter 20

ELI ROUNDED THE bend in the two-track leading through the woods to his cabin and jammed reflexively on the brakes. That was Willa's truck in front of his cabin. Willa had come to him.

Hope soared inside him, erasing the ugly taste the confrontation with O'Malley had left in his mouth. He snatched the phone off the dash where he'd set it so he could talk hands-free.

"Ben? I've got to go."

"Damn straight. Get the hell out of there. O'Malley's come fucking unhinged. If he thinks he's going to pin a fire on you—"

"No, I meant I have to get off the phone." He eased his DNR-issued tuna can up to Willa's bumper. It wouldn't keep her from getting away if she wanted to — she'd run over this car like it was a paper bag — but it might slow her down a little. "Something's come up."

"Fine. But, hey, real quick. How many more supervised removals do you have to do?"

"Two."

"Do them and get the hell out of there, Eli."

He wasn't going anywhere. "I'll talk to you later, Ben."

"You sure will."

He hung up and headed for the cabin, a curious mix of delight and trepidation dancing around inside his rib cage. He pushed through the front door. "Willa?"

Nothing. And it wasn't like she could hide, given that the entire interior of the cabin was visible from the front door. He stopped by the fridge, grabbed a couple of beers and stepped back outside. He rounded the corner to the back and found her on a ladder propped up against the back of the cabin, her ball cap poked up under the overhanging eave.

"There you are."

She didn't spare him a glance. She patted at the tool belt slung around her hips and came up with a power screwdriver. "Here I am," she muttered through the wood screws between her lips. She picked one out, centered it and drove it home with an unfussy expertise that sent a hot ripple of interest through him. She was good with her hands. It was a damn fine quality in a human being. Finer yet in a woman who might be convinced to use those hands on him again sometime.

"What are you doing up there, Willa?"

She centered and drove home another screw. Eli shifted, uncomfortably aware that he was enjoying this a little too much. He had one, maybe two more screws until that enjoyment became visible.

"My second observed removal," she said and zipped another screw into place. Christ. He put both beer bottles in one hand and so he could put the other in his pocket for camouflage. He was in trouble here. She slipped the screwdriver back into her tool belt — thank you, Jesus — and came down the ladder. She stood on the grass and squinted up at her work. "You should be mouse-free within the week."

"Really?" He handed her one of the beers. She took it and slugged back a good half the bottle at one go.

"Thanks." She pulled off her cap to swipe a sleeve over her face. "It's hot out here."

"No kidding," he murmured, momentarily mesmerized by all that dark hair spilling down her t-shirt. Little wisps had escaped her ponytail and they clung to her face, to her damp neck, and Eli caught himself reaching. He wanted to touch that glowing skin with everything in him, with a hunger so vast it might break him if he didn't grab the reins on it. He managed to abort the touch, pointed at her with his beer bottle instead. "How'd you get all that saw dust in your hair?"

"There's sawdust in my hair?" She pulled her ponytail over one shoulder and inspected it. "Oh, wow. Yep." She gave it a couple of brisk smacks, sending a shower of wood shavings flying and Eli mourned. He'd have taken minutes, hours to comb his fingers through that river of hair, freeing each individual shred and shaving. He'd have laid her in the grass and spread all that hair out like a blanket, followed each strand and color to its end just for the pleasure of it, and she'd chosen instead to shake it out like a wet dog. All that skill in her hands, he thought wonderingly, and she used none of it on herself.

But he kept his tone light when he said, "You built me a better mouse trap, did you?"

"You could say that." She lifted her beer again, a sip rather than a guzzle this time, her eyes cautious on his over the bottle. "I sealed up the cracks in your foundation and siding, then installed some one-way vents over the larger openings."

"One-way vents?"

"Think doggie doors that only flap one way."

"Ah. Exit only?"

"Exactly. Come on, I'll give you the tour." She bent, scooped up her cap and Eli took it from her. "Hey!"

He adjusted the back and snugged it onto his own head. "Payment for the beer."

She frowned "You want my sweaty ball cap?"

"I want to see your face."

She stiffened. "Eli—"

"What? It's a reasonable enough request, isn't it? To make direct eye contact with my contractor?"

"That's not what you want."

"What do I want then?" He stepped forward, close enough to crowd her. She smelled like warm woman and hot sun and cool, blessed peace. "Tell me what you think I want, Willa."

She scowled at him. "You want to give me things."

"I'll take the beer back if it makes you nervous." He smiled and slid the cap's brim to the back. Stepped closer yet because he knew it wasn't the beer making her nervous.

Her scowl deepened but she refused to back up. She had grit, his Willa. Eli approved of grit. He also approved of the way it put her boots nearly toe-to-toe with his own. The way it put her body close enough to scramble the air particles between them into a hot frenzy. The way it put her lush mouth and angry eyes perilously close to his. "That's not what I meant and you know it."

"What then? The mouse nest made out of dirty socks and clean — thanks be to heaven — tampons?" He tipped his head and gazed down at her. "What, too much romance too soon?"

She flinched. It was tiny, probably imperceptible unless you were watching as closely as Eli was.

"Back off, Eli." She gave him a bad-tempered nudge. "You're crowding me."

Heat streaked through him that had nothing to do with the weather. He took her beer, set it aside with his own. Stepped forward again. "I know."

"So back off." She did give ground this time, and her back fetched up against the cabin wall. She gave him another little shove, and the heat roared through his system like lightning, a jagged blast of brilliant desire.

"No." He caught her hand, held it to his chest. "But I am sorry."

"You're sorry?" Her eyes went wide. "Why?"

"Because I can't back off." He put his free hand flat on the rough wood of the cabin wall beside her head and leaned in. "Because I'm crowding you." He left her hand flattened on his chest and reached out to sink his fingers into the living heat of her hair. She sucked in a breath but didn't move. Didn't blink. She also didn't drop her hand from his chest. Something bloomed inside him, something bloody and hopeful and alive. "Because I was a dick just now, and made you feel stupid for thinking that mouse nest was a romantic gesture."

She gazed up at him, and the uncertainty in those giant gray eyes nearly put him on his knees. "Was it?"

"It's the most nakedly sappy gift I've ever given a woman."

"Oh." It was more breath than sound and it turned his knees to water. He put his jaw to her temple and breathed her in. She smelled like sunscreen and competence and peace. A jittery appetite rose in him, hot and hungry. It raced through his veins, urging him to take, to hunt. But he held himself in check. He filled only his lungs with her. She'd given him so much, so generously, so willingly. He hadn't given her enough in return, not nearly enough. She didn't want what little he'd given her. But he could give her the truth. It was the least he could do, and it might be all she wanted from him. All she'd take, anyway. So he'd give it to her.

"Jesus, Willa, the way I want you is insane."

She didn't speak but that stillness, that gorgeous, heavy *calm* of hers intensified. It waited. She'd opened a space for him, he realized. A second chance. A test? He had no idea. But he knew that everything hung on the words he chose next. Just like he knew that all those easy, charming words he used to be so good at wouldn't do the trick here. She didn't want his charm or his flattery or his tricks. That much he knew. But what did she want? What did she need?

"Don't leave me, Willa." The words emerged reluctantly from the bloody, rusty core of him. Shocking, raw, completely unexpected. He hadn't even known they were coming but once he heard them, he knew they were right. "You're trying to go and I don't want you to."

"Why not?" Her voice was a little rusty, too.

"Because I don't want to be alone anymore." He fisted

the hand in her hair and pulled in another rich, vibrant breath of her. The leashed need inside him growled and urged but he allowed himself only her scent. "For years, alone was all I wanted. It was all I deserved. If I was lonely, I didn't know it. If I was tired, I didn't feel it. If I was ashamed, I was serving my sentence, and I was okay with that. It felt like justice. That was my path. I'd earned it, and I was walking it alone. That was the plan anyway. Then you came along and I breathed."

He pulled her into him, dropped his face to the warm curve of her neck and sucked in another trembling breath. "God, for the first time in years, I can breathe. I don't know how you do it or why but you got into all the places I thought I'd built over, mortared up. You're just there, like smoke or rain or those stupid mice who can get in any-damn-where. You're just *there*, and God help me, I don't want you to go. I've been so lonely. Can't you just stay? Even for a little while?"

"You can't keep giving me things."

"Why not? You give me things."

"I do not."

"Then why am I on my knees here, Willa?"

"You're not."

"I am." He rubbed his jaw against the delicate line of her neck. "You know I am."

"You gave my father a job." She made it sound like an accusation. "You *invented* him a job." But her fingers were fisted in his t-shirt. He wondered if she even knew it, then decided he didn't care. She was holding on and that was all that mattered. "You're paying him to take walks. Don't tell me that isn't a gift."

"Okay."

"You need to stop it."

"Why?"

"Because I don't want it to be like that!" She froze, as if startled by her own outburst. Eli froze with her, waited for a long, suspended moment for her to run. To shove him aside and make a break for it. Instead she released a long shuddering breath and dropped her forehead to his shoulder. "I don't want us to be like that."

"Like what?" Tenderness flooded him and he opened the fist in her hair. Slid his palm to the nape of her neck and cradled her. Savored the warm weight of her trust.

"A transaction." Her fingers found the belt loop at his waist, hooked through it. "I don't want you to feel like you have to pay for whatever it is you're getting from me. I'm not paying you, am I?"

"What would you pay me for?"

"The, uh, orgasm?"

He smiled. "You melted my brain, Willa. We're even-steven on the orgasm front." He paused. "Except for the part where we didn't use a condom because you'd melted my brain. Tell me that's not going to be a problem. I'm disease-free but probably fertile."

"I'm disease-free myself, and lucky for us both, I'm not fertile at the moment. Give it another week and we could've been in trouble."

"Okay. Good to know." He traced the tense line of her neck with gentle fingers, eased her into his shoulder again. "Tell me, then, since we're so happily equal on the sex front, what do you think you should pay me for?"

Her response was a bad-tempered jerk of her shoulders.

"Just admit it, Willa." He rocked her slowly, wrapped her up in his arms and his contentment. "Whatever it is you do to me? I'm doing it right back to you." He drifted his lips to her temple, pressed them there. "I'm getting to you. Getting through your cracks the same way you're getting through mine. We're in this together."

"What *this*? What *this* are you even talking about?" she asked, and that was desperation he heard. Just a tiny thread of it, bewildered and raw. It delighted him, as it matched his state of mind so precisely.

"Hell if I know." He sighed happily. "I just know that my world looks different now. A roving band of mouse pirates makes hay with my favorite socks and instead of a mess or an inconvenience, I see beauty. I see inventiveness, I see creativity and I see necessity. I see you." He lifted his shoulders and let them fall. "I wanted you to see it too, because you're the only person I know — have ever known — who'd understand. Who would see what I saw." He treated himself to the hot spill of her hair, let it run through his fingers like rough silk. "I'm not alone when there's you. Not just when you're with me but in general. Now that I know there's you, I'm not alone. Ever."

"Eli." Her voice was an ache, sweet and impossible, deep inside him, so heavy with tenderness and understanding. He jumped in before she could say anything to shift the moment, to break that understanding.

"If I'm the same to you, then it would be a crime — it would be a goddamn sin — to walk away from it because you're afraid of it. Or because you think you don't deserve it, or because I don't deserve it, or for whatever reason you have and I'm sure you have plenty. This is a gift, to us from the universe. Are we really, after all the shitty luck we've had, going to reject a little piece of the good?"

She was quiet for a long time. "When you put it that way, it sounds ungracious."

Relief soared within him. "Damn ungracious."

"You don't understand this town yet, Eli."

"Christ, tell me about it."

"You don't know who I am here."

"I know who you are, Willa."

"You don't know what I am to these people."

"I don't care."

"I haven't cared either, not for years. But every story needs a villain and Devil's Kettle made me theirs. Or the Davises made me theirs."

"How?"

"It doesn't matter, because I didn't care. I refused to care. And so long as nobody cares about me, it all works. It doesn't hurt me." She hesitated. "But if you care about me, Eli—"

"I do."

"You shouldn't. It'll only hurt you." She shook her head. "You should just leave."

"I will." He smoothed a delicate wisp of hair away from her cheek. He would, too. "I'm not asking for anything permanent here, Willa. I don't have that to offer."

"I know. I don't want it."

"I know. But you matter to me and I'm going to let you." He paused to take his courage in hand. "I want to matter to you, too. Will you let me? Even knowing what you know about who I am, what I've done? Even knowing I'll leave soon? Can we just matter to each other for now?"

She opened her fingers, laid them flat against his chest and nudged him back. Suddenly he was looking into her huge gray eyes, at the hope and resignation tangled up behind them.

"What are you doing tomorrow night?" she asked.

Eli's heart cracked open under a flood of joy. "Why, Willa Zinc. Are you asking me out?"

"I am." She didn't smile. "Before we decide to…matter to each other, you need to understand who I am in the story of Devil's Kettle."

"Do I?" Concern tempered the joy and he laid his hand on top of hers on his chest.

"You do." She slid her hand out from under his and took back her ball cap. Snugged it on her head and pulled her ponytail out the back with her usual efficient grace. "Addy's doing a preview of the gallery's Devil Days show tomorrow night for the locals. You know about Diego Davis?"

"Who doesn't? What are they showing?"

"Couple things, some naughtier than others." She paused. "Some with roots that go deep and dark."

"Do they touch you?"

She shrugged. "Some. It's not what you'll see so much as what you'll hear." She stepped sideways, put a couple feet of hot, dry air between them. "Once you hear it all, then you can decide how much you want me to matter."

"Willa, you matter."

"Tomorrow." She split her ponytail in two and yanked it tight. "I'll pick you up at seven."

Chapter 21

FOR THE FIRST time in weeks, the sun went out. By
Thursday evening, clouds the color of old bruises were
sliding across the sky, but the heat refused to relent.
Stagnant, thick air spread itself along the North Shore like an
old blanket, suffocating and dry, while thunder grumbled
beyond the bluffs. It was itchy weather, close and
inescapable, the kind that drove dogs to madness and people
to murder. Certainly Willa had considered it while Georgie
had played Fairy Henchmother in her closet again.

Willa had decided to let her live but as a result she now
stood on Main Street wearing a high-collared, vaguely
Japanese-looking dress that managed to nod at modesty
while leaving no doubt as to the exact size and shape of her
body. It was also light and linen, and she had to admit it was
comfortable. Way more comfortable than the hour Georgie
had spent trying to coax Willa's stubborn hair into an up-do
of some sort.

"Jesus, it's like the loaves and fishes," Georgie had
muttered bitterly through a mouthful of bobby pins, as if
Willa had grown acres of hair just to spite her. "It just keeps
coming."

"Ball cap," Willa had said smugly. "Pony tail. It's a
classic for a reason."

"I wonder what part of the brain controls speech,"
Georgie mused vaguely and stabbed a bobby pin into Willa's
scalp like she was trying to penetrate the skull. She probably
was, Willa realized, and shut up. Fifteen minutes later,
Georgie spit out the pins, released her hair and said, "Fuck
it."

Which was how Willa had ended up in public with her arms and legs *and* all her hair showing. Not to mention her eyes. She felt exposed and naked, dangerously so. But she also felt undeniably...pretty. No, more than pretty. She felt sexy. Eli's eyes had slid down her body when he'd seen her, hot as a touch, then drifted back up again, and a slow smile had spread across his face. The kind of smile that sent a hot little shimmy through a woman's stomach. It sat there still, pulsing like an ember, and every inch of her exposed skin felt needful and hungry.

She'd let this dangerous part of her sleep for so long. She couldn't help that Eli had woken it up, but had it really been a good idea to let Georgie put it on display like this?

Nothing for it now. There was no way through tonight but forward. She circled the hood while Eli climbed out of the passenger side. He drifted hot eyes from the hair swirling around her shoulders all the way down to the toes peeking out of sparkly sandals again, lingering at all the most sensitive places in between. The hunger leapt inside Willa even as the worry twisted tighter.

"I like your shoes," he said, grinning at her feet.

"Shut up." She jerked her head down Main toward the gallery. "Let's go."

"They sparkle."

"I said shut up."

He did and she managed to walk the block and a half to the gallery without tripping on the glorified leather flip flops Georgie had insisted on. Some poor child had probably bedazzled them in a Vietnamese sweatshop instead of going to school but did Georgie care? No. Georgie liked the sparkle.

Soren Buck was standing on the sidewalk in front of the Davis Gallery when they arrived, his back to the display windows, his face to the sky.

"Looks like we might finally get some rain." He was a shaggy bear of a man, all barrel chest and lumberjack beard.

He looked exactly like the kind of guy who might own a bait shop, which he did. He didn't look like the kind of guy who'd commission a giant papier mache fish to leap through the second story of his shop where it would then hang out over the sidewalk like a bizarre awning, but he had. Bianca Davis hated that fish. Hated that nothing but Third Street separated the tacky kitsch of it from her precious gallery.

As a result, Willa loved that fish, and Soren Buck along with it.

"It sure feels that way," Willa said. Despite the clinging heat, she rubbed her hands up and down her bare arms. "I hope it breaks this weather."

Soren squinted out over the lake, then turned to the clouds sliding across the bluffs to their north. "It's going to break something."

"Yeah," Eli said, frowning at the clouds. "I've got that feeling, too. I just hope it's nothing too nearby."

Willa blinked at him. "What does that mean?"

"Nothing." He shrugged. "I'm itchy, that's all. Feels like lightning."

"It does." Soren studied him with deep-set eyes. "You're the Forestry guy."

"I am. I'm also the guy Gerte tried to slap into next week." He held out his hand.

"Heard you had a difference of opinion with Paul O'Malley, too." Soren took his hand, gave it a considering pump. "That would be Gerte's cousin, you know."

Eli closed his eyes briefly. Willa wondered exactly what kind of run-in he'd had with O'Malley. "I didn't know that. Explains why he seemed so familiar with Gerte's slapping hand, though."

Soren's eyes warmed to a near-sparkle. "Woman's got an arm on her."

"Believe me, I know."

Soren shifted his gaze to Willa. "Heard you told everybody you burned down Davis Place with a fancy coffee maker."

Willa didn't blink. "You heard right."

He nodded slowly. "Okay by me."

She patted his big shoulder. "You're all right, Soren. You coming in?"

"In a minute." His eyes went back to the clouds. "I'm going to watch the show out here for a bit yet."

"We'll see you inside then," she said and reached for the door.

"I'll see you." Soren chuckled. "But who'll see me when you look like that?"

Willa froze with the open door in her hand, uncertainty swamping her all over again. Oh, God. Had Georgie dressed her up like a hooker? Had she walked docilely into a social trap of that magnitude? Was she really that stupid?

Eli put a hand in the small of her back and nudged her inside. "You look incredible," he said, and kept his warm hand just there, just below her waist where anybody could see it. Where it sent all kinds of inappropriate signals to all kinds of inappropriate portions of her anatomy.

"I don't want people looking at me," she whispered desperately.

"Then you shouldn't look amazing." A white-draped table was set up to one side of the entry, topped with a forest of leggy champagne glasses and silver ice buckets. It also held one of the stranger sights Willa had clapped eyes on in a while.

"Oh good," Eli said. "There's a doughnut tree."

She blinked. "A what?"

He laughed. "There, by the champagne. Looks like the unholy union of a Christmas tree, a porcupine and a doughnut shop?"

He pointed his chin toward the stylized spiral of iron sitting serenely among the champagne glasses. The base was circular, maybe a foot and half in diameter, tapering to a lofty point some three feet above the table top. Every inch of it was studded with needle-sharp spikes, which might've been forbidding if each one weren't holding a perfectly glazed dark chocolate doughnut hole.

"That might be the most beautiful thing I've ever seen." She considered it seriously. "Or the most dangerous."

"My favorite kind of danger." A smile bloomed, slow and mischievous, across that angular face, and he took her hand. "Let's go."

A little dazzled by that unexpected flash of the boy he must've been, she let him haul her toward the alcohol and chocolate. She was aware of the eyes on them — on her — as they moved through clusters of people she'd known her whole life. Eli pressed a glass of champagne into her hand, and even as she took it, she could feel the raised eyebrows and speaking glances. She saw curiosity ripple through the crowd like a school of fish, darting this way and that, shifting direction on a dime. Low murmurs passed from person to person while Eli considered his options at the doughnut tree. Gossip spread, grew, sharpened its barbs and reached for her. So she sipped her champagne and reached for the peace of her thinnie, for the serenity of its countless eons. She put it in the center of her mind and the weight of it stilled her from the inside out, polished her so smooth that nothing could catch hold. She was time, she was air, she was endless.

"This one," Eli said and plucked a doughnut hole from a spike. "It's perfect." He passed it to her on a pretty little napkin and went hunting for his own.

She murmured her thanks and continued breathing. Just breathing. Suddenly her nose was full of cigarette smoke, black coffee and lilies of the valley, which could mean only one thing: Nan Davis had arrived.

"Well if it isn't Willa Zinc. Good lord, child! Look at you, all dressed up!"

Willa turned to find Georgie's grandmother at her elbow, all not-quite-five-feet of her. Nan Davis hadn't exchanged a civil word with her daughter-in-law Bianca in more than a decade, which put her and Willa on more or less the same team. But Willa hadn't survived as long as she had by underestimating Davises. The glaring exception being, of course, letting Georgie stuff her into this godforsaken dress. She kept the thinnie firmly in the back of her mind and freed up the front to perform the standard exchange of guarded remarks.

"Hi, Nan. You look—" With an unnaturally black cap of hair, a brightly painted mouth and a year-round Birkenstock habit, Nan looked like nothing so much as a bad-tempered hobbit. "—very nice yourself."

Nan barked out a rusty laugh. "No I don't. But I would if I had a figure like yours." She gazed directly at Willa's chest. "Where on earth have you been hiding all that?"

Willa sighed. The *where* of the matter was simple — a determined sports bra could flatten anything. The *why* was a bit more complicated but it had a lot to do with Nan's clear conviction that seeing something put it squarely in the public sphere, open for comment and judgment. It had even more to do with the subtle, assessing glances being leveled on her body to some degree by everybody else in the room. Nothing good ever came from this kind of attention. "The usual places," she said with determined lightness. "Given my line of work, this isn't a very practical look. Georgie insisted, though."

Nan's attention flew back to Willa's face, her eyes sharp. "Since when does Georgie tell you what to wear?"

"Since Addy made me a bridesmaid."

Nan seized a champagne glass. "Young man." She poked it at Eli's kidney. "Fill this."

"Yes, ma'am," he said, as if being ordered around by barky, chain-smoking hobbits were a daily occurrence. He handed Nan the doughnut hole he'd obviously just selected for himself, and obediently filled the glass. He gave Willa a probing glance and topped off the glass in her hand, too.

Filled one for himself while he was at it. He started to put the bottle back in the chilling bucket, then shrugged and just held onto it.

"Thank you." Nan sipped her champagne and smiled. "So. Willa. You're standing up for our Addison, are you?"

"She didn't really give me a choice." Willa shrugged. "You know Addy. Then she sicced Georgie on my closet."

"It shows." Nan gave her another shrewd up-and-down. "You look just like your mother."

Shock had Willa staring stupidly. She didn't look anything like Shay. Shay had been blonde and flamboyant, with curves for days and a wardrobe that was more costume than clothing. "My shoes are sparkling," she heard herself say vaguely.

Nan surveyed them with sympathy. "Yeah." She wiggled her own toes inside a pair of comfortably worn Birkies. "Too bad about that."

"I like the sparkly shoes," Eli offered.

"Who are you?" Nan asked.

"Eli Walker." He stuck the champagne bottle back in the ice bucket and held out his hand. "Gerte slapped my face off a few days back."

"That was you?" Nan tossed the doughnut hole into her mouth and shook with her now-free hand.

"That was me."

"Well, you *did* blow up the Dumpster and Peter's resort."

"That actually wasn't me."

"No?" Nan's penciled-on brows climbed. "Lainey said it was."

"Lainey said she *thought* it might've been Eli," Willa said.

"Why would she think that?" Eli asked.

"Because she threw herself at you in a tizzy of sexual frustration, you said no and she didn't take rejection like a lady." Nan smirked. "And this is Gerte's daughter we're talking about. Probably packs a decent punch."

Georgie said, "She does. I danced with her date at our junior prom and found out for myself."

"Georgie? When did you get here?" Willa frowned at her. "I thought you only appeared out of the blue when I was dressed inappropriately."

"Please. There aren't enough hours in the day." Georgie flicked back a shimmering sheet of white-gold hair, straight as rain and twice as slick. She leaned down to kiss Nan's cheek. "Hey, Gran. Enjoying the champagne?"

"I'm no Bianca fan but I'll give credit where it's due. The girl doesn't cheap out on the alcohol."

Eli said, "Who's Bianca, and why aren't we fans?"

"She's my mom," Georgie said. "And I am a fan, thanks."

"My daughter-in-law," Nan said, and her mouth soured. "Diego's mother." She jerked her helmet of hair toward the center of the gallery, where Bianca stood chatting. It was like looking at Georgie twenty-five years from now. Her hair just brushed her shoulders, an expensive swing of honey-gold lightly streaked with silver. *Diego's Angel* hung on the wall behind her, exactly where it always had, but a second, sheet-draped frame hung beside it now.

"Hey, is that *Diego's Angel*?" Eli asked. "I've never seen it in person." He tipped his head and frowned. "What's under the sheet next to it?"

Nan's lips spread in a tight smile. "That's what we're here to find out."

Georgie sent her a bland look. "It'll be a revealing evening, I'm sure."

A few yards away, Gerte was chatting with Sarah Schnickle from the Gilded Fish gift shop, and her head popped up like a hunting dog coming to point. "Revealing?" Gerte left Sarah without a word and stalked over to them. "In what way, Georgie? Because I swear on all that's holy, if you brought me out here to look at porn—"

"For crying out loud, Gerte." Nan sighed. "Nobody's

going to expose you to porn. Some of the stuff is probably R-rated, but Addy's already agreed to keep it in the *Diego After Dark* collection, which they're clearly advertising as an after-hours, ticketed-patrons-only showing. It's not going to drive God-fearing families off Main Street."

"We've got it all set up already, right through there." Georgie pointed at the white-curtained doorway she'd taken Willa through a few days earlier, and smiled serenely. "In case your curiosity gets the better of you."

"I'm hardly curious about your brother's smutty drawings." Gerte sniffed. "I would, however, be very interested to know what Bianca's got under that sheet next to *Diego's Angel*."

"Why?" Willa asked. "It's Addy's painting. It's Addy's business. If it isn't dirty, why do you care so much what it is?"

Gerte's eyes flew to her, then widened. "Good lord, Willa, is that you? Look at all that hair and…" Those eyes fell to Willa's chest. "…everything." She blinked and dragged her gaze back to Willa's face. "Where on earth have you been hiding it all?"

"That's what I asked," Nan crowed and poked her empty champagne glass at Eli again. "Hit me again, young man." Eli obligingly refilled her glass.

"Under her abysmal fashion sense," Georgie said and pointed at Willa's knees. "Look, she has legs, too."

Willa breathed and thought desperately of her thinnie. Eli put his hand in the small of Willa's back and grinned. "This must be the henchmaid you've been telling me about."

Nan snickered. Georgie lifted one perfect eyebrow. "Henchmaid?"

"I'm sure I meant bridesmaid," Willa said innocently. "But yes, this is Georgie Davis, Addy's maid of honor, Nan's granddaughter, Diego's sister and my closet's arch enemy."

"Eli Walker," he said and held out a friendly hand.

"Professional hiker, owner of the face Gerte slapped silly and Willa's date. I think we've actually met before. I was holding a dish tub at the time, though, so you might not remember."

"I remember," Georgie murmured, frowning. "You're really Willa's date?"

"I am."

Willa's cheeks felt hot but she kept the thinnie firmly in her mind and shrugged lightly.

Georgie stared. "But you're a man."

"Oh, right." Eli snapped his fingers and pointed at her. "I understand you thought Willa was a lesbian."

Nan waved that off. "We all thought Willa was a lesbian."

"Not that my sexuality is anybody's business," Willa pointed out.

Georgie snorted. "A town this size? Your sexuality is everybody's business." She turned to her grandmother. "Nan, you've got a newspaper. Write a story or something. Willa's dating a man." She blinked, struck. "Hell, Willa's dating."

Gerte was still staring wordlessly at Willa. Her eyes dropped to Willa's sparkly sandals then drifted back up to her face. "My stars, Willa, you look just like your mother! It's like Shay come back to life."

"She's not dead, Gerte," Willa said. "She just took off."

"Mmm," Gerte murmured noncommittally. "Speaking of your father—"

"I wasn't."

"—I hear he's back in town?"

Willa was saved from answering when Georgie lifted a hand and waved to Addy who was speaking to somebody on the other side of the white curtain dividing the public space from the private. "Addison! Come over here and meet Willa's date!" she shouted. "It's a *man*!"

Conversation died and every face swung her way. Horror

rose inside her — she definitely shouldn't have let Georgie live — and she lifted her champagne glass for a fortifying slug. Beside her Eli chuckled, then leaned down to brush a wisp of hair away from her hot cheek.

Addy craned her neck and blinked at Eli. She gave Willa big eyes and a thumbs up. Eli gave her an amused finger-wave.

"That's the bride-to-be, I assume?"

"That's the one," Willa muttered, mortified.

Addy pointed at Georgie and jerked her head toward the center of the gallery. She made an exaggerated sorry face at Willa, who waved it away.

"Showtime," Georgie said. "That's my cue." She scooped up a glass of champagne and drifted off in the direction of the draped painting.

Eli watched her go, then turned to gaze down at Willa. "You're not the villain of this story, Willa," he decided. "They don't hate you."

"No?" She smiled up at him fiercely. "What do you call this kind of systematic public shaming?"

He smoothed his hand over the hair spilling down her back and smiled sympathetically. "Family."

She stared up at him in mute shock.

"They give you shit all the time, sure, but just watch them circle the wagons if somebody else tries it." He drifted his knuckles down the line of her cheek and lifted a shoulder. "It makes no sense, I know, but that's family for you."

She closed her mouth. She suspected it was gaping. Was that really how family worked? They'd hurt you endlessly and right up close, but protect you from any minor hurt a stranger could launch at you from across the moat? Finally she shook her head. "Not my family."

Her family had only gotten half the memo, if that. They believed in hurting you right up close. Protecting you from strangers? Not really on the agenda.

"Not the one you grew up in, no. I believe that." He

dropped a companionable arm around her shoulders. Why was he touching her so much? And why was she letting him? But the weight of his arm was warm and comforting and she felt safe under it. And she'd been unsafe too often to reject even the illusion. "But you have this family, too." He nodded at the gallery full of people, watching with naked interest as Eli touched her. As Willa allowed it. "And they don't hate you."

Wouldn't that be nice? A forlorn yearning threaded through her skepticism. She didn't need to be loved, but it would be nice not to be hated.

"I'm a Zinc," she said simply, and killed the yearning with cold, brutal logic. "It's not my fault but believe me, I'm hated."

"I don't believe that."

She smiled bitterly. "You should."

Chapter 22

THE CLEAR TINKLE of a spoon tapping on crystal cut through the hum of conversation and the gallery fell silent. Eli turned with everybody else to the center of the room where the woman who was unmistakably Georgie's mother stood gazing out over the crowd with patrician satisfaction. *Diego's Angel* hung behind her left shoulder, and the rest of the family stood on the other side of the frame, their backs to the sheet-draped mystery canvas that held everybody's attention. Georgie stood nearest her mother, then came Addy, the real-life angel Diego had painted. She was less perfect than the woman on the canvas but so radiantly happy that the painting faded in comparison. Which probably had something to do with the man holding her hand.

Jackson Davis was obviously the groom-to-be in Willa's unholy bridal situation, and the eldest Davis brother, though he had nothing of his family's tall, angular elegance. He was about six feet, if that, but built like an oak tree and probably just as easy to move. If Eli remembered correctly, he was also Devil's Kettle's fire chief.

"Welcome, everybody. Thank you so much for coming." Bianca Davis clasped elegant hands loosely at her waist, a woman confident in her authority and comfortable in the spotlight. "Devil Days kicks off tomorrow, and I know you've all taken time you can't spare to be here tonight. I want you to know how much we appreciate your support. Tomorrow we'll unveil a collection of Diego Davis canvases never before shown in public, a collection that tells Diego's story in full, from the talented boy he was to the mature master he became."

She paused, grief passing over her face like a cloud sliding across the sun. Addy stepped forward to take her hand. She was a curly little riot of nutmeg hair and creamy skin next to Bianca's cool elegance but there was no mistaking the affection between them. The smile Addy gave her was a miracle of warmth and encouragement, and it melted away a stiffness Eli hadn't even been aware of in Bianca's posture. She didn't smile back but turned to face the crowd once more.

"It's fitting, I think, to tell his story in canvases. Diego painted the way the rest of us breathe. It was his oxygen. He didn't understand his own heart until he poured it out in oil and sweat on the canvas. And for that reason, we've kept a number of his works private. They were simply too revealing, and our loss was still too new. Some of his works, however, we weren't even aware of."

A murmur ran through the crowd again, and the air went electric, as if the lightning gathering above the bluffs outside were suddenly inside the room.

"As I'm sure you all remember, our family suffered a number of unfortunate accidents earlier this year, beginning with a fire in our carriage house."

It occurred to Eli suddenly that he remembered that fire. It had been late spring and Eli had just peeled off the Superior Hiking Trail hoping to find enough work to replace his failing camp stove. Not that he was broke. His Forest Service job came with a paycheck but as far as Eli was concerned, it was just one more stubborn root connecting him to his old life. And he didn't want to even remember the past, let alone finance the present with it. So his salary sat in the bank collecting interest while Eli survived day to day on the grill skills his mother had insisted were forever.

He'd been busing tables at the Wooden Spoon when the carriage house had gone down, and though he didn't talk much, he heard plenty. He'd gotten the distinct impression that Devil's Kettle was dubious about just how accidental that fire had been. He'd also overheard more than a little sympathy for the youngest Davis kid, who was rumored to be responsible for it. *The kid might look just like Diego but that doesn't mean he can paint like Diego, not that Bianca wants to hear it. If she was my mom, I might be tempted to burn something down myself.*

"Addison risked her life to rescue from that fire a canvas of which I had previously been unaware," Bianca said. "A canvas that undeniably puts Diego in his rightful place as one of the brightest lights of his generation. A canvas that also chronicles his descent into addiction, infidelity, guilt and shame. He named it *Broken*."

She stopped, swallowed visibly. Addy squeezed her hand and took over.

"Unlike Bianca, I knew *Broken* existed. But the subject matter was so raw, so painful, that Diego and I agreed to keep it private so long as our marriage endured." Grief crept into her smile but didn't dim it. She simply shone brighter. Eli was a little mesmerized. "Addiction stole his life before we resolved our marriage, and I spent the next couple of years trying to find my way. Trying to find my place. Eventually I found it."

She shifted that smile to Jax, who returned it with a slow devotion that Eli looked away from. It was so richly intimate that he felt like a voyeur just seeing it.

"My place is here, with you. I'm a Davis, twice over by next year, and I finally feel like I'm in a steady enough place to tell the rest of Diego's story. He didn't love me by the end. He didn't love anything more than his addictions, or at least that was what I thought. But I've studied this canvas over the past months. I've really looked at it with fresh eyes and a fresh heart, and I know now that Diego did love me. We weren't *in* love anymore but he loved me nonetheless. And he hated what his addiction had done to me. What it had done to him. What it had stolen from us, from the world. Diego's story isn't a happy one but it's true. It's beautiful, it's bloody and it's real. It gives, it takes, it hurts and it heals. In short, it was exactly like him. *Broken* is his final chapter, and it's brilliant. We hope we've given it the context here that it needs to shine."

She stepped to the side, grasped the sheet and pulled it free of the frame.

Even Eli gasped. It was like Diego had taken the joyful optimism of his *Angel* and run it through a nightmare machine. It was still unmistakably Addison on the canvas, and she lay across a rumpled bed in much the same attitude as in the *Angel* but that was where the similarities ended. This Addison was face-down, wracked with grief, her body exposed rather than revered. In *Diego's Angel*, she wore silk and the artist's devotion. In *Broken*, she wore ill-suited lingerie, the artist's dissatisfaction, and her own shattered heart. Grief and pain and disappointed expectations oozed from the frame and wrapped ugly tendrils around Eli's heart. He found himself rubbing his sternum as he gazed at it, trying to break free.

Georgie stepped forward. "Beginning tomorrow, *Broken* will be on permanent display right here on the central wall of the gallery, a bookend to *Diego's Angel*. But beginning tomorrow evening, we'll veil both it and the *Angel* and direct patrons first to *Diego After Dark*, the collection on display in the private gallery." She tipped her head toward the white curtain at the back of the gallery. "*Diego After Dark* is a selection of Diego's work we've never, as my mother mentioned, shown before. It begins with some teenaged pencil sketches and progresses chronologically through each era of his career, culminating in the *Angel* and *Broken*, side by side. We recommend you all experience the collection in this way, as it gives his later work such context and depth. The subject matter is graphic, however, so you're welcome to simply view the *Angel* and *Broken* if you'd rather. Either way, you'll see that Diego was both a complicated man and a great artist. We hope you'll join us in celebrating him."

The crowd surged toward the curtain.

"Should we get in line?" Eli asked.

Willa reached up as if to snug her ball cap down but it wasn't there. Her hand fluttered back to her side and she dipped her head. "I've already seen it," she said.

He tugged her hand until she looked up at him. "We can go, you know. If you don't want to be here, just say the word and we're out."

"No." She set her lips. "We'll stay. Addy asked me to be here. I'm not bailing on her."

"Okay. But, Willa, if you don't want—"

"I'm fine. I'm maybe not fully dressed, but I'm fine." She nodded toward Addy, standing bravely between both versions of herself, her smile tight, her hand secure in her fiancé's. "Let's go see how she is."

Two hours later, the gallery was nearly empty and Willa's feet ached intolerably. Having no role at this party, and no particular desire to look at any of Diego's work, Willa had appointed herself to the wait staff, freshening champagne glasses and restocking the doughnut tree while keeping a gimlet eye on Addy. Her friend's smile had loosened up over the course of the event — the bottomless glass of champagne Willa kept in her hand had probably helped — and lately even Jax didn't look like he wanted to toss everybody bodily into the street. Eli, bless him, had dutifully and silently pitched in, no questions asked. She might love him just for that, if she didn't love him already.

She froze there in the little kitchenette off the private gallery, an empty champagne bottle halfway to the recycling container. Did she love him already? Was she in love with Eli Walker?

"Here," he said behind her. She whirled, startled, and Eli stuffed a doughnut hole into her mouth. "There was only one left and I really want to recycle this box. Thank you for your sacrifice. If I ate one more, I was going to puke."

The chocolate melted sinfully in her mouth and she realized she'd never eaten the doughnut hole Eli had hand-picked for her hours ago. Nor had she finished her single glass of champagne. But she'd survived this night without anybody else comparing her to her mother or obviously ogling her chest, so she was calling it a win. She closed her eyes, dropped the champagne bottle in the recycling and took a moment to just savor the chocolate in her mouth and the man who'd put it there. Tomorrow was soon enough to worry about why he'd put it there, why he seemed to like feeding her, or why she seemed to like it when he did. Because he seemed to have taken an interest in her body, a very proprietary one. But whereas that sort of attention typically made her cringe, coming from Eli, it only made her insides shiver. In a good way. A hot way. A...happy way. And that should worry her. A lot.

Tomorrow, she assured herself. She would worry about all of it tomorrow.

Eli shoved the doughnut box into the recycling, put his fists in his lower back and stretched. "Good Christ. I'd forgotten how much people love free food."

"Free alcohol is worse," Willa managed, and swallowed her doughnut. "I think Nan alone put away two bottles."

Eli grinned and shook his head. "I wouldn't doubt it. I might be in love with that old lady."

"Send me a postcard from the Shire, will you?"

He laughed and Bianca appeared in the doorway.

"Willa," she said. "A word?"

She didn't wait for an answer but withdrew into the private gallery that housed *Diego After Dark*. Foreboding immediately soured the chocolate in Willa's stomach. She glanced at Eli. He lifted baffled shoulders, and they followed Bianca into the room where Willa had stared down Georgie the day before. The room from which she'd evicted a chipmunk a few days before that. The room where she'd last seen Matty, who was growing up so fast and so beautifully and so very far away from her.

Bianca saw Eli and stiffened. "If you'll excuse us." She smiled politely at him. "I'd like to speak to Willa privately."

Eli turned to Willa. "Your call."

"Stay. Please." But she folded her arms when he would've reached for her hand. She wanted that comfort, wanted it desperately, but knew she shouldn't take it. Couldn't afford to. Her gut had been telling her all week that something bad was brewing. That this sea-change in Bianca's attitude couldn't portend anything good for Willa's future. It looked like Bianca was finally ready to drop the other boot, and everything in her screamed to send Eli away. To protect him from the knowledge of who she was and what she'd done, but also to protect herself from the sight of disappointment and confusion replacing the affection and warmth in his eyes when he looked at her.

But wasn't that why Willa had asked Eli to come with her tonight in the first place? So he'd know who she was here? So he'd know everything? So the fragile seedling of love burrowing its way into her heart could get squashed before it did any real damage?

Bianca shrugged elegantly. "As you like." She strolled to the far end of the long, narrow room, past the thin ledge running the length of the wall on her right. The ledge was about chest high, and on it were perched frames of various sizes and shapes. Spotlights on the ceiling bathed each work in its own individual aura of golden light. A small chest of drawers stood against the far wall next to a discreetly closed bathroom door, and Bianca pulled from the chest three small frames. She placed them on the ledge with the other pictures, as if they would be the collection's new opening salvo. She stepped back and gestured for Willa to look.

Willa obeyed, her heart pounding, her mouth dry, but unable to do otherwise. They were pencil sketches, she saw immediately, their black frames echoing the bold, black strokes on thick, creamy paper. Bianca pressed a beautifully lettered placard to the wall above them that read simply *Diego at Fifteen.*

"I found these in one of Diego's old sketchbooks," Bianca told her. "I don't know why I'd even saved it. I'd flipped through it before and only found geometry proofs. It was in one of the boxes that tipped over the other day when you were working back here and that chipmunk got loose. I grabbed the sturdiest book from the pile to swat at it, and there they were." She waved a hand at the frames, then paused. "There *you* were."

"Wait, this is you?" Eli asked, leaning forward to examine the sketches more closely. Willa couldn't speak. She could hardly breathe. Hot panic skittered across her icy skin, scalding and merciless. She reached desperately for her thinnie, closed her eyes and poured herself into the effort. She found it somewhere deep in her soul, dragged it into ruthless focus and let the ageless peace of it sweep through her.

"Willa?" Eli asked again. "This is you?"

Chapter 23

SHE OPENED HER eyes and found him gazing down at her, those huge blue eyes filled with surprise and...concern? How odd. She tipped her head and studied the sketches. "These two I remember." She pointed at the first two frames where a few confident pencil strokes had captured a girl, fully nude and asleep in the summer grass. In the first, she had one foot planted on the ground, the knee upraised, one arm and a tumble of wild hair over her face while she slept. In the other, she'd rolled away from the artist's eye, and his pencil had flowed in one long, lovely line from her shoulder to her ankle, capturing the inchoate curve of a hip just beginning its reach toward womanhood.

"That one?" She waved a hand at the third sketch. The setting was the same, and the subject was still nude but the artist had focused on just her naked back this time. All that hair tumbled toward lush, rounded hips, and there was a knowing, almost coquettish arch to the spine, as if the subject were sending an invitation through her lashes to the artist behind her. "I don't remember that one at all."

She had her suspicions, yes. A memory, however? No.

"The sketches were undated," Bianca went on, "but we checked Diego's school records. He took geometry in ninth grade, so we're assuming these were drawn the summer between his freshman and sophomore years."

It had been the summer before freshman year for Willa. The summer before she'd begun high school, when the future was still something she looked forward to.

The curtain separating them from the main gallery twitched and Georgie appeared. "Addy and Jax are seeing our stragglers to the door," she announced. "I told them to just go home, that we'd lock—" She saw Willa and stopped. "Oh. You're doing this now?"

"What choice do I have?" Bianca lifted slender shoulders. "Devil Days opens tomorrow and these sketches are too important not to show." Willa felt Bianca's eyes on her, focused and sharp. "They're the prologue to Diego's entire career, and give this showing the context it needs."

"I thought you were going to talk to Matty first." Georgie drifted over to them with her usual lazy grace, though she wore an unhappy frown. Willa crossed trembling arms over her chest, tucked her cold fingers into her elbows and swallowed a lump of terror. For years, she'd wanted nothing more than to know Matty. To be allowed to love him. He wouldn't love her back, nor did she expect him to. She was practically a stranger to him. But what if Bianca finally stepped out from between them, and he hated her? Once he knew the whole story, how could he not hate her?

How could this not have occurred to her before?

"I would have spoken to him if he'd gotten home on time," Bianca said, rolling her eyes. "I only agreed to let him go on this silly field trip because that coach of his promised me he'd be here in time for tonight's preview." She flicked the irritation away with one hand. "Ah, well. It's probably better this way. We should know how Willa plans to respond before we start that conversation with Matty, anyway."

Behind the bathroom door, a toilet flushed. Bianca froze, her eyes going wide and latching onto Georgie's. Georgie shrugged, her eyes equally wide. The sink ran, and Bianca stepped gracefully in front of the new frames. The door opened, and Gerte stepped into the room.

"Beg pardon," she said. "Am I interrupting—" She leaned around Bianca to glance at the new frames on the wall. "Were those there earlier?" She stepped over to peer at them. "Goodness, no, they weren't. I'd have remembered these. Diego at fifteen, eh?" She pinched her lips together and shook her head. "Fifteen years old, and already getting girls naked in the grass. How very…unsurprising." She sent a smile of poisonous sweetness to Georgie. "You'd have been, what, thirteen or fourteen that summer?" She shook her head in wonder. "My gracious, what an adventurous year for the Davis children." She shifted that smile to Bianca. "You must be so proud."

Willa blinked at that one, momentarily lost. Then she remembered that most of the town suspected Matty to be *Georgie's* bastard, not Diego's. This would've made Georgie barely fourteen at conception, and Gerte was only too happy to shame Bianca for having raised such dirty children. Beside her, Eli stood in silence, his head swiveling like he was at a tennis match. Before Bianca could eviscerate Gerte with one of those icy set-downs she was so good at, the emergency exit swung open and Matty appeared, flushed and breathless.

"Hey," he called and wrestled his duffle bag and lacrosse stick through the narrow doorway. "Sorry I'm so late. Adam thought it would be funny to make a pot joke at the border and we almost had an international incident." The door banged shut and he hustled over to join them. "Is it over? Did I miss it?" There was a beat of taut silence, everybody evidently at the same loss for words. Matty frowned. "What? What's going on?"

"Nothing, dear." Gerte smiled primly. "Goodness, look at you! You're practically all grown up these days, aren't you? How old are you now?"

"I'll be fourteen in a few days."

Gerte sent a significant look toward the placard that read *Diego at Fifteen.* "Any girlfriends yet?"

"Uh, no," Matty stammered, baffled and embarrassed. "I haven't, I mean, I'm not—"

"Ignore her, Matty," Georgie drawled. "She's trying to slut-shame me, and you're just getting caught in the cross-fire."

"Why, Georgie!" Gerte widened her eyes innocently. "What a thing to say! I was only making conversation!"

"No, you were implying that if Diego could talk a girl out of her clothes at fifteen, and if I — as rumor loves to have it — could get pregnant with Matty here at fourteen, then we really ought to keep a sharp eye on this kid before he goes off the rails, too."

"Georgie, enough," Bianca said quietly. "Gerte, I think it's time to say goodnight."

"You're wrong, you know," Matty said to Gerte, his voice flat. "About Georgie. She's not my mother."

"Well of course she isn't," Gerte said quickly. "My word, who ever said she was?"

"Everybody." He laughed bitterly. "But guess what? I'm not stupid. I'm not deaf, either. You think I don't know that I'm adopted? You think I don't *know* that Georgie's your top choice for my birth mother? Did you honestly think a town like this could keep a secret like that?"

Gerte didn't say a word, only gaped at Matty like a bemused fish.

"I don't know what kind of sick thrill you get out of talking about it all the time, or out of calling my sister a slut. I don't really care, honestly. But since you're so curious, you might be interested to know that I actually do know who one of my birth parents is."

Willa's heart stopped. It froze inside her chest. Her hands and feet went dangerously numb and her lips tingled. Blackness pressed on the edge of her vision and she concentrated on pulling deep, even breaths into her lungs. Even as her head threatened to float away like a balloon, she breathed. Eli's hand found the small of her back.

"Easy," he murmured. "Steady."

"You do?" Gerte sounded sincerely shocked.

"Of course I do. I look just like him."

"But you look just like Diego," Gerte breathed, her eyes bouncing from Matty to the sketches and back. "Oh my lord, you're *Diego's*?" She turned those bewildered eyes on Bianca. "But if Diego's the father, who on earth is—"

"—my mother?" Matty jerked a shrug. "I don't know. But I'll bet she does." He aimed his chin toward the frames on the wall. A icy shock skittered along Willa's bare skin, as exposed in this dress as it had been in the summer grass. "I was born, what, the summer after he drew those? And if Diego was talking some girl into posing naked for him in the summer, he'd probably talked her into doing more by the winter. And if I'm right, if he did? Then that girl's my birth mother."

"He didn't leave any notes," Bianca said evenly, and she didn't twitch so much as a betraying lash Willa's direction. "He didn't even draw her face, so there's no way to know from these sketches who she is."

"Not unless you actually look at the sketches," Gerte said impatiently. She stepped into the frames until her upturned nose was mere inches from the drawings. "This is a small town and I know the north woods when I see them. I've lived here my whole life, haven't I?" She squinted at the sketch, then drew back to squint from a different angle.

Bianca exchanged a worried look with Georgie, then hooked a hand through Gerte's elbow. "I bow to your superior sleuthing skills, Gerte, but even you can't positively identify a fifteen-year-old sketch by a head of hair."

Gerte folded her arms and gave a satisfied huff. "I can when that hair's standing right in front of me." Willa's heart jerked once, then gave up and went still. Gerte tapped a finger to the wall next to the first frame, next to a lush tumble of sun-warmed hair and a slim shoulder in the grass, all of it suggested by nothing more than a few bold pencil strokes. "That's Willa."

"It's you?" Matty breathed, his eyes filled with

bewildered anguish. "You're my mother?"

Willa's heart tore in half. It simply ripped in two and bled for him, for the hope-streaked agony that filled his voice. She felt it happen across the vacuum of the thinnie, knew herself to be mortally wounded. She only hoped her borrowed composure held firm and carried her home before the storm broke and her own agony fell down on her like rain.

She turned to Gerte instead, that awful calm falling between her and the pain like a white curtain. "What's wrong with you?"

"Oh dear lord." Gerte stopped, her soft hand clenched in front of her throat, sincere distress in her pale eyes. She stared at Willa as if she'd never seen her before. "I'm so sorry. I shouldn't have said that. I was so surprised, it just popped out." She blinked, evidently as dazed as Matty. "All these years, I thought Georgie was the one who—"

"—who got pregnant at fourteen?" Rage, hot and red, beat its fists against that cold calm. Willa was aware of it there, but she didn't feel it. She might later but right now she was simply curious. "You thought maybe it was Georgie who was having sex when she was fourteen years old? When she was a child? That's not sex, Gerte. That's rape." Gerte flinched and Willa was aware of a savage joy beyond the curtain, a warrior's fierce satisfaction in scoring first blood. But shame as well. Shame tangled there, too, always. "Rape isn't really the kind of ammunition decent people use to score social points." She studied Gerte with academic interest. "So I'll ask again — what's wrong with you?"

"What's wrong with me?" Gerte's voice strengthened, her mouth firmed into a dissatisfied line. "What's wrong with her?"

She shot a finger toward Bianca, standing there staring just like everybody else. Bianca appeared to be beyond words for once, and Matty still gazed at Willa as if she were something he'd never seen before, or a difficult math problem he'd just finally understood.

"What's wrong with a woman who'd lead an entire town to believe such a thing? Bianca knew exactly how it would look when she swanned off to Europe with Georgie after Joe died. She knew exactly what we'd all think when she came home with a baby. Because life is strange and people are impossible but I think we're all clear on the fact that a woman doesn't celebrate her husband's death with a little European vacation, not even Bianca Davis. And she certainly doesn't carry a baby to term without being aware of it. For God's sake, she wears a size zero!

"So she *knew* we'd assume Georgie was the mother. But she also knew nobody would argue when she said the baby was hers. And why not? Because she's a Davis." Her mouth twisted with disgust. "She's a Davis, and she knows there's not a soul in this town who'd challenge her. She could say the sky was purple and everybody would rush to agree. *Yes, Bianca, it's lovely, Bianca, please don't bankrupt us, Bianca.*"

She pulled in a shaking breath, released it in a righteous huff. Color burned in her soft cheeks and Willa was aware of a pulse of sympathy threading through the rage and the pain on the other side of her borrowed calm. She knew what it was to be ground under Bianca Davis' pointy high heel. Gerte was wrong and misguided, and she'd let her rage poison her, but Willa understood.

"Her Diego was an entitled little monster, a cruel, selfish boy who grew into a cruel, selfish man, but nobody's allowed to say a word of that ugly truth because what would Bianca say? What would we do without the great Diego Davis and all the tourist dollars he's still bringing in from beyond the grave?" Gerte jerked a hand toward the sketches, toward the entire gallery full of works of undeniable genius. "So we don't say anything. We smile and we go along and we scrape out our little living by the grace of God and the indulgence of Bianca Davis." Gerte's eyes burned.

"So to answer your question, Willa, there's nothing wrong with me. I simply take every opportunity that comes my way to remind the Davis family that they're no better than the rest of us. They might be richer, but they're no better. And I'd think you, of all people, would agree."

"Why would you think that?" Willa asked evenly.

Gerte tipped her head and considered her closely. "You really do look just like your mother, Willa. Did you know that?"

Her fingers itched to tug on her non-existent ball cap. "No."

"You have her hair. I never noticed before."

"Why would you?" Willa had taken care to erase every bit of resemblance between herself and her mother. Shay had been a wild thing, a dangerous flame. And fire didn't concern itself with what it consumed. It just fed. Willa understood wild things too well to feel safe anywhere near Shay.

Bianca frowned. "Shay was a blonde."

"No, Shay wanted to be a blonde. Shay *chose* to be a blonde. But what God gave her looked more like that." Gerte nodded at Willa's loose hair, an avalanche that had defeated even Georgie. A pulse of shame surfaced through the fury burning away on the other side of the thinnie's calm. "Shay had hair for days, remember?" She sent a measuring look Willa's way, then turned to the sketches on the wall. "This one," she said, and tapped a finger next to the third sketch, the one of the naked back, the flirty invitation and all that wanton hair. "Your hair is just like hers in this one. You could almost be Shay."

"No," Willa heard herself say. "I couldn't be." She could feel Matty's eyes on her but she threw herself toward the thinnie's calm and didn't meet them. She didn't want to. Not yet. "Shay was—" She stopped, shook her head, unable — or maybe just unwilling — to complete the thought. She didn't need to. Everybody knew what Shay had been.

"Yes, she was," Gerte said, her lips thin and disapproving. "And then there was your daddy, drunk more often than not, and dangerous when he was. Peter must've been away at college by then, or nearly. Not that any one of them would've been much help to a girl in trouble. The only other person you could've gone to was—" Gerte's face went slack as comprehension dawned. "Bianca." The hand at her throat crept up to cover her mouth. "A woman who cares more about the Davis name than anything or anybody in the world. Whose answer to everything is money, money and more money." She stopped, thunder-struck. "Bianca bought your baby, didn't she?"

Matty said, "You sold me?" His voice, thin and shocked, threaded into the cracks in Willa's already-battered heart. His pain rooted and spread, became her own. The thinnie's peace strained under the crushing weight of it.

"My God," Gerte murmured, staring at Bianca. "You did. You bought a *child*. For shame, Bianca!"

Shock thickened the air, the rancid scent of Gerte's revulsion shot through with the sharp tang of Matty's confusion and pain. And that pain was overwhelming. Staggering. How could it be otherwise? Gerte had just informed the boy with no grace or compassion whatsoever that his own mother had *sold* him, for God's sake. Willa's chest was so tight she could barely breathe.

She met Eli's gaze almost as an afterthought. She'd nearly forgotten he was there, he'd been so silent. He was shocked, too, unmistakably, and those deep blue eyes held immense sorrow. But it wasn't cold, that sorrow, and there was no judgment in it. He wasn't disappointed or betrayed; he was simply sad for her. For whatever she'd been through. It was as if he could sense her pain across the protective canyon of the thinnie, and it grieved him.

Shock tried to rock her back but he threaded his fingers through hers and kept her close. His palm was wide and warm against her own, and it had gratitude curling up on the other side of the thinnie's buffer like a cat, content to wait until she opened the door between them.

"It was complicated," he said softly to her, and she nodded helplessly. He turned to Bianca, zeroed in on her somehow with an accuracy and an authority that must've served him well when he was still fighting fires. "It was a complicated and difficult situation."

"It was." Bianca moved so that Matty was sandwiched firmly between her and Georgie — the family closing ranks, Willa saw with a bittersweet pang. Matty was her blood but he wasn't her family. And she wasn't his. She'd sold that right years ago. And yet satisfaction glowed inside her like a hot coal. Maybe she wasn't his family but Matty had one in the Davises. They'd given him money and prestige when Willa could offer him nothing but her love. That would've been enough, maybe, the money and the reputation. But it made her sacrifice all the sweeter to know that he had love, too. Georgie studied Eli with a narrow-eyed awareness Willa might've found shocking if she'd had the bandwidth left for reflection. As it was, simply continuing to breathe required all her concentration.

"I'm sure you'll want to discuss it further," Eli said.

Bianca said, "I'll be in touch."

"I'm taking Willa home now."

"You do that."

He nodded to the Davis women. "Thanks for a lovely evening." He turned to Gerte with perfect composure. "You, on the other hand, are a poisonous old bitch and I hope you get everything you deserve."

Chapter 24

ELI SHEPHERDED WILLA onto the sidewalk, and when he held out his hand for the truck keys, she surrendered them without a murmur. Eli's heart ached. He didn't know what the hell had happened just now — he didn't know what had happened fourteen years ago either — but it was all connected and it had torn Willa apart. Her precious stillness was a ragged thing now, clinging to her in tattered shreds. Agony leaked from her, puddled in the air around her, and for the first time, Eli understood what she'd meant when she'd said sadness smelled like rain.

He handed her into the truck, and she sat docilely as a doll while he buckled her seat belt. He glanced up at the sky as he rounded the hood. Clouds swirled and roiled, deepening from green to purple as the sun sank into a steely lake. The storm was coming. It was coming and there was nothing Eli could do about it. Just like there was nothing he could do for Willa. She'd been wounded, deeply and grievously and in a way no doctor could heal. So he took the wheel and did the only thing he knew to do.

He drove her home.

He drove her home but he didn't take her inside. The air was a hot-tempered blast when he opened the truck door and stepped onto her drive. It shoved and slapped at him when he rounded the hood again and handed her down as well. He kept her hand in his and led her across the yard to the path they'd followed a few nights before.

"Do you want me to come with you?" he asked her. For a long moment, she only gazed at him, her fairy eyes wide and blank. And a near-perfect match for Matty's. He hated himself for seeing it. Hated that it was there to see. Hated even more that she'd been robbed of her innocence, while an entire town revered the bastard who'd stolen it.

The urge to do violence surged up in him, curled his free hand into a fist and had sweat popping out on his spine. And he knew once again that he wouldn't get out of this town without punching somebody. He prayed it wouldn't be Gerte, though lord knew she deserved it. If there was a God in heaven — an option that was looking less likely by the moment tonight — maybe He would raise Diego from the dead so Eli could punch him instead. Yeah, he decided. That would make a believer out of him. How about it, Big Guy? One little resurrection so I don't have to go to jail for beating down a poisonous old lady?

There was no answer. He wasn't surprised.

"I don't care," Willa said. She dropped his hand, turned and started down the path. Eli believed her. In that moment, she truly didn't care. Or she'd disconnected herself from caring. She was going to the thinnie, he knew somehow, to either put herself back together, or to fall apart completely. Either way, Eli would be there.

He fell into step behind her as darkness dropped over the forest, and let the rhythm of her footfalls guide him through the night. It was a near-perfect replay of the hike they'd taken a few days ago, but it wasn't his pain accompanying them this time, it was hers. And the darkness wasn't a gentle, welcoming presence this time, it was a naked blade. Thunder grumbled in the bluffs to their north, and distant lightning illuminated the clouds a split-second at a time. It was as if disaster were unfolding in slow motion, the clouds growing heavier, the darkness growing deeper, frame by inevitable frame. Eli could hear the spit and sizzle of sporadic raindrops hitting the dirt path all around him, could see the tiny individual puffs of dust each one sent up from the dangerously hungry earth with every flash of brilliant white.

It was beginning. It was breaking.

After a time, they stepped out of the woods into Willa's clearing. It was the perfect circle Eli remembered, minus the pocket of stars overhead. There was only a black, pregnant sky up there now, dropping lower and lower, pressing them harder and harder into the earth. The wind ramped up to a gusty howl and the trees swayed, jostling up against each other like passengers on a crowded train. The soft wood creaked ominously and Eli followed Willa to the center of the thinnie.

She dropped to her knees beside the rock, spread both hands over the flat surface. Lightning flashed and Eli saw the raindrops, fat and erratic, painting black splotches on the steely gray basalt. Her eyes were closed, and he hesitated. What did she need? What was she listening for? Did she hear it, that song he could almost hear that seemed so accessible to her? Was she soaking it up, healing herself? Filling the jagged rips in her soul with whatever the thinnie offered her?

Then she bent and laid her cheek against the rock between her hands. Her face crumpled with unimaginable pain and a sob escaped her that sliced Eli clean in two.

As if it had only been waiting for Willa to break first, the skies broke, too. A jagged bolt of lightning ripped open the belly of the clouds. Thunder roared and rain lashed down in great, pounding waves. The heavens released a decade's worth of rain while Willa unleashed a lifetime of pain. Eli flung himself forward, dropped down behind her, planted his knees on either side of hers and curled himself over her back. She was so small. He wasn't a huge guy but he covered her almost completely.

He pressed his cheek to hers and twined his fingers through her own cold, shaking ones. The rock radiated heat, evaporating every raindrop with a hot sizzle while Willa howled out her anguish. He couldn't hear her over the crash of the thunder but he could feel it rolling through her body, shaking her, taking her, bruising her. He breathed her in — the hot slice of her pain, the cool wildness of the rain, the

devastated helplessness with which she rode the tide of it all.
Icy needles of water sliced at his back, and the wind swiped
at him like a grizzly bear playing with its dinner. He braced
his forearms on the rock, on the unyielding strength of it, and
let the storm rage in the sky above him. Let the storm rage in
the woman below him.

He had no idea how long it lasted. No idea how much
time had passed before he became aware that while his t-
shirt might be stuck to him like a second skin, it wasn't
getting any wetter. The sky was no longer vomiting fury, and
the woman underneath him had gone quiet. She lay curled
against the rock with an exhausted quiescence. He lifted his
head, opened his eyes and saw the first star winking at him
from a hole in the thinning clouds.

"It's over," she murmured, and shivered. "I'm cold."

He wrapped himself more firmly against the delicate
curve of her spine, covered her body more fully with his own
and closed his eyes again. "I'm here."

"I know." She drew his hand to her cheek, pressed his
palm against her cool skin. "You got wet."

"So did you."

She sighed into the rock, which was still improbably
radiating heat. Eli imagined he'd see steam rising from it if
he bothered to open his eyes. "You're so warm, Eli." She
wriggled as if burrowing into him. Her bottom snuggled into
his crotch and a completely inappropriate spark of interest
flew straight to his dick. "You're always so warm."

Yeah, and getting warmer. He was an awful person. He
inched back, unwilling to watch her shiver but more
unwilling to press his growing erection into her bottom like a
horny teenager. "Let's get you home."

"No." She twisted her fingers through his, snugged him
tight to her back again. "Don't get up. Not yet." She arched,

lifting her bottom straight into exactly what Eli was hoping she hadn't noticed. He sucked in a sharp breath but she only gave a hum of female interest.

"I'm sorry," he muttered.

"Don't be." She circled her bottom against him in a primal invitation that heated his blood. "You feel good."

"Oh, Christ, so do you." Lust shot into his veins, and he found himself meeting her offered bottom in a counter-rhythm older than the rock she was sprawled on. Her hum of interest drifted into an appreciative moan, and need eclipsed reason. Hunger roared, sank sharp claws into his mind but he grabbed at his fleeing decency with both hands. "But I don't think—"

"Good. Don't think. Don't think at all." She captured the tip of his index finger with the moist heat of her curvy lips. His dick jumped and he jerked against her. Lust flooded him and he moaned.

"Willa, please," he managed. "Let me take you home. You need—"

"I need you." She squirmed underneath him as if hunger had her in its claws, too. As if the same needful ache that danced underneath his skin danced under hers, too, raw and demanding. She sat up suddenly, and he leaned automatically back to give her the room she wanted. He watched, fascinated and mute, as she yanked up the sopping hem of her dress and rearranged herself until her knees were outside his. Her bare legs, shiny with rain, glowed under the nascent starlight. He stared helplessly at all that smooth skin, at the shadowy hint of silk just barely exposed under the hem of her skirt. His palms ached with the need to fill his hands with her and take what she offered. To bury himself deep inside the living flame of her.

"Touch me, Eli." She took his hand, threaded her fingers through hers and bent over the rock again. He fell forward with her, braced his free hand against the warm stone. She brought their joined hands to her lips, touched his knuckle with her tongue, a butterfly-light shock. Electricity swept through him, gathering low in his belly, coalescing into a throbbing ball of want. She slid his hand to her breast, and the nipple puckered. It pushed into his palm through the fine fabric of her dress. Need howled inside him and he took the delicate point between his fingers, rolled it gently. She gasped.

"Touch me," she said again, and arched her spine, pushed her breast deeper into his hand, ground her bottom into his pulsing erection. "I want to feel something, Eli. Something good. Something joyful. I want to know that I can." She circled and sought, panting with frustration and need. "Help me, Eli. Give me this."

"Anything you want, Willa." He lifted his other hand from the stone and smoothed a wet spike of hair away from her pale cheek. Her lashes were dark crescents against her luminous skin, and he traced a knuckle down the edge of that pixie-pointed jaw. He drew his palm down the line of her spine next, past the rumpled mass of her skirt to the living heat of her thigh. He hissed out a breath but his hands were gentle, reverent. Because he knew he was telling her the naked truth. He'd already given her his own ugly history. He'd given her his pain, his sorrow, his shame. He'd given her his vulnerability when he'd asked her to stay. When he'd begged her not to run from him, from whatever this was that lived and pulsed between them.

He'd give her his body, too, if that was what she wanted.

He'd give her anything.

Willa pressed her cheek to the familiar warmth of her rock, twined her fingers through Eli's on her breast and shook. She wasn't cold, though, not anymore. For the first time in years, Willa felt clean. Clean and hollow and new. She'd emptied herself with the sky, poured all the secrets and pain, the loneliness and rage out onto this ancient, hallowed ground. And the whole time, Eli had held her. He'd held her through the storm that raged within, letting the storm outside beat its fists on his back while hers stayed warm and dry.

So, no, Willa wasn't cold. How could she be with Eli so hot and hard against her, his desire so pure and uncomplicated that it burned away all her stains?

"Anything you want, Willa," he murmured again. "I'll give it to you."

"You," she said, and she'd never known any higher truth. "I want you."

"Are you sure?"

She pressed her bottom into the hot ridge of his erection. "Try me."

He slid his hand out from under hers, moved it to the back to her thigh and Willa went still, lust sparking in her nipples, pooling hot in her center. He slid one finger under the elastic of her panties and nudged, his touch a gentle question against her most private place. She lifted and offered herself, met him with slick welcome. Eli hissed out a breath through his teeth, and sank that finger deep.

She arched and cried out.

He released a shaky breath. "Okay, so we're doing this."

"Only if you want to live."

He gave a soft chuckle and withdrew slowly. She spread both hands flat on the rock and whimpered but then he added a second finger and slid deep again. Her core quivered and her nipples tightened to aching buds of need. She didn't open her eyes — didn't know if she could — but she twisted sideways to offer them to him. She felt his gaze, hot as a touch, on those stiff, needy points pressing greedily against the wet fabric of her dress. "Jesus, Willa, you're so pretty." He cupped her breast with his free hand, plumped it in his palm and rolled the tip between his fingers. Even through layers of material, the sensation shot from her breast to her core. Her world skidded sideways, and she pushed back into the fingers of his other hand, still stroking deep inside her. But it wasn't enough. She circled and sought, hungry, needful, desperate. It wasn't *enough*.

"Please," she murmured, her mind a helpless sheet of desire. "Eli, please."

"Okay, I know. Just let me—" He urged her upright, found the zipper of her dress and drew it down. She raised her arms, allowed him to lift it away. It landed with a wet slap somewhere in the pine needles, followed by her bra. The night air flowed over her damp skin, steamy and lush, and Eli took her hand, pressed it to her own breast. He used her own fingers to pinch the nipple gently and his lips landed on the tender curve of her neck, hot and open.

"You take over here," he murmured and Willa obeyed without thought, rolling her nipple between her own fingers while sparks exploded behind her closed lids and shimmered through her body. "I'm going to be busy for a while."

He hooked his fingers into the sides of her panties — pretty pink things, thanks to Georgie — and slid them reverently down. He lifted one of her knees then the other, slipping the panties free of each foot with a care that put a funny clutch in her chest. There was another wet plop as they joined her dress somewhere in the woods, followed by Eli's t-shirt. Then there was the shush of his zipper. Foil ripped — protecting her again — and Willa's skin tightened deliciously.

Then his hands were on her hips, his lips on her shoulder and she bent once again to lay herself on the altar of her thinnie. She turned her face to the side, one cheek against the rock's rough heat, the other exposed to the swirling night air, wet and warm as a kiss. He nudged her knees farther apart, put himself between them and she hissed in an electric breath. The tip of his erection found her, plump and swollen and needy, and she moaned. Heat streaked down her legs, exploded in her mind, flooded that aching place between her legs that needed him. She pinched her nipple and felt her core quiver for him in welcome, in demand.

"Oh Christ," he said, and plunged deep. Satisfaction sang through her as he filled her, as he found all her empty, aching places and put himself there. Hunger roared in after it. It wasn't enough. She wanted more. She needed more.

"Eli," she gasped. "I need—"

"I know." His hands flexed on her hips. She could feel him shaking against the backs of her thighs. Or was that her? She didn't know. She was falling apart, disintegrating, sifting away like sand. He withdrew by slow, aching inches and her womb spasmed, clutched at him. He swore and sank deep again. And again. And again. Until there was nothing but him, nothing but the scent of his desire, so clean and pure, swirling in the steamy air rising from the earth all around them. Nothing but his skin against hers as he pushed himself into every empty corner, every lonely forgotten place. And when she was full, when he'd filled her, she clenched around him and exploded in a star-bright fury.

Chapter 25

THEY DRESSED IN fragile silence, as if there were a newborn between them they didn't want to wake. Eli had the oddest sense that there was. Something new and tender and exquisitely valuable had been born between them just now, something they should protect for the rest of their lives if it didn't fly away like an exotic bird.

She turned, swept her hair away from her back and presented him with her zipper. He found the tab and pulled it up slowly, reluctant to hide the delicate line of her spine. He pressed his mouth to the tender curve where her neck met her shoulder and she touched his cheek. Once upon a time, Eli might've felt the need to say something. Tonight he swam through the silence like a fish through water. There would be words soon enough. Ugly ones. Awful ones. Necessary ones. Right now, all Eli needed was her hand in his, and the gift of her smile.

She gave him both and they walked the night path home.

The little cabin glowed in the moon-dappled woods, and Eli glanced with surprise at his watch. A lifetime must've passed since that brutal scene back at the gallery but it wasn't even eleven p.m. yet. And Willa's truck wasn't alone in the drive. There was a shiny Range Rover, too, plus a sleek black beemer and an ancient Ford F350 that somebody had jacked out into a mini-pumper.

The Davises had arrived.

"The reckoning is upon us," Willa murmured beside him.

He tugged her hand and she stopped with him in the shadows at the edge of the woods. "It doesn't have to be." He met her eyes in the darkness, and they were like liquid silver. "We don't have to go in there. You can come home with me."

"I could." She smiled at him. "But I'm not going to. I always knew this would happen someday."

"But it doesn't have to be today. Not if you aren't ready."

She took his other hand and tugged him down until he leaned his forehead against hers. "I'm ready." The air between them was a private garden that twisted and swayed with the scent of rain and pine needles and her. "It's time." She hesitated. "Will you stay, though?" He opened his eyes and gazed down at her. Moonlight limned the angles and edges of her face in silver, and her hair was a wild fairy-tumble over her shoulders. "I don't want to be alone."

He cupped her cheek in one hand, an aching wave of tenderness tightening his throat. "As long as you want me."

She leaned into his palm, her lashes coming down over her eyes. "Thank you."

Eli couldn't help but notice as they started across the yard toward the cabin that she hadn't said how long that might be. An hour? A day? A week? The rest of his life?

But just like before, he knew with unerring certainty that he'd give her whatever she asked of him.

Thirty minutes later, Willa was freshly showered and seated on her lumpy old couch between Eli and Addy. Jackson Davis sat on the arm of the couch next to Addy while Willa's father brewed coffee in the kitchen with a quiet competence she didn't remember from her childhood. Somebody had dragged the straight-backed kitchen chairs into the living room while she'd showered, and Bianca perched on the edge of one like it was a throne, her spine a regal six inches from the back, her hands folded loosely in her lap. Georgie sat beside her mother with that liquid grace of hers, somehow making her creaky old chair look as comfortable as a hammock. Matty sat on the rug between them, his back against the TV stand, elbows propped on knees, big hands dangling limply between them. He frowned into space, as if digesting this new upside-down view of the world Gerte had thrust upon him. Willa's heart ached vaguely, as if the pain were trying to reach her from an immense distance. It was temporary, she knew. Like the aftermath of a traumatic trip to the dentist. The pain was coming. You only had to wait for it.

"Well," Bianca said briskly. "That was quite a scene at the gallery earlier."

"Gerte," Georgie sneered.

"Bitch," Matty muttered.

"Language," Bianca said and flicked his ear, then turned it into a caress. "Not that I'll argue with the sentiment." She sighed. "But it was bound to happen."

"What was bound to happen?" Matty asked dully. "I'd find out that you bought me from a fourteen-year-old?"

Willa experienced another buffeting gust of distant pain but nothing penetrated. Bianca smoothed a hand over Matty's dark head and he closed his eyes, to Willa's everlasting gratitude. She was temporarily immune to pain, not bullet-proof.

"I've spoken to Matty," she informed Willa. "I explained everything, and in much more accurate and compassionate terms than Gerte was able to summon. But he wasn't going to be satisfied until he heard it from you." She released a determined breath. "Obviously, my credibility with him isn't what it could be these days." She gave Willa a tight, close-lipped smile. "So here we are."

Willa studied her like she was a brand new entity, an unknown quantity she'd never tangled with before. She might as well be. There was an emptiness inside Willa now where all that hatred and resentment used to live, and it was so new, so vast. It was hard to adjust to the hugeness of it, the lightness. The absence. It was negative space, like a missing tooth or an amputated limb, and Willa was still trying to get her balance back.

The one thing she knew, however, was that she *would* get used to it. She'd been released from the prison of her secret, and she wasn't going back, not ever. Not even for Matty. It was time to tell the truth.

"I'll tell you everything," Willa said. "Everything I know, though I don't know all of it."

Bianca's dark eyes narrowed. "What do you mean, you don't know all of it? What could you possibly not know?"

Georgie touched her mother's clenched hands. "Mom. Let her talk." She waved lazily at Willa. "Go on."

"Before I start," she said to Matty, sitting so still and silent between his mother and his sister, "you need to know something." She waited until he lifted those gray eyes to hers, and the shock of recognition, of *connection* sang through her like a cracking whip. "I always loved you. I would've kept you if I could, if there was any way at all. But I was only a little older than you are now when you were born, and my choices were limited. By my age, by my circumstances." She shrugged. "I was a Zinc, you know."

She paused when Brett came into the living room, carrying a coffee pot and a handful of chipped mugs. She glanced at him, waited for the usual pinch of resentment but nothing came. She was still echoingly empty, but it was a clean, bright space with no room for an abandoned child's anger. She reached out and took the mugs from him, set them in a neat row on the coffee table at her knees. He flashed her a look of tentative gratitude. She met it, accepted it. He blinked in surprise.

"I'll get some milk and sugar," he said slowly.

"No, Dad," Willa said. "Stay. You need to hear this as much as anybody."

"I'll get it," Addy said and rose. Jax rose as well but she said, "No, you stay, too. It'll just take a second."

Jax subsided onto the arm of the couch where he'd been

221

perched beside his fiancée.

"I *am* a Zinc," Willa continued while Addy bustled around in the kitchen, "and in this town that's as loaded a name as Davis. Except where *Davis* means money and privilege and talent, *Zinc* means drunk and disorderly and possibly dangerous."

Brett folded into an empty chair, his head bowed. "That was my fault, Willa. You shouldn't have had to carry the weight of my mistakes."

She shrugged. *Should've* was a wish without the birthday candles. She continued talking to Matty, only to him. "This story — our story — isn't a nice one, Matisse. But if there's one thing I want you to hear while I tell it, one thing I want you to believe? It's that I *wanted* you. I never wanted anything more than you in my life. But you weren't my baby. I didn't give birth to you."

Addy froze in the act of placing a little pitcher of milk on the table. Her eyes were round and green. "I couldn't find any sugar," she said blankly.

"Excuse me?" Bianca's spine snapped even straighter if such a thing were possible, and her lips went white. "Of course you gave birth to him!"

"Screw the sugar," Jax said and tugged Addy onto the couch beside him again, threaded his fingers through hers.

Eli's hand crept up to rest against the small of Willa's back, his palm warm and strong and reassuring. It gave her the courage to ignore the blistering power of Bianca's fury and keep her focus on the boy they both loved. She spoke to him, only to him. He stared at her, those familiar eyes guarded, that beautiful face a careful blank.

"I was fourteen in the sketches we all saw tonight. Fourteen years old and dizzy in love with an amazing boy. A boy who looked just like you."

"Except for my eyes," Matty said slowly. "Nobody in our family has them. I always assumed I got them from my mother, but if you're not her—"

"You did get them from your mother." Willa tipped her head in acknowledgement. "I got mine from the same woman."

Matty stared, uncomprehending, but Brett jerked as if she'd struck him. "Shay?"

"Oh dear God," Addy said, her fingers going to her open mouth.

"You're not my son, Matty," Willa said gently. "You're my brother."

Jax said, "Holy shit," and even Georgie snapped out of her slouch to blink owlishly. Bianca went unnaturally still, her mouth open while the scent of her horror, cold and jagged, leached into the air around her. It all but burned Willa's nose but she still didn't take her eyes off Matty. Bianca dropped a hand to the boy's shoulder and he seized it with both hands like she'd thrown him a life preserver.

"Who's Shay?" he asked, his voice shaking.

Eli's thumb stroked her back, a silent infusion of courage and Willa went on.

"My mother's name was Shay," she told Matty. "She was beautiful and charming and selfish and vain, and when I was a little girl, I loved her. God, I worshipped her. I orbited her the way a planet circles the sun. She used to dress me up like a little doll and take me out to lunch or shopping. People would always stop us to say how pretty we were."

"I remember that," Brett murmured, his eyes unseeing. "She'd do your hair just like hers, put on those matching blue dresses, and come by the bar for lunch just to show you off."

"No, Dad." Willa smiled faintly. "Not to show *me* off, but to show off, period. If there's one thing a sociopath loves, it's attention. And she loved all the attention she got from the guys who hung around the taproom, all your cop buddies from your days on the force."

Brett flinched. Willa regretted causing him pain but his mistakes were his own to reconcile. She had her hands full with her own.

"But I got older and so did Shay." Her shoulders had somehow found their way up to her ears. She stopped, pulled in a deep breath, let it out slowly. Consciously let go of the past, and let her shoulders melt back down. "I hit puberty while Shay was looking down the barrel of forty, and suddenly, I wasn't so fun to take out in public. I developed early and kind of, ah, enthusiastically." Matty's cheeks went a dull red and he studied his knees carefully. "Men started to look at me with the interest they should've given her, and Shay couldn't stand that. Never mind that I had no idea what to do with that kind of interest. At that point, I hardly even understood it existed. But sociopaths can't really see things from any point of view but their own, and the only currency Shay understood or dealt in was sex. It was her trump card, and nobody else was allowed to play it. Particularly not her daughter."

"Jesus," Brett said wearily and dragged a hand down his face. "What kind of mother thinks about her own kid that way?"

"Look at me, Dad. This is her face, her body, even her hair. I wasn't her kid. I was the competition."

"And she hated you for that. She must have."

"Hate was all she had," Willa said. "Anyway, that was when she started…acting out."

"Sexually, you mean," Bianca said. She frowned first at Willa, then shifted that dark gaze to Brett. Willa frowned, too. Had she really caught the faintest whiff of sympathy? From Bianca?

"That was when she stopped threatening to have an affair and actually had a few," Brett said and rolled his empty coffee cup between his palms. "That was when I stopped having just a couple drinks every night and started having a couple dozen." His smile was thin. "Because when your wife tells you you're not man enough to satisfy her, that she's looking to supplement her diet so to speak, it's better to pass out on a bar stool than try to sleep in your own empty bed."

Matty dropped his forehead to his knees, clearly past his limit on mortifying adult confessions. Willa wished she could spare him some of it but didn't see any way around it.

"She preferred cops," Willa said.

"Ah, hell." Brett closed his eyes, drew in a long breath through his nose.

"I'm sorry," Willa said, sympathy beating its fists on the other side of all that empty space inside her.

Eli looked a question at her but Brett was the one who answered.

"I used to be a cop, remember," Brett told him with a crooked smile. "I couldn't play football anymore but I could still put the beat-down on a guy, and I was young enough to mistake muscle for courage. Stupid enough to mistake it for justice." He lifted defeated shoulders. "I'd love to say I learned my lesson but—" His jail sentence sat in that brief silence, ugly and unspoken.

"There was one guy in particular, a cop that used to hang around the bar flirting with Mom," Willa said. "Then one day, he was flirting with me instead. Harmless stuff at first, then progressively less so." Brett pressed a fist to his forehead and Willa hurried to say, "He never crossed a line, Dad. Never touched me. I didn't even understand most of it. I just knew he made me uncomfortable. But Mom understood. Mom caught every last little innuendo, and knew he was getting off on it. It didn't matter to her that he was indulging a vaguely pedophilic kink by talking sex to a twelve-year-old. All she knew was that he was looking at me, not her, and that was unacceptable. So she got his attention back."

"Christ." Brett knocked that fist slowly against his forehead.

"It became a pattern. Some poor guy would pay me a compliment and suddenly Shay's got him in the crosshairs. And like any sociopath, Shay was very, very good at figuring out exactly how to get what she wanted. At knowing exactly where you're weak, where she can apply pressure to get you to give it to her. And once you'd given it to her, she had no conscience about using your mistake as leverage to get more." She paused to glance at Brett's slumped shoulders. No help for it. "She had half the sheriff's department in her pocket."

"Fair exchange for letting them into her pants," Georgie murmured.

Matty made a pained noise. Willa's heart tried to break for him but she gathered up the stillness and clung to it. Wrapped it around herself like a blanket. Wished she could wrap him up, too. God, this must be hard to hear. She'd had years to come to terms with the horror that had been her mother. Matty's world must be blowing apart.

"That was pretty much how she saw it," Willa said.

"You paid for my defense lawyers." Brett dropped his hand and stared at Willa as if he'd never seen her before. "I don't know how you did it, but you paid."

Willa met his eyes. "You weren't getting anything like a fair shake from the legal system, and I knew why."

"I pled guilty, Willa."

"You *were* guilty. At least you felt guilty. Guilty enough to put your thumb on the wrong side of your own scale." She shrugged. "I put mine on the other."

"Why?"

"We might not've ever functioned like a healthy family but you're my father. I had an obligation. Plus I saw what it did to you, living with the weight of bad choices. I didn't want that for myself. I wanted better."

He closed his eyes again and fell silent. The entire room was silent, and it waited, hungry for the ugliness she was going to feed it.

"So Shay was sleeping around," she said, "rubbing Brett's nose in it and putting me in my place." She paused to gather her courage. "Then Diego happened."

Chapter 26

MATTY LIFTED HIS head and fixed her with those piercing eyes. His sharp regard echoed inside the numbness under Willa's sternum, and she rubbed at it, concerned. Was his pain breaking important things inside her? She supposed she'd know soon enough. Beside him, Bianca drew in a sharp breath, but pressed her lips together and stayed silent. Georgie just gazed at her, unblinking and tense. Addy's hand crept to her arm, rubbed it comfortingly.

Willa's throat tightened at the small kindness and she sent her a look of gratitude. Was surprised to find Jax gazing at her, too, with sad compassion mixed into the warmth she'd always found there in the depths of his bark-brown eyes. She'd always assumed Bianca had kept him in the dark, that he was only kind to her because he didn't know the truth. But now she wondered if that kindness was simply a building block of his character. Another thing to think about later. When she wasn't tearing several worlds apart. God, this was taking forever. She wished she could just download the whole thing into public knowledge instead of wading through the blood and the shit like it was yesterday.

"Or I guess I should say that Peter and Diego happened." She sighed, resigned to wading in. "They'd hatched some plot to cheat their way through math together. Not that Peter needed math help. Numbers are his first and only true love."

Georgie snorted. "Believe me, we know. I learned the hard way how Peter's mind works."

"Everybody does eventually," Willa told her. "I'm sorry he hurt you."

"He didn't." She waved that off with one languid hand.

"He pissed me off, no question. But he didn't hurt me."

Willa nodded. Hurt followed love, and nobody had ever imagined Peter and Georgie had been a love match.

Georgie said, "So what was Peter after if not the grades?"

"Social capital," she said simply. "It didn't matter how many tackles he made, how many grading curves he set. End of the day, Peter was still a Zinc. He and Diego had always been friendly but this would make them friends. This would pull Peter into a rarified orbit reserved for the Davises and their equals. Which wasn't us. By the time Diego came into our lives, Mom had been slutting around for a few years already, Dad was wasted most of the day and the fighting was constant. Violent. Everybody knows how often the cops were here, but you might not know how much Mom enjoyed leaning into the swing and showing off her new shiner for the responding officer."

Matty stared dully at her. "She did that? Really?"

"I'm sorry, Matty, I know this sucks to hear but it's true. Cops are protectors by nature, and Shay was a predator. She understood exactly what kinds of buttons the sight of a battered woman pressed in their psyches." She shifted her focus to Brett and said, "Not that I'm excusing you, Dad. You were so much bigger and stronger than Mom. You had a responsibility to keep it together." Brett nodded and eyed the hands in his lap with pure dislike. As if he were chained to them against his will. "But you were never the one who got physical first. And while Mom slapped me into next week pretty regularly, you never laid a hand on me, or on Peter as far as I ever saw. But you know what I did see? Shay hitting you and hitting you and hitting you, then leaning in when anybody who truly didn't want a shiner would've leaned out."

"That bitch," Bianca breathed. "That unmitigated, black-souled bitch."

"She was ruthless, she was smart, and she knew what she wanted."

"Which was?" Georgie asked, one brow arched.

"Exactly what Peter wanted. What he still wants." Willa lifted helpless shoulders. "More. Just always *more*."

"And Diego had more written all over him, didn't he?" Georgie said.

Willa's stomach twisted mercilessly but she ignored it and pushed forward. "Yeah, he did. He walked around in a cloud of charisma and talent, and everything he touched glowed. The way he saw things, the way he made me see things, the way he made me see myself, it was—" She lifted helpless shoulders. "Keep in mind, I was fourteen and inclined to be dazzled, but God, he was intoxicating. I could hardly look directly at him. It was like trying to look at the sun."

Addy's hand was warm and comforting on her arm. "He *was* dazzling, Willa. And he knew it. He used it."

"I know." She smiled ruefully. "I know it now, anyway." She shook her head and went on. "Sometimes he'd come by early, while Peter was at some practice or other and we'd sit in the yard. It was awful in the house, but it was springtime so we always sat in the yard. There was a little meadow I loved, this beautiful clearing at the end of a path in the back—" Eli's hand on her back tensed and she wished she could reassure him. Wished she could tell him that nothing awful had ever happened at their thinnie. Wished she could promise him that it was and always had been a place of beauty. But she'd scoured herself clean this night and there was no more room inside her for mistruths. She swallowed and went on.

"By summer it was our place. The silence there was so clean and warm, and the light was incredible. Or so he told me. We met there before or after his sessions with Peter. I'd lie in the grass and he'd draw me. He acted like I was doing him a favor by letting him but I knew better. I was being drawn by Diego Davis. Even then, it was staggering to be at the center of that kind of talent and purpose. That kind of desire. And it was desire, even if I didn't know it at the time. All I knew was that a beautiful boy with magic in his fingers was looking at me like I was something special. Like I was worth something. Like there was something rare and beautiful in me that nobody else could see. But he could, and with his magic pencil, he pulled it to the surface where everybody else could see it, too. I was so beautiful, so special. The line of my leg was just incredible, could I hike my skirt up a little higher? Your shoulder, Willa, it's art. I can't capture the line, can't quite get it right. Could you just slide your shirt down so I can see more? I need to trace, touch, feel..." She trailed off, shook off the memory. "Take." She blew out a shuddering breath. "He wanted to take everything I had, and when I'd given it to him — because of course I did — the mystery was solved. There was nothing else to be explored. He'd finished with me, and I was empty. Broken. Used and worthless."

"Oh, honey." Addy tipped her curly head onto Willa's shoulder. "I'm so sorry."

"I thought my mom would be furious with me when she found out but she wasn't. She held me while I cried, and I hadn't been held in so long. She said how she'd show him. How she'd teach him a lesson he wouldn't soon forget."

Willa laughed, and it was raw with pain. "I don't know what I thought she meant. I never imagined she'd revenge-seduce him, for God's sake. But she did."

Bianca only shook her head, her fingers still pressed to her eyes.

"How very Mrs. Robinson of her," Georgie murmured.

"She was that kind of mom," Jax said. Addy glared at him and he said, "What? She was. Guys talk and it was a generally accepted opinion that, of all the hot moms in town, Shay Zinc was the Lady Most Likely when it came to giving a young man his first taste of glory." He shook his head. "Damn. I can't believe Diego never told me that."

"I don't know if she meant to get pregnant," Willa said,

"but she did. I, on the other hand, didn't." She met Matty's eyes. He'd been silent, absorbing her words with total focus. "I've never been pregnant. Not with you or anybody else."

"But—" Bianca broke off, stared sightlessly at Willa. "But Shay told us Diego had gotten you pregnant."

"Of course she said that. If she told you the truth, not only would you have stripped her of custody without paying her a dime but she'd have gone to prison."

"Amen," Georgie said promptly. "Because child abuse."

"God, she played me so well." Bianca blinked, a scene clearly playing out in her mind. "It was early spring and she came to Hill Top House one day while you kids were all at school. Told me Diego had gotten Willa pregnant, and we were going to be grandmothers together. It wasn't ideal, of course, but a baby! A baby is always a celebration, she said. We would have to work out how to share custody, of course, but family was the most important thing. It takes a village and what a lucky child to have such a village." Bianca's mouth soured. "That was what she said, anyway. But I saw her looking around Hill Top House like it was up for auction. Like I was impoverished nobility, and she was the tacky American heiress my father had rustled up for me, propping up our years of breeding with her great bags of money. She thought she had me over a barrel, that I would have no choice but to welcome her into our family."

Jax laughed. "She had no idea who she was dealing with."

"She figured it out when I threatened to use every police report she'd ever filed to strip Willa of custody the minute that baby was born and paternity verified. The Zincs were dangerous, and I'd never let them touch any baby of Diego's, let alone insinuate themselves into our life. But, God, she was good." She laughed softly. "She never even mentioned money. She let me think it was my idea."

"What was your idea?" Matty asked slowly.

"A closed, private adoption. Diego was too young, too

talented. I wouldn't have him tied down by even the knowledge of what he'd done. Diego had his flaws, God knows, but he was going to fly. He was born to fly and I was going to see that he did. I'd be damned if I'd clip his wings because of a youthful indiscretion. I named an outrageous sum, far too much, but I had conditions."

"She'd take me away," Willa supplied. "Shay and I would have to disappear until the baby was born."

Bianca inclined her head. "The timing worked out. Matty was due in late August so Willa — God, *Shay* — wouldn't have started showing until May or so. Shay agreed to take Willa away the instant school let out. She told everybody they were going to visit relatives in Illinois but I paid for a little villa in Italy instead. Willa — God, *Shay* — would give birth at a private hospital there, and all the arrangements would be made for a private adoption.

"I booked a mother-daughter tour of Europe that summer for Georgie and me so I could spontaneously deliver one of those menopause babies you always read about while in Italy. Joe and I had planned to tell everybody Matty was our late-life surprise-a-baby. He'd always wanted one more baby, you know." She squeezed Matty's shoulder. "He'd have loved you so much, Matty. I wish more than anything he could've met you, even once. His death that spring was—" Bianca stopped, pressed her lips together and pulled in a deep breath. "Well, it was awful. But it was probably why people were so willing to accept — publicly, at least — that you were mine." She smiled crookedly. "Fate had taken my husband. Maybe it owed me Matty." She sighed. "There was talk, of course, but Gerte wasn't entirely wrong tonight. There are some advantages to wealth and social position, and I used every one of them to scotch the gossip."

"So did I," Georgie sighed. "I hadn't even gotten my period yet, but somehow I'd delivered a secret baby over the summer." She examined a lock of silky hair for split ends and tossed it over her shoulder with insouciant disregard.

"You can stare people out of that," she said, "but it's not easy."

"And you did it beautifully." Bianca leaned across Matty to touch her knee. "You make me proud," she said softly. "Every single day, you make me proud."

Georgie covered her mother's hand with her own and squeezed. Willa's heart ached. Nobody had ever been proud of her. She'd been so good, worked so hard, denied herself so much and all she'd ever gotten was contempt.

"It was worth it," Bianca said, and resumed her regal posture. Her hand, however, had drifted from Georgie's knee to Matty's shoulder. "It was worth every penny and every lie to keep Shay out of Matty's life."

"But you thought Willa was my mother." Matty lifted his head and stared at his mother.

"I assumed they were a package deal." Bianca stroked Matty's hair and turned to Willa. "Birds of a feather. You gave me every reason to think so."

"I did," Willa said. She stopped to swallow, to savor the steady weight of Eli's hand on her back. He'd been silent this whole time but his hand hadn't moved. Hadn't wavered. He was right there beside her, loyalty and uncompromising support in every second of that touch. Something squeezed inside her, something tender and dangerous. Something she hadn't felt in ages and didn't particularly want to feel now.

She turned to Matty. "After you were born, we had two precious weeks before we had to give you up. Shay would've handed you over the second they cut the cord, but you were a little early and the Italians insisted. I don't think I slept the entire two weeks." She smiled, her heart in bloody pieces at the memory, but in a way she'd never regretted. "I held you, I fed you, I rocked you. I sang to you, changed you, bathed you. I fell in love with you. Giving you up ripped my heart right out of my chest but by then I'd begun to understand. I'd begun to grasp what being a Zinc meant in Devil's Kettle. And it meant that I could never, ever keep you. Giving you to Bianca meant that you could grow up with money, privilege and a family that knows what loyalty is. What love is. Keeping you would mean robbing you of all that opportunity, and in exchange for what?" She gave a soft laugh. "A family so dysfunctional that when my mother disappeared, everybody — including my own brother — assumed my father had killed her?"

She forced herself to look straight into those eyes — her eyes, Shay's eyes — and meet all that accusation and pain head-on. "So, yeah, Matty. I loved you with everything in me. Which is why I did everything my mother told me to do. I let your mom believe you were mine, and I let her believe she could have you if she paid me. My mom took that money and did us all the massive favor of disappearing while I tried to figure out how to hold up my end of the bargain and stay away from you. I couldn't stop loving you, but I could stay away from you. And I did, faithfully." Her fingers were numb but she clenched her fists harder. "I only faltered once."

Those eyes narrowed. "Faltered how?"

Chapter 27

SHE DROPPED HER gaze. She couldn't look at him and tell this part. "You were born in August and Shay was gone by September, off spending her money, I guess. Peter had left for college by then, and Brett was as deep in the bottle as I'd ever seen him, what with everybody talking about how he'd killed his wife. By January, I was out of my mind with grief and loneliness. It had been nearly six months since I'd held you but I could still feel you in my arms, the soft, warm weight of you, the clean baby scent of you. It was like phantom limb syndrome, where an amputee can still feel their missing hand or foot or whatever, and it drives them mad. You were like that for me. I ached for you, but you were gone.

"Only you weren't. I could see you every day. I knew exactly where to find you. I knew it was the right place for you, too, and I tried to stay strong. I tried so hard but one night I broke. I went to Hill Top House and I rang the bell and I begged."

She spread helpless hands and gave thanks for that clean, bright space between her heart and the tears that wanted to rise. But God, they were right on the other side of the void, so close to the surface. "I was like a junkie who needed a fix. I must've been terrifying."

"You said you wanted Matty," Bianca said.

"I did." She blew out a breath. "I didn't want to take him from you, though. I only wanted to hold him. I was like a nursing mother who'd been separated from her baby. It was almost feral, the way I craved him in my arms." She smiled faintly. "I don't even know what I said. I only remember that

Georgie came into the foyer then, and she was holding him."
She shifted her eyes to Matty. "Holding you."

"You *were* feral," Georgie said. "Your hair was out to
there, and your eyes were—"

"Recognizable," Matty finished for her. "You couldn't
look at her without knowing I belonged, somehow or other,
to her. Isn't that right?"

"Yes," Georgie allowed, "but she wasn't fully with it,
either, Matty. You have to know that. She wasn't in her right
mind and she wanted you." She touched her brother's hair
with a loving finger. "And we weren't having it. You were
ours. As much ours as hers, anyway, and she was scaring
us."

"More importantly, though, I scared *you*," Willa told
Matty. "You cried."

"I did?"

She lifted stiff shoulders. "You didn't recognize me. You
weren't my brother anymore, you were hers. It was her arms
you wanted, her neck you hid your face in." She gave him a
plastic smile while her heart tried to bleed. "And that was
when I finally snapped out of the fever dream I'd been living
in the past six months. That was when my heart finally got it.
You were gone. Truly gone." She shifted her eyes to
Bianca's. "So when your mom offered me one final cash
settlement in exchange for my signature on a document
forswearing any future claim to familial rights, I signed it.
You were already lost to me whether I took the money or
not, and it was just me and Brett by then. With the way he
was drinking?" She shook her head. "I was essentially the
only adult in my life. Let's just say the money came in
handy."

"Jesus Christ," Jax murmured, and Addy just rubbed a
damp cheek against her shoulder.

Georgie stared. "I thought you came to shake us down. I
thought you came to ask for more money. I thought—"

"You thought I was monster enough to look at my own

child and see dollar signs. You thought I was just like Shay." Willa shrugged. "You had reason to."

"I hated you."

"And honestly, I respected you for it. If Matty had been mine, I'd have destroyed anybody who tried to hurt him." She lifted a brow. "I'm not going to thank you for it, though. You made high school a living hell."

"I'm not going to apologize any more than you're going to thank me." She shrugged. "But we both know what we know."

Willa nodded. That was as close to a peace treaty as she and Georgie would ever hammer out, she figured. "So I took the money, and did my part to make sure that nobody had any reason to ever look my way where Matty was concerned. I kept my head down, my hat on, my mouth shut. I went to the woods and stayed there as much as I could. There was comfort in it. Safety." She smiled faintly. "People think animals are dangerous but they've never been caught in the crossfire when the alpha females of Devil's Kettle go at it."

"Amen," Addy said fervently. Bianca sent her a sharp look and she made a face. "What? I love you, Bianca, but you're terrifying."

Bianca smiled smoothly. "Thank you, darling."

Georgie caught Willa's eye and delivered her own version of that slick, dangerous smile. "I learned from the best."

"Davis genes run strong and true," Willa admitted. She nodded at Matty. "He's yours to the bone. Outside of those eyes, there's not a bit of Shay in him."

Brett said, "Thank Christ."

"There's plenty of Diego, though," Addy put in. "Enough to worry me sometimes."

Matty smiled grimly. "And not enough to satisfy my mom."

"Untrue, darling." Bianca cupped a fond hand around his nape. "Seeing Diego's old sketches reminded me of how messy and unformed emerging talent is. You have to let it be born before you can guide it, and that means letting it take whatever shape it will." She patted his cheek. "You really want to draw graphic novels?"

A knife-sharp smile dawned slowly across his face, a budding version of Bianca's favorite weapon. He said, "Comic books."

She sighed but fluttered serene fingers. "Go for it. Gorge on it. Draw caped crusaders until you're sick of them. And when you're finally satisfied, when you're ready for more, we'll talk."

He eyed her cautiously. "No more Friday Art Academy?"

"Not until you ask for it."

"Sweet." He turned to Jax, his grin boyish and delighted. "What about my job at the station?"

Jax smiled back, as boyish and delighted as his brother, and Willa understood that this smile, too, was a Davis legacy. "Oh, your butt is still mine until school starts."

"Aw." But the disappointment was all for show. Underneath it was satisfaction and love. Matty knew he was adored. Knew he was wanted. Knew that he was part of something unbreakable and true.

"Don't take it so hard, kid," Jax said. "Graham Graves has his eye on you to help him run the hose for the Devil Days slip-and-slide."

Matty blanched. "He keeps asking me to lift with him."

"We're firefighters, son," Jax said solemnly. "We run the slip-and-slide shirtless."

He blinked. "I'm nearly six feet tall, and I weigh like 130 pounds."

"Hence the weight room."

Matty scowled. Jax laughed. Georgie rolled her eyes.

"Can we get back to business, please?" she said. "We still haven't dealt with the big question of the night."

Willa tensed. "Which is?"

"If Gerte has anything to say about it, everybody's going

to know I'm not Matty's mother by sunrise, if they don't already. They're going to think you are. So do we let that misunderstanding hold? Or do we rip the Band Aid off and go public with the whole thing?"

"Shay is a sociopath," Willa said slowly. "That means delusions of both grandeur and persecution. She knows in her bones that she was born to be rich and famous, and if she's not, it isn't because she doesn't deserve it. It's because everybody's jealous and they're undermining her. So if you think there's a chance in hell she'd let me be publicly named as mother to the kid who could grow up to be the next Diego Davis, you're wrong. It doesn't matter what you say, or what story you tell. If the news breaks that Matty is Diego's son rather than his brother? Shay's coming home."

"So we don't break the news," Bianca said firmly.

"I don't think you have a choice," Brett said quietly. He dropped his elbows to his knees and studied his linked fingers. "Unless Gerte's changed completely since I went to prison, half the town already knows Diego's the father by now. And possibly a reporter or two as well."

Peter Zinc pulled up to the unimaginative square of aluminum siding he'd grown up in and parked behind a small army of cars spanning the gamut from a sleek BMW to a firetruck. Shit. The Davises had beaten him here. He'd avoided the gallery tonight but gossip moved faster than fire in Devil's Kettle, and it hadn't taken more than five minutes for him to hear the whole story.

Jesus. Willa and Diego? He hadn't seen that one coming. Of course he hadn't. He pinched the bridge of his nose and tried to think back. He'd been so wrapped up in his own plans to get the hell out of this place, he hadn't had the bandwidth to pay attention to anything else. Between busting the grading curve in every class and busting his ass on the football field, he'd been too busy to check up on Willa. She wasn't his job, anyway. Christ, he'd been a kid himself. He'd had his hands full.

But if he *had* taken a minute to pay attention? If he *had* stopped his feverish marathon of maximizing opportunity, would he have wondered why exactly Diego had sought him out? Sure, Peter had known his shit, math-wise, but so had Diego. It had taken about three minutes to understand that Diego and numbers got along just fine. He'd assumed the kid just liked to fuck with authority, which Peter fully respected. As to why he'd chosen Peter for his partner in crime? Well, Peter was a Zinc, easily thrown under the bus if they got caught.

It was a risk Peter had been more than willing to take. Social capital, after all, was the one element of success you couldn't earn, buy or fake. It lay at the intersection of breeding, money, charisma and admiration, and you either had it or you didn't. Peter didn't, but an endorsement from somebody who had it in spades might correct that. Somebody like Diego Davis.

It had never crossed Peter's mind that Diego might be after anything beyond a convenient scapegoat. Jesus. Willa had been all of fourteen, skinny and needy and only barely civilized. Why would he have thought anything like that?

Because you knew Diego, his conscience whispered. Because you knew what he was. Because you know that even if he'd come right out and named Willa as his price for a golden ticket to social glory, you might've looked the other way. You might've.

Shame touched him with greasy fingers and Peter rolled his shoulders impatiently. God, enough. The past was the past, and there was no changing it so there was no point in raking himself over the coals for something he hadn't even been consciously aware of.

Besides, why rake himself over the coals at all when Georgie was inside? She'd do it for him, and happily.

And you deserve it, his conscience whispered mercilessly.

He switched off the ignition and started for the cabin, walking straight toward the past he'd run so far and so fast from.

Chapter 28

THE SILENCE GREETING Brett's weary pronouncement wasn't, to Eli's ear, either shock or disappointment. It was more like the moment between dropping the match and the flames roaring to life. It was an airless vacuum suspended in time, with no room to react, only to dread.

And into that moment walked Peter Zinc. He didn't bother to knock, just opened the door and walked in like he owned the place. Like he had a right to the family within it. A hot spurt of fury leapt up inside Eli and he forced himself to blow out a slow breath. Rage was sloshing around inside him like a restless ocean tonight and every revelation lifted the tide another inch. It was just looking for a handy outlet, and Peter looked awfully handy. But walking into one's childhood home without knocking wasn't, Eli reminded himself carefully, a punching offense.

"Hey, Willa," Peter said smoothly. He was a tall guy, like his dad, well over six feet, and lanky with it. He'd shaved his head down to a shine, and while Eli hoped it was a pitiful response to a receding hairline, he had to admit the guy had the bones for it. He was prettier than most women. There was, he supposed, some cold comfort in that. Peter shifted his dark gaze to his father. "Dad."

Brett shot out of his chair and stood uncertainly. "Peter. You're, uh, here."

Peter sighed ruefully. "I am." He looked around the little cabin, his dismissive gaze touching on the shabby couch, on the scarred kitchen table, on the ancient pine-paneled walls. On the sister he'd abandoned, sitting so composed and silent in the middle of it all. "And everything's just where I left it."

"It's good to see you," Brett offered.

Peter only smiled at that, and Eli wondered what it was with this town and the smiles that meant everything but welcome.

"Why are you here, Peter?" Willa asked. She studied him curiously. "You've been back in town for years now and you've never come here before. Why are you here now?"

"I heard the news," Peter said, and slid his hands into his pockets. "Guess you had yourself quite a night." He nodded toward Matty. "And I'm not talking about just tonight, either. Sounds like you and Diego had yourselves quite a summer back in the day."

Georgie surveyed her ex-fiancé idly. "You're such a dick, Peter."

"If you like." His smile grew and Eli wouldn't have been surprised to see a few extra rows of razor-sharp teeth, like sharks had. "But at least I had the decency to offer you marriage in exchange for the Davis name."

"Try the Davis money," Georgie sniffed.

"They don't come apart." He glanced at Willa. "Unlike, evidently, my sister's legs."

Eli wasn't even aware he'd moved until he found himself standing over Peter's prone body, his knuckles singing with pain, his brain alive with satisfaction. But his fists wanted more. He wanted Peter to get back up so he could hit him again. Punching was like salty snacks. Once you started, one was never enough.

"If you get up," he said tightly, "I *will* put you back on your ass."

"I believe you," Peter said. "Fuck." He sat up and touched a trickle of blood at the corner of his mouth. "You pack one hell of a punch for a little dude."

"There's more where that came from," Eli told him. "*Please* get up."

Peter laughed and Eli had the strangest impression that he

was tempted. Like he almost wanted Eli to punch his stupid face in, to whale on him until oblivion claimed him and he could float away on the blackness. Eli had known guys like that on the fireline. Part of the convict crews, usually, or guys who'd done time. Guys who sought out the pain and the risk because they thought they deserved it. It wasn't a job for them so much as penance. Or a daily round of Russian roulette.

It was enough to uncurl the fists at his sides, to push him back a step. He'd been, he realized with a dull shock, straddling Peter's expensive loafers, just waiting to swing again. Christ.

"Are you finished?" Jax asked him. "Because I've got next ups."

"Stop, both of you," Willa said. "He's just winding you up. Don't let him." Eli turned to look at her. She, however, was looking at Peter. "Stop stalling, Peter. What are you really here for?"

He drew up his knees and draped his arms across them. "I just learned I have a nephew, Willa. You don't think that's enough cause to visit?"

"You have a brother," she told him shortly, "and no."

"A brother?" Nothing in his face or posture even shifted, as far as Eli could see. One eyebrow winged up, though, and some seriously genius-level machinery kicked into high gear behind his eyes. It was...disconcerting, Eli decided. That kind of brain power wrapped up in such an emotion-free package. He sighed. "Shay?"

"Shay."

He palmed his face. "Christ."

"What do you want, Peter?" Willa asked again, her voice as blank as her brother's heart.

"A minute to digest this." He glanced at Matty, then at Bianca. "Seriously? Shay?"

"She led us to believe it was Willa." Bianca smiled tightly.

Georgie's smile was more leisurely but no less dangerous. "And Mom led the entire town to believe it was me."

"But it was Shay," Willa said softly. "It was always Shay."

Peter turned dispassionate eyes to his father. "Is that why you killed her?"

At the far end of the couch, Addy gasped sharply. She was probably the only person in this room with a pure enough heart and a clean enough conscience to be truly shocked at the accusation.

"I didn't kill Shay," Brett said wearily. "She took off. Once Bianca paid her, she left. Disappearing like that was just a flourish, a final fuck you to me and our marriage." He smiled sadly. "If I landed in jail for it, so much the better, I'm sure."

"You didn't, though." Peter's gaze didn't waver.

"Not for that, no." Brett lifted his shoulders. "I made my way there all on my own."

"You did," Peter agreed. "Well played, sir. I'm sure your father of the year trophy is on its way."

Georgie said, "You really are a dick, Peter."

He shrugged amiably. "Okay."

"Peter." Willa leveled a gaze at him that should've sliced him in two. "Either tell us what you're here for, or get out of my house."

"Fine." He unfolded himself to his full height, dusted off his trousers and turned to Jax. "The good people of Devil's Kettle have been trying to reach you for over an hour, chief."

"Why?" Jax was on his feet instantly. "I'm not on call."

Peter rolled a shoulder. "There've been reports of smoke from the state forest lands north of town, and the DNR wants somebody to go up there to check it out. You're the closest responder with wild land fire training, which means you got the short straw. Time to go, Smokey Bear."

Eli frowned at Jax. "Lightning strike?"

Jax sighed. "It was one hell of a storm."

"And you're riding one hell of a fuel load."

"You'd know," Peter said and sent that sharky smile Eli's way. "Heard you had words with Paul O'Malley the other day about just that."

Eli's hands wanted to fist up again but he breathed through the impulse. "Did you?"

"Sure did." The smile took on an ugly edge of mockery. "I'm a bartender these days. I hear everything sooner or later, but when you throw it down fifteen feet from the bar I'm tending, I hear it sooner."

Georgie rolled her eyes. "Everybody throws down with O'Malley sooner or later. Between him and Gerte? That family was born to beef."

"O'Malley's a cranky bastard, no question," Jax said, eyeing Eli. "Knows every inch of the forest, though, from Duluth to Canada."

"He might know it," Eli said, "but he's crap at managing it."

"Which is basically what he told O'Malley," Peter said, "only louder." His smile spread. "Evidently our boy Eli here is strongly of the opinion that a good forest fire is exactly what we need up here in Devil's Kettle. O'Malley, however, found himself disinclined to take advice on his forests from a reckless cowboy with a bad track record." He shifted his gaze to Eli. "Kind of a loaded retort, we thought. Google to the rescue. Turns out that you do have kind of a spotty history when it comes to fire."

"What does that mean?" Jax asked.

"Eli was a hotshot," Peter answered. "And not just a grunt but a captain. An awfully young one, according to the news coverage."

"News coverage?" Bianca asked, her eyebrows slowly rising.

"When you walk into a fire with a full crew of fit men and walk out alone, people want to know what the hell happened in between, especially if the guy calling the shots is your lone survivor." Peter lifted a shoulder. "Just look up *Cathedral Hill hotshot tragedy*. It's all there."

The usual pain rushed up Eli's throat, mingled with a regret so old and familiar it was almost comforting. But it didn't close his throat. For once, it didn't fill his head with the unbearable static of shame. Willa, with her stillness and her courage, had changed him. She'd drawn the poison out of him. Left the history and the regret but the toxic shame that drove him across miles was simply gone. His heart ached with the unbearable weight of gratitude for her.

"I heard about that fire," Addy murmured, her eyes large and full of sympathy. "It was in the news. *You* were in the news."

"It was a case study in my refresher course on wild land firefighting," Jax said slowly. "That was you?"

"That was me." Eli spread his hands and let them fall.

"So why isn't the DNR calling you to check out this lightning strike? You're a goddamn hotshot."

"I *was* a godddamn hotshot." Eli shrugged. "I quit."

"Quit hotshotting?" Peter asked. "Or quit fires? Because I have to tell you, Eli, it's starting to look suspicious, the way shit burns down around you."

Matty, still on the carpet between his mother and Georgie, laughed sharply. "Fuck you, Peter."

Bianca rapped him smartly on the head. "Language, young man."

"I got this, Matty," Georgie said. "Fuck you, Peter."

"Thanks," Matty said, rubbing his scalp.

"My pleasure," Georgie said, her smile a glittering blade. "Don't pull that garbage up in here, Peter. Everybody in this room knows who's responsible for those fires."

Peter held up his hands. "Guilty as charged."

"*Not* charged," Jax muttered, "and against my better judgment."

"Hey, I made Addy whole on Davis Place," Peter said.

"Which is why I'm now just a bartender who hears shit." He held up innocent hands. "I'm not saying I believe it, and I'm definitely not repeating it, but I thought you should know what's being said." He leveled his eyes on Eli's, and for the first time, Eli wondered if he was seeing the guy. "Especially if you're thinking of hanging around." His gaze shifted to Willa for a split second before coming back to Eli.

"He's not," Willa said flatly. "He's leaving."

Like hell he was. "Not yet, I'm not." He frowned at her. "I have one more removal to observe."

"We had sex," she told him. Brett dropped his head to his hands and sighed. "You're no longer unbiased. I'll request somebody else. You're leaving."

"What, and let Gerte convict me of arson in absentia? Yeah, I don't think so. I'm not going anywhere."

"Yes, you are. Because if that lightning strike turns into something real? If we end up with a forest fire? There goes Devil Days, and half the town's financials along with it. They'll be looking for somebody to lynch, and if Peter's reading it right — and that's kind of his specialty, reading people right — they'll be looking straight at you." She studied him carefully, her stillness back in full force, wrapped around her like an impenetrable fog. "So yeah, you're leaving now."

Chapter 29

ELI RODE SHOTGUN in Jax's mini-pumper, and used his phone to navigate the narrow dirt logging roads toward the plume of smoke barely visible against the night sky. It was brilliantly clear since the storm, and the sky was awash in stars, except for one ominous column blotted out by smoke to the north.

"Take the next left," Eli snapped and braced himself on the dash. "Here! Take the left, now!"

Jax jammed the brakes and hung a hard left. The mini-pumper began to climb and Eli leaned forward to squint out the windshield. "We're gaining on it. Grab the next turnaround and park. We'll have to hike the rest of the way."

"Got it." A few minutes of rumbling road later, Jax pulled into a glorified ditch. He opened the side panel of the pumper and pulled out an axe and a compass. He held them up, an eyebrow lifted in question.

"You know this area?" Eli asked.

"Not on foot in the dark."

"I'll take the compass."

Jax handed it over, watched as Eli took a bearing on the column of smoke. "Willa's not wrong, you know. You really should leave."

"I know." He dropped the compass's lanyard over his head and started into the woods. "I'm not going anywhere."

"Why not?" He could hear Jax behind him, the crunch of the other man's boots, his breathing easy even as Eli set a punishing pace. "You don't hotshot anymore, and if Devil Days goes south, your life won't be worth living. There's nothing a small town loves more than somebody to blame when shit goes sideways, especially a stranger."

"I know." He paused to confirm his bearing, and gauge the wind direction. Coming out of the east, which would push the fire straight west. If it didn't shift, the fire would pass north of town, but not by much. He consulted his mental map, identified a peak with a nice view a couple miles away that would probably give him a decent look at the fire. He shifted course and aimed for it. "I'm not leaving."

"Not yet?" Jax asked. "Or not at all?"

"I don't know." Dread climbed up his throat. He could smell it now, the acrid tang of pine pitch boiling. He'd done everything in his power to avoid that scent these past few years, but it was as familiar as a lullaby to the firefighter he'd once been. His shoulder itched for the weight of that axe he'd given up to Jax, or better yet a Pulaski, that handy axe/shovel combo that was the hotshot's Swiss Army knife. "That would depend on Willa."

"Would it now?"

He angled his body for the uphill climb, ate up the distance with maximum efficiency, exactly as he'd been trained to do. Jax's breathing behind him was a little harsher now, but still coming easily enough. The guy was in shape, Eli would give him that. In return, Jax gave Eli maybe a half mile of hiking before he pushed.

"In what way?"

"In what way what?"

"In what way does your decision to stay or go depend on our Willa?"

"*Our Willa?* Oh, fuck that." He stopped abruptly, rage seizing him by the nape and shoving him into Jax's face. He drove a finger into the guy's chest, savored the round-eyed surprise on his face as he fell back a step. "She's not yours. If she were yours, you'd have protected her. You'd have closed ranks around her like you did around your fucking brother."

"Which one?" Jax asked, his mouth a grim line in the darkness. "The one we bought from her, or the one who abused her?"

Eli's fist clenched and Jesus, he wanted to drive it right through the guy's smug face. Except his face wasn't smug, was it? It was agonized, ashamed. The guy was swimming in naked regret and true sorrow. And once again, Eli found himself with a stomach full of violence and nowhere to put it. "I was thinking of the one you bought from her, but now that you mention it, how about the one who abused her?"

Jax blew out a breath, scrubbed a hand down his face. "Diego was a genius," he said simply. Eli's fists curled up again and Jax stepped back quickly, his own hands coming up in defense. "No, listen. I'm not excusing him. I'm just explaining how it was. Because it wasn't just art he was good at. It was manipulation, it was lying. It was charming the shit out of people to the point that, even when they realized what he'd done, what he'd stolen or broken or disrespected, they were willing to write it off as the price you paid for proximity to greatness."

He shook his head. "I don't know how he did it. It was some powerful voodoo, and it drove me nuts when I was younger. But it's worse now. And you know why?"

He stepped closer, right into the punch zone should Eli still feel inclined. Eli understood that this was a deliberate move, a purposeful vulnerability. "Because he almost destroyed Addy along with himself." He huffed out a laugh, black and ugly. "So trust me, I'm not excusing him. Sometimes I think I'd bring him back to life just so I could kill him myself. Which is kind of funny, now that I think about it." He studied Eli closely. "I never truly hated anybody until I fell in love. Did you?"

"Did I what?" Bafflement swirled into the rage, left Eli disoriented. "Hate anybody or—" Oh, fuck. Fall in love. "You think I'm in love with Willa."

Jax laughed, not unkindly. "Buddy?" He clapped a hand

onto Eli's stunned shoulder. "You're worse off than any poor bastard I've ever seen, save myself when I realized Addy was Diego's." He shook his head. "Yeah, that was a bad moment. Fucking Diego."

"Fucking Diego," Eli agreed automatically, still reeling. "I'm in love with Willa?"

"Did I break the news?" Jax clucked sympathetically. "Sorry, dude. I thought you knew."

"I thought..." He broke off, shook his head. "Nope. I didn't know shit."

"Well, now you know. Congratulations."

"Thanks?"

"My pleasure, sincerely. But what I was asking was whether you'd ever really hated anybody before."

He laughed bitterly. "Besides myself?"

"Yeah."

Eli turned and resumed hiking, picked up the mile-eating pace he'd set. "No."

"Yeah, me neither." Jax fell in behind him. "How does it compare?"

"What, the way I hated myself versus the way I hate Diego?"

"Or the way you hate me or my mom or the rest of the town that failed Willa so badly. But yeah. How does it stack up?"

Eli considered that. "It's different," he said, his brain churning in time to the beat of his boots on the trail.

"How so?"

"I hated myself because I made a mistake. It was a terrible one and it cost men their lives, but I didn't make it alone. It was my idea, sure and maybe I was being a cowboy, or maybe I was just young and bulletproof, or maybe I was chasing glory but..." He stopped, really thought it through for the first time in years. "But I didn't manipulate anybody. If I was a cowboy, we all were."

"Occupational hazard," Jax offered.

"Yeah, maybe. I gambled with lives that weren't mine to gamble with but every single one of the guys on my crew knew the plan and they all anted up. If I'd sent somebody else to take watch, he'd have been the one to walk away. It never crossed my mind that I was taking the safe way out. If anything, I thought I was putting myself closer to the fire."

"Whereas Diego fully intended to take something that wasn't his," Jax said softly. "He saw something pretty, something shiny, and he wanted it. I'd forgotten how shiny Willa could be until I saw her tonight with her hair all wild and her eyes out from under that damn cap. Diego wasn't one to deny himself anything, and he wouldn't have thought twice about taking whatever he could talk out of Willa."

Rage flared anew inside him, lit up his brain like the Fourth of July. "Just because she didn't say no—"

"—doesn't make it right," Jax finished. "Of course it doesn't. It makes it worse. It's just evidence of how badly he fucked with her mind and preyed on her vulnerabilities."

"Amen," Eli muttered.

"And the rest of us being so willing to believe the worst of her, and of her family? We're in the same boat as you. We never intended harm but we sure as hell didn't make the right call. And we'll have to live with that call, same as you live with yours."

Eli looked up, saw the dark shoulder of the knoll just ahead of them. The forest gave way to exposed basalt near the peak, and it was going to be a scramble. He paused, shot a look back at Jax, at a member of the family that had systematically ostracized Willa for nearly half of her life. And saw a man struggling to rise up under a crushing burden of guilt and shame, a man who clearly wasn't used to either one. A man who knew exactly what it was to love a woman who'd been damaged, selfishly and repeatedly. Who knew that he'd either been unable to protect her, or simply hadn't.

"What's your point, Jackson?"

"Just figured you should know that not a soul in this town

has any moral high ground on you. We're not going to condemn you for one bad decision." Jax smiled, a flash of charisma in the darkness. "Not saying people won't react emotionally should this fire we're chasing impact Devil Days or — God forbid — the town itself. But if you're going to be staying around for a while, if you're going to convince Willa to think about gambling long-term on you—"

"I am." It wasn't even a decision. It was a certainty that rose up from some dark, primal place deep inside, and it felt right in a way that Eli had almost forgotten existed.

"—then you need to convince her you're a good bet."

"And if I'm not?"

"You're as good a bet as any of us. Better, probably, because you take your failures so damn hard." Jax pointed his chin at the craggy peak ahead of them. "Let's not fail today, though, okay?"

"If I've learned one thing about fire, it's that failing isn't always up to us. It's not even mostly up to us."

Jax slapped him on the shoulder, a manly thwack that brought Eli back to the days when he'd had a team, a crew. Brothers. "Goddamn," he said, "I knew I liked you. Let's get after that bitch."

Eli cleared the ridiculous tightness from his throat. "Yeah, all right."

Fifteen minutes of slippery scrambling later, he and Jax stood panting on a naked dome of basalt, gazing down into a small valley alive with flames. A nasty, fitful wind snatched at it, scooped up a handful of flames and tossed them gleefully forward, lighting scout fires that sprinted toward the next crest like it was the finish line and they were running for gold.

"Jesus," Jax breathed.

"I don't think he's going to be helpful here," Eli returned grimly. "We need Boise."

Addison said, "He's not leaving, you know."

Willa looked across the cab of her truck at Addy, who'd elected to ride into town with her since Jax had abandoned her for a wildfire. And taken Eli with him. She didn't bother to misunderstand.

"Yes, he is." She eased her truck into her favorite spot underneath Soren's giant fish and killed the engine. "I know what you're thinking—"

"That he's stupid in love with you? That you're stupid in love with him?"

She closed her eyes, and gripped the wheel hard. "—and you're wrong."

"I'm not." Addy folded her arms and scowled. Willa could feel it filling up the cab, all that righteous indignation. "*You're* wrong."

"About what?"

"He's not leaving you, Willa."

Of course he was. Everybody left Willa eventually. "It's not like that, Addy." She opened her eyes, forced out the breath she'd been holding, the one that wanted to wrap itself around her throat and rip free the tears that had been sitting there for hours, for years. She thought she'd cried them all out at the thinnie but what do you know? She had more, and all it took was the thought of Eli leaving to bring them to the surface.

She pasted on a smile that she hoped looked indulgent. "It's nice that you want that for me. You're a real friend." The only one she'd probably ever had. And goddamn, here came the tears again. She swallowed them down. "But Eli and I aren't like that. Neither of us wants that. I went into this with my eyes wide open, okay? He's not staying here, or anywhere. That's not his path. And I don't want anybody permanent. That's not my path. There was some incredible chemistry, and we acted on it. But it was with the specific understanding that we were temporary."

"Screw temporary." Addy threw off her seatbelt and

twisted to face Willa. Her angular little face blazed with determination. "He put Peter on the floor tonight, and I have it on good authority that that's not easy to do."

"I'm sure it's not," Willa murmured, astonishment still echoing inside her at the memory. Nobody in her life had ever stood up for her, let alone thrown such a vicious punch on her behalf. And Peter hadn't even threatened her. He'd just made the sort of snide remark people had been making about her — or her mother — for years. "But emotions were running high and it's my understanding that men enjoy punching one another occasionally."

"They do." Addy put her warm, soft hand on Willa's forearm. "But Eli didn't hit Peter because he felt like it. He's not even from here. He doesn't give a crap about anything that happened fourteen years ago. He gives a crap about you. He laid Peter out because Peter is your brother and he didn't protect you. Nobody protected you, and we all should have."

"You didn't even live here then."

"I don't care." Her chin came up, trembled ominously then firmed.

Willa wanted to laugh but was afraid it might come out a sob. "You really are a good friend, Addy."

"And I mean to keep it up, which is why I'm not going to back down on this. Eli Walker loves you. He's in deep. And you might both think it's temporary, but I've been there. I know what temporary is, and what forever feels like. And when I look at the two of you, when I look at the way he looks at you, and the way you look back at him?" She squeezed Willa's arm. "It doesn't look like temporary, Willa."

She closed her eyes again, bent until her forehead touched the steering wheel. "Fuck me."

Addy's laugh was as warm and sympathetic as her hand. "I know, sweetie. That's just how I felt."

Willa rolled her forehead side to side on the slick steering wheel and moaned. "He has to leave, Addy. They'll crucify him here." She sat up, met those sympathetic eyes. "If there really is a fire, O'Malley will use the Cathedral Hill thing to smear it all over him."

"I know. But you'll stand with him."

Willa dropped her head to the wheel again. "How the hell is that going to help him?"

"Because I'll stand with you." She touched the back of Willa's head, light as a breeze, comforting as a blanket. "And so will Jax, and Georgie and Matty and Bianca. Because we're yours now. You're ours. We're family."

Willa lifted her head, baffled. "We are not."

"Of course we are. Matty's my brother. Matty's your brother. That makes my family your family."

She stared. "I don't think the Davises are going to see it that way."

"The hell they won't." Addy's smile was sleek and sharp in the darkness. "Nobody does family like the Davises. Just you wait."

"Yeah, I will." Till hell freezes over. "Let's just get inside, okay?"

Chapter 30

"I STILL DON'T understand why you need me here,"
Willa said as Addy unlocked the Davis Gallery's front door.
The lights were low, but the widow display glowed softly,
Diego's work whispering as always of mystery and power
and secrets. She hated the way it still tugged on her soul, the
way his painting reminded her of how badly she could want
things she knew she shouldn't have, how she yearned to
touch things that oughtn't be touched. She thought of Eli,
and sighed. Lord help her, after all these years she still loved
forbidden things.

"I told you." Addy led her through the night-time gallery
and held aside the white curtain for her. "You're family
now."

Willa balked at going into the *Diego After Dark* display.
She stopped to frown at Addy instead. "And I told you,
you're wrong."

Addy smiled beatifically. "I'm never wrong." And she
shoved Willa inside.

Bianca and Georgie were waiting for them there, perched
side by side on the edge of a shiny white table.

"That's true," Bianca said lightly. "She never is."

"Though God knows we wish she were sometimes,"
Georgie said, and smothered a delicate yawn with one hand.

"Like now," Bianca said, and smiled with a fierce fury
that hit Willa like a bullet. "But she's not. You're ours now,
Willa."

She stopped, shock locking her up from legs to lungs.
"I'm what?"

"Ours." Bianca's eyes were hot, angry. "Welcome to the

family, dear."

Georgie smirked and held out her arms. "Get in here, Willa. Time to hug it out."

Bianca sent her daughter a dark look. "This isn't funny, Georgie."

Georgie shrugged and dropped her arms, her lips still curved in a lazy grin, her eyes still sparkling with something far sharper.

Addy rolled her eyes and said, "Do it, Willa. Go give Georgie a big fat hug. She deserves it."

Willa folded her arms — they still worked, thanks be — and took a moment to consider each of the women in turn. To consider the bloody mess this night had made of her soul. Rage boiled up inside her, white and stark and clean. A rage she hadn't allowed herself to feel in years, if ever. It was the nuclear-strength grief of an abandoned child mixed with the bewildered agony of a girl who'd given her heart and her body to a predator, both of them shot through with the aching loneliness of a young woman whose family had just shrugged out of her needy grip for the last time. It was all of them, clumsily stitched together with a staggering hunger for love, and set ablaze by Bianca Davis's cold-blooded attempt to use that hunger against her.

"No," she said flatly. Her voice didn't even shake, which was vaguely astonishing, because the trembling inside her should've registered on the Richter scale. Things were crumbling in there, fault lines opening up, canyons appearing, mountains moving, islands rising. Jesus, it was seismic. It was the tectonic plates of her soul playing bumper cars, and all because somebody had claimed her. Even somebody she hated. Or used to hate.

"I'm not yours," she said to Bianca. "I'm not your family, or your anything else."

"Willa, wait, she didn't mean—" Addy started and touched Willa's arm.

"I know exactly what she meant." She stepped away, and

Addy's hand fell helplessly to her side. Her dismay was nearly palpable. It came to Willa's nose like the scent of wet rocks but she blocked it out. The rage rode over it easily. "She wants to put me under the Davis umbrella because she loves Matty and wants to make sure I'll go along with whatever lies she wants to spread this time. And she thinks I'm such a damaged bootlicker that after all these years and all this abuse, I'd be grateful for the offer. That I'd jump at the chance to be a Davis, oh glory hallelujah." She smiled grimly. "Well, guess what? I'm not interested. I don't need your family. I don't need your name or your money or your approval. And what's more, I don't want them." The words were pouring out now, barreling from her in a cleansing storm. "So if you have some plan to make sure my mother never sets foot back in this town, just tell me whatever the hell it is you need me to do or say or be. I'll lie through my teeth and I'll do it for free, but not because you want me to. I'll do it because Matty's mine as much as yours."

Bianca shot to her feet, her black eyes blazing but Willa said, "Oh sit your skinny ass down. I don't want to take him from you. You're his goddamn mother, and believe me, I know better than anybody what it is to lose a mother, even a shitty one. I'd never do that to anybody, let alone him. Jesus, Bianca, what don't you get about the fact that I *love* him?"

Bianca only glared at her, her fury an icy whip in the still air that stung Willa's nose like a January morning.

"She knows you love him," Addy said softly. "But she loves him, too, and knows she played dirty to get him. It worries her, so you worry her."

"I'm not worried about her." Bianca's chin came up imperiously. "There's not a court in the country that would—"

"Of course there is," Addy cut in with a terrible gentleness that stopped Bianca cold. "She's Matty's blood relative. If she wanted to petition for visitation, a court would hear it. And probably grant it."

Bianca glared but Georgie said, "Mom. You know she's right. She's *always* right." She slid Addison a languid sideways look. "Bitch."

Addy shrugged modestly and turned back to Willa. "Believe me, she knows you love him." She rubbed a hand up and down Willa's cold arm. "That's why she's so frightened of you."

"I'm hardly frightened of Willa Zinc." Bianca lifted her eyes to the ceiling. "But I was prepared to pay for the privilege of her cooperation." She dropped her gaze to Willa. "As usual."

Willa bared her teeth. "You bought me once, sure, but I'm not for sale anymore. Not ever again. So why don't you take your precious family name and shove it up your—"

"Willa!" Addy caught her by the elbow. Willa realized with a shock of horrified delight that she had taken a threatening step forward. And oh, holy hell, had she actually cocked her elbow for a swing? Judging from the way Bianca had jerked back, her eyes huge and amazed, Willa thought she probably had. She grinned and dropped her fist.

"Easy, B," she said. "I'm not going to hurt you."

"B?" Georgie rolled her eyes lavishly. "Christ's sake, Willa. You don't get to use nicknames if you're not in the family."

"Shut it, Barbie," Willa said, still gazing at Bianca.

"You can both shut up," Addy snapped at Georgie and Bianca. Willa blinked, shocked. Addy didn't go after her in-laws. Not ever. "After what I heard tonight? After the way you've spent the last decade and a half making Willa's life an unconscionable misery? I think Willa can do whatever the hell she wants, and I'm her head cheerleader." Bianca and Georgie both dropped their gazes to the floor, and Willa's shock deepened. Addy was legendarily fierce in defense of her family, but Bianca and Georgie *were* her family. If she was taking a bite out of them over Willa, and they were letting her, then the only conclusion was that…Willa really was family, and not just in Addy's compassionate imagination. As if Addy could read Willa's mind, she concluded, "Plus, Willa's totally in the family." She grinned. "Barbie."

"Shut it, you," Georgie replied idly, but those sharp, sharp eyes were on Willa.

"But I am going to warn you," Willa said to Bianca. "Don't ever try to use my heart against me again."

"Your heart?" Bianca echoed blankly. "When have I ever—"

"Every single person I've ever loved has walked away from me," Willa said. "They've used me, hurt me, stolen from me, or just decided I wasn't worth loving back." She thought of Eli, of the way he'd curved himself over her back while she'd cried herself raw at the thinnie earlier. Thought of the way he'd absorbed the storm's fury with his own back, absorbed her bottomless pain with his own wounded heart. She'd told him to leave, she thought with a pulse of wonder, and he'd said no. Flat out refused. And something fragile and new had sparked to life inside her, something that had uncurled thread-thin roots into the cracks in her soul. Something that even now was trying to grow. Something dangerous and beautiful and precious and terrifying. Something that gave her the strength to face down this woman who'd been the instrument of so much of her pain. "It's the kind of childhood that would've messed up most kids. I mean, look at Peter."

Georgie snorted. "Point taken."

"I should be just that cold, just that selfish, just that greedy. But I'm not, and do you know why?"

"Why?" Bianca asked stiffly.

"Because I loved something. I loved Matty. Loving him saved me, and that's what you don't get. You don't need to bribe me to protect him, for God's sake. I'd do that anyway. I'd die to keep him safe. He's my family, the only one I've got. The only one I want."

"You're wrong." Bianca smiled again, smugly. As if Willa's violent rejection of her family name had satisfied her on some level. "You're ours now."

Willa stared, her mind simply refusing to accept an about-face of this magnitude. "Why do you keep saying that?"

"Because it's true." Bianca waved a languid hand. "You're Matty's sister, and Matty is my son. Ergo, you're my child as much as he is."

Willa shook her head slowly, her bewildered heart thudding harder than it should. She was nobody's. Nobody's but her own. "Just tell me what you need from me, Bianca."

"It's not what we need from you, dear," Bianca said. She folded her hands at her waist and studied Willa closely. "It's what you need from us."

"I don't need anything from you."

"Yeah, you do," Georgie said. She hopped lightly off the table and came to stand at her mother's shoulder, peered at Willa with an identical expression of satisfied calculation in those pale blue eyes. "The press is coming for you, Willa. They'll be here by tomorrow."

"Which is why we need to figure out how to protect you," Bianca said, and her smile died. "Because I will be good and goddamned if I let Shay get wind of this and damage another of my children."

Dawn was just touching the sky when Eli trundled his inadequate excuse for a car through the state forest to Cabin Six and found Willa's truck parked at his porch. His heart leapt inside his chest even as he braced himself for the fight. Willa had told him to leave and he hadn't left. He'd done the opposite, actually. Dug in hard. And the fire chewing up the forest a bare fifteen miles northeast of town was only half the reason why. Maybe not even half. The balance of what was keeping him in Devil's Kettle was waiting for him inside his cabin, probably ready to tear him a new one for still being here.

He grinned, and it was the first time he'd felt remotely cheerful in the last twelve hours. Normally he got up this time of day to put a dozen or so punishing miles on his boots and on his soul. Then he'd pop a tent somewhere and not even pretend it was home. Coming home to Willa instead — even to a gloves-off show-down with Willa — beat the hell out of that solitary tent in the woods. He killed the tuna can's sorry little engine and went inside. And froze just inside the door.

She was on his bed, asleep. He toed off his boots and eased the door shut, hope blooming inside him. Her suitcase stood at the foot of the bed, and she'd helped herself to his sleeping bag. He decided he'd own sheets by lunch time if she wanted to share his bed on the regular. A bed, too.

She lay on her side, her back to him. She slept in a tight ball, knees up, fists under her chin, gripping the sleeping bag like she was afraid somebody might snatch it. Her ponytail spilled over the edge of the cot, a tangle of black silk that nearly brushed the floor. Eli had no idea why she was here but he didn't care. She was here, in his bed, and he was so goddamn tired.

He scooped up all that hair and smoothed it over the pillow. She frowned in her sleep and stirred but Eli eased himself onto the cot, stretched out along her back. He hooked his chin over her shoulder, wrapped an arm around her waist, breathed in the scents of sunscreen and wild things that clung to her always and closed his eyes.

Chapter 31

LATER — MINUTES, HOURS, who knew? — he felt her surface. Her consciousness touched his, brought him back to his body in time to feel her slip into hers again.

"What time is it?" she murmured, her voice rough with sleep.

"Barely sunrise, last I looked," he said, and drifted his fingers over her forearm. "Go back to sleep."

"Where have you been?"

"Slapping my glove in O'Malley's face."

She took a moment to process that one. "Really?"

"Figuratively."

"That's a relief." She burrowed deeper into his arms. "Don't duel him for real. He's a decent shot."

"Who's shooting?" He tightened his arms around her, savoring the warm weight of her there. Rubbed his cheek into the cool spill of her hair. "I'd have picked chainsaws."

"You challenged. He picks weapons."

"Shit. Really?"

"Really. Good thing we're being figurative then, huh?" She stirred and he loosened his arms. She rolled to face him. Her nose was about two inches from his, her cheek pillowed on his biceps. "What exactly did you slap with your metaphorical glove, anyway?"

"His authority." He leaned in and rubbed his nose against hers. She smiled and something that had rusted shut ages ago cracked open inside him. God, Jax was right. He was totally in love with this woman. Like really, stupidly, dangerously *gone* over her. "Jax and I went up to look at the fire last night. It's small right now but ugly, and with nearly fifty unburned years of fuel just sitting out there, dry as shit? It's going to grow. O'Malley needs to get after it with everything Boise's got. Yesterday, if not sooner."

"How far away is it?"

"Fifteen miles to the northeast, but there's a westerly wind."

"Which pushes it our way?" She frowned. "Crap. Devil Days opens today. Is it bad enough to keep the tourists home?"

"Might be." He hesitated. "It'll pass north of town by at least ten miles if the wind doesn't shift, but—"

"But if it does?"

"It won't be just Devil Days that's in trouble, Willa. It'll be the whole damn town."

"Holy hell."

"I know. But O'Malley's a local boy. He knows Devil Days is this place's Black Friday."

"It's more than that. It doesn't just make us profitable. It makes us viable. Without those tourists, this town doesn't survive."

"And he's not going to do a damn thing to derail that." Bitterness crept into his voice. "Especially not on the advice of an ex-hotshot just looking for a flashy chance to redeem himself."

Willa sat up. "He said that?"

Eli rolled onto his back and stared at the ceiling. "He wasn't happy that I went over his head and got Boise involved."

She laid a hand on his chest. "I'm glad you did. Devil Days is important but not as important as people's lives. Nobody's going to make a living if Main Street burns down, for God's sake."

"Yeah, that was my thinking." He tipped her a wry smile. "I'm in the minority, evidently."

"The majority sucks." She flopped back down beside him and joined him in frowning at the ceiling. "I hate the majority."

Eli propped himself up on one elbow, smoothed a wild lock of hair away from her cheek. "Get outvoted recently, Willa?"

She scowled. "You have no idea."

"Does it have anything to do with why you're sleeping on this lumpy old cot when you have what I'm sure is a lovely, comfy bed in an actual house?" He hesitated. "Particularly after you told me in no uncertain terms that you expected me to be gone by morning?"

She glanced at him. "I said that?"

"Almost word for word."

"And yet here you are."

He drew a finger along her jaw, from the secret hollow under her ear to the point of that pixie chin. "Here I am," he agreed.

"Why?"

Because I fell in love with you so hard I couldn't leave if I tried. Because my heart is scattered all over the lawn like I'm having a goddamn yard sale. Because that sleeping bag is my home and I can't fucking breathe when I think about you not being in it next time I lie down.

"Do you really want to know?"

She blinked those huge gray eyes seriously. "Probably not. But I think you should tell me."

"You tell me something first."

She considered that. "You need a minute to warm up to it?"

He laughed softly. "Yeah."

"Okay. What do you want to know?"

"Why are you in my bed?"

She scowled again. "Bianca said I couldn't stay at home anymore."

He lifted a brow. "Since when does Bianca tell you where you can live?"

"Since she decided she's my stand-in mommy."

Eli stared. "Your stand-in *mommy*?"

"It's a long story." She sighed. "Suffice it to say the reporters are coming for me." She cut him a disgruntled sideways look that he wanted to kiss off her face. "Being Diego Junior's mommy is evidently a high-profile gig."

He arched a brow. "But you're not Diego Junior's mommy."

"I know that. And you know that. But the press doesn't know that. All they know right now is that a mean old lady is talking smack about how Diego Davis's brother is really his love child, and they all want to be the one to score the first interview with the supposed mother."

He slid an arm across her waist, danced his fingers up her ribs. "I see." He eased his thigh over both of hers, resisted the urge to rub himself against her like a horny dog. "So you decided to hide from the reporters in my bed?"

She sighed. "I'm not great at people."

He scowled. "The hell you aren't."

"I'm good at you." She fisted a hand in his t-shirt, pulled him down to her mouth. He fell into the kiss with dizzy abandon, eased back reluctantly when she broke it off. "Other people? Not so much."

"Screw other people." He leaned in for more, then stopped. "That came out wrong."

"I took it right." She sighed and leaned her forehead into his. "But let's be honest, Eli. The reporters are swarming, and I'm not exactly captain of the debate team. Bianca thinks it would be better for Matty if I were really hard to find just now." She shrugged. "She's not wrong."

"Works for me." He eyed her mouth — curvy, sweet, not nearly well-kissed enough — and moved back in.

"Nope." She scooted to the edge of the mattress, that sleeping bag in both fists under her chin again. "You've stalled long enough. Now it's your turn." She studied him, those big gray eyes wide and implacable. "Why did you stay, Eli? You don't owe me anything, and I know you didn't start that fire. This place should've been in your rear view hours ago." She pursed her lips as if she was getting ready to taste the truth in his words. As if she could smell it on him. "Why isn't it?"

"Because I didn't want it there."

"Why not?"

"Because you're here." He reached for one of those fists, eased her grip finger by finger, threaded his own fingers through hers. "This is your home, and I want to be where you are."

"Why?" It was a whisper this time, and the knuckles of the hand still gripping the sleeping bag were white and tense. He pressed her palm to his heart, left it there and speared his fingers into the wild spill of her hair instead. Her ponytail elastic had given up the ghost sometime during the hours they'd slept and her hair fell from his hand like a black river, full of eddies and swirls and invisible currents. Her eyes drifted closed with pleasure. He knew how she felt.

"Because I'm in love with you, Willa." Her eyes snapped open at that and he shrugged sheepishly. "I know, right? It ought to be impossible, given that I've known you about two minutes. But there you have it. I'm in love with you. And do you know how I know it's the real deal?"

"How?" Her lips shaped the word but evidently sound was beyond her. Eli grinned. He was pretty sure that was how he'd reacted when Jax had acquainted him with this fact a few hours earlier.

"Because I *can't* leave. Oh, I know I should. O'Malley and Gerte are probably huddled over the coffee pot in the Wooden Spoon right now, discussing what to charge me with. Her honor's at stake after I called her a nasty old bitch at the gallery—"

She grinned suddenly. "You did, didn't you?"

"—and then I called O'Malley's judgment into question in front of the big boys at Boise. That family's not going to be happy until I'm good and punished, and I have a feeling they know what they're about, punishment wise."

"They do," Willa conceded. "Lord, do they. Gerte is second only to Bianca when it comes to Devil's Kettle's Most Frightening. I don't know much about O'Malley, except that Gerte doesn't screw with him, which means he's probably meaner than she is."

"Great." Eli sighed.

"Which means you really ought to get out of here, Eli. At least until this fire is resolved."

"Yeah, that would be the smart thing to do, wouldn't it?" He shook his head. "But if I run from this, I run from you. I leave my trouble behind, sure, but I leave it here where you have to deal with it. Alone. And that shit's not happening. Not on my watch."

She gazed at him for a moment. A long sweaty moment, during which Eli realized that he hadn't the first clue what she was thinking. He became aware suddenly of that stillness of hers. It had crept unnoticed into the air around them, had grown into a palpable presence between them, pure and absolute. It wrapped itself around him in soothing tendrils, gentled the tide of humiliation and panic trying to rise inside him. But it also made it utterly impossible for him to get a bead on where her head was. Where her heart was.

"Eli," she said finally. The hand she still had pressed to his heart fisted on his t-shirt but her eyes were as remote as the mountains he'd grown up in. "That's without a doubt the most beautiful thing anybody's ever said to me."

"But?" Eli was in love but he wasn't a fool. He knew a *but no thanks* when it came rumbling down the tracks.

"But we discussed this. This thing you and I have? It's been amazing, and I don't have a single regret. But I'm not in the market for anything permanent." She released his t-shirt, smoothed the wrinkles she'd put there and reached up to cup his jaw. "And neither are you."

"I wasn't." He put his hand on top of hers, closed his eyes at the feel of her strong, capable fingers against his skin.

"Then you happened."

"No, then a bunch of drama happened. And you're a good guy, Eli. You have a solid family, a good heart and a conscience as big as the sky. Losing those men broke your heart but it didn't break you. You're still above the ground, working for your uncle even though you don't want to, emailing your mom occasionally because you know she worries, getting too involved in small town dramas because a girl you slept with has a rotten history." She smiled softly. "But this is my home, not yours. There's no shame in walking away from trouble that isn't yours, and this trouble isn't yours. I'm not yours. And you're not mine. I just woke you up." She rubbed her thumb over his cheekbone. "You woke me up, too. We're leaving each other better than we found each other, which is more than you can say for most impulsive affairs. We got damn lucky, so let's not ask more of this than it can give us. You're free finally. It's time to go."

Eli studied her for a long moment. Then he leaned in and laid his lips to hers. Her stillness wrapped around him like a duvet, thick and warm and drugging. It wanted to lull him to sleep, to complacency. He eased back, smoothed a lock of hair behind her ear. "That was a good speech. You almost had me, too. It's that stillness of yours. It's like a tranquilizer. How do you do that, anyway?"

She blinked innocently. "Do what?"

Eli wanted to kiss her again but told himself to focus. "Produce it. The stillness."

She frowned. "I don't know what you're talking about."

"I think you do. I think it's a defense mechanism. I think somewhere along the line, you learned how to wrap up everything inside you — all the wildness and the appetite and the want — and lay it down to sleep. It probably seemed safer that way, and believe me, I get it. Your childhood was a fucking mine field. You did what you had to do to survive, and now you're like one of those frictionless balls from

271

physics problems, rolling through the world without really touching anything or anybody. It's no wonder you're so good at your job. Animals are all about the non-verbals, and yours are like a tranquilizer dart. I'm a little embarrassed now at how well it worked on me."

She jerked away from him — tried to, anyway — but Eli held on. He was planning to hold on forever but he'd settle for finishing this conversation. He rolled her under him in one swift move, sleeping bag and all, propped his elbows on either side of that astonishing hair of hers. The stillness broke, wisps of it dissipating almost visibly under the heat of her anger. And something else. Her fear? His heart clenched.

She said, "Let me go."

"Willa. I get that you're afraid."

She glared up at him. "I'm not afraid."

"Of course you are. You'd be stupid if you weren't."

She narrowed hot gray eyes. "Excuse me?"

"I just told you I love you, for Christ's sake. With your history? I might as well have pulled a gun on you."

She shoved at him but he twisted the sleeping bag around his hands and gave her more of his weight, pressed her deeper into the mattress. She squirmed under him and a spark of interest flared to life deep in his belly which he firmly ignored.

"I'm not afraid of you, goddamn it."

"You shouldn't be. I'd never hurt you."

"I know that." But she twisted her face to the side.

"No, you don't." He nudged her jaw until she sighed and met his eyes again. "But I want you to. I want you to believe that with everything in you."

"Eli, please." He felt the stillness gathering again, felt her revving up that mystical engine of hers that created the black hole that sucked in everything she didn't want to feel. Or didn't want anybody to know she felt.

"You're doing it again. The stillness thing."

"I am not." She set her mouth stubbornly and looked

away while it rose up between his heart and hers like a fog, impossible to touch, to strike, to defeat. "This is going nowhere."

"But it could." Anger bloomed inside him, red and choking. How could he fight what he couldn't touch? "God, Willa, it *could*. If you'd just stop—" He broke off, struck.

"Stop what?"

"Protecting yourself." He sighed and closed his eyes. Dropped his forehead to hers. "God, listen to me. I'm such a jerk. That stillness is the only thing in your life that's never let you down, isn't it? It's kept you safe when nobody else tried or even cared." She stiffened under him and he rubbed his cheek against hers. "It was the first thing I loved about you, too. That day you told Gerte off for slapping me? You were amazing. You defused a potential mob without breaking a sweat. The stillness isn't a flaw, it's a superpower, and I'm a dick for implying that it's standing between you and happily ever after. It's not."

She lay under him, rigid and wary, but the stillness stalled, as if listening. As if giving him a chance to make his case. "What are you even talking about, Eli?"

He kissed her. He put everything into that kiss, too. The snarly temper, the bitter fear, the overwhelming ocean of love sloshing around inside him for her. The desperation to get through to her, to make her feel what he felt so she'd understand it. Believe it. Risk her own heart on it.

He tried to get his arms around everything banging around inside his heart, tried to corral it into some coherent mental image he could telegraph to her somehow. All he could think of was her thinnie, but not the magic, night-blooming bower she'd taken him to that first night. No, he thought instead of the storm-lashed altar where they'd come together so fiercely the night before, the place she'd gone to cry herself dry under a raging, relentless sky. The place where he'd given her proof that when shit cut loose, when she was weak, when she was broken, he'd be there. She

273

could come undone twice a day for the next forever, and he'd be there every time, gathering the pieces up in loving arms, helping her glue it all back together when the sun came out again.

He could almost smell the sizzling rain, feel the sting of it shredding through his t-shirt. He remembered the vulnerable warmth of her shuddering back against his front as he shielded her from the worst of the storm, as he wished like hell he could shield her from whatever it was that had raged within her. Love crested inside him, threw back its head and howled like an animal, and he poured it all into his kiss. Prayed he'd found the language that might convince her wary, wounded soul to reach for him.

"Eli?" Her voice was a broken whisper, a shaking wish.

"I know," he said and pressed his forehead to hers, his eyes shut, his soul hers. "I'm sorry. It's ridiculous."

"It's too much."

"I know." He slid his fingers into her hair, let it sift slowly away. She allowed the touch with the wary stillness of a feral cat, as if pleasure were an unfamiliar concept. His heart squeezed. She'd earned every ounce of that wariness, and he'd spent precious little time showing her the simple pleasure of being petted. He didn't deserve her, and yet... "But I can't help it. It's yours, all of it. It just is."

"I don't know what to say."

"Don't say anything." He lifted his head, met those fairy eyes, still filled with uncertainty, but with hope, too. Hope, he decided, looked good on her. She should wear it more often. He'd see about making that happen. "Just understand that I'm not going anywhere. I'm going to be here next week, next month, next year, exactly as in love with you as I am now." He rubbed his nose against hers again. "Just think about it."

She studied him owlishly. "Maybe you should kiss me while I think about it."

He grinned. "Your wish. My command."

Chapter 32

DEVIL DAYS HAD arrived, and with it the teeming masses. Tourists and art lovers had easily tripled the town's population by Friday afternoon, something Eli had vaguely expected but hadn't truly understood until he tried to report to the fire station. Boise was in town and Eli's presence had been demanded. Ben's royal summons had cut short Eli's morning hike, but as the only available parking was halfway to Canada, he figured he'd make up the distance, no problem.

He eventually found a spot on the north edge of town and hoofed it for the fire station where Ben had set up his Incident Command Post. He smelled the Sugar Rush before he even saw it, a hot pink fishing shack wreathed in a hot-oil-and-sugar scented cloud that had doughnut lovers swarming like groupies at a rock concert. As he threaded his way through the crowd lined up outside, he caught sight of Walt Kovacz at the counter inside, slinging doughnuts with mad efficiency under his signature bandana do-rag. He worked the cash register with one hand, poured coffee with the other and still managed to give Eli a cheerful chin-jerk in greeting.

Eli waved back. "Get the lead out, Walt!" he called. "People are hungry out here."

The crowd murmured its agreement and Walt flung open expansive arms. "And I shall serve them all!" he boomed in a surprisingly *Ten Commandments* voice given his skinny chest. "My deep fryer overfloweth!"

The crowd shouted its approval and surged forward. Eli laughed and kept hiking. There was a crowd outside the

Davis Gallery, too, though Eli didn't know whether they were in line to see the art or to buy tickets for that night's *Diego After Dark* showing. There were a handful of TV reporters, too, doing stand ups in front of the window display, speaking with a hushed earnestness that suggested Gerte had done her work and done it well.

Bianca had been right — the rumor mill was in high gear, and the press had come to feed. He took a moment to be grateful for Bianca's foresight, and the bossiness that had Willa snugged safely away in Eli's cabin, far away from the reporters and their ravenous appetite for other people's business.

He arrived at the fire station and found news vans there, too. He ducked his head, attached himself to a couple of locals heading toward the door and tried to look invisible. It had been over two years since he'd walked out of the Cathedral Hill fire alone, and he didn't think anybody would recognize him, but he'd been flooded with interview requests for months after that terrible day. He hadn't granted a single one, but he was still getting the occasional email from New York City talking about book deals. He'd gotten one just the other day. He'd deleted it, just like he'd deleted all the others since the moment he'd become the sole survivor of a high-profile disaster.

So there was no reason this pack of reporters would know his face now, but the back of his neck itched all the same until the fire station's dented steel door finally closed behind him.

And suddenly Eli found himself immersed in a world he understood but had sworn never to set foot in again. A world full of young men and bullet-proof bravado that smelled of sweat, smoke and coffee strong enough to power a nuclear submarine. A world that, at the moment, was full of raised voices, creative profanity and giant computer monitors devoted to satellite maps and the weather. A world he missed, God help and forgive him.

One of the men he'd tailgated into the building arched a bushy brow at him and jerked an impressive mustache toward the center of an open space that looked like it normally served as a kitchen/dining area. "That your boy? The new Incident Commander?"

Eli looked and found his uncle squaring off with O'Malley in front of one of those giant monitors. "Yeah. That's Ben Bayfield out of Boise, my boss, my uncle and all around pain in my ass." He sent an arched brow back toward Mustache Man. "That your boy he's yelling at?"

"O'Malley?" Mustache had at least three decades on Eli, and the belly to match the mustache. He rubbed that belly now while he considered the question. "Known him since we were both tadpoles, sure. He was one hell of a point guard back in the day. Saw the whole court all the time, you know?"

"Yeah," Eli muttered. "I got that impression."

"Found Jesus in Vietnam, though."

"Is that where they're keeping him these days?"

Mustache chuckled. "Never ran across him there myself but O'Malley sure found somebody. Hasn't been the same since." He smoothed his 'stache and studied Eli closely. "Some experiences will do that to a man."

The back of Eli's neck went itchy again but he arranged his face into noncommittal lines. "War being one of them."

"Among others, I imagine." Another freighted moment passed during which Eli realized that Peter had been right. Every single person in Devil's Kettle with an internet connection had flagrantly Googled him, and was now fully briefed on his life story. Great. Eventually the guy held out a hand. "Mason Kennebec. Volunteer firefighter."

"Eli Walker." He shook. "Just passing through."

Mason laughed and clapped a meaty hand to Eli's shoulder, hard enough to make him stumble. "Not the way I hear it."

Eli blinked, startled. Evidently Google had nothing on

Devil's Kettle's grapevine. You hold a girl's hand at *one* gallery opening and the entire town knows your relationship status? Did he mind that? He considered it, and a grin bloomed up out of his very soul. No. No, he didn't mind one bit. "No, you're right. Sorry. Force of habit."

"A girl will turn your world upside down, kid."

"Turned mine right side up."

"Yeah? I always said Willa was good people." A smile lifted his 'stache. "You'd be a fool to leave, then. Good woman's tough to come by." He delivered another three-ton shoulder clap then dug an elbow into Jax, who'd appeared on his other side. "What's going on there?" he asked, nodding toward the center of the room.

Jax said, "Bayfield's taken over as Incident Commander, which demotes O'Malley to Public Safety Supervisor." Mason winced. Jax shrugged. "Boise wants the fire, Boise gets the fire."

"Yeah, yeah." Mason waved that off. "So what's the beef?"

"IC Bayfield wants to put out an evacuation order that covers Devil's Kettle proper."

Mason's eyes went round. "What, the town? Jesus, the fire's fifteen miles off! And it's Devil Days!"

"Yeah, that's O'Malley's position." He tucked his fingers into his pockets and frowned at the massive weather monitor splattered with slow-moving color. "Forecast's for dry, dry and more dry, and the wind can't make up its mind. Puffs a little from the east, then the north, then the east again. Edges around to the south every now and then."

"It's the lake," Eli murmured. "Body of water that massive is one big question mark when it comes to weather. Keeps you warmer than you ought to be in the winter, colder than you ought to be in the summer. Puts storms on the spin cycle." He shook his head. "Any damn thing could happen."

"Which is what Bayfield's saying." Jax leaned forward to eye him around Mason's bulk. "O'Malley's of the mindset that the hotshots Bayfield called up should have the fire well in hand by nightfall without causing undue alarm."

"Or disrupting the inflow of tourist dollars?"

Jax shrugged. "It's a concern."

Eli dragged a hand down his face. "Yeah, I know."

"They here yet?" Mason asked while O'Malley drew a finger across the swirling map between the fire and the town, and Ben rolled his eyes. "The hotshots?"

"Yeah," Jax murmured. "There's two crews cutting a line north of the fire right now."

"North?" Mason frowned. "Why north? The fire's only a problem for us if it moves west."

"But the Devil River's already sitting there to the fire's west, and it's doubtful the fire could jump a couple million gallons of water."

Eli wasn't so sure about that, but he didn't say so. He wasn't a firefighter anymore and didn't want anybody to think he was interested in changing that.

Jax went on. "Between the river, a Forest Service road to the fire's east, and Lake Superior to the south, she's pretty much contained by geography. O'Malley figures the hotshots and their fire line will put the lid on that box. If he's right, it should stop that thing in its tracks."

Eli wasn't sure about that, either, not with a fuel load this heavy and this dry. Ben — now drawing his own imaginary line on the map, significantly closer to town than O'Malley's — didn't look convinced, either.

"How much of the forest is involved?" Eli asked.

"About a hundred acres at this point, and uncertain which direction to grow with the wind all indecisive. But when the wind picks up—"

"*If* the wind picks up," Mason said placidly.

"According to Bayfield, it's a when." Jax shrugged. "And when it does—"

"—it's going to make eating up a hundred acres look like popping a breath mint," Eli finished for him. "Fuck." He glanced at his uncle, at the veins starting to show in his forehead, at the muscle ticking in his jaw. None of these were good signs. He was going to punch O'Malley any minute, and while Eli wouldn't lose any sleep over that, it probably wasn't the most productive start to negotiations.

Jax rocked back on his heels. "Think you can get between those two without getting bit? I already went. Have about eight fingers left."

Eli sighed. "I doubt it. O'Malley hates me and Ben—"

—*was a tough guy to convince*, Eli was going to say. Unfortunately, Ben was also a tough guy to hide from. Especially when you were family.

"Eli!" Ben stopped excoriating O'Malley's character and intellect long enough to grab Eli in a fierce, back-pounding hug. Average in height, wiry of build, with endurance for days, Ben was Eli thirty years down the road. It was both comforting and a little eerie, Eli had always thought, to be hugged by your future self. "You're a sight for sore eyes, boy." He pulled back for a critical up-and-down. "Goddamn, don't they feed you up here in the north woods?"

"I've had some fine pie," he returned, glancing at O'Malley. The guy looked like he could tear a bite out of either one of them at any time. "O'Malley's cousin Gerte down at the Wooden Spoon does a crust that would make Mom weep envious tears."

"That so?" Ben eyed O'Malley with straight-up dislike. "Good enough to risk the lives of hundreds of tourists?"

"There's no risk to Devil's Kettle proper," O'Malley snarled. "And while sacrificing a year's worth of income for an abundance of caution might make you look like a real hero to the national press and to the feds you answer to, the folks around here won't thank you for it. We're real familiar with risk, and this is one we don't mind taking if it means we can keep our doors open one more year."

"You speak for every citizen, do you?" Ben's smile was more a baring of teeth than anything friendly. "You've got it on good authority that they'll just sit whistling in their homes while this fire burns to the fucking harbor?"

"It's going nowhere near the harbor," O'Malley said, stabbing a finger at the map again, this time at a line of blue between the town and the fire fifteen miles up the shore. "See that? That's the Devil River right there. That's a couple million gallons of water running between us and that fire every minute. You've got two crews of the nation's finest wild land firefighters cutting line to its north, and a nice, wide Forest Service road on the east. There's nothing to the south but water, so assuming your hotshots know what they're about, this fire's in a fence already!"

"A fence it could jump in a heartbeat if that wind picks up," Ben said grimly. "Which is why we need to get all these goddamn people out of its way!"

"They're not *in* its way, Bayfield!"

And they'd circled back to the beginning. From the expressions on the faces watching the match, Eli figured it wasn't anywhere close to the first time they'd covered this ground.

"What's the forecasted run for today's fire?" Eli asked, suddenly beyond weary.

They both turned to him with glares that were near-identical. Eli didn't think either man would thank him for pointing it out.

"Why? Are you offering to get out there with the hotshots and cut line?" Ben snapped. He sent a poisonous look O'Malley's way. "Because I could use a set of eyes I trust on this fire."

"I'm done hotshotting," Eli said. "And you know it."

"Are you?" O'Malley sneered. "Because this feels like a picture perfect opportunity for you to get back in the game." He glanced toward the door, on the other side of which the press had assembled. "And I do mean *picture* perfect."

Ben's jaw tightened ominously but Eli said, "Hey, Ben." He waited until Ben had reluctantly brought his attention

back to him and away from thoughts of punching.
"Seriously, what are you forecasting for the fire's run
today?"

Ben scowled. "We were just discussing that."

"No, we weren't," O'Malley said tightly. "Nothing in the
data suggests the fire could run more than four to five miles,
dead west."

"Unless the wind picks up," Ben added just as tightly.
"Then you could see a run of fifteen miles or better."

"Which is not only unlikely, it's unprecedented,"
O'Malley snapped. "I already have teams of forest rangers
clearing the Superior Hiking Trail, along with the state and
national forest campgrounds inside the *reasonable and
predicted* four-to-five mile clearance radius. We've put out a
reverse 911 to every cell phone attached to a camping
permit, or to a registered through-hiker on the Superior
Hiking Trail inside that same zone, along with another four
to five miles beyond that, just to be safe," O'Malley said. "I
see no earthly reason to clear a city five miles beyond *that* of
all its residents plus the hundreds of tourists happily and
safely spending money there."

"No, I'd guess you don't," Ben said almost pleasantly.
Eli's gut clenched. Ben didn't do pleasant. "Otherwise you'd
have done something about the forty-plus years worth of
dry-as-shit forest you're sitting in the middle of, you
incompetent ass-scratcher."

"Excuse me?" O'Malley growled.

"No. I won't excuse you. There's no excuse for you.
Because you had one job, O'Malley." He held up a single,
furious finger. "One fucking job! All you had to do was
manage the fucking forest. Strike a balance between burn,
suppress and protect. But for some godforsaken reason, you
decided to let go of the wheel and pile up enough fuel for
this place to go up like a Roman fucking candle the instant
God dropped a match." Ben leaned in, drove that finger into
O'Malley's pectoral. "So frankly, I give exactly zero fucks

about what you see or don't see. All I want to hear from you is *yes, sir*, then I want to see your ass get busy clearing civilians."

O'Malley gave him an ugly smile. "With whom, IC Bayfield? My state forest rangers are the only staff we have with both deep backcountry knowledge of the area and fire training, but it'll take them all day just to clear the forecasted run zone. I could start them on the next five-mile radius tomorrow but that still wouldn't get anybody to work clearing the town until Sunday, at which point Devil Days will be wrapping up anyway." He spread his hands helplessly. "So unless Boise can rustle us up some extra resources with fire training and north woods experience, you can want whatever the hell you like. You're not going to get it."

"I'll go," Willa said, and stepped from the crowd that had concealed her.

"Willa?" Shock had his head snapping around to stare at her. "What the hell are you doing here?"

"Offering to clear tourists out of the danger zone." She didn't look at him but kept her gaze level on O'Malley and Ben.

"Who the hell are you?" Ben asked.

"Willa Zinc," she said. "Zinc Pest Control. I grew up in these woods, and I spend a lot of my professional life dealing with the animals that live in and around them." She stepped up to the map O'Malley and Ben had been snarling over like feral dogs. Eli watched her, still stunned into silence. He'd left her at home, safe and sound and *asleep*, obeying Bianca's very prescient suggestion to lay low. What was she doing volunteering to walk into a forest fire?

"I can't speak to how the fire's going to behave, but if you're concerned with the general public outside the five-mile evac zone O'Malley's already set up, you'll want to focus right here." She leaned forward and tapped the map just west of the river.

"Devil's Kettle Trail and Monument," O'Malley said and nodded stiffly. "Yes, it's very popular."

"It's a disappearing river," Willa told Ben, "and one of Diego Davis's favorite subjects."

"I don't know who Diego Davis is, and I don't give a fuck." He paused. "But there's a disappearing river?"

"Yep. It's kind of awesome, too. Which is why I'd lay good money that ninety percent of the people in the woods around the town of Devil's Kettle this weekend are on a day-hike to the Kettle it was named for. Let O'Malley's rangers focus on clearing the country between the fire and the river. I can clear the Kettle trail between the river and town."

"By yourself?" Ben asked, his brows crunched together in a way that suggested he was thinking hard. Diplomacy had never been Ben's strong suit but he was making a mighty effort, Eli knew. He was clearly turning Willa's suggestion over in his head, looking for flaws. Dread filled Eli's gut but he was turning her plan over in his head as well, and couldn't find much to object to, other than the fact that the woman he loved had just volunteered to walk *toward* a fire he desperately wanted her to walk *away* from.

Jax stepped forward. "I'm in."

Willa grinned at him. "There you go," she said. "I have a partner."

"I'll go, too," Eli heard himself say. "I have a per diem guy I've been using, covers tough ground at speed. If he's in, the four of us can cover the ground twice as fast." And get Willa back to the cabin twice as quickly.

"I know it's not ideal," Willa told Ben, "but it doubles the ground O'Malley's people can cover, which means we can at least get the people closest to the fire out of the way. So?"

A long moment of tense silence passed. Finally Ben said, "Fuck it. Go."

"Don't forget the radios," O'Malley said, and spread his lips in a stiff smile. "If you're clearing the trails, you're on Public Safety. Which means—" He caught Eli's eye, gave him a good, hard stare. "—you report to me."

Chapter 33

"GIRL," JAX SAID from the passenger seat of Willa's truck, "you have people skills I never guessed at."

Eli sat in the middle, directly to Willa's right, her gearshift between his knees, his silence thick and unhappy. Willa shifted uneasy shoulders. She wasn't sure what to do with a silent Eli.

"It wasn't people skills," she told Jax. "Two grown men were going after each other like angry raccoons. I'm not great at people, but I know raccoons."

"Well, you defused that situation, slick as snot," Jax said as Willa pulled into the gravel drive of her cabin. "It was impressive." He nudged Eli with his shoulder. "Wasn't it?"

"Yeah," Eli muttered. "Impressive."

Jax got out and strolled over to the porch steps where Brett sat tying his boots. He pulled a map from his back pocket and spread it on the porch where he and Brett began pointing and debating the way men did whenever a map made an appearance. Willa sat clutching the steering wheel, confused and uncertain. Eli didn't say a word, nor did he make eye contact. He just slid across the bench seat and got out the door Jax had left hanging open for him.

By the time Willa reached the porch, the men were already negotiating for territory. "I figure we'll park in the Kettle Loop lot," Jax said. "Brett and I can take the south trail, Willa and Eli can take the north trail and we'll meet at the Kettle. That way we can catch hikers coming and going." He looked up. "Okay with you all?"

"Okay by me," Brett said.

"Fine," Eli said shortly.

"Sure," Willa said, but her stomach wasn't so sure. Eli's fury — because he was definitely furious with her — wasn't settling well. She watched him stride to her truck and pull four DNR-issued backpacks from the bed. He came back and dropped two on the gravel at her feet. He tossed the other two to Jax and her father.

"Water, first aid, some protein bars and a fire shelter," he said while they all slid into their packs and adjusted the straps. He handed Jax a radio. "Public Safety is channel three, Incident Command is channel five. Air Support is channel seven. Report to Public Safety with your location every half hour."

Jax hooked the radio to his belt. "Got it."

"Don't take any chances. You hear or see anything resembling fire, you hear radio chatter about the wind picking up, you smell so much as a goddamn campfire, you haul ass back to the parking lot, no questions asked." Eli pressed his lips together, and Willa's gut clenched yet tighter. Eli wasn't happy about this. He really, really wasn't happy. Why would he be? He'd given up hotshotting. He'd given up on fires. The prospect of walking into the one simmering in the woods north of town clearly had him digging deep for a steely courage that hung in the air around him with a metallic tang. And he was taking a mostly untrained crew of civilian hikers with him? Guilt surged inside her like a storm-whipped lake.

"Haul ass back to the lot," Jax confirmed. "Roger."

Willa said, "Eli, wait."

"No time," he said. "You drive."

Willa bumped carefully up the dirt road that led to the Devil's Kettle Loop Trail parking lot, the apologies bottled up in her throat slowly fermenting into righteous anger. She kept one eye on the road and one on her rearview mirror, where she could see Eli speaking to Jax and her dad in the truck bed. He'd elected to ride back there with them, ostensibly to go over how to deploy their fire shelters but Willa doubted it. Eli was angry at her. Well, fine with her. She was angry right back.

She pulled into the lot, hands in fists on the wheel. There weren't many spots available. Hikers and art enthusiasts, all with their own reasons to worship at the Kettle, were out in force today. Would be all weekend, unless the fire simmering away in the northeast had its way and came down for a visit.

By the time she'd found a spot and slammed the door, the men were already standing at the tailgate, tightening their pack straps.

"Eli," she said, more firmly this time and headed toward them. She'd be damned if she'd let him be all pissed off at her for being exactly who she was. She'd agreed to hide from the press and she was keeping her word, damn it. But sitting in Eli's stifling little cabin like a rat in a trap was far likelier to kill her than a bruising, backcountry hike several miles from a fire she probably wouldn't even see. And she wouldn't apologize for that. Nobody had asked him to join her. He'd volunteered for that gig all by himself, the martyr. "Eli, I want to talk to you."

Eli kept his focus on his pack. Brett was the one who looked up.

"Willa, hey." Her dad stepped away from the group and made as if to touch her elbow. She blinked, startled, and jerked to a halt. He stopped, too, and put both hands up. "Sorry. I wasn't going to—"

"No, it's okay." She frowned and thought that one over. It *was* okay. She'd just been surprised. In the week or so Brett had been home, he'd made no attempt to play the dad card. Hadn't tried to hug her or touch her or offer her advice. And before that? She searched her memory for some instance of physical contact, affectionate or otherwise, but came up empty. Shay was the one who'd done all the hugging — and the hitting — as far as Willa could remember. "What do you need?"

His hand dropped awkwardly to his side and he shrugged. "I just wanted to say—"

"What?"

He met her eyes with a bright determination that startled her more than the aborted touch. "I want to thank you."

She blinked. "For what?"

"For letting me know you. I wasn't any kind of father to you, Willa, even when I was around. You didn't — you don't — owe me a thing but when I showed up out of the blue, you didn't turn me away. You gave me a bed and a computer. You gave me a chance. I didn't deserve any of those things but you gave them to me anyway, because you'd raised yourself better than Shay or I ever could have." He shook his head, his eyes dangerously moist. "You've been through so much. I had no idea but even if I had, I doubt I'd have been any help to you." He pressed his mouth tight. "It should've made you hard but it didn't. You didn't let it. You made yourself strong and smart and generous and kind instead. And I'm so damn proud of you."

She stared, utterly speechless. Brett hooked a thumb over his shoulder and barreled on. "Eli's a good guy," he said. "Solid. He'll make you happy and you deserve that. You won't be like me and Shay. We were broken from the get go, her and me."

She closed her mouth — it had been hanging open — and glanced at Eli. "We're broken, too."

"Everybody is, in their own way. But Shay and me, we made each other worse. You and Eli make each other better. Any fool can see that."

She shifted her eyes back to his. "Why are you telling me this?"

He shrugged uncomfortably. "Life's slippery. You should say things while people are in front of you."

She studied him, then frowned at Eli, now bent over the map with Jax. "Why is this sounding like a farewell speech?"

"It's not. But I see you and Eli circling each other and I worry that you might let the way Shay and I were color your thinking. That you might not believe you could do better. But you are better, Willa. So much better. You said last night that you don't want to live with mistakes, mine or anybody else's, so I want to tell you right now that letting go of him would be a mistake."

She lifted her eyes to the sky, spotted the purplish column of smoke spearing into the blue in the distance. "What about this, though? What about today? Are we walking into something here we shouldn't?"

"Eli wouldn't let us go if he didn't think it was okay." He met her eyes directly, and they were clear. Sober, not a hint of doubt. "He's solid, Willa."

"No, he's not." She wondered if she was talking to Brett, or to herself. "He's broken, just like you and me and everybody else."

"Exactly. He's not pretending otherwise, though. You can trust him. Whatever he's carrying, he's strong enough to carry it into these woods and back out again."

"But he doesn't want to." And she knew it. The knowledge settled inside her with the inevitability of a stone dropping to the bottom of a lake. "This is the stuff his nightmares are made of — an unpredictable fire, an untrained crew, both of them his responsibility. And I don't understand why the hell he'd take it on. But I'm going to find out." She stepped around her dad, then paused. Reached out and put a hand on his shoulder. "But hey, Dad?"

He stiffened under her touch, a deer scenting a threat. "Yeah?"

"Good talk. Thanks."

He closed his eyes briefly, and released a breath so faint that Willa felt more than heard it. "Yeah," he said. "Okay."

Eli folded the map while Jax stepped away from the truck bed and gave Brett a smile. "Ready, partner?"

"Ready," Brett said.

Jax clapped his shoulder. "Let's get after it, then."

"Channel three," Eli called after them. "Keep us posted."

"You, too." Jax dropped a big hand to Willa's shoulder on his way by, gave it a squeeze. "Stay safe."

"Same." Willa watched him split a sheaf of leaflets with Brett, little blue *Trail Closed* notices to be tucked under windshield wipers and stuck on campsites. She turned in time to accept her own stack from Eli.

"Let's blanket the parking lot then hit the trail," he said.

"Why?"

He frowned. "So people will know to get the hell out of here?"

"No, I mean, why are we doing this?"

"You tell me." His eyes were bright and angry on hers.

"Because I have to hide from the press and I suck at the indoors," she shot back. "I was three seconds away from calling Georgie to see if she'd come pluck my eyebrows when I decided to see if I could be of some service to my community instead."

"Damn." Eli sent her a sideways look and began tucking leaflets under windshield wipers. "That bad?"

"That bad. So I know why I'm doing this." She shoved one under a wiper herself and stalked to the next car. "Why are *you* doing this?"

"Because I love you, Willa."

Her eyes skated from his and she heard him tuck another slip under the nearest windshield wiper. "You keep *saying* that," she muttered and slapped another notice on another car. "I don't have the first idea what to do with it. Or what to say about it. Or what to say to you when you say it."

"You don't have to say anything." Eli hit the last car, then stuffed the leaflets in his pack and started toward the sign at the far end of the parking lot that read *Devil's Kettle*

North Loop. "You just have to trust that I mean what I say. I love you. And that means that I'm going to protect you whenever and wherever I can."

"Not if it means walking into your own personal nightmare! For God's sake, Eli, go home!" She caught his elbow, stopped him before he could put a single boot on the trail. "You don't have to do this!"

"Sure I do."

"No, you don't! Not for me!" She glared at him. "Love shouldn't cost you that much. It's not worth it." She dropped her voice, forced out the truth she hadn't wanted to face. "I'm not worth it."

He leaned forward, put a hard, angry kiss on her mouth. "Yes, you are." He drew back and glared at her. "Plus I'm fine. I wouldn't do it if I wasn't, so just trust me, okay? Now we promised Ben and O'Malley that we'd clear this area by sunset, so it's time to shut up and get hiking."

Chapter 34

ELI TURNED AWAY from Willa's skeptical eyes and started up a dirt trail rutted with millions of bootprints and veined with exposed tree roots. The shade swallowed him up, cool and dim and quiet. For a moment, he didn't think she'd follow, then he heard her fall in behind him. Relief flooded him, and he stretched his legs into the smooth, mile-eating pace that was as familiar to him as a lullaby. She could've walked away from him, he knew. She had every right, honestly. She'd been through some serious shit this past twenty-four hours. Put that next to the fourteen or so years she'd already lived through, and she could be forgiven for deciding that she was better off without a man who wouldn't negotiate. Couldn't negotiate. Not on this.

He wasn't proud of himself. He was proud as hell of her, though.

They'd hiked in cool silence for the better part of a mile before she finally spoke.

She said, "Okay."

He sent her a startled look over his shoulder. "Okay? Okay, what?"

She shrugged. "Okay. I trust you."

Hope surged inside him, nearly overshadowed the thin, omnipresent trickle of terror that connected his soul to the distant fire like some hideous umbilical cord. "Trust me to what?" he asked. "To know my own limits? Or to know when I'm in love?"

"Either," she said simply. "Both."

She hadn't said *she* loved *him*, but it was a start. Her trust drifted warmly to the floor of his stomach, and smoldered there like embers stored away for the evening fire. The trail narrowed to a single-file footpath as the miles fell away, choked with gooseberry leaves as big as elephant ears. Wild raspberry vines snatched at his pant legs, dragging at their pace even as Eli's mood soared.

A pair of hikers appeared on the trail ahead of them, a college-aged man and woman wearing matching packs.

"Hey," Eli said when they overtook the pair. "Sorry, guys, you're going to have to turn back." He pointed toward the northeast, though the tower of smoke wasn't visible through the dense green canopy. "We have a wildfire in the neighborhood."

"We know." The woman frowned. "But that's at least ten miles from here. I checked." She pulled a phone from her pocket and held it up like evidence.

"True enough." Eli smiled. "It's just a precaution at this point, but the wind changes on a dime this close to the big lake. The DNR doesn't want anybody to get into a situation."

"But we drove seven hours to get here." She thumbed the phone's screen and made a frustrated noise. "No service, of course. But I checked the radar back in the parking lot. The fire's nowhere near here and we've been planning this hike for a month."

"I'm sorry." He handed them a blue slip. "Not my decision."

The man took the slip, studied it. "This recommends evacuation." He exchanged a look with his girlfriend. "It doesn't mandate it."

"Well, no. This isn't a mandatory evac," Eli conceded. Great, a couple of law students. "Not yet. But as I said—"

"Well if it isn't mandatory, and you're not the police—" The woman cast a triumphant glance at Eli's civilian clothes. Didn't even bother looking at Willa. "—I think we'll just go ahead and take the vacation we planned."

"I wouldn't recommend that," Eli said.

"What are you going to do, arrest us?" She smirked. "Put us in park ranger jail?"

"No, ma'am." Eli blew out a breath and shifted his shoulders under the weight of responsibility for these clowns descending upon him. "I have no authority to detain you."

"If you don't mind, then?" She arched a brow at the trail Eli was now blocking.

Eli glanced at Willa, who stood silently at his shoulder, studying the pair with bemused detachment.

"It's their skin," Willa said finally and nodded up the trail. "Come on. These two want out of the gene pool, it's cool by me."

"Excuse me?" The woman's face flushed. "I'd like your name and position, please. I'll be speaking to your supervisor when we're off the trail."

Willa smiled. "Yeah, good luck with that. We're volunteers, lady. We're out here because some really smart people who know their shit think you ought to get off this trail now. You obviously think you know better." She shrugged. "There's no law against stupid, and even if there was, we're not law enforcement, as you so astutely pointed out. Now if you don't mind, I'm sure this trail is full of folks who aren't suicidally bone-headed, so we're going to go find them." She nudged Eli again, clearly his signal to move on. But it chafed, leaving anybody out here, even the suicidally boneheaded who clearly weren't going to listen to reason.

"Be safe," he said to them. "If you smell smoke or hear fire, head back to the parking lot at a run, understand?" He accepted the woman's glare as his due, and started up the trail again. Willa fell in behind.

"Have a nice hike," she called back to the baby lawyers.

"We will," the woman called back. "And screw you!"

"That was pleasant," Willa said.

"Yeah," Eli muttered.

"Law students?"

"That was my guess."

"I hate lawyers."

"Now I do too."

"I hated them before." Willa sighed behind him. "They talk and talk and talk, and it never amounts to anything but a massive bill."

"I hope those two don't have to pay for today."

"Me, too. If only so you don't tie yourself in knots over them."

He threw a glance over his shoulder. "I'm not tying myself in knots."

She returned his look with a cool, steady silence.

He looked away first, found himself staring at the path under his boots, watching it fly away underneath him like a river, a current carrying him closer and closer to the flames. "I'm not in knots," he muttered. It sounded like a lie even to him.

Behind him, she exuded that stillness of hers, serene and unconcerned. "I know I'm not the only reason you're in these woods, Eli. If I were, those idiot pre-lawyers back there wouldn't have bothered you. They sure as hell didn't bother me."

He frowned. "What do you mean?"

"You're really upset that they won't get off the trail."

"Of course I am. If the wind picks up, they could be in a lot of trouble."

"We all could be." He felt rather than saw her shrug. "They're adults, though, and they've been warned. They clearly want to take their chances. Why not let them?"

"I *am* letting them." He shifted his shoulders under the straps of his pack, their presence in the woods an itch he couldn't scratch. "They're still hiking, aren't they?"

"Yep. But you hate it. It's making your skin crawl. You've been twitching since we gave up on them."

"I'm not twitching." He caught himself wanting to adjust his pack again and suppressed the urge with ruthless self-control. Christ, it was nearly unbearable.

"You are." The stillness thickened, wrapped itself around him. The itch eased almost immediately.

"Stop it."

"Stop what?"

"Sedating me."

"Stop guilt-tripping out over a couple of idiots then."

"I'm responsible for those idiots!"

"Exactly." She grabbed his elbow, dragged him to a halt. "Eli, exactly! The guy you were, the one you've been trying so hard to walk away from? He's still in here." She tapped him just above his sternum strap. "And he's a good guy. He's not an arrogant cowboy or a thrill seeker. Not anymore. You're here today because I dragged you here, sure. But it's also because you have the skills and the knowledge to save some lives, and a sense of responsibility that won't let you walk away when you can help. It's a Venn diagram, right?"

"A what?"

"You know, those charts with the overlapping circles? Everything in life can be explained by a good Venn diagram."

He stared at her. "Okay."

"So you've got these circles, these problems, okay? Here's one for *My uncle and O'Malley want to punch each other.*" She drew a circle in the air. "And here's one for *The reporters want to eat Willa.*" She drew another circle. "And here's one for *Hotshot training I no longer want to use,* and another one for *I'm hardwired to care about people, either because I'm a firefighter or because I'm a bartender.*"

"All that in one circle?"

She shrugged. "Make it two circles. I don't care. This is your chart."

"Okay."

"So this situation happens with the reporters and the fire and me, and all the circles — all the problems — start to move closer together." She lifted her arms, gathered in all the air-circles she'd drawn in a tight bundle between them.

"Pretty soon they're bumping up against each other, and there's no way to separate them out into individual issues. The only thing to do is find the one place in the center where all the circles come together, where all the problems touch." She stabbed a finger into this imaginary overlap, this confluence of all Eli's problems. "That's your solution, the only one. And in this case, the only way to solve all these problems, to satisfy all the pieces of you — the nephew, the firefighter, the bartender, the protector, the lover — was to walk into the fire again. So you screwed up your courage and you did it. It was the last thing you wanted to do, but you did it. And that's fantastic."

She flung her arms around him and hugged him hard. He hugged her back, dazed and baffled. "Your circles were separate for so long, Eli, and you only let one of them matter, the one that said you weren't worthy of the work you loved. You were a puzzle and you were broken. You've finally put yourself back together. So yeah, I'm proud of you. I'm in awe of you."

He stared at her, lost for words. A breeze stirred the thick, still air, and pine needles slid against each other with a quiet chuff. And somewhere underneath the sharp green scent of fir and hemlock and aspen, Eli smelled it.

Smoke.

"Oh shit," Eli said and grabbed Willa by the upper arms, his eyes flying wildly around the serene green forest. Cool, lush, still. Too still.

"What?"

"Do you smell that?"

She tensed in his hands. "Smell what?"

"Smoke."

She inhaled deeply. "I don't smell anything."

Eli dragged a breath into tight lungs. Nothing. "Neither

do I. Not anymore." He snatched the radio off his belt and turned up the trail again. Started off at a near jog. "But I did. And that's not good."

Willa fell in behind him as he keyed the radio. "Public Safety? Public Safety, this is Team Alpha in the voluntary evac zone, do you read me?"

The radio gave a belch of static then a crackle that dissolved into words. "...Safety, repeat?"

"Again, Public Safety, this is Team Alpha in the voluntary evac zone. We're scenting smoke intermittently. Request update on fire movement?"

The path flew along under his feet, blurring into a river of dirt and roots and rocks that barreled him along without any effort on his own part. It had its own gravity, dragging him into its orbit, pulling Willa along behind him.

"...out of the northeast at...to ten miles per hour...time," a voice said. A woman. A vague image of a redheaded dispatcher came to mind. He'd seen her at IC, hadn't introduced himself. "...now involves 200 square acres...estimated daily run of—"

The radio squawked violently and the dispatcher cut out. Eli spun the channel knob, searching for a signal.

"—Team Three," a new voice emerged from the chaos. "We've got eyes on..." The voice cut out but dread gripped Eli by the throat.

"Public Safety Team Three?" the dispatcher responded. "You have eyes on the fire?"

"Roger," a woman — one of the park rangers sweeping the mandatory evac zone — said through a film of static. "We've cleared...campsites in this section...ninth is supposed to...vacant." Even catching every third word or so, Eli could tell she was panting, her voice uneven. She was running, Eli realized, his gut twisting. "...going to check it...be safe but...smell smoke...really dark...We can—" Another sharp blast of interference cut her off.

"Team Three?" Eli could picture the dispatcher sitting up

sharply, pressing the earphones tighter to her head. As if that would cut down on the interference. "Team Three, what is your current status?"

"…loud, like a roar all of a sudden then…see flames…still two miles from safe zone…"

Eli's lungs seized up. "Fuck," he said with a sinking inevitability. Urgency beat like blood inside him, and suddenly he was running. "It's going to go over them."

"What?" Behind him Willa broke into a run as well, her hiking boots thudding into the dry earth like his heart knocking against his ribs. "The fire? It's going over who?"

"One of the Public Safety teams in the mandatory evac zone. A pair of O'Malley's rangers." A stark clarity descended on him, and everything sharpened, slowed. His lungs loosened and his breath cycled smoothly now even as the scent of smoke filtered again through the trees. "They're two miles from the safe zone."

"Where's the safe zone?" Willa demanded.

"We're in it."

"I thought we were in a goddamn jungle of ladder fuel?"

"We are."

"How are we the safe zone, then?"

A cliff shearing away to the Lake Superior shoreline lay beyond the tree line a few hundred yards to their south, and the hotshots were cutting fire line along a basalt ridgeline to their north that rose up out of the woods like a spine running from Canada all the way to the town of Devil's Kettle. The river was ahead of them by a mile or so, an iffy fence a determined fire could jump in seconds if it wanted to. "There is no safe zone."

He flipped to channel five — Incident Command — and the radio exploded.

"—goddamn run of at least seven miles, and the wind's up—"

"—gusting to…miles per hour—"

"—tanker planes en route, drown that motherfucker—"

"—Moving the Barker Mountain Hotshots west to…cutting line on the south bank…River, contain this bitch before—"

He flipped back to the Public Safety Channel, keyed the mic. "Team Bravo, this is Team Alpha, do you read?"

Static gurgled from the radio but then Jax's voice surfaced. "Got you, Alpha. Go ahead?"

"Fire's on the move," he snapped, relief a cool rush in his veins. "Get back to the parking lot and get the hell out. Now."

"Roger that. Meet you there."

"No, it's too close to us. We'll deploy in the river. Keys are in the truck. Get back to town. We'll see you there after."

But the connection had gone to shit again, and when he keyed the mic, he got nothing but static.

"Shit!" He glanced left. He knew the ridgeline was there through the trees to the north, rising up and up, playing havoc with the radio signal. Frustration was a greasy knot in his throat. There was no way he could break into the radio traffic on the IC channel, not with the fire blowing up. Public Safety was out of reach for the moment, too, or until he could get to higher ground. But he'd gotten Jax and Brett off the trail so he hooked the radio to his belt and picked up the pace. He wasn't sprinting but it wasn't far off.

"Eli, wait!" Willa's voice was ragged behind him, her breath coming in snatches. "Where are you going? Shouldn't we turn around?"

"We can't." His brain — still in that state of artificial calm — had been performing calculations in the background since the minute he'd heard that poor park ranger running. It had been efficiently identifying risk factors and escape routes, creating and playing out scenarios, estimating his and Willa's pace and progress toward the river. "We're only a mile from the river at this point, maybe less. We turn around now, we're running through two miles of ticking time bomb back to the parking lot, and no guarantees once we get there that we can outrun the fire to town."

He felt the weight of her silence as she digested that info, as it rejiggered her reality and not in a good way. Eli was familiar with that unpleasant process. "What do we do?" There wasn't a hint of panic in her words, and pride flickered inside him. She was breathless, yeah, and more than a little afraid, but she was calm. Alert. Ready to think and survive. And she was looking to him for guidance. Because she trusted him.

Eli was going to reward that trust. He was going to keep her alive. He swallowed a greasy ball of horror at the thought of the baby lawyers on the trail behind them, but Willa was his first priority. Maybe if he got her squared away he could go back for them.

He picked up the pace yet further. "We've got to get to the river."

"But that's toward the fire!"

"That's toward a couple million gallons of water."

"Water that's freezing cold, wicked fast, and running straight into a bottomless hole?"

Eli blew out a breath. "That's the stuff."

"Shit," Willa said, and picked up the pace. Then suddenly she grabbed his pack and jerked him to a halt. "Oh Jesus," she moaned. "The baby lawyers."

"Screw the baby lawyers." The words were bitter in his mouth but he didn't regret them. "We have to run now, Willa. Right now."

"We have to get those idiots off the trail."

"No, we don't."

She didn't bother answering, just turned and bolted back the way they'd come at a dead sprint. Eli's blood ran cold at the sight of her putting even another foot of distance between herself and the safety of the river, but his heart swelled with love for her. Because he knew she wasn't risking her life for the baby lawyers. She was risking it for him. She'd said it herself earlier — if things went south, they'd made their choice. And while Willa could probably live with that, she knew that Eli couldn't bear the burden of even one more death. She wouldn't ask him to. It hadn't even crossed her mind to ask him to, not even with her own life on the line.

Goddamn, he loved this woman. He was going to kill her later, but in this moment, love was all he knew.

Chapter 35

WILLA BUSTED AROUND a sharp bend in the trail and nearly took out the female lawyer. Hands fisted, mouth sour, the woman was marching down the trail with more determination than enjoyment. When Willa appeared, she stopped abruptly, then sneered.

"You again," she said.

"Me again," Willa agreed, panting.

"What, did you forget something?" She folded her arms, kicked her weight to one hip. "Overlook an insult you wanted to deliver?"

Eli caught up and Willa glanced at him. "I already regret this," she told him.

"Regret what?" the woman asked acidly.

"Saving your lives."

The woman rolled her eyes. "Listen, I don't know what kind of peon power trip you're on here but if you think you can intimidate us into—"

"Cara, wait." The other baby lawyer stepped up, put his hand to Cara's elbow.

She shook him off impatiently, her eyes hot and pinned to Willa. "No, Tim, I won't wait. We have every right to be on this trail and if you think I'm going to let this woman push us off it with her incredibly and persistently unprofessional behavior—"

"Can you be a professional volunteer?" Willa wondered aloud. "Is that a thing?"

"Do you smell that?" Tim asked.

Cara gave an elaborate sigh. "Smell what?"

"Smoke." His eyes flicked to Willa's, then to Eli's.

"That's smoke, isn't it?"

"Yeah," Eli said grimly. "It is."

"Wait, smoke?" The woman's eyes flew to Eli. "How could it be smoke? The fire's ten miles from here!"

"The wind picked up," he said. "Best case scenario, the fire's four miles away. Worst case? Two."

Willa could smell it now, too, an invisible haze threading through the trees. Between their boots, a patch of sunshine faded from bright lemon to a sickly ash as Willa watched. The woman didn't seem to notice any of this. She pressed her lips into a line that struck Willa as both skeptical and habitual, and produced her phone.

"Seriously?" Willa stared as the woman flicked competently at the screen with both thumbs. "You think we have time for a fact check? Lady, listen. This is the North Shore, and we're eight miles from the nearest town. There's no service, okay? There wasn't service before and there's no service now. Plus there's a goddamn forest fire close enough to *smell* so will you please put that away and move your ass?"

She continued to tap intently, her eyes never leaving the screen. "If you swear at me one more time—" she began.

Eli reached out, snatched the phone from the woman's hand, and heaved it into the woods.

"Unbelievable." Cara stared, outraged, her hands still shaped around the missing phone. "You people are unbelievable. I am *so* going to have your jobs."

"You're welcome to them." Eli smiled grimly. "But I should warn you, they're kind of thankless."

"Plus, they aren't even jobs," Willa put in. "We're *volunteers,* damn it."

The woman glared. "What did I say about the swearing?"

Willa turned to the boyfriend. "Is English not her first language?"

He dragged a hand down his face. "It's not the language, it's the authority. She has a problem with authority."

Cara tilted her chin. "I have no problem with authority properly rendered. But this is a blatant overreach and I have no intention of—"

A sudden wind pushed through the trees, and Willa had to brace her boots against the nasty slap. Cara broke off, seeming to notice for the first time that the air had gone an ominous pearly gray. Smoke, Willa realized with a pulse of dismay, was curling through the trees like the thinnest fog, hardly visible except for the way it muted the green.

"Okay," Eli said, "Time's up." He took Cara by the arm and turned her up the trail the way he and Willa had come. "You don't have to stop talking if it makes you feel better but it's time to run now."

Cara dug in her heels and tugged on her elbow. Eli kept it. "What, *toward* the fire?" She stared. "Hell, no. We're heading for the parking lot." She jerked her elbow from Eli's grip. "Come on, Tim. We're out of here."

She marched by him but Tim didn't fall obediently into line. He stood there, frowning thoughtfully into space. Cara stopped on the trail and threw him an impatient glance. "Tim, come *on*."

The forest swayed and shifted around them, dancing with the fitful breeze. Willa became dimly aware of a throb in her bones, some kind of terrible subsonic vibration she'd never experienced before. An instinctive burst of dread filled her, welling up from the part of her brain that didn't need to name a threat to perceive it. She shifted on her boots, sidling under the itchy urge to run toward the parking lot herself.

"I'm sorry, Cara," Tim said finally. "But I'm not going to die because you have daddy issues."

Her mouth fell open. "Daddy issues?"

"The river is this way," Eli said, jerking his head the way he and Willa had come. He eyed the narrow strip of sickly yellow sky above them, lined in spiky pine crowns. That terrible buzz in Willa's bones grew until her fillings ached. "I'd suggest we run."

Tim looked at Cara on the trail behind him. "I'm running," he said. "Are you coming or not?"

"Fuck you, Tim," she said, furious tears filling her eyes. But she yanked her pack straps tight and started jogging toward the river. Tim followed.

"Thank you, Jesus," Eli muttered.

"Amen," Willa said, and started running.

It happened with breathtaking speed. Later, Willa would have no clear memory of it, just a series of frozen images lodged in her brain like a row of crooked teeth. They ran single file, boots pounding over the hard-packed trail while that buzz in her bones grew and twisted. And then it wasn't in her bones anymore. It was too huge. It was inside her, outside her, all around her. It was a roar, consuming and ravenous. It was, she realized with a pulse of terror, the sound of the fire. It was ripping and devouring, chewing through centuries of forest, decades of fuel, tearing its way toward them with a gleeful roar that inhabited the very air.

Then suddenly the oxygen disappeared. She felt it go — an eerie rush like the tide going out. Her ears gave a vicious pop and her lungs made a startled lunge into the vacuum where the air used to be. Her heart knocked against her ribs, terrified and starved. Then a dingy twilight dropped over them and they were running blind, sprinting into the dark toward a river they couldn't see but their lizard brains could somehow sense. That itchy urge to turn around and race for the parking lot was gone, and all Willa knew was a pounding need to race toward the ribbon of salvation twisting and dancing through the forest like a finish line. She couldn't possibly smell the water — there was no air, nothing to carry the scent — but her brain remembered. Instinct whispered. The scent of wet rocks and lush greens was survival, and it slipped through her fear, wrapped itself around her and pulled. *This way, this way, this way.*

Then the air returned all at once, a wall of hot smoke that punched her in the face. Her lungs seized on it automatically — oxygen! — then hacked it immediately back out again. Her eyes stung, her chest ached. She dropped her head into the foul blast of it and kept running, skimming only the thinnest layer into her lungs.

Something bulleted out of the black blanket of the sky as she ran, caught her squarely on the shoulder with a muffled pop. She clapped a hand to the sting and lifted her face to the sky, squinted uncomprehending into the punishing blast of hot wind.

Rocks were falling out of the sky all around her. They were pelting the dirt at her feet and rolling away like marbles. She blinked watering eyes and focused. No, not rocks, she saw finally. Hailstones. The fire was making its own weather, just like Eli had said. An incongruous moment of wonder caught her by surprise and she watched them fall to the trail in dirty gray plops. One crunched under her boot with a strange, hollow delicacy, and a shock of bone-deep revulsion shot through her.

Oh Jesus, oh God, oh *hell*. These weren't rocks. This wasn't hail or rain or even fire. These were birds. Tiny, hollow-boned songbirds were falling, singed and smoking, out of the sky. They littered the ground at her feet, the smallest and first victims of the coming fire. She cried out and Eli said, "Don't stop. Willa, you can't stop."

Ahead of her on the trail, Cara screamed and skidded, then went down hard on her butt. Tim yelped and leapt sideways and Willa said, "Jesus!"

A deer tore out of the forest a foot from Cara's boots, his antlers ripping at the branches, his large liquid eyes full of panicked urgency. Cara threw her arms over her head and Willa waited helplessly for her to be trampled. But then the buck gathered itself and gravity fell away. The deer sailed over Cara's head, hit the trail with a thud of hooves and a puff of dust and bounded down the trail toward the parking lot.

Tim hooked his hands through Cara's pack straps and yanked her to her feet, shoved her forward. "Keep going," he shouted, and Willa realized that they were all shouting now. The roar of the fire had built into a scream. It filled her head and jittered through her veins, it inhabited her muscles and drove her feet into a sprint.

The scent of sanctuary was stronger now, sliding underneath the smoke and heat and dying birds. The trail gave a sudden lurch under their feet in the dark, angling steeply uphill and Willa cried out in relief. This was the last climb, she knew. They would crest their last hill and the Devil River was just a slippery scramble away, hiding in a deep notch between two piney ridges. She couldn't see anything but she knew the trees were thinning as they climbed, knew the horizon would break free fifty yards ahead. Twenty-five. Ten.

The breath sawed in and out of her lungs, hot and useless. Her chest ached, her legs shook, but still she ran. Tim's pack was close enough to touch and she knew he had his hands on Cara's, driving her forward. Eli was right behind her, too, she realized suddenly, his hold on her own pack the only reason she hadn't hit her knees half a dozen times in the past thirty seconds. A wave of love for him crashed over her.

"Come on, come on, come on," he was muttering behind her. "Just over the hill, Cara!" he shouted. "You're almost there!"

Then suddenly the trees were gone. They were standing on a sharp basalt ledge with a view that had been drawing hikers for a hundred years. And they could finally see.

The world was a deep pulsing orange, and the forest on the other side of the river was a spiky black silhouette, backlit by an advancing wall of flames. A fist of fire reached between the trunks as Willa watched, wrapped itself around the base of a two-hundred-foot pine and lifted it casually out of the ground. The tree exploded into fire, flew into the sky like a rocket and tumbled down the steep embankment toward the river. Willa cried out or tried to, but the air was blisteringly hot, as wavy as old glass. It scorched her throat and killed her voice. Plumes of fire floated through the air like clouds, rode the swirling updrafts, leapt from tree to tree like squirrels. They rained sparks, tiny fires floating out of the sky to drill through her clothes, bite at her skin. And there below them was the river.

It spilled among a jumble of rocks, black and rough and fast, racing toward the cliff, toward the lake below. But just before the edge, a massive hole opened up in the basalt, a perfectly round void the river had drilled from its own stream bed, a gaping maw into which the river fell and disappeared. It was a hundred yards downriver from them but the current was fast and greedy. One bad step could toss a hiker into it and—

"Go!" Eli shouted and reached around Willa to give the baby lawyers a mighty shove. They slid and stumbled down the slick, mossy rocks, and Willa followed. The river leapt and boiled at the base of the hill, the wind ripping waves up out of the surface and slapping them back down again. She didn't break stride when she hit the edge, refused to let herself think about the hungry Kettle waiting downstream. She just threw off her pack and tossed herself into the water.

It swallowed her with an icy shock that closed her throat and sent a fresh fear trembling down her spine. If the Kettle didn't kill them — or the fire — the cold water might. Lake Superior didn't drown people so much as freeze them to death. The water was only waist-deep where they'd crashed into it, so she shoved herself to her feet. The current snatched and pushed at her, though, and her boots slid in the loose rocks tumbling along the riverbed. She went down hard. Water filled her nose and mouth and a thread of panic stitched through her starving lungs.

Then Eli's hand was on her collar and she was hauled

half out of the water. Her upper body landed across a large, flat rock in the middle of the river, her hips and legs still submerged. Eli was standing in the water in front of the rock Willa was clinging to, his back to the current, his chest to the rock. She could hear the baby lawyers shouting somewhere downstream, so presumably they hadn't tumbled to their deaths in the Kettle.

"I have to help them with their fire shelter," he shouted.

"What?" Her throat was on fire, her arms breaking out in goosebumps even as they burned in the heat.

He shoved a flat packet into her hands. "Here, hold onto this for a second." He wrestled himself and the sodden pack he was still wearing out of the water until he was sitting on the rock beside her. He took the packet from her numb hands, ripped it open and gave it a hard shake. The furnace-blast of wind filled it and it snapped open. It looked like a tent/sleeping bag hybrid made of aluminum foil. He dropped the mouth of the fire shelter into the water and let water flow into it until the bottom sank. He hopped off the rock on Willa's side this time, dug his boots into the gravel and braced against the current. He slipped the shelter over Willa's boots and pulled it up to her shoulders until she was wearing it like a sleeping bag.

"Here," he said, and threaded her hands through a couple of webbing loops near the top. "Use these to hold the hood down over your head until I get back. And Willa?" He grabbed a handful of her t-shirt and hauled her forward, pressed his mouth to hers with fierce promise. "I'm coming back. Do you hear me? *I'm coming back for you.*"

Then he stepped away from the rock and let the current sweep him toward the baby lawyers. She clung to the rock and watched him disappear.

He'd left her.

Chapter 36

SHE SHIVERED, THE air hot enough to scorch her throat while her legs went numb in the icy water filling her shelter. Tears — stupid and helpless — gathered in her eyes. She was going to die. They all were. But she was going to do it alone. A laugh broke through her tears, bitter and unsurprised. Of course she was going to die alone. Why should her death be any different than her life? She closed her eyes, rested her cheek on the rock and let the hood of the fire shelter slip down to her shoulders.

She didn't blame Eli. He loved her. He'd said so and she didn't doubt him. But he was who he was, and protecting others was as integral to his survival as oxygen. He couldn't save himself before making sure everybody else was okay, even a couple of barely-adult idiots with better debate skills than survival instincts.

But at least the question that had been eating him alive since losing his entire crew had finally been answered: He wasn't capable of enriching himself while risking others. It was a brand of selfishness that simply wasn't in him. So there was no way he could leave a couple of bone-heads to their stubborn fate while the slenderest hope existed that he could save them *and* her, along with himself. Even through her pain and terror, she was aware of a deep, glowing satisfaction. Eli was finally whole again, doing exactly what he had been put on this earth to do — protecting the helpless.

It didn't, however, change the fact that death was coming for them, relentless and ravenous. Nor did it change the fact that Willa was going to face it alone because everybody she cared about had something more important to do, somebody more important to save. As usual.

Even as the thought crossed her mind, she could taste its bitterness. It was an ugly thought, selfish and wrong. But fuck it. If she wanted to spend her last few moments alive feeling sorry for herself, she had every right.

A morbid curiosity opened her eyes for her. Would she see death coming, she wondered, or would it surprise her? She had a feeling death was always a surprise, no matter how resigned you thought you were. She watched without interest as animals boiled out of the flaming forest on the far side of the river, appearing suddenly through air gone opaque with heat and smoke. They flew from the woods — rabbits and raccoons racing and bounding along the ground, squirrels driven out of the tree tops. A wolf bolted out of the tree line maybe twenty yards upstream, yipping in agony, its coat in flames. It crashed smoking into the river, fought through the shallows then hit the current and began to swim.

A spasm of hope caught her off guard. Not hope for herself, but for that wolf. *Come on, come on,* Willa thought, watching it dig in against the pitiless current. *You can do it. You can beat it. You can win.* And for a moment, she thought maybe it would.

The wolf struggled toward the far riverbank, its lips peeled back with effort. It was small for a wolf, probably a juvenile, and the river dragged nastily at it, snatching and grabbing. The wolf fought, though, finally gaining its feet on the rocky bottom. Willa's heart leapt in triumph as it dragged itself toward the shore. But then it stopped, teetering in the shallows, gauging the jump it would have to make out of the water. The rocky bank it faced was so high, the ledge so steep.

"Please," she murmured as the wolf gathered itself for that last crucial leap. "Oh, please."

It lunged, and fell short. It folded to its knees, beaten, and surrendered to the current. The water snatched at its limp body, swirled it back into the heart of the river straight toward her. A horrified pity flooded her, and she cried out. To the wolf, for the wolf? She had no idea. But the lonely heart in her reached out as the battered wolf floated by, and suddenly her hands reached out as well. She watched it happen as if her body belonged to somebody else — the wolf's body tumbling down the river, then her hands slipping free of the webbing loops connecting her to the fire shelter and reaching out. She understood, even as the current stripped the fire shelter off her and sent it spinning downstream, that she wasn't close enough to catch the wolf. Just like she understood that she would leap to meet it.

She did. She shoved away from the rock, dropped into the icy water, and snatched her arms around a limp, beaten wolf.

She went under, tumbled over and over until she didn't know which way was up. Until she'd lost any inclination to even figure it out. She was dead; they all were. And it was ridiculous to think a glorified sleeping bag could change that.

Eli had tucked her into one all the same, of course, just like he was tucking the baby lawyers into theirs. It was useless, and Willa figured he knew as much, but his soul demanded he try.

And in that dark, airless moment of surrender, Willa finally understood.

Eli was going to die a good death, the kind of death that would honor him. And by wrapping her arms and her mind around a bewildered, terrified animal, by giving it comfort in a way that only she could, Willa was going to do the same.

Love pulsed through her, filled her empty lungs and glowed deep inside her soul. The water was punishingly cold and the wolf was a sodden weight in her arms but she wasn't alone anymore. Eli was with her. They would die separately, yes. But they wouldn't die alone. They couldn't. Not with their souls whole and love between them.

And it *was* love. He'd said he loved her, and he'd been right. She loved him right back. If she died with one regret it was that she'd never told him so. But he knew it. Somehow, she believed, he knew.

Her boots struck something hard and unyielding, and instinct had her taking the shock with her knees. She gripped the wolf by the scruff and pistoned her legs. She shot upward. Her head broke the river's madly roiling surface and she dragged a desperate breath into screaming lungs. She shook her head hard, cleared her eyes and realized she'd been sucked into a small eddy created by a dead tree that had fallen across a bend in the river. The Kettle hissed and roared just around the bend, and the center of the river sprinted madly toward it. Willa's heart gave a thud of horror. It had been nothing but the purest luck that had landed her and her soggy wolf here in this relatively protected eddy instead of flinging them over the edge into oblivion.

A few feet of gravelly sediment had collected in front of the fallen tree trunk, creating the closest thing to a beach the North Shore had to offer. The river tugged on her, trying to pull her back out into the current and sweep her gleefully into the Kettle. She snatched at the dead tree instead, and hauled herself out of its grip. She dragged herself into the shallower water and dragged the wolf up with her. She couldn't tell if it was alive or dead but she couldn't do anything about that. All she could do right now was make sure that her face and wolf's were out of the water while keeping the rest of their bodies as submerged as possible. She doubted it would make a difference in the long run — dead was dead — but she'd protect the both of them as best she could.

She cradled the wolf to her chest, buried her face in its sopping scruff and thought about her thinnie. The fire shrieked and gobbled, its roar a seismic trembling that inhabited the air she was trying to breathe. It was driving itself into her lungs, breath by super-heated breath. The wolf stirred suddenly in her arms, whimpered restlessly, and Willa rubbed her cheek against it. "Shhh, now. I'm here.

You're not alone."

And she would make that mean something.

She threw her mind fiercely toward the serenity of her fairy ring, to the impossible age of that rock and the unshakeable calm that came with it. She felt it creep into her soul, that calm, and allowed it to spread its cool fingers through her body. Death and life and death again spiraled out in endless parabolas in her mind, one feeding into the other into the other until Willa was just one more star, stitched into the incomprehensible pattern of the universe. Ending to beginning to ending, turning around and around, forever and ever, amen. Everything within her settled, surrendered, and she cast that stillness over the wolf in her arms like a quilt. Tucked it around them both. She was aware of the heat and the scream of the fire but the thinnie and its unassailable wisdom stood between it and her. In her heart there was nothing but calm and love.

Eli, she thought, and smiled. She whispered his name in her mind like a prayer, like a benediction, like an amen. *Eli*. She sent it out into the universe, too. To him. She understood the impossibility of it, but if there was any chance that he could hear her, she wanted him to know that her last thought was of him. That it had brought her peace and immeasurable joy.

And she heard in return, *Willa*.

"Willa!"

It wasn't until Eli actually fell on top of her that she realized his voice wasn't just in her head.

He seized her by the shoulders, hauled her upright and shook her. "Willa! *Willa!*"

She didn't bother trying to speak. Her throat was too burned, her relief too acute. She simply threw her arms around him and released a cry that tore loose something deep inside her. It was a shocking sensation. Eli had already turned her inside out, or so she'd thought. Surely there hadn't been a single piece of her soul that he hadn't exposed to the pitiless light of day. Evidently there had been one, a crucial pocket of bitterness and fear hidden away. A little nugget of doubt sowed deep in her soul, a seed that had needed one last abandonment to bloom.

Eli's return obliterated it. Ripped it out by the roots and flung it out to be swallowed whole by the Kettle.

His hands on her shoulders were like vise grips and he shook her, hard. "Jesus Christ, Willa! You scared me to death! Why didn't you stay on the rock? *Why didn't you stay?*"

"I've stayed my whole life!" she shouted back, surprising herself. She hadn't known the words were coming until she heard them, ragged and burned. "Stayed and stayed and stayed, hoping somebody — anybody — would come back for me! Nobody ever did, okay? Nobody ever came back!"

"Yeah? Well I did." He glared at her. "I said I would, and I did." He let her go and leapt to his feet. He snatched up the sopping wet fire shelter at his boots — her shelter? Had he rescued it from downriver somehow? "God, Willa. Do you know what I thought when I saw this floating toward the Kettle?" He gave it a violent shake. "I thought you were in it! I thought you were going to die while I stood there and watched!"

"Well I didn't!"

"And you're not going to, either!" He dropped to his butt in the water beside her and shoved his boots into the slimy mouth of the soaking wet fire shelter. Then he grabbed her boots and shoved them in as well, and started dragging the whole sodden mass up over their thighs. "Budge up there, Willa. Neither of us is huge but these things aren't really made for two. We're going to have to get cozy."

She lifted her bottom obediently and let him slide the thing underneath her with a sense of unreality. She'd given up. She'd accepted death, but here he was, yelling at her and fighting for their lives. For *her* life.

"You really came back for me," she said wonderingly, and it settled inside her like a warm stone. It sank straight to the bottom of her battered soul and set up a serene, steady glow.

"Of course I did." He glared at her.

"Of course you did." She laughed, a sharp burble of sound that rode the line between joy and disbelief. "I love you, Eli Walker."

He rolled his eyes. "Now she tells me."

"You knew already?"

"Of course I knew." He hiked up his own butt and pulled the shelter up to their waists. Found the webbing loops attached to the hood and threaded his hands through them. "But it's nice to hear you say it. I love you, too."

"I know that now. I really do."

He cast a glance toward the opposite bank. The fire had roared forward, was gobbling up the last few yards of forest and gathering itself for the leap over the river. "This is going to get ugly, Willa. We're going to have to just ride it out." He hesitated. "Do you trust me?"

"More than anything," she said promptly, and it was true. That last pocket of doubt had been torn away and she was his.

"It's time to lie down, then. I have to drag this thing over our heads and we're going to lie here, belly down, until we hear the hotshots calling our names, you understand? The water's going to protect us as best it can but the air outside this shelter will be hot enough to kill us if we open it up too soon, never mind the fire. Are you claustrophobic?"

"Does it matter?"

"Not really."

"I didn't think so." She drew the wolf's limp body into her arms. "She's coming, too. I won't leave her."

Eli stared at the half-burned wolf and sighed. "No, I

know you won't."

"She was so brave," Willa murmured. "You should've seen her swim."

"I'm glad I didn't. I don't think I'd have lived through the sight of you going after her. All right, face down." Willa tucked the wolf into her body and rolled until she was lying on top of it, her cheek pressed to the sharp gravel of the bank. Eli spread himself over her back, his knees on either side of hers. He stretched his arms as wide as the shelter would allow, pressed his cheek next to hers and punched his fists into the silt on either side of her and the wolf, dropping them all into a dark, hot pocket of mud, water and noise.

For a heart beat, maybe two, the world was still and suspended. Then the fire fell on them. It leapt from the forest behind them, rained down onto the bank around them like death. It took the skies for its own — wind, air, and cloud, they were all fire. It raked at their fragile shelter, rattled it violently, twisted and shoved at it like a tornado. She closed her eyes, wrapped her arms around the wolf and pressed her back into the heat and strength of Eli above her. He was protecting her with his own body once again, she thought wonderingly. And even though the wolf took up precious space and oxygen, he'd never even suggested leaving it outside. If this was it, if this was the end of Willa's road, she didn't have the first complaint.

A thought occurred to her suddenly and she twisted her head so she could shout in his ear.

"Eli! The lawyers! Are they all right?"

"I got them deployed a little ways downstream. They were damn close to going into the Kettle but that girl's a fighter. Got herself and her boyfriend to the bank instead. If they stay inside the shelter, they'll be as all right as we are."

Which wasn't making any promises but she laid her cheek back in the mud, satisfied. Eli had done everything he could for them. He wouldn't have any complaints either. She kept one arm around the wolf, but wrapped her other hand around one of Eli's wrists, and added her strength to his to hold their whisper-thin sanctuary tight.

Chapter 37

PETER SLIPPED INTO the Wooden Spoon, found a space on the wall and put his back against it. When the fire had turned nasty so abruptly, O'Malley had sent out a shelter-in-place directive for locals, but declared Peter's bar a temporary shelter for the tourists. This meant that while Peter was selling a shitload of beer, he was also violating the taproom's maximum capacity by a long shot, along with his own personal space requirements.

After an hour or so of that nonsense — Peter had never been a people-person, per se — he had volunteered himself to step next door to the Wooden Spoon to see if he could get an update from Gerte, O'Malley being her cousin and all. Turned out most of the town had had the same idea and it was as ass-to-elbow in here as it was at the taproom. He felt his shoulders trying to crawl up to his ears and consciously relaxed them. He was steeling himself to slap some charm on his face and approach Gerte when the door banged theatrically open.

Peter turned to find Matty standing in the doorway, panting, his eyes — Willa's eyes — huge.

"The wind turned!" he announced. The crowd sagged visibly with relief, and a ragged murmur went up. "I was just at the fire station, and I heard Mr. O'Malley say so. The wind's straight out of the south now, pushing the fire up toward the Boundary Waters. He's calling on the Gunflint Trail guys and the BWCA rangers to start evacuating any campers they can find but we're safe! The fire's going the other way!"

Georgie was suddenly right there between Peter and

Matty. He would have loved to say that he hadn't noticed her before, lounging in the back booth the Davis family favored, but of course he had. He noticed Georgie everywhere.

She curled a hand around her brother's elbow. "What about Jax?" she asked urgently. "Jax and Willa? Eli and Mr. Zinc?"

"Wait, what?" Suddenly Peter was right there next to Georgie. He had no memory of moving, knew only that he now had her by the elbow, his head strangely light. "Willa's in the forest?"

"Jax and Mr. Zinc just got back to the fire station," Matty told his sister. "So did the park rangers evacuating the fire zone. A couple of them had to deploy their fire shelters, but they did it in the river so they were okay."

"Thank God." Georgie closed her eyes and breathed a moment. Then she gripped her brother by both shoulders and said, "What about Willa and Eli?"

He hesitated, swallowed visibly. "We're not sure."

"Not sure?" Peter's voice sounded miles away even to his own ears. "Not sure about what?"

Those gray eyes flicked his way, then went back to Georgie and held. "They were on the Kettle trail and the fire caught them," he said. "Jax thinks they might've made it to the river, too, and deployed their fire shelters there but—"

"But what?" Peter's face was numb, and his fingers tingled ominously. Was he going to pass out? Surely not. He'd never passed out. He'd been knocked out a few times but his brain had never just given up on consciousness of its own accord. Maybe he was hyperventilating. He pulled in a slow breath and held it, counted to ten before he let it go.

"Well, nobody's been able to get them on the radio," Matty said reluctantly. He shifted on his enormous sneakers but held Peter's eyes bravely. "There was a hotshot crew ready to start cutting line near the trailhead where Willa parked. Now that the fire's turned, they're moving north. But Mr. Bayfield said he'd send them up the trail to the river, to see."

"To see?" Peter asked. His head was clearing, thank Christ. He could feel Georgie peering at him and didn't care for the scrutiny. "To see what?"

"If Eli and Willa are there."

"Their bodies, you mean?"

Matty glanced uncomfortably at Georgie, who frowned at Peter. "Don't be a jerk," she snapped. "Now's truly not the time."

"Okay." Peter shrugged. Loss was a gaping wound inside him. Why hadn't he known he cared about Willa until it was too late? Why hadn't he felt anything when it mattered? What was wrong with him? "I'll be a jerk when it's more convenient for you. How's Tuesday?"

She ignored that. Ignored him. Better, Peter thought. Much better.

"Matty," she said, "go back to the fire station. Text me when you know more."

"Right." He pivoted on the spot and dashed away, the door jingling merrily shut behind him.

"You." Georgie pointed at Gerte. "Can you confirm what Matty just said?"

Gerte held up her cell phone. "Already did. Wind's straight out of the south, fire's moving north, Devil's Kettle's out of the woods, so to speak."

"Great." She nodded decisively and pointed at Peter this time. "You. Go next door and charm the tourists. Sell a bunch of beer, then wait for O'Malley to give you the okay to tell them we're all clear." She lifted her voice. "Same goes for all of you. Get out there and make some money."

A cheer went up and shopkeepers hustled for the door. Peter found himself standing like a rock in the middle of a stream, splitting the current. But he couldn't make his feet move. Willa was gone. He was living in a world without his sister in it. The one and only person on the face of the earth who knew what his childhood had been. Who knew because she'd lived it, too. But where Peter had drowned in it, Willa had made herself a boat. She'd risen above it, and ridden the current to someplace that even Peter in his extensive fantasy life had never dreamed existed — happiness. And now she was dead and he was alive. Without her.

Goddamn, the world was a fucked up place.

"Peter." Georgie was right there in front of him. He blinked and focused. Bright blue eyes, nearly on level with his. She must be wearing heels. "Peter, are you all right?"

"Of course." He stretched his lips into his company smile. "I'm fine."

"Bullshit."

"Maybe." He pushed the smile harder. "But nothing makes money like tragedy, and you know me and money. So excuse me while I go profit off my sister's death, as instructed."

He stepped around her and headed for the door.

"She's not dead."

He stopped. "How do you know?"

"I hated her too much for too long," she said quietly. "If she were gone, it would leave a hole in my universe. I'd *know*."

"I hated her more," he said, just as quietly. "I thought I'd know, too. But I don't know shit, and neither do you."

In the end, it was the wind that saved them. Or maybe the lake, being the architect of all wind on the North Shore, had saved them. Either way, shortly after the fire jumped the river, the wind had spun around the compass, settled in the south and blasted straight north. It forced the fire to flee up into the Boundary Waters, leaving Devil's Kettle in peace. Leaving Eli and Willa — and an unconscious wolf — sweating inside their own personal oven, breathing shallowly and waiting. Waiting for the air to cool, the wind to change, the fire to come back, the world to end. Who knew?

Then suddenly, somebody was rattling their fire shelter. "Ahoy the shelter!" a voice boomed. "Olly olly oxen free. Anybody home?"

Joy leapt inside Willa. Holy hell, had they really survived?

"Two of us," Eli shouted back. "Plus a wolf."

"Whoa." The rattling stopped.

"It's unconscious," Willa shouted.

"And a long story," Eli added. "Can we come out now?"

"I think you'd better."

Eli flexed his fingers and released the loops that had held the shelter safe over their heads. Willa slid a finger under the edge of the hood and lifted it a cautious inch. What had once been mud was desiccated hard-pack now, veined with cracks and ash. The air was intensely hot but breathable and Willa lifted the hood away from their heads. Eli lifted himself off her, and she felt forlorn and light without his sturdy weight. He helped Willa to her feet and she stared at the utterly transformed forest all around them. Tree trunks stood like black spikes arrowing into the sky, every branch burned away. Great basalt boulders had split at the seams, falling away from each other like slices of an orange.

"Good God," she murmured. "It broke the rocks."

"Didn't break you guys." A sooty-faced hotshot beamed at them, his teeth a brilliant flash of white in his dirty face. He slapped Eli's shoulder. "Long time, no see, Eli. Who's your pretty friend?" He didn't wait for an answer, just keyed a radio and spoke into it. "I got Eli Walker here with a pretty girl and a wolf. Shit you not."

The radio shot back, "Awesome, because I got some chick who won't stop yapping about how Eli stole her phone. Get him over here to shut her up, will you?"

Willa wasn't sure how Eli managed it but she suspected it had something to do with the fact that he knew every single firefighter on the hotshot team that rescued them. By the time they'd sucked down enough oxygen to satisfy their paramedic and hiked down the trail to the parking lot — in the company of a couple of filthy baby lawyers who'd been firmly persuaded that filing a lawsuit against the people who'd saved their lives would be criminally ungrateful — a helicopter was waiting for them.

A woman in a jumpsuit hopped off and ran in a crouch to meet them. "I'm Dr. Lawson," she shouted over the rotor blades. "I'm looking for a Willa Zinc?"

"I'm Willa Zinc," she croaked. Christ, her throat was sore. "But I'm fine. I don't need a doctor."

"I'm not a medical doctor, I'm a vet," the woman said. "I'm with the International Wolf Center in Ely. I understand you have a wolf for me?"

Willa stared in disbelief, first at the vet, then at Eli. He shrugged. "I wasn't sure they'd be able to send anybody," he said. "Didn't want to get your hopes up if they didn't. Consider this your third supervised removal." His smile was very white in his dear, dirty face. "Congrats."

"Where is it?" the vet asked. "The wolf?"

Willa, still speechless, hooked a thumb over her shoulder to the pair of hotshots who'd rigged up a litter for the wolf she'd saved. Hoped she'd saved, anyway. Dr. Lawson hustled over to the litter, and Willa hustled after her. "She's pretty bad off," Willa rasped, "but she's a fighter. You think you can do anything for her?"

"Jesus God," the doctor said, looking over the unconscious wolf strapped to the litter. She shook her head. "She's going to need every bit of fight she's got in her." She nodded to the hotshots holding the litter. "Load her up, guys. It's going to be a long night."

There was a blast of filthy air as the helicopter lifted into the sky and shot west toward Ely. The chop of the blades died away and suddenly there was nothing but the crackle of the hotshots' radios. Eli's hadn't survived its swim in the river, and the fact that civilization still impatiently existed shocked her somehow.

"Come on," said one of a dozen sooty-faced men Willa couldn't tell apart. "Hop in the buggy. We'll take you to town. Bet there are some folks who'll be glad to see you."

Willa exchanged a look with Eli. She wasn't sure about that, and neither was he.

"What about the baby lawyers?" Eli asked and Willa only barely resisted a fond eye roll. Of course he'd still be concerned about those ungrateful snots.

"They went with the other buggy," another hotshot said and she recognized him as the paramedic who'd literally stood over her while she breathed obediently into an oxygen mask. "You're welcome."

Eli grinned at him. "Thanks, Heathrow."

"Heathrow?"

The guy smiled, and it transformed him from just large and filthy to strikingly charming. "I'm an Anglophile."

"Listen to him," Eli said. "He's an *Anglophile*."

"Good on ya, mate!" called another hotshot in a Disney-thick cockney accent. "We can throw some shrimp on the barbie later, what?"

"That's Australia, asshole," Heathrow called back. He kept his eyes on Willa and Eli. "Seriously, you two. In the buggy."

Eli shrugged and Willa shrugged back. Next thing she knew they were crammed into the back row of a converted passenger van big enough to hold an entire football team. It smelled the part, too. She thought she might be sitting on half a bag of Funions and somebody's tangled earbuds. They jerked into gear and the driver put his foot down. He was maybe nineteen and whooped with delight every time they caught air off a pothole. Eli dropped an arm over the back of the seat as they jounced along, picked up the grimy end of her ponytail and toyed with it.

"So," he said casually. "You're in love with me."

She considered the back of the seat in front of her with great care. "Did I say that?"

"You did. Right before I saved your life."

"Maybe it was gratitude talking."

He studied the ends of her hair gravely. "Maybe it was."

She slanted him a sideways look. This was Eli. He'd come back for her. Nobody had ever come back for her until him.

"Then again," she said, "maybe it wasn't."

"No?" He looked up, met her gaze with all that deep, sad blue. The sorrow was still there, she saw, all of it. And it still packed a punch that shoved the breath from her lungs, but it was different now. Not less, just…mellowed, maybe. Softened. And it was all tangled up with a new-born hope that had her heart crawling up her throat and trying to fling itself into his lap.

"Maybe it was true love."

The smile started deep in the bottomless blue of his eyes, spread like the sunrise until it finally curved his lips. "True love? Is that a thing?"

"I never thought so. I do now."

He tipped his head, considered her while he flicked the end of her ponytail with his thumb. "Why?"

"Because you came back." Her throat tried to close on a rush of emotion but she coughed it away. Heathrow shot them a narrow-eyed paramedic look from two rows up. "I'm *fine*," she told him. He gave her a jerk of the chin that said *we'll see* and Eli tugged her ponytail until she met his eyes again. "You came back," she repeated helplessly.

"Willa." He wrapped her hair around his hand until her forehead rested against his. "I will *always* come back for you. If I had my way, I'd never leave but I can't promise that. Life's too…" He moved his shoulders vaguely to fill in the blank. "…uncertain for promises like that. But as long as

I'm alive, I'll come back for you."

She wrapped her hand around his. "I have a life here, Eli."

"I know. I'll have one, too."

"How?"

"I don't know yet. But we'll figure it out."

Joy tried to close her throat again and she swallowed down a cough. She didn't want Heathrow giving her the evil eye again. "Okay," she whispered and pressed her mouth to his. "Okay."

Hoots and whistles filled up the van.

"What?" the driver shouted and aimed for another pothole. "What?"

"Eli just got engaged!" somebody called back.

"Or something," somebody else said.

"Or something," Eli said and smiled into her eyes.

"Our something," Willa said and kissed him again.

"Damn," somebody else said wistfully while the hooting and cheering started up again. "I have got to get me a girlfriend."

Chapter 38

THE HOTSHOTS DROPPED them off on Main Street before turning north and roaring toward the leading edge of the fire. Eli stood on the sidewalk beside Willa and watched the van take the corner on two wheels. The squad boss riding shotgun banged on the ceiling and shouted with glee.

"They're excited," Willa said, bemused. "They're filthy, and they must be exhausted. I doubt they've seen a bed for forty-eight hours."

"Or more," Eli said.

"But they're acting like toddlers who heard there might be marshmallows."

"Well, there's a fire." Eli waited for the envy, for the bite of nostalgia. They were a band of brothers, marching off to fight a war Eli had spent his life training for. A war he loved. He glanced at the woman beside him, filthy and exhausted herself, reeking of smoke and wet wolf, and knew he didn't want to be anywhere but right beside her for the rest of his life.

"That makes no sense," she murmured, squinting down the street.

"None," he agreed cheerfully. "Want to rise from the grave now?"

"No time like the present, I guess."

He waved grandly toward the doors behind them. "Wooden Spoon or the Devil's Taproom first?"

"I doubt there's anybody in either place who'd be particularly glad to see either of us." She tipped her head. "Let's hit the fire station. I'm sure the hotshots let your uncle know we're fine but I'm not sure he'd communicate that one to O'Malley or Jax."

"Yeah, Ben knows his way around a grudge." Eli offered her a courtly elbow. "Shall we?"

She took it with a muddy hand. "We shall."

The door to the Wooden Spoon flew open before they could take three steps, and Georgie strolled onto the sidewalk. She propped a hand on one skinny hip and gave them both a languid once-over. "Lord have mercy, Willa. Dirt just finds you, doesn't it?" She sighed. "Well I'll give you this. At least you're dependable."

Willa blinked at her, then — improbably — a smile curved her lips. "You, too, Barbie."

"Shut up," she said without heat. She stepped forward, gingerly took a pinch of Willa's sleeve and tugged her toward the Wooden Spoon. "Get inside, both of you." She smirked. "Addy's going to hug you both to death and she's wearing this unspeakably awful t-shirt. I want to see her ruin it."

Willa laughed and allowed herself to be led toward the diner. "Of course you do."

"Wait." Georgie paused just outside the door. "Your brother's next door. Maybe you should see him first."

Willa shook her head. "Nah. Addy actually likes me."

"Peter likes you, too. He's your brother."

Willa huffed out a disbelieving chuckle. "That's exactly why he doesn't like me." She grabbed the door and pulled it open. "You first, your majesty."

Georgie frowned but went inside.

"Hey." Eli put his hand on Willa's arm. "Why don't I go next door and let Peter know you're still breathing?"

"Go ahead." She fisted his t-shirt and pulled him down for a smacking kiss. "Meet me here?"

"Sure thing."

The door closed behind her and a roar went up from the diner that made his heart swell. Willa's wounds were nothing that would heal in a day but neither were they

331

hopeless. The community would open to her as she opened to it, slowly, carefully, steadily. Eli smiled to himself and stepped into the Devil's Taproom.

He made his way to the bar where Peter's head waitress was pulling pints and doling out that sandpaper charm of hers. She caught sight of him and her eyes went wide.

"Holy hell," she said. The pint she was holding under a tap overflowed. She hastily turned it off and set down the dripping glass. "I heard you died!"

"You heard wrong."

She paused, glanced behind him and paled. "Willa?"

"Still breathing, too. She's next door, getting hugged to death by Addison while Georgie rejoices over the loss of Addy's ugly shirt. Or something like that."

The woman barked out a sharp, relieved laugh. "Oh, thank Christ. Peter's in the office. Go let him know."

"Will do." He followed the bar to the end, and took a left into a dim, narrow hallway. Just past the bathroom doors, he found a door marked *private*. He lifted a hand to knock then paused, as Peter was clearly on the phone.

"Listen, I'm afraid I can't help you, Ms... I'm sorry, what did you say your name was again? Ms. Gates, right. Julia. Well, as I said, Ms. Gates, I really don't know what you're talking about. If my sister had had Diego Davis's love child at fourteen, I think I'd have noticed. If my former fiancée had done the same, I'd probably have noticed that, too. Devil's Kettle, for better or worse, is a very small town. Middle schoolers don't just give birth here unnoticed. If Matisse Davis is adopted, that's news to me."

He paused. "I have no idea why you'd have heard otherwise, unless you've been talking to Gerte Torsen, who's had a bug up her butt about Bianca Davis since time immemorial."

Another pause. "Well, I doubt your anonymous source can speak to the issue more definitively than I can, seeing as I lived with Willa during the year in question."

Another pause. "I'm sure you'll do as you see fit, but be advised that I do have a lawyer on retainer and I like seeing her earn her daily bread. So research all you want but be careful what you print, Ms. Gates."

There was a clunk, as if he'd tossed his phone onto a messy desk.

"Yeah," Peter muttered, "fuck you, too, lady."

Julia Gates hung up her phone, tapped her pencil to her teeth and considered her options. She hadn't survived the shark-infested waters of art reporting by underestimating pretty boys like Peter Zinc, after all. She'd done enough research before dialing him up to know the lawyer talk wasn't for show. The gentleman did, indeed, have a lawyer on retainer, which was no surprise, considering the scope of his business ambitions. That he frequently used his lawyer was less surprising yet. All her research pointed to Peter Zinc being the solitary sort. The very few people he invited into his life served a very pointed purpose.

His ex-fiancée, for example — the pampered Georgie Davis — had been meant to prop up his failing finances, and look good doing it. His lawyer — an attack dog in designer heels, or so Google would have it — functioned as hired muscle but was also flawlessly beautiful. When Peter had a choice, Julia mused, he chose pretty. Function first, but looks ran a close second.

Which was probably why he'd never bothered himself much with his only sister. Willa Zinc was small, dark, and utterly unremarkable. If she'd ever spoken two whole words on the public record, Julia couldn't find them and her research skills were relentless, especially where Diego Davis was concerned. But Julia was interested in Willa for two very important reasons.

First, her eyes were truly remarkable — large, silvery,

strikingly unusual. And she shared them with Matisse Davis.

Second, Peter, after having largely ignored his only sibling for the bulk of their adult lives, was suddenly playing the protective older brother. Julia could only guess at what had motivated such a dramatic about-face, but coming as it did so close to this startling tip she'd received? A tip claiming that Diego had had a son? That the child had been raised as Diego's brother? That Willa Zinc might be his mother?

Julia smiled. It was all just too fascinating to ignore.

Plus she had a score to settle with Diego's prissy little widow and his evil mother who was evidently — and falsely, Julia was ninety-nine percent sure — claiming to be Matisse Davis's biological mother. Wouldn't it be just lovely to invite them both to the press conference where she revealed the boy's true mother? All she had to do was find the woman.

She picked up her phone and began dialing.

Eli was glad to see Peter toeing the party line Bianca had laid down with the blood-hungry reporters. From everything he'd gathered, Peter didn't have a history of exerting himself when it came to Willa's wellbeing so this was a welcome change of pace. Eli knocked and nudged the door open. He found Peter sitting behind the desk, feet up, fingers linked over his stomach, staring bleakly at the ceiling. Eli leaned against the doorframe and said, "Hey."

Peter leapt to his feet like somebody had cattle-prodded him and stared. All the color dropped out of the guy's face. "You." His hands went to fists at his sides and he took a jerky step forward.

"Whoa," Eli said, and held out a palm. He had no illusions about his prowess as a street fighter. He'd cold-cocked the guy last night but Peter wouldn't go down so easy this time. Eli had no intention of going down at all. "Easy. Willa's fine. She's next door, letting Addy squeeze her neck."

"Wait, she's alive?" The guy tipped his head like he'd never heard the word.

"Fine," Eli assured him. "Coughing like Nan Davis but otherwise, healthy as a horse."

The color drained yet further from the guy's face and he swayed.

"Jesus!" Eli leapt forward and reached for him, but Peter had already slid to his knees in front of the trashcan. He gripped it with two big hands and froze there. The fluorescent light gleamed off the sickly sheen covering his shiny scalp. "Are you all right?"

"Give me a minute," he muttered, his knuckles knobby and white. After a long moment, he sat back on his heels and swiped his sleeve over his face. "Fuck me. Thought I might puke for a minute there."

Eli dropped to his haunches to study the bigger man. "You actually love her, don't you?"

"Shut up."

"No, you do. You love your sister." He frowned, thinking it over. "Why doesn't she know that?"

Peter laughed. "I didn't even know it until I thought she was dead. Why should she?"

"You should tell her."

"Hell, no." Peter shoved back to his feet and stalked to the back of the office, stared at a shitload of framed diplomas. "The last thing Willa needs is another Zinc in her life. Besides, what's the point? I'm leaving anyway."

"You are?" Eli pushed warily to his own feet.

"Yeah. As soon as I find a buyer for this shithole."

"You're selling your half of the bar?"

"Trying to." He smiled bitterly. "Believe me, I'm trying to."

"Does Willa know?"

"Of course. I offered her first dibs. She told me to stuff it up my ass."

Eli smiled. "Of course she did. People aren't exactly her gig, you know."

"Yeah, I know."

He eyed Peter closely. "You seem to be pretty good at it, though. At the whole thing — the bar, the people, the business. Why give it up?"

"Because I hate it. I hate every fucking second I spend smiling for assholes who can't count and think if they buddy up maybe I'll give them something for free."

Eli shrugged. "That's the job, man."

"Yeah, I know. But I hate it and Willa sucks at it, so what are we supposed to do? Brett was awesome, of course, but we all know what this place did to him, so that's never happening." He rolled his shoulders irritably, like the bar was a tangible weight he carried. "It goes against the grain to unload a healthy, profitable business but Jesus Christ, I'm jumping out of my skin here. After the arson thing and the Georgie thing, and now this—"

Eli wondered what *this* was. Suspected it had something to do with his new-found attachment to family, but didn't think now was the time to push for clarification.

"—I've just got to get the hell out of here. I'm suffocating." He shoved both hands into his pockets and spun to face Eli. A considering light gleamed in his eye. "Hey, you want to buy a bar?"

"What?" Eli stared.

"Half a bar, anyway. It's a family business, you know. You're already in the family — or will be, if I'm reading this right."

"You are," Eli allowed, the idea already taking hold. He'd grown up in a restaurant. He knew the business. He was looking for roots.

"Why not make it official? Make me an offer. We could work something out."

Eli rubbed his chin, considered that. He'd all but ignored nearly three years' worth of paychecks while hiking his head straight. He probably had a solid down payment already sitting in the bank.

"I'd give you the family price," Peter said. "Come on, man, I'm desperate here. After this all I have to unload is a sheep farm and I'm out."

Eli paused. "You own a sheep farm?"

"It's a long story." Peter sighed. "So how about it? Are you interested?"

In going halfsies with Willa on everything from a bed to a bar to the rest of his life?

"Maybe," Eli said and grinned. Willa was going to kill him, and he couldn't wait. "Yeah, maybe I am."

ABOUT THE AUTHOR

Once upon a time Susan Sey was a software trainer with nice clothes and free time, but now she has kids. She lives with them and her incredibly patient husband in St. Paul, MN, where she produces smart, sexy contemporary romances on an annual basis. She loves ice cream, her family and happy endings, though not necessarily in that order. She does not enjoy laundry, failure or mowing the lawn, but rises to the occasion as necessary.

You can find her on the web at www.susansey.com, on Facebook or on Twitter. Or drop her a line at susan@susansey.com. She dearly loves a good letter.